HOSTAGE TO FREEDOM

RICHARD SORAPURE

Chapter 1

Peter Dempsey looked back wistfully at the open door of the old pre-war bungalow, clad with black-painted timber and white stucco facade. The house, perfectly preserved as if in a time capsule, was just one of many similar colonial houses in Singapore's Adam Road district from the 1930s, blending fashionable Tudor with Anglo-Indian artistry. Such opulent dwellings, referred to as good class bungalows by the estate agents, were once popular as married quarters for the forces who danced the jitterbug as the clouds of war spread their tendrils through the Malay jungle and crept closer to Singapore. A house where time stood still, facing the ghostly stare of history. Peter loved its unspoilt beauty and privacy from the tall angsana trees hiding the distant housing developments. The sound of the cicadas drummed out their chorus from the magnolias as the embassy staff moved about their tasks. Inside, the amah stripped the sheets from his bed and opened the windows wide to let in the earthy fragrance of recent rain. The overhead fan stirred the humid air. Outside, the gardener swept up dead leaves and ran a strimmer over the tough lalang grass on the hill.

The chauffer hauled Peter's case into the spacious boot of the limousine. Too early for his return flight to London in mid-afternoon, but he had unfinished business. Peter watched the house disappear from view as the car rolled down the drive. No one would miss him. After two years, he only had memories.

'Airport, Mr Dempsey?'

'Later. First take me to the embassy, Tanglin Road.'

He needed to see Margery again. The driver was a recent recruit—not his usual man. However, he could not resist fatuous comments about the weather as a build up to the critical question.

'Mr Dempsey, sir. Do you know who is replacing you?'

'Not the slightest idea. Probably someone the High Commissioner owes a favour to or a fresh graduate.'

The circumstances of his dismissal still irked. They reassured him the reposting to the embassy in Cairo was a promotion. The driver took the hint and lapsed into silence. His return to the consulate a day after leaving surprised the staff. Why come back again? He greeted his friends with a cursive wave and headed for his old, now empty office, on the pretence of checking the desk drawers. While he sat scanning emails on his computer, Margery came in with a cup of tea.

'I have to change the password—since you have left us.'

'Is the High Commissioner in yet?'

'What, at 11 o'clock? What a joke! No way—he is taking Mountbatten for his morning walk.'

Mountbatten was the High Commissioner's old and smelly black labrador. Sometimes the High Commissioner brought the dog into his office, where he curled up beneath the picture of the Queen and wagged his tail whenever there was a visitor.

'What brings you back? Sad to leave us?'

'Yes. I didn't have time to speak yesterday. I wanted to see you before I catch my flight.'

Margery, who had been standing, close to his desk, turned around and headed for the door to take the mail into the vast office where the High Commissioner idled away a few hours catching up on the news and slotting in the odd meeting between cups of tea.

'He is not due in until lunchtime. Are you in a hurry? With all the secrets you know, you need a thorough debriefing.'

Peter recalled the last time they had entered that hidden sanctum one weekend. Raiding the High Commissioner's office for a daring glass of whisky had escalated to intimate behaviour. Was she inviting him to a repeat?

'I'll just finish my tea and delete the history on my computer.'

'In real life, that's what we cannot delete.'

The telephone interrupted with a call from the guard. It was irregular to return after leaving—in fact, a breach of security. Margery placated the man, and he made a tactful retreat, suspicious but powerless. She dealt with handling staff, scheduling meetings, correspondence and phone calls— a powerful position. Anything computer-related was a black art the High Commissioner bypassed. Why should he bother when Margery handled everything so well?

Peter checked his emails. The in-box was empty, but he deleted the folders. There was nothing incriminating. The IT department would check and recover the files he had recycled and examine every email and photo, just as they tracked his phone conversations. He knew a few tricks and cleared the computer, especially the browser history, which was not work-related. Reluctantly, he switched off for the last time and scowled at the security camera. Margery was shuffling around in the office, and he hurried to join her.

An antique partner's desk dominated the room. Sunbeams, falling through the open window, spread out behind Margery to create a strange halo effect. A lustrous spice of old leather mixed with the smell of polished mahogany filled the air.

She acknowledged him with a quick smile but continued checking the post as he settled into an English Regency dark brown tub chair. Peter felt honoured to sit in such a historic chair. In a flight of imagination, he imagined Stamford Raffles, the founding father of Singapore, sitting here. But this was unlikely. Although Raffles founded Singapore in 1819, it was 1827 before they built Singapore's oldest surviving building, the Old Parliament House, and 1887 before they renamed Emerson's Hotel on the seafront Raffles Hotel. Poor Raffles, who died of apoplexy in 1825 at 45, never saw his name associated with a girl's school, a shopping mall, a Mass Rapid Transport Station, and a brand of cigarette.

Peter waited for her to finish. The only sound was the rustling of letters and the flash of the paper knife as she opened the mail. In Margery's hand, each bold slice heightened the tension between them. She was taking her time, letting the silence build up like a dam holding back a flood. At last, she spoke, as if to herself, forgetting the young attaché was present.

'Hmm. Renewal fees are due at the Singapore Cricket Club—very expensive. That's better, an invitation to a drinks reception to welcome the new ambassador for Brunei.'

'They will probably offer him cold tea.'

'No. You are wrong. These so-called dry countries provide the best champagne. No expense spared.'

That was better—a conversation at last. Why was she wasting time dealing with the mail now? Surely, that could wait.

'The old man can't even open his letters. Clearly you do everything for him.'

Margery peered over her glasses. Her lips parted in that surprising way he found endearing.

'Not everything, Peter. While you are sitting there, why don't you get yourself a drink?'

'*Déjà vu*. Like last time.'

He laughed as he reminded her of their earlier amorous encounter in the old man's office—still fresh in his memory from two weeks ago. Peter looked over to the bookcase and located a 21-year-old bottle of Lagavulin malt and a clutch of Stuart crystal tumblers. He slipped off his jacket and wandered over, pouring a generous slug into his glass. She shook her head, refusing his offer, but her eyes took in the trim figure and the damp patch in the small of his back where the flap of his white shirt stuck.

'No ice?'

She feigned annoyance.

'Peter. It is not correct to add ice to a malt whisky.'

He smiled at her predictable reaction. On the surface, there was no change, but possibly a mistake to return. He drained the whisky and got up to leave.

'I'm sorry I have to go.'

She put down the letters and pushed back the chair. Was the squeak on the parquet floor the soundtrack to a last act? She too could sense things were different, but the reality had not struck home. It was not right to walk away like that.

'I hope your new posting in Cairo goes well. Such a shame that piracy case with the Fletchers got so complicated. You did nothing wrong—quite the reverse. And the homecoming party you arranged for them was brilliant! They sacrificed you because of the cock-up by the Americans.'

'It's all history. Put it down to experience. At least I am an expert on piracy in Southeast Asia. When the cases involve commercial vessels, that is straightforward to deal with, but when amateur treasure hunters get involved, things are trickier. I should write a book about it.'

While he was talking, she walked around the desk and leant against the table, facing him, her arms folded.

'Good idea for a project. It's bound to be a best seller. Maybe we will meet again—perhaps in London or Cairo?'

She was a few inches shorter than Peter. His hands moved out to hold her, but she drew back. Sensing his disappointment, she moved closer until they locked in an embrace. Damn, he thought, as other sounds intruded. Footsteps were approaching—the shuffling, soft footfall of a man with a familiar cough and the staccato rhythm of a dog's nails hitting the floorboards. They heard Mountbatten panting and barking as his master reached the door. Peter and Margery broke away in panic as the handle turned. Fortunately, the hound entered first, waddling and grinning in that doggy fashion, endearing to dog lovers and repelling to others. The High Commissioner followed seconds later. Mountbatten snarled at Peter and rushed to defend Margery.

'Peter, what are you doing here? I thought you had left us,' said the High Commissioner.

Both Peter and Margery started talking at the same time.

'I just popped in to sort your mail,' said Margery.

'I dropped by to empty my computer of old emails and stuff,' said Peter, 'and to say goodbye to Margery. Sorry, sir, I seemed to have startled Mountbatten. I need to hurry as I have an afternoon flight to Heathrow. A fortnight at my parents' house in Sussex and then onto Egypt.'

'Bad dog. Leave him alone,' Margery tried to interest Mountbatten in a dog biscuit, but he ignored her and went for a tour of the room, sniffing suspiciously.

'Peter, we are *so* sorry to lose you. Our loss will be Cairo's gain,' said the High Commissioner, offering his hand. 'I'm sure you will get used to the horrendous temperatures and pollution!'

'Thank you, sir, for your kind thoughts.'

'Don't mention it. Also, you will not have any piracy issues. Captain Saiëd in Alexandria deals with all of that. You must visit the pyramids. I found them disappointing but fine if you like ancient tombs.'

'Before I go I was wondering if you had any more updates from Zamboanga?'

'Strictly off the record, Peter, that attack on the treasure hunters looking for the *Siren* has helped us. After the American forces over-reacted, there was more hostility from the Abu Sayyaf terrorists. Can't blame them, can you? The Americans have put a lot more marines and equipment into cooperating with the Filipinos. The alliance is much stronger and, if we play our cards right, I'm sure they will ask our SAS chaps to help them wipe out the rebel camps in Basilan and defeat the enemy.'

Peter agreed this was an excellent result. However, there was little chance of success. The Abu Sayyaf had been campaigning for a separatist Muslim state in the Philippines for so long. The conflict kept dragging on with occasional kidnappings and beheadings of foreigners when the relatives argued over the ransom. He was leaving the office when the High Commissioner handed over his jacket, which he had left abandoned in a heap on the Regency chair.

'Cold in London—you might need this.'

He was blushing with embarrassment. He wanted the earth to swallow him up. As he headed out to the reception area, Margery followed. The girl at the desk looked surprised but thought it best to ignore any dramas.

'Sorry. The old man was adamant.'

'Thanks for offering to resign if he didn't reinstate me.'

'Yes—but he called my bluff. He mentioned a local woman they were keen to hire. Just a ploy, but I couldn't risk that happening. I'm unhappy he wouldn't listen.'

'That's okay, you tried.'

She scribbled an address in London in case they were both in the UK over Christmas. Margery hated Singapore in December as the stores on Orchard Road competed to recreate snowy scenes of a traditional Christmas, often going to ridiculous lengths. The children and the cash tills loved it. But so artificial. Peter promised to take his leave and meet up in London. Perhaps hire a car and drive around with long walks in the countryside and visits to friendly pubs with roaring log fires.

She kissed him in farewell—a kiss that united them as they parted with a chance to meet again. For him, everything had gone wrong since the day he phoned Julie Fletcher in the early hours with news of Michael's kidnap by pirates.

Midday already—hard to believe he had only been at the embassy for an hour. He fetched his case from the lobby. He was disappointed there was no official car available, though they ordered a taxi for him. There was no hurry, but he preferred to hang about at Changi Airport rather than prolong awkward partings.

The High Commissioner wandered through to the front desk looking for Margery. He asked if Peter had left. She stood with a vacant stare in a mix of emotions: sadness at Michael's departure, but happy they would meet again. Tactfully, he did not remind her he was still waiting for a cup of tea.

'Yes, sir—he is downstairs waiting for his taxi.'

'Splendid show. We have a new chap starting next week, but it will be a hard act to follow on from Peter. I was so sad he had to leave us.'

Chapter 2

Michael Fletcher, husband to Julie and father to Alex, reached his apartment at Pagoda Villas at 6.30 p.m most evenings; half an hour before the sudden onset of sunset which always surprised, like the final page of a novel. They rented an apartment near the island's north coast, equally close to Changi village and the Loyang Marine Base where PanAsia Services employed him as a geophysicist. This consistency was a new thing, and the reason was a lack of work. The afternoons dragged slowly, but he resisted leaving before 6 p.m. Once home, he liked to sit on the terrace, drinking a cold beer. The swimming pool of their condominium outside the ground-floor apartment was alive with families splashing about before the evening meal and homework. Moths and insects swarmed around the lights as the heat of the day faded, and darkness crept in.

He treasured the peaceful time to unwind from the office—a chance to sit and chat. But tonight was different. Julie was in one of her silent moods. He had grabbed his customary can of beer, a Tiger or an Anchor. When she ignored his mumbled greeting, he slammed the fridge door to cut through the tense silence. Now he sat alone on the balcony on a rattan Planter's chair.

She remained inside, turning the pages of a magazine, skimming through with unfocused eyes. Michael had left the terrace ajar and let the hot air pour into the room, driving out the air-conditioned coolness—a petulant response to her moodiness. These bad-tempered spats had become more common. He wondered if the relentless heat and humidity were getting to her.

If she had analysed her situation, then the constant narrow climate change was one factor. She yearned for greater extremes, some variety, but what bothered her most was boredom with the predictability of each day. She no longer recognised the man she had married years ago. Where was the love, where was the spark to energise her days and nights? Hell, he had even forgotten their anniversary.

'You're quiet,' said Michael, attempting to lighten the mood as he returned for a second beer. These days a single can of beer was never enough. 'Alex not back?' He asked the obvious. Their eighteen-year-old son might be in his study. Julie sat on the sofa, her knees drawn up and her head resting, staring into space.

'What's the matter?'

'Nothing to concern you, obviously.'

'I come home to a moody silence and I should know what the problem is?'

'What day is it, Michael?'

With a shock he realised that it was their wedding anniversary!

'It's a surprise—I hadn't forgotten our anniversary. I have booked dinner at your favourite restaurant on Boat Quay.'

'The Maharajah? We haven't been there for years.'

'We can go to Orchard Road first and take a stroll—enjoy the cool night air.'

'I was sure you had forgotten.' She let him pull her to her feet and kiss her—a gentle peck, tired and passionless.

'I'll grab a shower. What time did you book?'

'Nine o'clock,' he lied.

After a thirty-minute taxi ride, the Fletchers were in the heart of Singapore's Orchard Road, mixing with the tourists. Eighteen years since their arrival in 1984 and the new Singapore was a modernised, transformed city. But at what price? Michael tried to recapture those earlier times and their heady excitement at the sights, sounds and smells of the city.

Those old shophouses, with their chaotic displays of cheap souvenirs, were no more. Planners had suppressed the unkempt streets, like a disorderly schoolboy squashed into a starchy uniform, to produce uniformity and a better shopping experience. Now wide pavements led pedestrians to modern air-conditioned retail centres, the same as any other city in the world. By the Paragon Centre, the packed crowds dawdled, mobile phones glued to the ear, forcing them into the street. Inside the vast, marble interiors of the complexes, shoppers drifted in and out, browsing in wonder at this brave new world.

But the sepulchral splendour of the retail cathedrals contained no bargains, dulled the senses and pandered to the market's misguided perceptions. The presentation was slick and polished, and the latest electronic goods encouraged more sales. Reaching Centrepoint, the crowds had thinned. Michael recalled an old pub and restaurant called The Pavilion. The mock Tudor style building had survived World War II and the occupation by the Japanese, only for city planners to turn the plot into a Pay-and-Display car park.

'Why do they have to change everything?' grumbled Michael. Many of the renovated shophouses were still empty, with no tenants prepared to fork out the inflated rents.

'You can't keep old places going out of sentiment,' said Julie. 'To attract tourists, they need to upgrade and modernise to stay ahead of the game.'

'But they convert interesting shops into sterile, over-priced outlets nobody wants.'

Julie nodded. She had not been too interested in revisiting their original haunts, and she was flagging. The oppressive heat was taking its toll. Michael suggested they find somewhere for a cold drink. They headed off in pursuit of a gem from the past, the old Mitre Hotel. After a brief walk, he rediscovered it, hidden away off Killiney Road, on a dark, tree-lined drive. The building, dating from the 1930s, was in the typical Bugis colonial style. Once it must have been a grand construction, imposing, busy, with rubber planters and tin miners visiting Singapore from their plantations and mines in Malaya. Now it was a sad place patronised by low budget backpackers and unemployed oil workers—the only customers to tolerate the damp from the leaking roof and the stained mattresses in the squalid rooms.

They passed a young couple sprawled across a moth-eaten sofa studying "The Lonely Planet Guide." Through a haze of smoke, they offered a drug-induced greeting before collapsing in giggles.

The pale light faded away towards an unlit corridor housing the accommodation. There was a small backlit bar counter attracting a few customers. Frayed rattan blinds hung over every window. In the pervading gloom, a mouldy carpet fought for existence with a few torn stitches covering parquet wooden flooring, black with age and grime.

Michael knew the recession had hit the oil industry hard. But it shocked Julie. Out of the shadows, a skeleton-thin *ah chek* staffed the bar counter. The old man flashed a lopsided grin through a mouth riddled with rotten teeth as he served the customers sprawled on their stools in a pall of cigarette smoke as they idled over their drinks, lingering for the rain to stop, standing by for the next job, or waiting for closing time. Julie's eyes widened in horror as she gazed at the crowd of single men, seedy and flushed from excessive drinking.

'Two Tiger beers please,' said Michael, getting the order in before Julie could flee. She glared at him but stayed silent.

The customers formed a solid block of hunched backs—their attention riveted on the barman's assistant; a Chinese teenager in tight shorts and a tighter top stretched to display a straining cleavage. They ignored us with deliberate indifference—except for the girl. She had a ready smile and uncapped two beers with a spurt. Her youthful laughing eyes told us, without words, we were welcome.

'Make way for the Sheila.'

The Aussie had noticed our English accents.

'Did you take a wrong turn? Don't get many ladies in here,' he leered, his puffed sweaty face and narrow piggy eyes noting Julie's discomfiture.

She quickly recovered from his rudeness. 'Well, that's a first then. Also, my name is not Sheila, Bruce.'

The Australian contemplated her as if she were a quaint, rare species. Was she so naïve that she didn't understand polite Australian banter? He was in his late forties with a beer gut, greasy, wild look and nicotine-stained fingers. Michael sensed they should back off as fast as possible to avoid further confrontation.

The fat Aussie smiled. 'No offence meant, miss. Mitch Austin, pleased to meet you.'

'None taken—I'm Julie, and my husband, Michael.' The crowd reacted with great merriment, with several of the barflies parroting her reply.

Michael steered her to a quiet table on the fringes, well away from the group.

'This is a popular bar with deep-sea divers in the oil business. They hang out here to pick up gossip on jobs.'

They stopped their conversation as the girl brought their drinks. Julie narrowed her eyes at the girl's flirtatious manner, wriggling her bum as she performed an impressive display of wiping the table.

'It wasn't necessary to bend over like that, although I can see it gave you a thrill.'

'She was just doing her job,' said Michael.

'Hmm, some anniversary drink,' she looked at her glass of warm beer with distaste.

The overhead fans made no impression on the blanket of tobacco smoke hanging over the bar. The rhythm of the cicadas drummed their mesmeric message, masking the distant traffic hum of traffic. Little lizards, which the locals called *cicaks*, sidled up against the walls—enormous eyes focused for the slightest movement of a fly or moth, as they remained immobile. Only the panting of their sides betrayed their tension before long tongues darted out to snatch their prey.

'This dive is filthy,' whispered Julie through gritted teeth. 'And I don't like the atmosphere. Can we leave?'

Julie's lack of appreciation was disappointing.

'We came here eighteen years ago.'

She looked startled and ill at ease—it wasn't her kind of place. She could not recall coming here before.

'I can't remember. Maybe it was smarter back then.'

'Let's move to the Maharajah,' said Michael, finishing his drink. In reality, nothing had changed much over the years apart from the air of decay. It was always the same. Julie pushed her beer aside, untouched.

'I hope you have never brought Alex here.'

Their son knew the best pubs and clubs in Singapore with no encouragement.

'No, he prefers flash bars with loud music. Our tastes are different.'

'Good, could we go somewhere clean and modern, please?'

'I told you. Boat Quay.'

After a stroll along Orchard Road, they picked up a taxi at Centrepoint. He held Julie's hand—a gesture neither had done for ages. It felt foreign, and she broke away to peer into an empty shop.

'Why all the attention? You are even treating me to an anniversary meal! Now I remember you forgot last year. You spend longer at work with Danica than at home with me.'

She laughed to defuse her remark, but sometimes he stayed late on urgent tasks requiring Danica's help with his survey reports.

'Danica?' said Michael in disbelief. 'She is just one of our staff—a pleasant girl. Her boyfriend is in the Singapore navy. But you are right. We have been nowhere much for ages. When Alex leaves school, we will have more time together.'

She did not reply. Perhaps it was a mistake to relive the past. Had it been a gilded past? Back then, they lived for the moment, untroubled by plans. Not slaves to money—but happier.

In practical terms, Michael could not mention an underlying problem. The recession was hitting hard, and unless a miracle came along, he could lose his job at PanAsia Services. As the only expatriate geophysicist on the team, his salary was triple that of the locals. He would be first to receive marching orders if the situation did not improve. Of course, this was nothing new. Cycles of boom and collapse depended on the oil price, and since the peak highs of $120 a barrel in 1980, the last 22 years had struggled at values less than $30 a barrel. Aware of the trend, Michael had left a previous company focused on oil and gas for his present job, concentrating on engineering and construction projects. But even this sector was under-performing. They might as well enjoy the present before they had to pack their bags and head back to the cold, grey shores of England. He put aside his depressing thoughts as they approached the Maharajah beside the Singapore River. They had space with a table outside on the terrace. The waiter promised it was the best, most romantic view and they were lucky to secure a spare table in such a top-notch North Indian restaurant.

Chapter 3

Michael's bus sped past Changi prison, a grim site where the prisoners in the old blocks used to stare through the bars at the passing traffic, envying the latest cars and changing fashions. The authorities set the recent building out of sight, keeping the captives hidden away from the tourists. The Japanese had imprisoned 50,000 POW after the Fall of Singapore in 1942 in the former British army barracks at Selarang. Michael imagined the jungle and scattered kampong houses at the time of the occupation. The north of the island was no stranger to suffering—ghosts still hovered in the air, a presence in the mist and the driving rain.

The bus ran along Loyang Avenue, stopping at each of the large condominiums to take onboard expatriates bound for the Loyang Offshore Marine Base. Except for today, that did not happen. No one boarded. They blamed the global recession. The depressed oil and gas prices permeated every business with a lack of confidence and gloom. The shipyard in Changi was quiet, with more stray dogs scuttling about than people.

Michael was never too early at the office in Loyang. His ideal timing was after Danica, the secretary-cum-draughtswoman, but before Lucas, the boss. Today he was last to arrive. It was one of those times that can afflict any industry. The order books are full. There are plenty of exciting projects and hum of energy, a nervous rush to meet deadlines and produce reports. Then the company loses work, the current jobs complete, with nothing new to replace them. The freelancers leave, the Christmas party cancelled and senior staff sacked. The survey company's French owner, Lucas Miffré, could see no end in sight to the recession. From bidding an average of twenty tenders a month, activity had dwindled to a trickle.

With a sigh, Lucas glanced across to his full-time employees. Michael was alongside Danica, the skilled cartographer transforming Michael's rough plots into professional looking charts. But the new workstations and mapping software were much quicker. Sadly, he must let Danica go unless things improved. Michael too—he was too slow to adapt. Best save a fortune and replace him with a Singaporean. However, few Singaporeans had the basic skills in written English, which was not surprising when the normal language was Singlish—a mishmash of Chinese, Tamil, Malay and Pidgin English.

Michael ambled off for a coffee and, from force of habit, returned to hand Lucas a cup of a strong Indonesian brew, thick enough to stand a spoon vertically. Lucas told him to sit and stop wavering in the doorway. He lit up a Gitanes to generate a smoke haze convivial to creative thought. It was unusual for Lucas to engage in official chats like this, so Michael feared the worst, As he expected Lucas discussed the dire economic state which was affecting the survey companies leading to staff being retrenched. He could see no end in sight to the lean period, but ever the optimist he believed conditions would improve.

'A grim forecast,' said Michael. 'Alex is finishing his A-levels and leaving school this summer so we won't have to pay fees anymore, but the rent at Pagoda Villas is steep. We may have to move out at the end of the tenancy and find somewhere cheaper.'

Lucas was unmarried, so saved the costs of family life, but he could not afford to be emotional on behalf of his employees. Although not ruthless, he had a business to run.

'Pagoda is a nice condo, and good value as Changi is not a high-cost zone. It's never a satisfactory plan to downgrade. Best if you moved to a larger place. With two bedrooms you can't even accommodate friends.' Michael wondered where this was leading. Was it the preamble before he sacked him?

'If the recession continues, we can negotiate a lower rent with the landlord,' Michael was clutching at straws. In Singapore, rents never decreased. But an extra bedroom at the same price in a less desirable district such as Tampines was possible.

'Julie's father keeps threatening to visit. He was in Malaya during the communist insurgency, so nice for him to see how things have changed.'

'You should send him an invitation. We never appreciate our parents when they are alive, only when they are dead.'

Lucas stubbed out his Gitanes. 'Well, less talk of the economy. I have stumbled on a solution to our problems: a profitable survey job we can do ourselves. If no one hires us, why not grasp a wonderful opportunity for a private venture?'

'Intriguing,' said Michael.

'Do you know Jim McCall? He has helped on a few jobs.'

'No, I don't think so.'

'Jim came for a holiday last month and stayed at the Mitre Hotel in Killiney Road—a cheap lodging house.'

'Yes, a shabby place. We had a drink in the bar recently for our wedding anniversary. It appalled Julie, but they should preserve a few of these ancient places before the developers destroy them.'

'You took your wife to the Mitre for your anniversary? That's grounds for divorce! Derelict and dirty, a cheap hang out for backpackers, divers and their tarts. The owners want to sell it for redevelopment. It's worth a fortune in that location, but one partner is holding out. Meanwhile, no repairs get done, and the building is rotting away.'

'It looked decrepit.'

'Jim likes these rough places. He goes for the cheapest lodgings he can find. Except when travelling with his wife when he spares no expense. Well, one night in the bar he met up with an old diving pal, a fellow Australian called Mitchell Austin from Perth.'

Michael remembered Mitch at the Mitre. Was he a permanent fixture?

'The Australian had made a few hundred dollars from selling an antique Chinese dish to a dealer in Holland Village. He claimed he recovered it from a shipwreck many years ago.'

This was a high price for a single plate and Lucas explained the bulk of the hoard was still on the seabed offshore the Philippines, but no one knew the location except for this diver. It was possible there were thousands of plates in pristine condition. Jim had encouraged Mitch with more beer, but the Australian shut up like a clam. However, he admitted he found this plate in the Sulu Sea with a survey company called Nereus.

Lucas said that Nereus got into financial difficulties and their personnel left when the owner went bust. Lucas bought the survey equipment for a song. They had no boats, just a tired echo sounder, a side-scan sonar system and soil sampling apparatus. After studying their old reports, he discovered Nereus had worked near Brutus Reef, off the southern Philippines, so it was obvious Mitch Austin must have been on that project.

'You say we have a report of the location?'

'It's confusing as Mitch said the divers kept the discovery of the shipwreck secret. They planned to return and salvage the booty themselves.'

'When was the job?'

'Around 1986—a hydrographic survey with soil sampling of the seabed and a side-scan sonar search. I suspect the team were looking for the wreck of the *Siren* and they disguised this to evade the Filipino authorities.'

Lucas handed over a slim bound report plus charts. Michael picked up the faded document and glanced through the pages, appalled by the poor presentation of photocopies held in a ring file. The ammonia prints had turned yellow with age but still had excellent clarity.

'What a strange name for a boat. Sirens were mythical creatures of half bird and half woman who sang seductive songs to lure mariners onto the rocks and kill them.' Lucas laughed. 'Yes, that's right. Odysseus had his men tie him to the ship's mast to hear their song but not fall under their spell.'

Michael glanced at the report. 'There is no mention of the *Siren*.'

'True, my research shows the boat sank with a fabulous cargo.'

From his briefcase, he retrieved an article and translated, selecting chunks and ignoring less relevant details. 'This is from a French website. "Built in 1751 at La Rochelle. *Sirène* was a fighting ship of seventy-six guns. In 1758, the British captured her in a skirmish and refitted her for the British East India Company. They renamed her *Siren*." I'll skip this boring part.'

Lucas sipped his lukewarm coffee. 'Listen, the account becomes most interesting: "At one thousand tons, she was twice the size of many other traders of her time. She made three Far East trips, selling English tin and cotton on the outboard journey and bringing back tea, spices, gold and Chinese porcelain on the return trip".'

'Possibly the same boat if the route is correct.'

'Yes. The vessel sailed to Canton. For extra ballast, she took on a big consignment of china. She had room for two hundred crates—at least 250,000 pieces worth over twelve million dollars at current prices.'

'That's a huge cargo.'

'It's conjecture based on comparisons to other East Indiamen. On the return leg in 1764, near the Philippines, she ran aground and sank, drowning most of the crew apart from the officers. They always survive! I think she sunk on Brutus Reef, and the purpose of the job was to locate the wreck.'

'But it could be anywhere. Did they find the plate during that survey?'

'Yes, according to Mitch.'

'And did they return to retrieve the rest of the treasure?'

'We don't think so. Mitch discovered the other divers are deceased.'

This shocked Michael. 'How did that happen?'

'The original team hired a ship in Singapore to return and salvage the cargo—apart from Mitch. They left him behind because of a row—lucky for him as the boat sank in the Java Sea, drowning the crew except for two survivors. It was an insurance scam, as the weather was calm. The owners scuttled her deliberately for a false claim.'

Lucas lit up another Gitanes and offered Michael one, which he accepted, and they sat for a few moments in a haze of smoke. Danica started coughing.

'*Aiyah*, you men. Why block air-con and throw smoke?'

Lucas smiled and shut the door of their office, hoping to placate Danica. But she continued to cough and left for fresh air.

'So a sizeable hoard of valuable porcelain is ready for plucking. Check out the Nereus report for any clues. We can put a team together to find it.'

The evidence appeared thin. Lucas told Michael they could raise personnel in Singapore and they would need him as the geophysicist.

'But will it be a legal enterprise?' Michael was aware many treasure hunts were not.

'We are in contact with the National Museum in Manila. We must follow a strict procedure. It allows us to export seventy per cent of the total hoard, and thirty per cent remains their property—a well-tried formula. Mind you, nothing can start until we apply for an exploration licence.'

'I see. I didn't think it was that easy.'

'Mike Hatcher recovered Ming dynasty porcelain from the wreck of the *Geldermalsen*, offshore Indonesia,' said Lucas.

'I know the case—the Nanking sale in 1986. It launched a whole rash of treasure hunts, most of them unsuccessful.'

'The haul fetched over ten million pounds at auction in Amsterdam. People are hungry to buy iconic treasures.'

'Phew. That's a fortune.'

'There is risk and up-front costs with the vessel, personnel and equipment. We have everything available in-house, and can mount a campaign far cheaper than others.'

'How soon could this happen?'

'I hope by August if we get the permits. We must cooperate with archaeologists and respect heritage.'

'I will discuss it with Julie.'

'Take your time; we need you.'

Back home at Pagoda Villas, Michael felt restless. The mad rush for an elusive search of a shipwreck in a hazardous country was foolhardy. He told Julie the story of the *Siren* and the business proposition—a roller coaster ride if he committed. She was incredulous and suspected the challenge to locate the valuable porcelain was a waste of time. She wondered how long he would be away offshore.

'I don't know; maybe two or three weeks.'

'As everyone, apart from your friend Danica, is joining the hunt, you better not refuse. If they fail, and the search is fruitless, you still get paid, so nothing to lose. And if you hit the jackpot, our financial worries are over forever.'

'True, but the Sulu Sea is notorious for piracy.'

'If it's dangerous, don't go—one's life is the most important consideration. But if the cargo is as valuable as Lucas claims, you might recover a fortune.'

'Money never used to concern us.'

She looked awkward and said they needed to think about the future. When Alex went to university, how could they afford to pay for the fees? The apartment was too expensive, and Michael was not earning enough in his job. This left him more confused. He could tell Julie the company was in dire straits with no work, but what was the point? He didn't want to offload his worries. The best strategy was to see how events developed over the next week. With luck, Lucas would abandon the plan.

Chapter 4

Unknown to Lucas, a keen collector was the buyer of Mitch's Dragon plate—a man who could spot the genuine article from a fake copy. Tong was the leader of the Singapore branch of the still active Wah Chan Clan—a secret society first established in Malaya in the nineteenth century. The clan had a lengthy history of profiteering from extortion, illegal gambling, prostitution and drug trafficking. But from the 1960s, the police had curtailed most of their operations or driven them undercover. Their new direction was to preserve the Chinese heritage and keep alive the local tongues. In Singapore, English was now the premier language taught in schools, with Mandarin delegated to second place. Despite this, the dialects of the Hokkien, Teochew, Cantonese, Hainanese, Hakka and smaller groups struggled to survive against the onslaught of English and mainstream Singlish, the popular Singaporean version of English.

Many believed that businesses were free of their influence. However, prostitution, gambling and drug taking were still active in the traditional neighbourhoods, yielding rich pickings for criminal gangs. Chinatown and Bugis remained under the control of Wah Chan. Here the Chinese owners of the nightclubs and bars paid the clan a small retainer to ensure good trading prosperity. This morning Tong met with his associate, Yap, to discuss plans for the coming week. In the Triad hierarchy, Yap acted as a henchman or enforcer. A former member of a Hakka association clan in Singapore, he fell out after a disagreement and moved to the Wah Chan Clan. Their headquarters was in an old shophouse in Pagoda Street, a convenient spot in Chinatown. First on the agenda at the daily session concerned a bar near Bugis Food Court. The new owner was a Singaporean of Tamil ethnicity. It was unusual for a non-Chinese to operate such a business in Bugis. The man renovated the nightclub. He transformed the dark, windowless premises and stained velvet lounge seating into a flash restaurant serving snacks and beer to Western tourists. Next, he sacked the ladies with revealing split cheongsam dresses—the key attraction for the sleazy patrons. Instead of a seedy club open to dawn, it kept honest hours and closed by midnight. After striking a deal with a travel company, it ran a roaring trade, attracting tour groups from Japan and Taiwan—a respectable crowd.

'His takings are huge,' said Yap. 'Even the *ang mohs* are drinking at the bar. But he turned down our standard package for protection of his workforce and premises. The last owner paid. No problem.'

'It's a sign of the times,' said Tong, with a sigh. 'Ignorant people get more brazen and think they can ignore normal traditions. How many staff has he got?'

'A *bapok* barman, a Hainanese cook and a young girl. A small team—but busy!'

'The key will be the gay barman. The owner doesn't work there?'

'Never, but he visits most evenings with his cronies. Should I arrange something to convince him?'

Yap's narrow, expressionless eyes never changed, matching the firm set of his thin and hollow cheeks. Impossible to guess his age—he was forty-five but could have been anything from thirty to sixty. Like the stereotypical villain, a knife scar cut across his left cheek from eye to mouth.

'No. Not yet. Give time for business to grow. Who is he?'

'An Indian businessman called Davinder Raja Singh. Youthful and arrogant; he has other businesses, so just a hobby to please his wife.'

Tong looked thoughtful. He told Yap to check out Davinder and his family, including where he lived.

'This other business—what is that?'

'Davinder got boastful. He is a marine surveyor with a small team. Most of his work is with a contract with the Port of Singapore Authority for hydrographic surveys, but he is also chasing the more expensive oil and gas market.'

'Impressive,' agreed Tong. 'A man with ambition. Dig up what you can, but as Confucius says "The cautious seldom err".'

Wherever Tong went, he attracted glances of surprise, even shock. A short, broad-chested man with close-cropped hair, an expressionless face and a searching stare from reptilian eyes. Regardless of the temperature, he dressed in a formal black suit with a crisp white shirt and tie. The clan society tie was a warning statement to those who could read its message not to mess with him or his operations. After his morning meeting with Yap, he spent a happy hour researching the base marks on the plate to discover its age. He suspected it was from the late Ming dynasty, early 1600s, but he needed a second opinion. The best place to start was a return visit to Meng's antique shop in Holland Village, an expatriate favoured shopping experience near Tanglin, close to Orchard Road.

Holland Village contained many outlets catering to tourists lapping up cheap oriental trinkets and curios such as opulent Persian carpets, Korean medicine chests and pictures of the Singapore River. But there were also conventional stores such as beauticians, hairdressing salons, shoe shops, a pet shop with sad cats and the Jelita Cold Storage supermarket. Something for everyone.

But this district was outside Tong's comfort zone. He took the stairs up to the second level of the Holland Road Shopping Centre, ignoring the choice of a lift or an escalator, as Tong preferred his own space. The antique gallery contained a disappointing mix of tourist rubbish, hiding a few genuine pieces of interest. He looked critically at the shelves as the owner chatted to two Malaysians. He overheard the men trying to trade a Chinese silver dollar of Yuan Shih Kai, dated 1919. It was in a worn condition, and Meng offered them only twenty dollars—about right as the coin would sell for fifty dollars. Disappointed, the men headed for the door.

'Where did you get it?' asked Meng.

'On a wreck, off Malaysia,' said Mahmood, the older man. 'My brother and I work for the oil companies, but this was a recreational dive.'

'If you discover any valuables, bring them here. I will give you a decent price, lah.'

'Twenty dollars?' complained his younger brother, Suleiman.

'Guys, I have loads of silver coins, but they must be in perfect condition.'

Tong opened his wallet and whisked out a fifty-dollar note. 'I'll buy it.'

The Malaysians stopped in their tracks, stunned at such generosity. Tong handed them his business card. 'Come and see me in Chinatown, 42 Pagoda Street, tomorrow at midday. I may have a job for you. The name is Tong.'

After the men departed, Meng bundled out a tray of Chinese coins for Tong to study. *Wah lau*, pay so much for rubbish coin. Show him quality stuff and man pay fortune!

But Tong waved them aside. 'Last week, I purchased what I believe is a Ming dynasty serving dish from a young lady. Have you more of the same?'

'Yes, I recall the plate—an article with dancing dragons and fascinating history. The girl who served you is my daughter.'

'A fascinating history, you say? How so?'

Meng looked embarrassed. Had he revealed too much?

'Your daughter said an Australian diver sold you the item as part of a haul of similar porcelain. I can't remember the wreck's name.'

Meng gave a nervous laugh. 'He never mentioned where he found it. I know Mitch well, and he tells a marvellous story! It was a one-off deal. Just a single serving platter, I regret. I don't think we claimed it was a Ming, did we?'

'No, but for the price I paid and the markings on the base, it seems likely. Does the Australian live in Singapore?'

Meng rubbed his forehead, deep in thought, as he struggled with the dilemma. He never cared to disclose sources, especially to strangers, but this man was different. He recognised the clan tie with its Triad associations. Protection and extortion rackets were still active in parts of the island.

'The diver's name is Mitch, Mitch Austin. I don't have his card, but he lives at the Mitre Hotel off Killiney Road—propped up at the bar.'

Intrigued by meeting the fat Chinese man the day before, Mahmood and Suleiman arrived at midday outside the nondescript building in Pagoda Street of the Wah Chan Clan. Mahmood studied Tong's business card—a mix of Hanzi characters and English. The men inched forward nervously, unsure of what lay behind the door. The paint peeling off the front entrance belied the opulence hidden within the building. There was no bell or knocker, so the men opened a brown mahogany door, ornate and decorated with carved dragons, and entered an unlit room, lined by rosewood chairs set around an enormous table. At the far end, smoke from joss sticks circled lazily from the porcelain figurine of a horse-mounted warrior, as if issuing from its flared nostrils.

Once they became accustomed to the light, they noticed Tong seated in a haze of spiralling incense. Attired in his habitual tight black suit, too small for his plump frame, Tong glanced at the brothers with a lizard-like stare from eyes sunk deep. With a wave of his hand, he gestured them to sit. As they slid on the hard rosewood carved seats, the sun slanted through the skylight, blinding them.

A young girl drifted out of the shadows and poured the men tiny cups of Jasmine tea. As quietly as she came, she vanished, and neither man saw her go. The sound of teacups scratching on the saucers was the only noise in the tense silence. Tong raised his eyes as if waking from a dream. He drank a dark coloured liquid—a special Hainan black tea.

At last, he turned his full attention on the men. He could offer them a job, which did not involve diving. If they were reliable and trustworthy, it would be an honour to help the clan with this simple task—an information gathering exercise. His sentences came out in asthmatic stabs. Almost as an afterthought, he asked them their names.

Tong told them of an Australian diver called Mitch Austin. He stayed in that old hotel on Killiney Road, the Mitre, a hangout for the unemployed. Divers frequented the place so they would feel at home. Tong instructed them to strike up a friendship. The Australian had sold an antique plate to a dealer in Holland Village. It was a rare piece, possibly unique, from a shipwreck. They needed to find the name of this wreck and its location as it contained a valuable cargo of porcelain. The brothers looked dubious.

'White people keep to their own,' said Suleiman. 'Why talk with us? Those guys work on major projects. We just small fry.'

'Maybe, but times are harsh. This Australian diver is unemployed. Why else stay at the Mitre? Buy him a drink and see how it goes.'

'Neither of us drinks alcohol,' said Mahmood.

Tong looked exasperated.

'The fee for this job is five hundred dollars in advance with the same again, if successful. For that, I think you drink beer.'

The Malaysians smiled. The Chinaman was a gullible eccentric, happy to overpay for a coin. This should be easy. Tong stood up and walked across to the sideboard, gesturing the men to follow him. For a heavy man, he was light on his feet and moved fast. He removed a cloth to show the stunning plate.

'This is the serving dish. The design and quality are excellent. Discover the name and location of the shipwreck. That is your task. Do not fail me.'

Chapter 5

Lucas was rushing along the corridor when he ran into Michael, soaked to the skin from a sudden downpour.

'Why are you so wet, did you walk to work?'

Michael wiped away damp strands of hair, obscuring his vision. He had travelled by bus. But his stop outside the Marine Base was a few hundred yards short of the office and he got drenched running through the monsoon. Looking like a drowned rat, he squelched to the washroom to rub off the excess rain colliding with Danica as she left the cloakroom.

'*Aiyah*, why so late this morning? It's best to take your shower at home and not here.'

Refusing to rise to the taunt, Michel ignored her as he stripped off his wet clothes apart from his brief underpants. He was dabbing dry with paper towels from the machine when Danica reappeared with a towel.

'Fetch, lah.'

She lingered in the doorway, forcing him to collect it. He saw she was playing a game with him.

'You normally choose the bus so you are used to its schedule,' she argued, to justify staring at him. He had an attractive figure—damn fit for an *ang moh*.

'The rain was torrential, so I planned to bring my car, but the bloody thing has a flat battery. I am only an hour late. Not the end of the world. So I'll stay later tonight to make up for it.'

He pulled up his trousers over still-damp pants in a hurry to escape her interrogation. What a disastrous day! After wasting time on the car, he tried, unsuccessfully, to call a taxi. But in heavy rain, taxis took a holiday, so it forced him to catch the bus. It was normally a reliable service, running every twenty minutes except for today when it was a forty-minute wait.

He prepared a strong coffee to recover and sat back at his desk, letting the caffeine hit wake his brain. Danica was smiling to herself, enjoying his discomfort.

'Michael, is it convenient to talk?' Lucas called from his office.

He lifted his sodden legs, hurried through to Lucas's office and sat by the window to let the sun dry his damp clothes. Lucas ignored Michael's soggy state and launched into an update. Things were moving quicker than expected. The search for the *Siren* might start earlier than planned..

'How much sooner do you mean?' Michael was surprised. He thought the scheme had cooled off.

'Jim McCall, the party chief, is flying in from Australia next week to sort out the equipment and team. He knows the Philippines. Your role is to interpret the data, to point us in the right direction. We aim to sail from Singapore by the end of July—six weeks from now. Does that time frame suit you?'

'It's unexpected. We don't have a clue of where to search.'

'We can't start until the museum issues an exploration licence. I count on you to visit them in Manila with me. Give them an idea of our investigation locality—no need to be too precise. There should be no problem. Once they understand we are serious, they will rubber-stamp everything.'

'Why has the time frame changed? We don't have enough information to make a convincing case.'

'Another group has got wind of our plans. I bet it was a leak from the museum. For such a huge value cargo word spreads fast.'

'I mentioned it to Julie, but no one else.'

'And your son? Add together those they talk to, and by now half of Singapore will know!'

'Alex knows nothing.'

'Are you so sure? I bet your wife has told him.'

Michael looked thoughtful. On balance, that was likely. Alex was certain to have blabbed to his friends at school. But so what? They based the whole wreck scenario on hearsay and rumour—no one could take it seriously. There was a tense silence, which usually triggered Lucas to light up another cigarette, but this time he drummed his fingers on the table.

'We need to speed up the project. Doesn't that old report from Nereus show us where to survey?'

'Yes, Lucas. They retrieved sand samples from the seabed and found pieces of broken pottery. There is a photo, which shows Chinese hallmarks from the Ch'ing dynasty on a base fragment. It is possible the site is the wreck of a trader that came to grief on the rocks nearby.'

Lucas looked thoughtful, weighing up the possibilities.

'That is helpful news—why didn't you mention it earlier?'

'Danica and I visited an antique dealer in Katong. We took along the photo and he identified the hallmarks straight away. Don't worry; I was discrete.'

'Okay—promising because the age matches. But I'm not sure if it's enough. Did the old survey report list any diving locations?'

'Yes, but they are useless with no descriptions or results from the dives, just geographical coordinates.'

'That's a start, isn't it?'

'Yes, but the accuracy is uncertain. There are several WWII shipwrecks in the Sulu Sea, so it will be hard to find the *Siren*.'

'If it's too vague, they'll send us packing,' said Lucas. 'Vargas, our agent in the Philippines, stressed the museum is much stricter, and we need solid evidence to get an exploration licence. They are eager to gain artefacts, but a scrap of old plate in a soil sample isn't enough.'

'Why don't I go to London, to the British Library? They store the historical records of the East India Company and may hold documents of the *Siren*.'

'Are you sure?'

'No, but I can phone them to see if it's worth a trip.'

'An excellent idea. So obvious—why has no one else done that?'

'Most treasure hunters are recreational divers who strike lucky,' said Michael. 'They don't research as that takes time and effort.'

'Okay, we will book you a flight to London early next week. You have nothing pressing like a parents' meeting?'

'No problem. Alex is on study leave for his A-levels so Julie can supervise him at home. I will start at the British Library and then to other institutions such as the British Museum, the National Maritime Museum and the Public Record Office—wherever the trail leads.'

'Good. Will Julie mind you travelling to London without her?'

'No, she has to watch Alex. Left alone, he would invite his friends over to party and trash the place. The desk study will help us make a decent case, but I am doubtful of finding the right location.'

Michael still had safety concerns because the southern Philippines and Mindanao was a high-risk region and a bunch of treasure hunting foreigners would look conspicuous.

'Michael, do not use the term treasure hunters. It has negative connotations. We are scientists looking for a wreck of architectural significance. Don't believe what you read in the papers. The Sulu Sea is much safer since the Americans are helping the Filipino armed forces root out the terrorists in Basilan. Why bother us doing a marine survey?'

'Let me discuss it with Julie. I hope the research will help.'

'Vargas tells me another group is seeking a permit to search for a wreck in the Sulu Sea. I suspect they are after the same wreck. A respectable antique collector in Singapore approached the museum yesterday. Just a coincidence? I wonder what information he has.'

The Fletcher's apartment at Pagoda Villas was a typical ground-floor two-bedroom unit built in the housing boom of the late 1970s. Its best feature was a large lounge with sliding glass doors opening out to a sweeping vista of the communal gardens and swimming pool. Hidden beneath a fold in the topography was a range of facilities including a small shop, a cafe, gym and squash courts. Out of sight, the complex extended with moderate low-rise developments of six floors interspersed with landscaped grounds, a pond, a children's playground. What else? Oh, yes, there was even a hairdresser and a Club House. It was as if they were on a permanent holiday at a luxurious resort.

Michael fetched a beer, surprised to find Alex wandering across the lounge in shorts and a T-shirt. His period of study leave at home had started already. Surely, the idea of paying huge school fees was for the school to ensure his boy did some work under their roof rather than his.

'School is the best place to revise. The boarders can't escape,' said Michael, scowling at the interruption.

'Dad, I've been working all day. I need a break. Most of us are day students with only a tiny number of boarders— it's not like Eton.'

Michael handed him a can of Anchor beer, and they wandered out to the balcony to enjoy the fresh evening air. The poolside was busy with the shouts of children until seven o'clock. Later, an unnatural calm settled over Pagoda Villas before a few noisy expatriates arrived for a boisterous swim. As they watched, a man with long black hair and an unshaven face, stripped off to a pair of tight Speedos. Noticing them staring from their veranda, he waved at them, and dived into the pool, settling into several lengths of an energetic crawl.

'What did he say?' asked Alex.

'Oh, just *Ciao*. He is an Italian called Luigi who is always trying to chat up your mother.'

Alex laughed. 'He's a young and fit guy, so that's understandable.'

'Haven't you got studying to get back to?' asked Michael, lighting up a cigarette.

'He was over here earlier.'

'What!'

'Yes, Ma couldn't start the car, and he was helpful and started it straight away.'

Michael looked amazed as he walked to the fridge for another beer. At least there was no need to send the Volvo for repairs with a useful handyman on their doorstep.

'So I guess your mother has gone shopping?'

'Yes, she said she will be late, so cook a frozen pizza, or if you don't fancy that we could go out. She is meeting up with friends in Holland Village—you can imagine that!'

It annoyed Michael. He was looking forward to a quiet evening at home, but a better choice was the hawker centre in Changi. The Indonesian stall served perfect beef rendang, and Alex loved the chicken rice. In addition, a bottle of beer to complete the feast at a fraction of the price Julie and her friends would pay at an over-priced joint in Holland Village.

'Ma says you are planning to hunt for treasure off the Philippines.'

'We plan an archaeological survey to locate an old shipwreck. It is confidential, but I imagine your mother told you.'

'True. But I have not blabbed to anyone. Your secret is safe with me. Dad, as I will finish school soon, I was wondering if you need help. Tell Lucas I am free to come along as a general dog's body or assistant. What do you reckon?'

It stunned Michael into silence.

'That's crazy. You lack training or experience in offshore work.'

'I'm sure I can lift heavy gear and learn to run the equipment. There must be simple tasks.'

Alex at eighteen was taller, fitter and stronger than his father. It would be a wonderful experience for him. However, the project was not without risks and his mother needed to agree. They had to pick the best moment to discuss it with her. It was up to Lucas, and maybe they had enough experienced personnel without risking someone green.

'I will suggest to Lucas we could use an unpaid research assistant. But the most important thing is to concentrate on your exam revision. If you want me to fork out £1,000 a year on tuition fees back in the UK, you better get good grades.'

'Great. No need to pay me apart from beer money.'

'Don't count on that, Alex, or mention the job.'

'Thanks, but you assume I plan on a UK university instead of staying here. The National University of Singapore is great.'

It was true Michael's preference was for a British university, and he thought Alex felt the same way. He shrugged his shoulders.

'Whatever. Wherever you choose, the offers will depend on your results. University is a wonderful opportunity to gain enough experience to command a good salary in an attractive job. It has kept me in solid employment ever since we came to Singapore.'

Alex yawned as if tired of the lecture. 'Okay, Dad, thanks for the advice; and whom shall I say has been smoking if she asks?'

Chapter 6

PanAsia's office at Loyang Marine Base was typical of many on the industrial estate. Three rooms on the first floor radiated out from a narrow corridor where the receptionist sat at a small desk. At ground level, the warehouse stored the survey instruments and various items of equipment.

Danica and Michael occupied one open-plan space overlooked by the compact room where Lucas lurked, polluting the air with his cigarette smoke. They had dispensed with the receptionist as the current recession made her superfluous. Her empty desk remained—a gesture of hope for a better future.

It was an ideal location to mobilise a vessel of convenience. Early this Monday morning, Lucas strolled along the quayside to inspect a boat for a geophysical survey. If suitable, they might use the same ship for the hunt for the *Siren*.

Mornings in Singapore were one of the best times to capture a brief calm before the everyday stress of the working day. Lucas strode alongside the sleepy berths where a wide variety of vessels lay idle. A few cats and scruffy dogs shuffled past the boats or chanced their luck for a snack at the guard post. A short distance away, a small plot of surviving mangrove teemed with bird life. However, the ever onward march of urbanisation might soon eradicate this last vestige, leaving only the outlying islands of Pulau Ubin and Pulau Tekong with relict mangrove swamps. The night chorus of the Malayan bullfrogs was silent now, and only the shrill stutter of the cicadas filled the air as dawn gave way to another day of unrelenting heat. Lucas shook his head sadly, imagining a future with an enlarged and modernised port destroying the original habitats hanging on so precariously—a sterile future of wealth without beauty.

Pacific Glory's owner, Subramanian, was late. It suited Lucas, as he wanted a chance to look her over, so he wandered across the gangway for a quick inspection. First impressions were not good. The superstructure was rusty and a glance around the cabins and galley areas showed poor hygiene and safety standards. A scuttle inside a kitchen cupboard revealed a rat disturbed by his inspection. A sleepy mariner came out of the heads, pulling up his trousers in a panic. He explained the crew were on leave. Lucas was ready to give up when the ship owner appeared.

'Ah. Mr Miffré, is it? I am sorry to be late. Our office is on Marine Parade, but the East Coast Parkway was a nightmare. The traffic gets worse despite the Mass Rapid Transit system's plan to ease the congestion. I am Subramanian, but please call me Subra,' Subra offered his hand, which Lucas reluctantly shook, 'and let me introduce Captain Singh.' Subra was in a smart suit in contrast to Singh, who wore a sweat-stained T-shirt, shorts and flip-flops.

The captain mumbled his excuses and headed off to the bridge. Lucas was unimpressed by Subra's lame excuse and told him he could not charter the vessel in its current condition.

'I assume the certification is up-to-date and you have a crew list of experienced personnel?'

'I understand you need a small boat for a diving survey?' asked Subra. 'We will renew expired certificates. We have a pool of qualified mariners who move between our different vessels, depending on the demand.'

The vessel was disappointing. It might do for the short sand search job off Malaysia, but for the longer project in the Philippines Lucas doubted if the survey team could cope with the cramped conditions and poor state of the accommodation.

'The vessel has got to stay at sea for at least thirty days. We are waiting for the go-ahead, but I need a boat for Malaysia—a quick job; and then onto the Philippines. One of the jobs involves diving, but the main task is for geophysical surveys which requires a larger team and more complex equipment,' explained Lucas.

'The Philippines is a long way. The transit takes two weeks, so a lengthy charter period will need port calls for fuel and fresh provisions.'

'Yes, we understand that. We plan a stop in Labuan.'

'Labuan is Freeport and easy to use. It is preferable to refuelling in the Philippines. The ports are poor with a risk of dirty fuel—not to mention other problems. How many scientists are sailing?'

'Our party for the Malaysian project is six persons and should last five days. But the vessel has to accommodate double that for the next job. The team will fly to Zamboanga to join the boat.'

'By golly, Zamboanga, in the southern Philippines—in Mindanao?' asked Subra.

'That's right. Is that a problem?'

Subra was unhappy—the region was notorious for criminal gangs, piracy, and kidnappings. It was such a dangerous place they would have to arrange extra insurance and ask for a higher day rate.

'Mr Miffré, our best way forward, is for your team to do an audit on *Pacific Glory* and tell us your requirements. We are happy to give you a quote and make allowance for our added costs to reach your specification.'

'Fine. But I will view other vessels in the meantime.'

'We purchased this boat recently and plan to upgrade it. We are keen for your business, so let's fix the things needing attention.'

Lucas crossed the rudimentary gangplank back to the jetty. Even the ramp was substandard, made of poor quality, splintered wood and lacking a safety net. He hurried towards his office. It was a ten-minute walk, but the hot weather dissipated the morning's coolness. Despite living in Singapore for many years, he still found the contrast between the outside furnace and the inside freezing air-conditioning difficult to cope with.

Lucas arrived at the Spindletop pub, which had a choice of hawker stalls on the ground level and a Western-style restaurant on the first floor. He was undecided which to choose when he heard Davinder, the manager of a rival survey company, rushing up the hill.

'You look over-heated,' said Davinder. 'Fancy a drink? We can compare notes on what work is available.'

'Well, just a quick one. Shall we go upstairs? It's cooler. I think we are too late for breakfast and too early for lunch.'

The staff directed them to the lounge bar—a charmless cubby hole with Formica partitions and an unused dartboard. They ordered soft drinks in the dining room. This annoyed the server, trying to lay the tables. Better the usual undemanding clientele of dockworkers, seismic crews and office personnel than these two. Spindletop's standard menu never changed and avoided dangerous innovations, which might upset the customers.

Davinder wiped the sweat from his glistening forehead with a large white handkerchief. 'It's sweltering! I thought I saw you onboard the *Pacific Glory*. You're not thinking of hiring her, surely?'

'Why do you ask? Have you used the boat?'

'Lucas, don't touch it with a barge pole!'

According to Davinder, there had been trouble when the vessel was surveying off Kalimantan and hit a mound of coral. She lifted off on the high tide and they aborted the work and returned to Singapore. But the captain kept this secret and omitted a hull inspection—a legal requirement—when she reached port. Davinder, unaware of its history, hired the boat for a minor job, and it drew in water and nearly sank. The end client was furious and refused to pay the survey bill, so Davinder stopped payment to the ship's owner. As a result, they went bankrupt and had to sell the ship to the present owners.

'And no doubt Subra picked it up very cheap,' said Lucas.

'I think they have fixed the hull, but if you want a word of advice, avoid it,' warned Davinder. 'There are many spot-charter vessels available. What jobs have you in mind?'

'We are mobilising for a small hydrographic survey off Malaysia.' Lucas was vague and careful not to mention the Philippines.

'I've got a vessel finishing next week. Nothing else coming up apart from a risky lead from a client. I will give him a high quote and hope he goes elsewhere.'

'Could that be a rich Chinese investor?' asked Lucas.

'How do you know? Just yesterday this guy called Tong phones me looking for a vessel and gear for a shipwreck search.'

Lucas reassured him. 'It's okay, he hasn't spoken to us, and if he does, we won't interfere. You discovered him first.'

'Well, thank you, but I haven't even met this Mr Tong yet. We had a brief phone conversation.'

'Where does he want to survey?'

Davinder relaxed. Lucas was fishing. 'Sure, there's no harm in telling you. It sounds like a treasure hunt somewhere. We got burnt on a similar job off Indonesia last year, so I am not keen unless they pay in advance.'

'I don't blame you. It's best to keep away from risky work, even though times are desperate. What boat are you off-hiring?'

'The *Eastern Pearl*. A standard utility vessel, forty metres long, shallow draught, twin screw, accommodation for sixteen persons, A-frame, good sized back deck space and clean.'

'Ideal for our purpose. Who are the owners?'

'Wong Kai Chee Marine—based in Jurong Shipyard. I think the owner is Phillip Wong. He is in charge of daily operations.'

'Thanks, Davinder. I will fix up a visit when she returns to Singapore. She sounds suitable for our small study.'

The Spindletop was filling up with customers for lunch, so the men gave up their table. In reality, both companies were fighting for survival, and Davinder feared the lead from Tong was his only choice. If he wanted a survey, he must pay up-front. Mr Tong had promised to contact him again next week once he had completed more research.

It was not a concern for Davinder. He had other business interests such as a bar in Bugis Court—formerly a shady nighclub. After refurbishment to improve its image, trade had blossomed. His wife had discovered it was for sale, chased by debtors, so he had purchased at a knockdown price. Once it was running, he could step away and leave to others to manage. Davider had done well, despite the recession, with his small team of local surveyors. Demand for hydrographic surveys had seen him expand the company to take on a large variety of work in the region. He felt pleased with himself. A pleasant glow surrounded him and his family in a protective bubble.

Chapter 7

Tong invited Suleiman and Mahmood for a progress update over a convivial lunch. They arrived at Hung Kang, an authentic Teochew restaurant in North Canal Road in Singapore's Chinatown, one of Tong's favourite haunts. The brothers expected a tricky meeting because of the latest developments revealed in yesterday's papers.

The divers waited, glancing nervously at the door whenever a customer entered. Reluctant to order anything before Tong arrived, they refused to buy drinks when the staff pestered them.

After a long wait, Tong's rounded figure squeezed through the doorway and headed for his table—one he had reserved for its privacy at the back of the restaurant. Without apology, he joined the Malaysians at the marble-topped Peranakan style table and waved aside the menus, which the server handed out.

'I have been coming here for thirty years,' said Tong. 'They have ruined Chinatown. The planners restore the old shophouses, but the tenants cannot afford the new rents. All the old people leave. This place survives because they serve Teochew food, keeping faith with the original style. I regret many of the old craft shops have gone. Where are the puppet makers, the old bakeries and the kopi shop? Dead—all dead. They call that progress, but I call it is a crime against our heritage—a sacrifice of poor people exploited by a government in league with grasping developers.'

Throughout this diatribe, the Malaysians maintained a puzzled silence. Tong ordered a choice of typical Teochew dishes: crab rolls, fish maw with sea cucumber, and prawn balls with chives. He lowered his voice even though they had a private table, with no immediate neighbours. Yesterday's report in the papers of a body of a tourist fished out of the canal concerned him. Just a vague account from the Straits Times which mentioned the Rochor area, but he wondered if this could be the Australian diver, Mitch Austin? He lived nearby. Maybe they had not heard the news as STV did not mention it. In fact, the Chinese and Malay papers ignored the story. There was no mention of foul play, so the police assumed a nasty accident.

'Did you see the newspaper?'

Mahmood and Sulieman looked uneasy. They exchanged glances, and both nodded, but remained silent.

'Then update me on your progress since you met the diver.'

'Mr Tong, you may be right—the body in the canal could be Mitch,' said Suleiman. 'But he was alive when we left him in Geylang. The diving business is a small world, and we had mutual contacts—so easy to discuss. We recalled past jobs—as you do. But no mention of treasure hunts or dives on ancient wreck sites.'

Tong filled his glass from a bottle of Tsingtao beer, but ignored the brothers. The conversation paused as the waiter served up several platters of Teochew cuisine—each dish lightly seasoned and subtle in flavour. The Malays gave face to Tong by pretending they enjoyed it, but they preferred spicy food to this bland Chinese style. Tong helped himself to the dishes with rapt attention, nodding at the divers to follow suit. His silence unnerved them. With no reaction, it felt as if their account was ignored as unbelievable.

Suleiman told Tong that their luck changed when Mitch met an Australian diving friend in the hotel bar and, after many drinks, started boasting of a treasure hunt many years earlier when he had found a mint condition Ming serving dish sticking out of a sand-covered crate from a hoard inside a sunken shipwreck. A legendary find! He told his friend they planned to return to salvage it, but his partners double-crossed him and sailed off on their own the following year. However, the ship sank in an insurance scam, scuttled by owners for its inflated value, and the treasure hunters drowned.

'And you believe he gave up and never returned to salvage the cargo?' Tong asked in disbelief.

'We asked him that,' said Suleiman. 'He said he returned to Australia for many years, got married and settled down so it was out of his mind. The marriage broke down and he returned to Singapore last year, but things have been tough and it forced him to sell the antique plate. He suddenly realised he should do something about it.'

'He was always drunk,' added Mahmood. 'Mitch wanted to go to Geylang, to the red-light district. We offered him a lift as we live nearby. He asked us to park outside a KTV lounge. I can't remember its name, but the girls sing loud Cantopop stuff. No regular karaoke—this is a shady club. You know the type where the bar girls serve cheap brandy in Martel bottles to the guys and keep sober by drinking lukewarm tea? Expensive, man.'

Tong nodded impassively. Good news that the wreck was untouched, but the brother's criticism of bars and clubs did not interest him. Tong's business interests supported many similar bars and clubs in Chinatown. With the help of the clan, the KTV girls and the mamasam could earn a good living. An urgent drum of his fingers on the tabletop persuaded Mahmood to resume his story.

'The girls encouraged Mitch to spend his money and loved his tales of diving on treasure. But, when a rich Japanese businessman came in—a big spender, they left to sit with him, so we joined Mitch. Drink had loosened his tongue, and he swore to return to salvage the valuable cargo, ripe for plucking. Better than waste time with Sarong Party girls! When he returned, he could find it—no problem. The mamasam was sending angry looks. Bad enough to burn a hole in your head. Mitch had spent his money, and she needed the table for other clients.'

The brothers persuaded Mitch to move to a quiet table, eager not to leave when so close to success. They ordered more drinks for Mitch, now in a mellow state—a fine balance of controlled euphoria before the inevitable decline into incoherence. Anyone offering to buy him a drink was a friend.

'We hit the jackpot,' said Suleiman. 'Mitch mentioned an old shipwreck called the *Siren*—an ancient trader from England. The wreckage lies near to a small chain of islands west of Basilan Island. The sea shallows to a metre at Brutus Reef and, after the impact, broke free, before sinking further east. He was sure his successful dive was halfway between the rocks and Dassalan Island. You can see the map I drew.'

Suleiman unravelled a folded white table napkin, which he retrieved from the back pocket of his jeans.

'Yes, your treasure map,' Tong opened out the tattered napkin, 'it is vague, but I suppose all we have. I have never heard of this *Siren* but suspect an East Indiaman—a China tea trader, a surprise as the Sulu Sea was not the usual trading route. The English boats traded with India and Canton, so why come here? It is strange. Why did he suddenly confide in you?'

'We talked of joining forces to find the treasure. Three divers plus all we needed was a boat. We said this to lead him on and never mentioned your interest. Playing him like a fish,' said Sulieman.

The brothers explained that they both left the KTV lounge at one o'clock in the morning. Mahmood drove straight home alone, and Suleiman walked in the rain to sober up. He took his time, in no hurry, as he feared a fierce scene from his wife if he returned drunk in the small hours. His plan was to slip in when she was sound asleep. The divers were unsure if Tong believed their story, as he remained inscrutable. Mahmood played with his table napkin, rolling it up and unravelling it.

A tense silence filled the restaurant with only the sound of background chatter and rattle of chopsticks against uplifted bowls. It was confusing to Tong as the meeting between the brothers and Mitch was in Geylang, far from where they found the body. He wondered why they thought the corpse was that of the diver.

'The KTV lounge only gives salty nuts. Make you thirsty but not satisfy. At one in the morning, nothing open, so perhaps he went to Newton Circus?' suggested Suleiman.

'It is possible—but strange. Without money, how could he hire a taxi? You are just guessing because you said you left before him. And how to buy a meal? It is very mysterious. That tourist trap at Newton never shuts. If the drowned man is the diver, it was in no one's interest to kill him. He could have helped us, and that was a clever move to suggest joining forces.'

However, Tong suspected the men were not telling him the full story. Had they taken Mitch to Newton Circus, tried to extract more information, fought and dumped him in the canal? Unlikely, as they had achieved their aim. He reached inside his black jacket and retrieved his wallet.

'This is the balance of what I owe you. Do not talk of our arrangement; especially not to the police.'

The men relaxed now they had their money.

'You are suspects—the last people to see Mitch alive. Do not involve me. I have a respectable standing within the clan, and my associates would be unhappy if you talk. Do you understand?'

'Yes, Mr Tong. What shall we say if they question us?'

'You are both divers, and the Mitre is where out-of-work divers and their whores drink. Tell the truth. You met up with a friend. On the day of his death, you gave him a lift to the KTV lounge and left him there. I recommend you leave Singapore for Malaysia to pick up work until the pressure is off.'

'Will you raise a team to look for the wreck?'

'It's not that easy. The Filipino authorities have to sanction the search. If we move ahead, are you interested?'

The divers agreed to help, despite their concerns. The Malaysians had their money and could walk away and forget the whole strange experience.

Leaving the restaurant, Tong showed them the Thong Chai medical building off Eu Tong Sen Road, praising the standard of the exterior renovation while castigating the mishmash of Chinese and western influences of the interior. At the entrance portal, they noticed a crowd of waitresses, like welcoming Sirens, ready to entice their clients into the chic chinoiserie. Tong spat at the sidewalk in disgust, narrowly missing an American couple seeking the genuine old Singapore. Little did they know the fat Chinese businessman hawking in the road was as close as they would get to it.

Chapter 8

Lucas visited the Jurong shipyard on a scorching morning. The derelict vessels alongside the quayside reflected the blinding heat so fiercely he shielded his eyes from the glare. Nearby, a scruffy dog lay in the shade of a crane whose rusty jib reached hopefully for the sky. Idle for so long, it might never work again. Compared to Loyang, this shipyard was in a state of deep depression.

Vincent Wong, a young over-weight man, waited patiently for Lucas at the gangplank. Lucas was running late. About to leave, Vincent greeted him with a surprised smile and a weak handshake. The men boarded *Eastern Pearl*, the vessel recommended by Davinder. Onboard, they met the captain, Mohamed Jaffar—a Malaysian from Ipoh. Jaffar proudly showed the men around the bridge. It was spotless and equipped with the latest equipment. Despite his pompous and verbose manner, his professionalism impressed Lucas. Without work, Jaffar had sent the crew on leave. Most of them were regulars. She was an impressive boat, with ample accommodation to a high standard—clean looking and tidy.

A welcome surprise in a run-down shipyard. Even the charter fee was lower than he expected. Lucas haggled the price down by fifty dollars a day, but would have paid a higher price without complaint. He agreed to hire the vessel as soon as the museum issued an exploration licence. The wreck search could follow on from the Malaysian job.

Michael spent a fruitful time at the British Library in London. He located the original ship's log for the *Siren*. In 1763, the East India Company had a monopoly for the China trade in the lucrative tea market. Over 30 sailings a year sailed from Long Reach, near Gravesend, on the perilous journey around the Cape of Good Hope and across the Indian Ocean to Whampoa near Canton. Besides attacks by French and Dutch men-of-war and pirate ships, they ran a risk of frequent storms, disease and infection wiping out the crew.

A helpful member of staff located the archives of the East India Company from 1600 to 1800. At the end of every voyage, they required the commander to hand over a copy of the ship's logbook to East India House. The British Library's India office now held the records. After a search for the 1763 and 1764 sailings, he located details of the last voyage of the *Siren*. This included the manifest for goods loaded in Canton. Although the bulk of the cargo was tea, the commander took on a quantity of export porcelain and Chinese gold. She must have been top-heavy like a clumsy elephant. Had the over-loading made her unstable?

The commander's journal recorded an account of the disaster. The vessel hit a reef. Despite taking on water fast, the *Siren* freed herself and anchored up south of the rocks. The commander, the mates, midshipmen, purser and boatswain were lucky to escape in the pinnace before the boat foundered and sunk. The journal recorded that the *Royal Talisman,* travelling in convoy, rescued twenty survivors from the nearby Pilates Island. Michael guessed this desolate refuge might be the modern-day Pilas Island. One hundred and twenty sailors fell to a watery grave.

Observations in the journal showed compass bearings, and the distance measured in leagues from nearby islands for the last resting place of the vessel. Certainly a challenge to work with such imprecise information. Brutus Reef is a shoal with jagged, submerged rocks. It might be the burial ground of many other boats, making it even harder to trace the *Siren*.

Michael studied the various trading routes. The passage from England to China took about eight months via the Azores and the Cape of Good Hope before heading east to Sumatra or Singapore. After a stop to restock supplies, vessels passed through the Malacca Strait, before crossing the South China Sea to Canton. The return trip was via India, depending on the season and strength of the monsoon. With port calls, the voyage could last eighteen months. A round trip via the Philippines would be at least two years. So why take this longer route?

The Spanish traded between Spain and Manila. To avoid any conflict with the Spaniards, the British favoured a route to the north, avoiding their territories. On this trip, the captain followed an unfamiliar course into Spanish controlled waters. Possibly London had commanded him to take the passage for commercial reasons. Perhaps they wished to open trade to Batavia and compete with the Dutch East India Company? Michael could not trace an accident report. Although the records were incomplete, he wrapped up his research. What a puzzling case! Whatever the plan, the mission had gone wrong.

He must convince the museum to sanction the survey. Here was the proof of a valuable cargo. He needed to study the maps and work out coordinates to see if they tied in with the 1986 survey—a daunting task. Even if he located the wreck site, others might have recovered the porcelain. All might be in vain with nothing to show.

This year the monsoon was a pale thing, erratic and fleeting. That afternoon, a sudden downpour forced Julie to shelter inside the Goodwood Park Hotel. The storm drains boiled with muddy rain and overflowed. Soon the floods subsided. Abandoning her shopping trip, she drove back to Changi. Julie marvelled at such violent weather changes. In the grounds at Pagoda Villas, she admired the red-veined caladiums and spiky heliconias still spotted with raindrops. The sound of the Tropics—the drumming chorus of the bullfrogs, invisible in the undergrowth, was like drum beats in an orchestra. Now the cicadas joined the performance. The buzzing vibrations of the male are hard to classify. Some call it a screech, others a buzz, or a whine or a chirp. It is a loud expression of male availability to attract a mate. She was lucky to live in a beautiful setting. So why so restless?

Julie forced herself to relax and enjoy the welcome change to be alone. She stripped to shorts and a T-shirt and lay back on the rattan planter on her veranda with an ice-cold gin and tonic. Such a guilty pleasure to laze about. This was the pattern most evenings. She blamed the narrow range of daily temperature fluctuations and high humidity, which typified Singapore's constant weather. With Michael at work and Alex at school, the interminable days were dull. At night the cycle changed. Just when she longed for a quiet rest, they invaded her space expecting food, drinks and sparkling conversation. Tonight, with both men away, was a bonus. Despite the offer of home study leave, Alex had been bored and returned to school. Best to make the most of a rare situation.

With Michael enjoying his leisure time in London, Julie scanned the faces by the poolside. She longed to see the attractive Italian from Block 42. Luigi usually took a swim in the evening, covering several lengths at a sprint, showing off his prowess. He was such a clown! Alone tonight, she wondered with a thrill of anticipation, if he might dare to approach her? He often did, casually, when Michael was with her. Restless, she'd love to talk to anyone. Especially Luigi. He had been so helpful starting the Volvo after Michael ran the battery flat. She recalled that surprise encounter with a warm glow. Was she reading too much into a brief meeting?

After starting her car, he was quick to leave with a matter-of-fact wave as he continued jogging around the perimeter of the gardens. But it was a start. A breaking the ice. She looked forward to seeing him again. It was just a question of when.

Luigi might walk right past her apartment. Fantasising about the man made her wonder if Michael was faithful to her on his trip to London. She had no one to swop small talk. No one to release the day's tension, like a spring uncoiling. Tiring of her own company, she glanced at the pool, willing her lean young Italian to show. But there were only a few children, released from homework, joyfully splashing. If the recession continued, Michael might lose his job. In this business he was very busy, or twiddling his thumbs with boredom. Nothing in-between. In the early years, he worked in the oil industry. He was often away on overseas projects for months. Tough times when Alex was a baby, and she had to cope alone. Now it was the reverse. He was always here when not needed! She could not face a return to the UK. To blend in anonymous and dull with her fellow neighbours in that rain-lashed land was a grim prospect. Surely, that was a bad move? She needed to step into the unknown. Confront fresh possibilities and experiences. Life was a search. If you sat back and became complacent, stuck in an endless repetition, then something was wrong.

On impulse, she slipped into an old swimming costume. She studied it critically in the bedroom mirror. It hugged her figure in all the right places and made her look younger and more attractive. But the backless view displayed her pale back. The sun was too harsh for a desirable golden tan, so she had to put up with dull white skin. She had not worn it in ages, preferring a more restrained little black number from Marks and Spencer.

However, tonight was different. With a carefree toss of her blonde hair, Julie headed for the poolside. She passed a shy Japanese woman with her daughter. They beamed a cheery smile and said hello. The mother spoke little English so any attempts at conversation ended in smiles and head nodding. Her husband worked late, as was the way with the Japanese expatriates. They loved to frequent bars without their wives. Singaporean Aunties wandered by in flip-flops, dragging their feet and staring in every direction like clucking chickens. Filipino maids gathered for a chat, as the kids in their care ran wild on the lawn and chased the mynah birds. In short, a typical evening at Pagoda Villas.

The lights lit up the pool with a magic glow. Most of the children had left. The few adults remaining spoke in hushed tones. Mostly they swam a few lengths in concentrated isolation. To break the silence, she jumped into the deepest part. A loud splash followed by a slow crawl to the shallow end to look up towards Luigi's balcony. But there was no trace. Perhaps it was too early, and he was not back from work? Julie continued her swim with a languid backstroke. All Luigi had to do was wander out onto his balcony, and he would see her, but there were no lights from his window. After an hour of listless swimming, all her fellow swimmers had departed. A coldness descended, and she returned to her apartment.

Chapter 9

The Singapore Airlines flight landed at Kuala Lumpur's Subang airport in the pouring rain. Mr Tong always travelled in business class. The seats in economy were too small and constricted for his broad girth, and he appreciated the better service, as befitted his status. A creature of habit, Tong stayed at the Shangri-la Hotel and liked to arrive early with time to relax before any meeting. After booking into his usual suite, he looked forward to a leisurely lunch in the restaurant before his appointment at the museum in the afternoon. There were eight restaurants to choose from, but Tong knew from experience to avoid the pretentious ones where the chefs indulged their creative interpretations of classic dishes. Strange flavour combinations often spoiled the goal of a spectacular presentation. Innovation was the scourge of otherwise decent hotels.

Tong opted for lunch at Shang Palace, which specialised in Cantonese cuisine. He avoided the dull set menu, and ordered a light meal of hot and sour Szechuan soup with prawn and shredded sea cucumber followed by a simple platter of Dim Sum with small dumplings made with shrimp, chicken, scallops and spring rolls. To finish, he ordered a pot of Pu'er tea, the fermented beverage from Yunnan province, to settle the digestion. He expected a more elaborate dinner later as a guest of honour at the Kuala Lumpur Clan Association, the original founding society before they branched out to Singapore. The influential network stretched over the world, paying no heed to boundaries or countries. Wherever there was a Chinese business community and a Chinatown; there were plentiful opportunities.

After lunch, he caught a taxi to the National Museum to meet Dr Khian Chiew, an expert at identifying antique porcelain, especially of the Ming dynasty.

Tong had wrapped his dish in bubble wrap and secured it in his pilot case for extra protection. On the flight, his case was by his feet; unwilling to risk it in the hold or the overhead locker.

The six characters on its base suggested it was a valuable piece. Despite paying an extortionate sum for the plate, Tong suspected it was worth much more. He hoped the ceramic's expert would confirm its authenticity. If so, he might commission a salvage operation of the cargo. On arrival at the museum on Jalan Damansara, Dr Chiew showed him to his office. After the opening pleasantries, Tong unwrapped the serving dish with great care. The blue and white enamelled design, incorporating prancing dragons and an unusual motif, was in a form Chiew had never seen.

'Ah, six marks on the base,' said Chiew, as he turned the plate. 'And the double-lined square border.'

'I looked up the characters in reference books,' said Tong. 'But I can't find it.'

Chiew moved the plate closer to the anglepoise lamp and used a magnifying glass to study it in greater detail.

'If I am correct, this plate is the middle period Ch'ing dynasty from the time of Kangxi—from 1662 to 1722. What I love is the quality of the reign marks. They are so sharp and deep coloured. Only the palace could commission such a fine piece—the highest level of Imperial porcelain.'

'You mean it belonged to the Emperor?'

'Yes, the Emperor would have commissioned it. It is a single specimen, but most likely part of a set. Maybe he kept it for himself, or to donate to an important dignitary. How did you find it?'

'From a dealer in Singapore. A diver recovered it from a shipwreck.'

'Was the ship found in Malaysian waters?'

'No, I don't believe so,' said Tong, unwilling to divulge more than necessary.

'It's odd to uncover such a fine piece in a wreck. The china exports to the West were of inferior quality.'

'You are correct. Do you remember the big Nanking cargo auction at Christie's in Amsterdam back in 1986?'

'Yes,' said Chiew. 'The Englishman Hatcher made a fortune.'

'Most of it was cheap Imari used for export. The prices were ludicrous, but the Europeans lapped up everything because of the mystique surrounding the search for the *Geldermalsen* and skilful marketing by Christie's auction house.'

'The unscrupulous treasure hunters lack respect for the archaeological significance of the wrecks. They plunder and destroy our treasures for illegal gains.'

'I am a lifelong collector of antiquities to preserve our Chinese heritage,' said Tong. 'The European traders carried private trade. It was a captain's perks, purchasing better quality china. Sometimes the fee-paying passengers took home fine collectables. Amongst the dross, there might be something exceptional such as this plate of Imperial porcelain.'

'Yes, I see you have researched the field. But the piece could be a forgery. If you like, I can check to prove the authenticity.'

'Are you able to run tests now?'

'It's best to analysis fragments of pottery from the wreck scene. Do you have any shards?'

'No, Dr Chiew, I only have the single plate.'

'A pity—XRD, XRF and SEM are excellent laboratory techniques to identify the clay minerals and pigments, but destructive so an insignificant piece is best. Without fragments, these tests are inappropriate.'

Chiew tugged at the few wispy hairs of his sparse moustache, removing and wiping his glasses. Aged thirty-five, he had the demeanour of an obsessed academic, young and ageless until one day he would wake up grey and old, having achieved nothing. It was his constant fear. His research into early dynastic porcelain had resulted in many papers published to mild critical approval, but this was different. If correct, this was the best find of his career. Although cold from the air-conditioning, he was sweating. He turned his attention back to Mr Tong.

'If you like, I can examine the marks on the base and take pictures to send to a colleague for a second opinion.'

Chiew had a compound microscope mounted at a side table. He racked the microscope to its full height and selected the twenty times magnification to detect the potter's stamp. Chiew took a series of photographs as he moved the plate around to get the best illumination. He pointed to the symbol like the figure of a running man.

'This Chinese mark means great. It is the normal first character used in both the Ming and Ch'ing dynasties. The second character confirms the piece is from the Ch'ing dynasty. These two stamps are the potter's hallmarks. I need a reference book to discover the place of manufacture. The last two marks clinch the identification as being Guan Yao or Imperial ware; so excellent news!'

Chiew racked the lens to a higher magnification as he studied the marks and took a further series of photographs. Tong glanced at his watch. Chiew's breathless scrutiny had lasted five minutes. In the rising tension, Tong dared not disturb him.

'The dish is in exceptional condition with no obvious deterioration.'

'No fading of the original colours?'

'That is correct. Remarkably pristine—like it was made yesterday! However, it depends on the conditions on the seabed. If clays bury the porcelain, it preserves better. It is more likely this plate is the product of a special heat processing used for the highest quality. This is a most exciting discovery. I hope you recover the rest of this priceless set.'

Tong felt his spirits lift at this excellent news. 'We plan to salvage more from the site.'

'Please inform me of the progress. Aside from the monetary value, it will generate historical and scientific interest. I can document your finds or get leave of absence to go on your mission.'

'Thank you, but we have a research team in mind. You appreciate that, as the find is not in Malaysian waters, we must use the local expertise. But we will contact you for further help, if required.'

Mr Tong took his leave. It had been a most useful meeting. The plate had surpassed his expectations. Now he needed to locate the rest of the set. As the sea conditions preserved the single plate, the others should be pristine. Dr Chiew had provided enough proof—no need to consult the expert further. The fewer people who knew, the better.

The clan had invited Tong to attend a *wayang* that evening at a small temple near Jalan Petaling, the centre of Kuala Lumpur's Chinatown. The puppet theatre was the front for a more sinister initiation rite of new disciples to the Wah Chan Clan. Compared to Singapore, the KL branch was far more active. In Penang and Kuala Lumpur, there were at least 40,000 members of various secret Triad organisations. With little effective control by the police, gang membership was thriving with drug smuggling, extortion, gambling and prostitution in the hands of organised crime. In the past, the traditional Chinese societies ran the Triad gangs, but Indians had infiltrated the structure and refocused on crimes that are more violent. For example, Malay Indians took over the Chinese Hua Kee and renamed it Gang 04. Other splinter groups such as Gang 36 controlled most of the drug dealings. The crime wave and killings were becoming rampant, and the Home Ministry were fighting back with success.

Tonight's initiation ceremony followed the age-old traditions. They brought the disciples into a back room of the temple, clad only in white sheets and in pairs. Outside the crowds jostled and crowded to watch the *wayang* performance oblivious of the secret rites about to take place.

Each pair of initiates was forced to advance on their knees and bend under five trestle tables representing portals. At each portal, armed men with parangs questioned the candidates and asked what they were seeking. The correct response was that they sought their brethren, after which the men allowed them to pass to the next four portals with repetitions of the same question. Finally, they filled a bowl with the fresh blood of a white cockerel mixed with red wine. The Master of Ceremonies pricked the middle finger of each candidate's right hand and shook the blood into the bowl. Each candidate with hands tied behind his back then leant forward to drink from the jar placed on the floor. After this, the candidates had to recite the 36 secret oaths requiring obedience on pain of death.

Tong was familiar with the rite which followed a similar form as first prescribed by the early settlers from China and was little different in aims from other societies such as the Freemasons. It was a mistake to imagine the initiation rites were merely a formality. Instant retribution to traitors enforced unquestioning loyalty.

After the ceremony, the clan served up a sumptuous twelve course banquet with a roasted suckling pig on a bed of jellyfish as the top dish.

Chapter 10

Michael smiled, pleased to have completed his research into the loss of the *Siren*. He could look forward to a free weekend visiting his parents in Sussex. It was sad that Julie could not join him. With more notice, they could have taken a week of their holidays. But times were tough at PanAsia Services, and Lucas was too mean to pay airfares for the family to the UK.

Michael drove out of London early on a sultry July afternoon to escape the routine crawl to the provinces. Cars crept forward until the roadworks on the M25, where the stalled traffic admired the overhead gantries and flashing speed limit signs. The queues inched slower than drying paint. Bored at the lack of action, he cast sideways glances at his fellow motoring sufferers, noting the habits of nose picking, ear scratching, hair tidying and mobile telephone chatting used to idle away the time.

Michael's imagination left the traffic jam and moved alongside the skipper of the *Siren*, as she eased south with the island of Basilan three leagues to the west. A balmy day near noon on Tuesday, February 14, 1764. A slight westerly breeze blew off the land, bringing a haze of smoke from loggers burning the forest. Despite the wind blowing from shore, the vessel kept crabbing towards a line of rocks, driven by a strong current. It was too close for comfort. The commander had never sailed this passage off the Philippines. In his wisdom, Robert Clive, head of the British East India Company, ordered him to pioneer an unfamiliar route for the return leg from Canton to London.

Although the helmsman followed a new heading away from the rocks, the strong current still forced them closer to shore. Together with the mate, they searched for any sign of white tops breaking over a submerged reef. The commander passed the wheel to a sailor and drew out his telescope to pan the waters. In the bow, a seaman took frequent soundings with the lead line, watching for any sudden change of slope. At the top of the mast in the crow's nest, a junior apprentice—a teenager on his first voyage—kept a keen lookout. Other seamen, clustered in groups on the main deck, scanned the ocean, both port and starboard, and in the helmsman's blind zone. The commander breathed a sigh of relief. He expected to be free of the offshore reefs in daylight and break out to the open sea.

Forty minutes later the current strengthened coinciding with a Spring tide, which forced the boat closer to a submerged reef not shown on their chart. A shout from the sailor at the bow warned them of the shoaling seabed. There was a sickening grating and grinding as the ship's hull scraped the coral reef. The crew rushed onto the main deck in alarm and lowered the sails. Meanwhile, the chief mate organised a team to inspect the bilges for damage.

The commander ordered them to hold the position until the rising tide lifted them off the reef and they dropped anchors to stop any more movement, which might have sunk the boat. But the anchors tore away without gripping. After twenty minutes, the tide rose, but instead of breaking free, the coral cut more jagged holes into the hull and water poured in too fast for her pumps to cope.

Desperate, the commander ordered the men to hoist the sails. The crew heaved the cannons through the gun ports and into the sea to lighten the load. They met with success, and the ship lifted off the reef. However, fate dealt another cruel blow. From nowhere, a violent Sumatra storm blew with high seas and winds of forty knots, pushing the boat back on the rocks and coral, which cut into the hull like a knife thrust to the belly. They lowered two longboats, manned with the most muscular oarsmen who attached lines to free her on the rising tide—a successful manoeuvre and the *Siren* rose again.

The commander made a last-ditch effort to run inshore to beach her on an island and salvage the cargo, but he was running out of options. Several leagues away, the *Royal Talisman* saw the disaster but held off for fear of foundering on the reef. With hope fading, he ordered the crew to abandon ship, and, as they lowered the pinnace, seawater poured through the hatches, escaped air hissing, bubbling and boiling. The sea swallowed up eighty seamen like a closed trapdoor until the surface erupted with men and pieces of wreckage amid a vortex of spiralling debris. Grabbing the ship's logbook, the commander left with most of his officers, defying the convention he should stay with his stricken vessel. There was only time to launch two longboats and the pinnace. They rescued a few, but the despairing arms of many more, reaching to the sky, sunk away, until the sea settled above their grave.

As the ship sat upright on the seabed, the sand waves into which she fell first cushioned her fall and then entrapped and buried her. Within a few years, trains of dunes hid the last traces of the *Siren* and her valuable cargo. The skeleton of the teenage apprentice stared out blindly from his crow's nest, and fish flew into his gaping mouth and left via the open eye sockets.

The main mast stuck a defiant finger and the uniform of the boy shrank over his bones, flakes of his red shirt danced in the current, the bright colours shimmering as shafts of sunlight pierced the waters. At last, masthead and the apprentice fell in a graceful arc to a seabed repose, and sand and coral encrusted his skeleton.

Michael came out of his daydream with a start as the car behind hooted. The traffic was flowing, and it rained as he joined the A3 south towards Portsmouth, and then the A283 for Petworth and Arundel. He expected hold-ups at the usual bottlenecks, and doubtless more roadworks. Hidden speed cameras racked up fines along trouble-free stretches where frustrated motorists tried to make up for lost time. The ring of his mobile phone interrupted Michael's musings with a call from Julie.

'Where are you?'

'I am near Guildford. There's the normal Friday afternoon crawl, so I expect it will be another hour before I reach my parents.'

'Well, give them my love. You must have finished your jolly in London if you are going to Sussex. When are you coming back?'

'I plan to catch the Monday night flight from Heathrow so I'll see you on Tuesday. You could meet me at the airport. I think we land at seven in the evening.'

'Lucas rang me. He needs to speak to you.'

'You're getting faint. Hold on—I'll pull off the road. Can you still hear me?'

'Yes, you are much clearer now. I said Lucas is chasing you.'

'Did he say why?'

'No, I imagine he wishes to know how your research is going. He has this meeting in Manila, and he hopes you will be back in time. But most likely he needs to bring you up to speed on the Mitch Austin case.'

'Mitch Austin, the diver?'

'Yes. Listen to this. I am reading from the Straits Times: It says: *"Identification of Rochor Canal victim: Papers on the corpse recovered from the Rochor Canal yesterday have identified the man as Mitchell Austin, an Australian citizen. Any witnesses or relatives should contact their nearest police station with information. Inspector Lim of CID stated they could not prove the cause of death at this stage. They will conduct an autopsy as required by law."* Isn't that amazing?'

'Mitchell Austin, My God! The same fellow we met at the Mitre.'

'It's definitely that rude man. I expect he was drunk and fell into the canal.'

'I see—that's incredible news.'

It was a puzzle how Mitch had fallen into the Rochor Canal. Killiney Road was some distance from the canal. Michael felt dazed at as he realised the key person who had triggered their search for the *Siren,* and had the best idea of its resting place, could no longer assist them. Julie interrupted his thoughts and asked how his research was going.

'Very productive—I have a few loose ends still to tie up, but enough to convince the museum to issue the permit to survey.'

'Great. It's midnight in Singapore, so give Lucas a call tomorrow to stop him fretting.'

'Will do. I can phone him later. These mobile calls cost a fortune.'

'Sorry. I'll take the hint. I'm missing you.'

The search for the *Siren* was developing into an obsession. As Michael unravelled the records from the British Library and pieced together its last voyage, it became more and more fascinating for him. She felt he had overwhelmed her resistance. Now Alex wanted to join the survey—her worst fear! Only eighteen and stubborn, just like his father!

Michael controlled everything in their lives. Now, this risky venture gripped him, and it worried her it might not work out well. By comparison, her mild pursuit of Luigi was only a distraction. What a lucky stroke their paths had crossed! In her mind, she replayed the chance meeting when he had fixed her car.

She was in a rush to drive to Cold Storage and had forgotten the car was unreliable. Just as she was struggling to start the engine of the old Volvo outside her apartment, he had come jogging past shirtless and wearing a pair of Ralph Lauren chino shorts. What luck he was running past just when she needed help. He pulled up by the open window of the car. Julie sat back with exasperation and brushed the sweat off her forehead.

'I think the starter motor's jammed. It won't start, and the battery is nearly flat. I am so cross. I asked Michael to fix it.'

He reached inside, brushing past her bare leg, causing her an immediate frisson as he fumbled for the bonnet release. He apologised as her leg shot out in an uncontrollable lunge and his face collided with her knee. Blind to the pain, he gripped the lever to free the bonnet, which popped open with a metallic clang. After inspecting the engine and tweaking a cable, he ordered her to try the ignition again. The Volvo purred into life.

'You've got the touch!' Julie simpered, still tingling from that casual, but she suspected, deliberate brush. She was struggling to get out of the driver's seat to thank him, but he had closed the bonnet and was fleeing.

'No problem—just a loose connection!'

He glanced at his watch and jogged off fast to make up for lost time, leaving Julie speechless. What a wasted opportunity for a longer chat! And he had ignored her when she took a languorous swim on that idyllic evening. True, his balcony was too far off to recognise her. Ever since, she kept surveillance on the swimming pool and the gardens of the condominium, but Luigi had vanished, to have trotted away on another route or held captive by a jealous wife or girlfriend.

Chapter 11

Davinder turned off Balmoral Road and up the driveway to the fake Tudor clad exterior of the Sloane Court Hotel. The restaurant and guest rooms were in the same style as similar establishments in the Home Counties of the 1950s, with black timber beams and hunting prints. Despite the name, this was tropical Singapore, a colonial survivor defying the new luxury high-rise apartments rising on the bones of the past.

The two-story hotel plot was a developer's dream, set back at the end of a drive lined by a garden with mature trees softening the edges to the adjacent tower blocks, which cast a perpetual shade. On one side, demolition had left a vacant void ready for the next addition, like a cavity waiting for a golden crown. Sadly, it was only a matter of time before they flattened the Sloane Court and erected multi-storey flats on the valuable site.

The restaurant was busy for Sunday lunch, and Davinder squeezed into a parking space. An ancient swing creaked as two small boys giggled and pushed at the rusty frame, urging it, like a tired old horse, to go faster. Whining and moaning in protest, the children forced the swing ever higher until their parents, squatting on the lalang grass, became concerned. The father jumped up and steadied it, telling them to stop.

Davider ordered a large Tiger beer, ignoring the more expensive imports purchased by the unwary. He grabbed a bowl of salted peanuts and sat at a table, waiting for his guest. The chef peeped through the kitchen door—an old grey-haired man in his eighties. This was a Hainanese family-run business—the last survivors catering to an unchanging menu of Chinese, Malay, Indian and Western cuisine. Tong entered the restaurant and identified Davinder with a restrained smile. In conformance to the Chinese custom, he avoided shaking the man's hand—a deplorable Western habit.

'Pleased to meet you. I hope it hasn't inconvenienced you at such brief notice?' asked Davinder. Tong was a short man with a square chest packed into a tight suit.

'I have never been here, but I hear favourable reports.'

'Yes, the food is excellent. There's a choice of local or Western cuisine.'

Tong scrutinised the menu and settled on a mixed grill preceded by mushroom soup. Davinder opted for a chicken curry.

'Mr Davinder, as I explained on the phone, we wish to uncover an old shipwreck. We need your best price for a survey vessel and expert team to find it. I believe your company can help us?'

Davinder took out a new business card from his wallet and handed it to Tong. His wife had come up with the name, which he was not that keen on. He relied on a tight-knit network of clients who knew him by name.

'Equatorial Surveys. We run surveys for wrecks, both modern and historical. Is this wreck in Singapore waters?'

'No, in the Sulu Sea near the Philippines.'

'Wah, the worst place possible,' said Davinder. 'The Sulu Sea is risky from the Muslim separatists, Abu Sayyaf. It will push the marine insurance up, and we have to pass those costs back to you. In addition, you must arrange the survey permit.'

'Understood, we have contacts to expedite this. Can you locate skilled people prepared to go there?'

'Our local surveyors may refuse, but our pool of young Australians will work anywhere.'

'I prefer we use Asians as much as possible. Too many Caucasians are conspicuous.'

'Okay. We'll see who is available. What are the water depths in the survey zone?'

Tong unfolded an Admiralty Chart with a pencilled rectangular block, which marked the proposed concession. It impressed Davinder. He had done his homework. Davinder studied the map with interest, noting the chain of small islands and reefs stretching from Brutus Reef towards the large island of Basilan. The best choice of vessel was the *Eastern Pear,* with enough space for a survey team and a shallow draught ideal for the survey area. But he had stupidly recommended the boat to Lucas for his work in Malaysia. Davinder wondered what time frame Tong had in mind.

'We hope to start once they have approved the exploration permit. Hopefully, we can achieve that by the end of next week. How long does it take to sail between Singapore and the Southern Philippines?'

'At least fourteen days—more if the weather is poor.'

Tong studied his beer. 'We leave as soon as possible— ideally in two weeks' time.'

Davinder sucked in his breath. 'That's pushing it. I doubt if *Eastern Pearl* will be free, but another choice is the *Pacific Glory*—an excellent vessel. Our lump sum price includes the personnel and gear needed for your job. Once we arrive on site and set up the equipment, we charge a day rate for the survey. For jobs of this nature, we need a fifty thousand dollar deposit paid upfront before we leave.'

Davinder studied Tong to see the impact of these words. Shipwreck searches were a gamble because the clients were reluctant to pay if the search was a failure.

'That is outrageous,' said Tong.

'I am sorry, but you are a new client. Dishonest people try to take advantage of us—not that I doubt you. The deposit paid upfront means the last bill is less.'

It was rare to impose such stringent conditions, but Davinder hoped the demand for a large deposit might put him off. However, Tong accepted it and moved on to further questions.

'What equipment do you need to locate a shipwreck?'

'We will survey where you instruct us. I recommend a magnetometer, side-scan sonar and a seismic profiler to look for possible buried objects below the seabed and a differential global satellite positioning system, what we call a DGPS. It's the standard these days, and accurate. If the equipment finds no contacts, we still expect full payment because our costs are the same, success or failure.'

This annoyed Tong. He reassured Davinder that the Singapore branch of the Wah Chan Clan guaranteed payment for the survey and had funds set aside. If they demanded such a large sum in advance, they might arrange this, although highly irregular. Tong agreed that if they performed the work correctly but without success, then he would settle the bills, regardless. Their research gave confidence of success.

'I can contact you next week with our proposal and recommendations. If you are searching for a historic wreck with a valuable cargo, we cannot survey without approval from the relevant government. Our company has to see a copy of your permit.'

Tong looked put out.

'Do not worry. We need to keep details secret. As soon as we have the licence, we will let you know.'

'You understand, I have to ask these questions. I don't want problems later.'

'The boat must sail direct to the site, complete the project and return to Singapore,' said Tong.

'It's irregular. We usually fly our people to the nearest port to join the vessel. If personnel travel onboard it will push up the cost and we might have problems with the clearance requirements.'

Tong shrugged.

'Our agent in Manila can sort out the logistics.'

This worried Davinder—best to give a top price, and hope Tong would go elsewhere.

At the same time as the men were discussing their plans, Lucas Miffré was at Jack's Steakhouse in Ang Mo Kio—a new town of ugly high-rise tower blocks. Jack's was always a busy restaurant and popular with families. Today, in an excellent mood, Lucas celebrated with their speciality, a large prime fillet of New Zealand steak. Michael had confirmed his research was complete. It was amazing the detail he had unearthed from the British Library. They had a clearer idea of the fate of the *Siren*. Lucas felt confident the pieces were falling into place—the boat and the team. He regretted not updating Michael with disturbing news about the Mitchell Austin case. Lucas's contacts in the press had passed him more details. The autopsy results had recorded blood alcohol levels in Mitch's body of twice the legal limit, but for a habitual drinker like Mitch, this was just a steady level.

Had he tripped, bashing his head against a lamp post, and then toppled into the water? It was a mystery why he was near the canal. The police claimed he had gone for a late meal at Newton Circus and was walking off his excessive drinking. Lucas reckoned this was unlikely, so had someone killed him to discover the lost location of the *Siren*?

He ignored these concerns as he savoured the steak and flirted with the waitress, a short, cheerful Chinese girl with long black hair. She kept looking at him with amused half-interest from beneath her fringe. She had persuaded him to buy a bottle of the promotional Jacob's Creek, but she could see he hated the wine.

An entire bottle was too much. Its unsubtle blackcurrant laced flavour left a cloying taste. Amazing that people could drink such awful stuff. In Singapore, the wine was expensive, so only the worst quality was affordable to the young National Service personnel who frequented Jack's Place. Australians must keep their best and sell the trash abroad. The French exported their finest and drunk vin ordinaire at home.

'*Meidan*,' Lucas asked for the bill. He knew a few words of Chinese. In multi-lingual Singapore, he liked to show off his knowledge of the languages and dialects, although English was the key to effective communication.

'You haven't finished,' the waitress admonished him like a naughty boy.

'It's too sweet for me. I should have ordered a more expensive wine. You can finish it.'

'*Aiyah*, I don't drink wine.'

'But you recommend it! Why not try? See if you like it.'

'Do you live in Ang Mo Kio?' she asked.

'No. I have a house in Serangoon Village. How do you know I live in Singapore?'

'Well, despite your French accent, I don't judge you as a tourist. Visitors never come to Ang Mo Kio, so you must work here.'

She had made a correct assessment. There was nothing much to attract tourists to the soulless multi-storey blocks that formed one of Singapore's largest satellite towns.

'Serangoon Village. I love it there. So quiet and old-fashioned; especially those eating-places by the bus terminal. My mother used to take me to the wet market. After her shopping at NTUC, we took char siew rice at a stall. I think they called it the Sputnik Restaurant.'

'It's still there. But the name has changed.'

They chatted for ages and after he had settled the bill, adding a large tip, he handed over his business card. His French name fascinated her. She volunteered her name as Kim Choo. Regrettably, she had no business card. But maybe she would serve him next time if her shift coincided with his visit.

Chapter 12

It surprised Michael to see Lucas drive up to Pagoda Villas on a Sunday morning. Was there no escape from the office? Lucas looked at Michael's dripping wet swimming trunks, indifferent at disturbing him unannounced. They stopped at the bar fridge for two beers. Eleven o'clock and blazing heat, a wonderful excuse for a drink. Lucas pulled the ring on a can of Anchor and emptied half the beer in a single gulp. He explained that the National Museum wanted them to attend an urgent meeting for Monday afternoon. Very short notice. He hoped Michael's research was complete in time to attend—anyway, a foregone conclusion because Lucas handed him a ticket for an early flight. They could stay overnight at the Manila Hotel, near the museum. Fortunately, Michael had finished his research and Danica had prepared a slide presentation for him. He was expecting this meeting, but not so soon.

'Our first approach to the curator was positive, but the person we have to win over is the head of the archaeological section—a Dr Da Souza. Christina Velasco works in his department. When I spoke to Da Souza yesterday, he told me they scrutinise applications. After nasty experiences with treasure hunters, they are much more circumspect.'

'You can understand their caution,' said Michael.

'Yes. Now, listen to this. After Dr Da Souza gave these negative vibes, I rang Miss Velasco. Christina is a senior research worker. If the job is approved, she will travel with us. Do you remember I mentioned another consortium from Singapore is seeking a wreck?'

'Yes, that's the reason you brought the project forward.'

'Christina told me this group is also after the *Siren*. They have a vessel ready to start. *Merde*! Can you believe this? Dr Da Souza is wondering why, after an unsuccessful survey sixteen years ago, two separate parties wish to return.'

'Is it the crowd who approached Davinder?'

'Yes—a man called Tong from Chinatown. I am guessing his source of information is Mitch. Or should I say, *was* Mitch since the police have confirmed the body in the canal was the Australian.'

'If they are relying on Mitch's word, they won't have concrete evidence,' said Michael. 'My success locating the ship's manifest will impress them.'

The veranda door slid open and Alex, dripping water on the floor after a morning dip, wandered past without a backward glance and carried on to the bathroom. Michael looked embarrassed, but Lucas just smiled, relieved that his single status spared him the experience of moody teenagers.

Black clouds swallowed up the blue sky, and a cool draught of air preceded a sudden deluge forcing a mass evacuation from the pool. In a moment, a lake formed on the tiles surrounding the swimming pool and a torrent cascaded over the steps as children squealed with delight. Alex threw on some clothes and returned to the lounge, drying his hair with a towel. Michael suspected he was hanging around for a beer but ignored him.

Lucas lit up a cigarette and stretched out on the sofa, making himself at home. Julie hated people smoking in the house, and Michael and Alex looked nervously at the door, hoping she would not return. Alex placed a saucer on the table next to Lucas to catch the ash before it landed on the floor.

'What are the sea conditions like in the Philippines?' asked Alex.

'The survey is outside the typhoon belt. August is the hottest month, although the offshore breezes make it more comfortable, but expect heavy showers. Fantastic your mother has agreed you can join us. It will be a great experience.'

'Thank you for the opportunity. I am a powerful swimmer if that is any use.'

'The divers should train you up to help them. But safer for you to keep dry on the boat. It might worry Julie if she knew you were swimming with sharks.'

In the road, the downpour caused a queue of drivers hooting their horns as traffic ground to a standstill. The rain had stopped as abruptly as a slammed door, and the black clouds parted as the sun lit up the canopy of the tall albizia trees alongside the roadside verges—the only evidence of the cloudburst, the swirl of muddy floodwater filling the deep storm drains. Traffic picked up speed and shot sheets of water into myriads of droplets like sparkling diamonds in the sunbeams. The darkness lifted, and the tropical sun bathed the balcony, causing steam to rise from the tiles.

'Where is your lovely wife this morning?' Lucas asked.

'Gone shopping to Cold Storage, Jelita. She will be sorry to miss you.'

'That's a lengthy trip. Why not go somewhere closer?'

'She isn't keen on the local supermarkets. She meets up with friends in Holland Village. It keeps her happy.'

'So far I have avoided married bliss,' said Lucas, inhaling his Gitanes and blowing out a cloud of choking smoke. 'I suppose I am too set in my ways. Well, I must go.

Meet me at the check-in counter at Terminal 2 tomorrow. Here is the ticket confirmation in case we are separated. Best to book a taxi tonight. You know it's impossible in the morning.'

Julie returned, looking exhausted and trailing loads of shopping bags. She sniffed the air. Although they cleared the ashtray, her keen sense of smell detected smoke. Michael told her Lucas had dropped by with a ticket to Manila for a meeting at the museum. They agreed it was strange to visit on a Sunday. Why not phone?

Julie walked out to the veranda. The heat of the sun was evaporating the recent rain. A group of her friends frolicked in the swimming pool, and others were grilling king prawns and spider crabs over a barbecue and waved her over to join them, but she felt too tired. Clouds of fragrant smoke billowed out in waves, and a pair of cats inched closer, their eyes pleading for attention. Nearby, the ornamental pond attracted small groups of maids who squatted on the ground chatting together. Children, in their care, dangled at the edge, or ran around in excited circles. The water was shallow, but the sides were rocky, so the maids kept a nervous eye, pulling the toddlers to them or shouting warnings to be careful.

Despite the peaceful scene, Julie appeared tense. Every day the same pattern. Predictable and boring; life was flashing past like a bus, and she had missed the ride. Michael and Alex could be part of an exciting survey to locate the precious cargo of an ancient shipwreck—a challenge Michael was reluctant to join. Why should they visit a beautiful, unspoiled destination with no thought of her? Mostly she worried about the risks of the area.

'Michael, I mentioned to a friend about your project in the Sulu Sea. He says it's one of the most dangerous seas in the world for pirate attacks. Is that true?'

'Who said that?'

'Oh, just someone I bumped into by the poolside—no one you know.'

'Whoever it was, he was trying to scare you. Best not to mention our affairs to others.'

She had nearly blurted out how she and Luigi spent time by the pool one evening after his helpful repair of the car—all harmless, naturally. Julie sensed the conversation was running away from her. It was easier to agree with him and not raise his suspicions. She ran off to the fridge to fetch more beers.

'And I am not alone. Danica told me the Sulu Sea is dangerous and attacks on boats are common with many cases never reported.'

'I don't know where she got that idea.'

'From you, Michael. Perhaps you are more honest with your girlfriend than with me?'

What rubbish, Danica was a colleague, and their relationship was appropriate for the workplace. No point in replying to such a ridiculous accusation. But he should not put Julie through this stress. What was driving him to get involved?

'Let's see how the museum meeting goes tomorrow. If my research convinces them to issue a permit, that's a result.'

'Makes sense,' she agreed. 'Can you fetch the rest of the shopping in from the car?'

Before lunch, they took a stroll around the gardens of the Pagoda Villas complex. After a few minutes, a sudden clap of thunder interrupted their walk. Large droplets of water fell from the sky, and the barbecue parties fled for cover. It was so sudden they took shelter in the ground level void deck of the nearest block of flats. They looked through the curtain of rain at children running and laughing through the downpour. One boy struggled with an umbrella, inverted and twisted. He let it fall like a bird, folding its dying wings, as it sunk into the sodden grass. Clearly, the heavy rain would not stop, so Michael and Julie sprinted back to the apartment. Although it was only a brief run up a flight of steps, they were both soaked to the skin in seconds.

Alex, who was playing table tennis with a friend on the void deck, noticed his parents rush back to the apartment. From this dry vantage point, he saw the storm unwind, and watched their embarrassing antics.

Wet and breathless, they collapsed on the sofa. Although Michael liked the condominium, it was like living in a goldfish bowl with a constant stream of locals and expatriates splashing about in the pool or wandering past their veranda. Better to move elsewhere with more privacy. This climate was so unpredictable—one moment you were too hot and then too cold. Julie fetched a bottle of Tiger. She never used to touch alcohol, but things change. She was feeling amorous, yielding to the lethargy of the afternoon and lack of plans. Michael had left the sofa and collapsed on the bed. The late nights working at the office were making him tired and irritable.

She removed his damp T-shirt and massaged the stress from his shoulders. He responded and mumbled something into his pillow, but she saw he was asleep, his deep breathing settling into an annoying snore. In case he was pretending, she gave an angry kick. He remained oblivious, although his snoring abated as he turned his head a fraction towards her, as if at the point of waking. Then he rolled over on his side, sinking deeper into the mattress, immovable as death. It was a pity to waste beer, so she drank it. No doubt about it, he was so selfish.

Chapter 13

Michael woke early, from a vivid dream of their survey boat tossing around in a violent storm with water pouring across the decks and flooding into the accommodation. They were sinking and panicking. He searched for Julie and Alex without success, a crumb of comfort. Instead, there was emptiness, a regret which death would not cure, only perpetuate. Despite the piercing chill of the air conditioning, he was sweating. With dawning clarity, he turned it off and opened the blinds. His head was muzzy, and nose blocked, but opening the window a crack let the heat flood into the bedroom.

Returning to bed, he lay beside Julie, savouring the silence. During the night, she had discarded the thin sheet and curled into a ball. He smiled, recalling how tiredness and exhaustion had overcome him, but sleep had not refreshed him. Staring at the ceiling, calm eluded him. Too early to rise, too late to snooze, he sat up worrying over the day ahead, restless as his mind ran over his planned presentation to the museum. Now on the threshold, he wished he had not agreed to get involved with the project, a search that had little chance of success.

Outside the sun had risen, although its orb was low on the horizon and obscured by buildings. Instead, a flat, grey, lifeless light replaced the gloom. With a tired sigh, he went for a shower. The water was never warm enough—just lukewarm to tepid. The soap refused to lather, but he forced himself to shave, taking time to wake up and dress for the coming meeting.

His noise disturbed Julie. She glanced at the clock, and uttering a groan, buried her head in the pillow.

'Sorry. I have to rush. The taxi is on the way. I will be back tomorrow evening.'

'Tomorrow evening! I thought Manila was near Singapore.'

'It's a four-hour flight. With the travelling and meetings, Lucas said best if we stay overnight.'

'Well, have a brilliant time,' she muttered.

Lucas and Michael checked into the Manila Hotel, close to the National Museum. After the meeting, they planned to see the finds from the *San Diego,* a Spanish galleon sunk in Manila Bay in 1600 after an attack by a Dutch warship. The museum housed a display of 34,407 artefacts from the wreck, including porcelain, storage jars and cannons.

'If we find a valuable cargo like that, it'll be worthwhile,' said Michael.

'The museum is keen to work with us, provided we follow the legal protocols. If they think we are opportunist treasure hunters, they won't issue a licence.'

'Does the museum want involvement? At this rate they will run out of room to store stuff.'

'The museum keeps a percentage of the finds. They send exhibits around the world for display, which generates an income. The collection attracts visitors—so they gain from every angle. The discovery of the *Siren* is opening a time capsule for academic research which far outweighs the monetary value.'

'That sounds a good argument to impress them.'

Hopefully, the rival group from Singapore was following a false lead. How could they know where to look? At least Lucas had the 1986 survey report, even though it was vague and unhelpful. He worried the museum would wonder why return to an area which was unsuccessful? Of course, modern equipment gave data that was more accurate. Michael's research had unearthed the cargo manifest proving a large and valuable cargo.

'We should stress the first survey was only a low key study by an inexperienced party,' said Michael.

'Well, we can try that approach. Care for a drink at the bar? The Taproom is a copy of an English pub to make you happy.'

'Okay, let's test the atmosphere.'

'Afterwards, I'll take you to Makati for a meal. There are many excellent Spanish restaurants. It is also the red-light district, but as a happily married man I am sure you will resist all temptations!'

Michael impressed the museum staff with the fresh information on the manifest. The cargo included a large consignment of china including complete dinner services, tea sets, servers, bowls and other sundry items. Dr Da Souza considered antique porcelain from this period unremarkable compared to discoveries from Thai, or Vietnamese junks active between the fourteenth and sixteenth centuries. He found the study of early ceramics more rewarding. His junior colleague, Christina, specialised in the blue-and-white china developed during the Ming dynasty from 1368 to 1644. Judging by the date of the wreck of the *Siren*, the porcelain was from the later Ch'ing dynasty.

Michael was struggling to stay focused—after a late night, he did not feel too well. Possibly the rich paella had under-cooked seafood lurking. He drank plenty of water and resisted the urge to be sick as he rushed through his presentation.

He showed them a slide of the proposed survey block, which research pinpointed as the likely position of the wreck. Next, he reviewed the planned equipment and its capabilities. Michael concluded his speech and invited questions.

The door opened, and the director of operations sat at the table, excusing his lateness. Dr Da Souza gave a quick précis of Michael's talk to put the senior man in the picture. Although decisions on issuing permits rested with the director, he deferred to his assistant, Dr Da Souza.

'Thank you, Dr Fletcher, for your lucid presentation. Monsieur Miffré told us of another investigation performed at this site in 1986,' said Da Souza.

Lucas nodded in agreement. 'Yes. That is correct. Nereus ran a survey, but there was no trace of a shipwreck. We understand it was an environmental project.'

'But what did they discover?' asked the director.

Michael tried to reply, but he had not finished. 'You didn't mention it during your talk. Did the divers recover any objects?'

Michael thanked the director for his question. That Dr Da Souza assumed he had a PhD was embarrassing, but he let that go. In fact, his greatest need was for a medical doctor, and after a quick apology, he rushed off to the toilet. Lucas took over as if it was a regular occurrence for Michael to disappear at brief notice.

'Yes, to answer your question,' said Lucas, 'we found a diver in Singapore who was on that job. They abandoned the project after finding minor artefacts but no sign of a wreck. With modern survey equipment, such as a state-of-the-art magnetometer, we have an improved chance of success.'

'So your magnetometer detects metallic content?' asked the director.

'Yes, correct.'

'But we know the wreck was wooden, as were the chests containing the tea and porcelain. Where is the metal?'

'The East Indiaman had cannons, iron cooking pots, weapons and hoards of coins. Ferrous objects are hard to detect because of corrosion and marine growth, which lowers the magnetic strength.'

'So this equipment may be useless because of insufficient metal?'

'Yes, I suppose so. But it's what we normally use. Our geophysical systems locate anomalies and then we follow up with a diving team. Research shows the wreck of the *Siren* is in this locality. The earlier study found nothing of value with a non-focused investigation.'

Da Souza looked annoyed—the director was sidetracking the discussion. He engaged the director in a private conversation interrupted when the door knob turned and Michael returned, looking as pale as chalk.

'Dr Fletcher, I hope you are better?'

'Yes, thank you. Much improved.'

'We suspect several World War II wrecks in the Sulu Sea—most of them are Japanese.'

'We ran an Admiralty wreck search. Their database flagged up many shipwrecks in the vicinity. I'm sure I have a slide somewhere.' Michael peered through his briefcase. After ineffective fumbling, the director saved him from further embarrassment.

'Never mind. If we give permission to proceed, we will lose Miss Velasco. We need her help at a new exhibition starting in September.'

'She could join the boat later once we have successful finds,' said Lucas.

The discussion annoyed Christina, with no one asking her opinion. Michael was making a rapid recovery. As the meeting headed for a close, the staff agreed, in principle, to issue an exploration licence.

However, Da Souza looked uneasy. 'We received an approach from a consortium in Singapore to hunt for the same wreck. Explain how two groups chase the same quarry?'

It was Lucas' opinion that a diver from the original survey passed information to this group. Probably drunken ramblings as the diver had recently drowned in a canal in Singapore in suspicious circumstances.

The museum team looked shocked.

'I love a mystery,' said Christina.

'We can't issue licences to both of you,' said the director. 'There might be a turf war. This gentleman is meeting us on Wednesday. I suggest we defer issuing any licence until we have listened to his presentation.'

'Can we ask who this party is?'

'I can't divulge that information.'

'Once you release an exploration permit, our names will be in the public domain.'

'True. But we wouldn't want to put you at risk if this group is wiping out divers.'

'I didn't say that. No one has suggested any connection between the diver's death and this consortium,' said Lucas.

'Your competitor is a porcelain collector,' said the director, 'and the head of a reputable clan society preserving the cultural history of Singapore's Chinatown, so take care what you say.' Lucas looked contrite. Dr Da Souza wound up the awkward end of the meeting.

After a rejuvenating coffee, Christina took Michael on a tour of her department, leaving Lucas to complete the paperwork. Michael admired two small Chingbai jarlets dating from the thirteenth century Song dynasty found on a junk near Palawan. Christina showed him a jar identical to one in St. Mark's Cathedral in Venice, brought back by Marco Polo from China. Next, she passed him a flagon for holding water retrieved from the wreck of the *San Diego,* a Spanish galleon sunk by the Dutchman, Admiral Olivier van Noort, near Fortune Island and salvaged in 1994.

'Where is Fortune Island?'

'It's a small island in Manila Bay owned by a rich businessman. He made a copy of the *San Diego*. Now he can charge tourists to gawp at the display. Worse still is a human skull and other bones they claim are from a sailor who drowned in 1600, but it's no such thing.'

'Gruesome.'

'I prefer to work with you. So many rogues exploit our history.'

'True,' said Michael. 'So you hope to sail with us on the *Eastern Pearl?*'

'Not if the museum has its way. They want me to stay for this boring exhibition.'

She smiled and motioned for Michael to follow her to the next research laboratory. Several PhD students sat at desks writing up their theses or thumbing through reference books to identify obscure fragments of pottery. It was rare to see visitors, especially tall and pale specimens, and many stopped in their tracks to stare at him or laughed nervously. Michael could hear Lucas in the distance, so headed towards the familiar voice once he had chatted with a few of the students. He felt a bit of a fraud, pretending he was a knowledgeable expert.

Christina touched on his need to leave the meeting but noted he had made a quick recovery.

'You coped well with that brief bout of gastroenteritis—so embarrassing having to run out during your presentation! You must avoid the street stalls and even ice in drinks. We can eat anything, but your immune system needs time to adjust! Where did you pick up the problem?'

'Lucas took me to a Spanish restaurant in Makati district. I can't remember its name, but we had paella with mussels.'

'Michael, paella is high-risk. Just watch how they cook it, tossing in raw mussels, squid and prawns and giving it a quick stir. The heat has no chance to kill off the bacteria! And you should avoid Makati Burgos Street!' Christina gave him a knowing smile and Michael looked uncomfortable.

Lucas rejoined them to continue the tour of the research facilities. Michael had made a wonderful impression, but they still had to convince the director—someone it was hard to move. It worried him they had not done enough to push their case. Lucas had run background checks on Tong. Although his activities had a respectable front safeguarding the Chinese heritage of Singapore, it had a sinister secret side and he was a ruthless operator.

In Chinatown, many of the clubs paid regular contributions to the clan. The society used the Triads to extract the fees, and in return, the businesses prospered. Those who refused to pay found it detrimental to their trade. Initially, a few broken windows or they might scare the customers—subtle ways of intimidation, and some not so subtle. Lucas had heard rumours of a club operator in Ann Siang Road who had resisted the clan for several months. His patrons deserted in droves until he agreed to their demands. Business improved overnight, but it was short-lived. One day they torched the premises in the small hours—the man burnt to death along with his wife and two children. This was not Tong's clan, but it showed what was possible. The Triads used any legal or illegal method for making money. If just half the rumours were true, Tong was a dangerous adversary. Lucas did not swallow the director's artful attempt to sanitise him. Michael reacted with disbelief that Triads were still active in Singapore. Like the Mafia in Sicily, the legend lived on stronger than the reality.

Chapter 14

After twelve days of inaction, Lucas was frantic at the lack of positive news. He phoned the museum daily to check progress, but Dr Da Souza was always out, and never replied to the messages left on his phone. *Eastern Pearl* had completed her minor Malaysian job and the team, including Jim, returned to Loyang Marine Base. They could not afford to keep the vessel on hire if the Philippine project ran into lengthy delays. The personnel earmarked for the job had arrived in dribs and drabs: two young surveyors from Australia were running up huge hotel costs, and even the local Singaporeans and Malaysians were complaining. Any long delay and they might lose key people.

At lunchtime, Jim and Michael headed to Charlie's bar in Changi for lunch—a well-established attraction attached to the Changi Point hawker centre where a vast variety of stalls catered to many nationalities with Chinese, Indonesian, Malay, Indian and Western specialities. The bar specialised in a large choice of beers from all over the world. As usual, trade was brisk with staff from the marine base, tourists, locals, national service recruits and seismic crews. They ordered beer and fish and chips and relaxed at a table on the walkway.

'Michael, great to have you onboard. George Choy is an excellent engineer. I have worked with him before. The rest of the team are multi-tasked and some have diving experience. And Christina from the museum. It's unusual for mixed crews in Asia. The skippers say ladies bring terrible luck.'

'Alex, is keen to join the survey. He's eighteen and just finished at school.'

Jim frowned, drawing a cool draught of beer before removing the foam with a swipe of his hand. 'Lucas mentioned it. I cannot see a problem, provided we have enough bunks on board. As long as he doesn't start whingeing if the going gets difficult.'

'Will things get tough?'

'No, but it won't be a picnic.'

'But I hear the area is a high-security risk?'

'You mean the Abu Sayyaf crowd? They are just a rabble. Piracy is unlikely—the main pirate pitch in Southeast Asia is the Malacca Straits between Sumatra and Malaysia. But that's too far away. Closer to Sabah can be a problem.'

'Hard to believe in modern-day pirates,' said Michael.

'Opportunists looking for easy targets such as fishermen after the personal effects of the crew or the cargo. They will target traders, supply boats, any floating object from small yachts to giant tankers, but they won't kill unless you resist.'

'How to counter this threat?'

'Keep vigilant and plan on extra security onboard if Lucas thinks we need it.'

'I suppose the dangers can't be too great if the museum risks one of their staff.'

'Correct. Christina is only twenty-two years old. Just finished at university. Most of this piracy stuff is scare talk. Sure, it exists, but not a huge problem.'

Before returning to the office, they had another round. With every sip, Jim's reassurances were a comfort. The threats were just dramatic exaggerations. Jim had never encountered blood-thirsty pirates. Michael decided not to dwell on the risk.

Michael left Charlie's bar and returned to the office. Jim would stay at Charlie's for the rest of the afternoon. With only Danica holding the fort, it was an excellent opportunity to take a more in-depth study of the only surviving copy of the Nereus survey report. Danica was busy at the drafting desk, deep in concentration. Michael focused on the diamante studded skinny jeans stretched tightly over her backside as she leant over the desk. Feeling quite *chio* in her new jeans, she remained prostrate in distracting pose. The jade bracelet caught the light as she shifted her arm to select a fine-nibbed Rotring pen to put the finishing stroke to the chart. Michael admired her precise touch and fluid movements, like a languid leopard. She was an artist at work—producing perfection with a pen. Julie suspected him of a wild, passionate affair, which was crazy. For a start, Danica was in a long-term relationship with a guy from the Singapore navy. For Michael, she was a working colleague on a purely professional basis with mild flirting. Understandable when she tempted him daily. He coughed to attract her attention.

'Danica, have you seen this report?'

Michael opened the faded, yellowing text pages and unfolded a map. She crowded next to him, close enough to detect the alluring scent of unfamiliar perfume with a strong chocolate orange aroma, so striking he dared to ask its name. She laughed with delight.

'Sin and Salvation,' she said. 'All the rage in Singapore. But I don't like it—so *chao*. Who wants to smell like a fruit salad?' Michael thought it was bewitching and tropical. She grinned and picked up the report gingerly, like a cat with a mouse.

'Before my time. What an awful report—so scruffy and ancient from before computers.'

Dismissively, she dropped it on the table and turned back with a flourish, stretching across the desk to resume work. With a silent sigh, Michael retrieved the document. An appendix presented a summary of dive locations with geographical coordinates, but with no results except a star marking one location. Perhaps this was where Mitch had found the valuable plate? A useful plan showed the limits of the survey bounded by several small islands.

For the first time, Michael noticed the proximity of the site to Basilan Island. The island where Abu Sayyaf, the group with links to the ruthless Al-Qaeda terrorist network, had held the US missionaries, the Burnhams, hostage after snatching them from a beach resort in Palawan. They had quickly beheaded Guillermo Sobero, another American hostage, before a long period of silence. It had recently been on the news that Martin Burnham had died when Government troops stormed the rebel camp in a raid. His wife Marcia survived.

Michael should pass these details to Alex to decide if he still wanted to join the party. One thing to risk his own life, no sense in risking his son's. Best not to inform Julie, especially with the Burnham killing so fresh and with kidnappers still on the loose.

At four o'clock Michael was planning to escape from the office early when Danica came back and dumped a load of geophysical records from the Malaysian sand search on his desk. She told him Lucas wanted him to work on the report in case the job in the Philippines kicked off soon. They agreed to work late together.

Michael and Danica were still in the office after seven o'clock when Lucas returned. Impressive dedication to work so late, he thought. The lack of action on the permit was annoying Lucas. Michael volunteered to phone Christina and got through straight away.

'Michael, you must be clairvoyant. My first day back from Sydney. You are lucky to catch me at the museum tonight, but I had to attend a boring lecture. Also, more drama!'

'What happened?'

'After your visit, we wanted to issue you the permit. But we had to see Mr Tong.'

'Yes, he came a few days later. Did he put in a convincing case?'

'No way! He said they could locate the wreck from private research, which he refused to elaborate on as less scrupulous treasure hunters might steal the artefacts. Although he was sure the museum staff were trustworthy, he couldn't risk it.'

'What a nerve.'

'With him was a ceramic's expert from Malaysia. Dr Kian Chiew. I had never heard of him, but Da Souza says he has written many papers—usually co-authored. Anyhow, I guess he knows his stuff. They produced this most extraordinary serving platter, a Ch'ing dynasty dish, ornate with dancing dragons. It had six marks on the base, and the expert said it could be Imperial porcelain. Chiew identified it as from the reign of Emperor Kangxi. Kangxi was the longest-reigning Chinese Emperor and was only seven years old when he took control.'

'The diver, Mitch, salvaged the plate. He sold it to a dealer in Singapore. Tong must have bought it from him.'

'Yes, he said he purchased it from a shop in Holland Village. What sort of name is that? Is it the Dutch quarter in Singapore?'

'Not exactly. It's a popular shopping district named after Hugh Holland, an English architect who designed the buildings about a hundred years ago.'

'I see. But imagine that! The owner never realised the true value.'

'The diver found dead in the canal.'

'Tong denied knowing that—all news to him. He explained how he was shopping, saw the plate, and recognised it as a valuable piece. Our line of questioning annoyed him.'

'Well, that's no surprise. I am sure Mitch was not reeling around drunk when he died, but I suppose we will never know the truth. Christina, is Tong searching the same spot as us?'

'That's the funny thing. Tong wants a block a few kilometres north of Brutus Reef, and yours is due south. You can't both be correct, so maybe you are looking for different wrecks?'

On merit, Christina explained, they accepted PanAsia's application and rejected Tong's submission. Dr Da Souza had sent in the recommendation to the director over a week ago.

'Normally he would rubber stamp our decision. However, while I was away in Sydney, Tong approached the director with extra details. The director said the strategy was excellent, and he was keen to award the permit to Tong's group. He said it was pointless to award your people a licence as you were searching in the wrong place!'

'Rubbish! He cannot do that. If they use Equatorial Surveys for the wreck search, they may charter *Pacific Glory*. If so, they will have lots of trouble. Lucas looked at the old bucket in Singapore and said it was a death-trap.'

'Da Souza adjusted the limits of the two areas to give no overlap and issue permits to both of you. Both blocks are the same size. I am to go with you and someone else from the staff on Tong's boat. I believe they mentioned they will use *Pacific Glory*.'

'An amazing solution, but I'm not sure whether to laugh or cry. When will we know?'

'Don't quote me, but your local agent should learn today. You are using Vargas, aren't you?'

'Yes. Christina, thank you for your help. We look forward to a successful project.'

'Michael, if we discover more of the Imperial porcelain it will be fantastic.'

Back home later that evening, Michael sat outside on the veranda. It was quiet; children dispatched to homework or bed, and the pool was empty except for that Italian friend of Julie's who had just completed several fast lengths before climbing out at the deep end to rub dry with a small towel. He waved across at the Fletchers with his usual friendly flair.

'Those trunks leave nothing to the imagination.'

'They are revealing,' said Julie. 'So obvious too. I think he is probably gay.'

She passed Michael a can of Tiger and a bowl of salty redskin peanuts with *ikan bilis*, the small dried fish that are a delicious snack with beer.

'You're late tonight. Alex has gone to see a friend, but we left you pizza in the oven.'

'Thanks. I'm not hungry. Yes, sorry for being unpunctual—I should have phoned. I was data processing for a Malaysian sand search. We are expecting the permit for the Philippines job at any moment, so it's a big rush.'

He filled her in on the latest developments with the treasure hunt. Despite trying to sound optimistic, she sensed his concerns and asked if he was having second thoughts.

'The survey is near Basilan Island, which is where Abu Sayyaf has a stronghold.'

'Who are they?'

'A militant band fighting for independence for the southern Philippines. The group has been active for ages and could pose a risk to us. We should let Alex know so he can choose if he still wants to come.'

'So you mean it's okay for you to go but not him?'

'No. Lucas wouldn't consider the job if he thought it was dangerous, but we should give Alex the facts.'

'You do that. You always do just what you want, so my opinion doesn't matter.'

Julie walked over to the veranda rails, turning her back on him.

'Michael, I can't decide for you. No one would blame you if you backed out, even at this late stage. Alex is mad keen to work on this caper, so if it goes ahead, you must get Lucas to arrange proper security and look after him. If he gets hurt, I will never forgive you.'

He walked up beside Julie at the veranda. She brushed a hand over her eyes, wiping away a tear.

'I'm worried we are blindly heading into this project. What's driving me to do this?'

'That's natural—it takes courage or stupidity to work in such a dangerous area.'

She headed back inside the apartment.

'Don't worry about me.'

This outburst puzzled Michael. Were they drifting apart like boats, once sailing together, now diverging? If they found the valuable cargo, their financial worries would be over, but was the price worth paying?

Chapter 15

Saturday morning found most of the team crammed into the office waiting for George Choy, the survey engineer, to arrive. The museum had just approved their permit, and the vessel could leave. Once they had installed the equipment, they should be ready to sail early Sunday. The surveyors would meet the boat in Zamboanga when she arrived in the southern Philippines in two weeks, and Lucas and Jim planned to arrange security a few days earlier. Vargas could offer armed guards from one of the less active Muslim separatist groups. The more violent terrorist organisations might tolerate them if they hired these guards for protection. Lucas explained Mindanao was twenty-seven percent Muslim. The fight for autonomy from the Philippines first started twenty-five years ago and led to the deaths of over 100,000. In the west, hardly anyone knew of, or cared about, this faraway conflict. For the best guarantee of success, they should follow Vargas' suggestion and ally with the separatist group. George Choy had slipped in unobserved. Although retired, George was a lean and fit Chinese Singaporean, over sixty years old. Out of respect for Lucas, he had agreed to join the party. His greatest value was familiarity with the Philippines, gained from many jobs in the Sulu Sea.

'If pirates attack us, the Philippine security forces pose the greatest danger if they mount a rescue attempt,' said George.

'George, meet Michael, our experienced geophysicist,' said Lucas, shrugging off this comment. 'He joined us two years ago but, before that; he was working with other survey companies. He and his son Alex will be on the survey.'

'Provided the talk of danger doesn't put them off,' added Jim.

Alex shook hands with George, in awe of the older man, and aware of his own lack of experience. This chat of pirates and terrorists was just an act. Last night, his decision upset his mother, but since meeting the team, he felt reassured.

'We will run a safe operation,' said Lucas. 'I believe George is the only one to have surveyed in the southern Philippines before?'

'I worked further north, but it went well. We had a problem with snakes. The surveyors set up shore stations on an uninhabited island which was crawling with them.'

'Snakes? Right George, if anyone has a pathological fear of snakes, pull out now. I'd appreciate it if you didn't— any last-minute changes will delay the start, and imperative we depart as soon as possible.'

Lucas looked at the faces of the assembled company for any signs of dissent or uncertainty. Jim swallowed, stared away out of the window, busy with a roll-up cigarette. George remained impassive and unreadable. He had meant the snake remark as a joke. Why was Lucas making such a fuss out of it? Alex caught Lucas's eye for a moment, probing for a sign of weakness, so Alex locked his eyes on the wooden parquet floor, refusing to display any emotion.

'Which survey company is Tong using?' asked Jim.

'Equatorial Survey—Davinder's crowd. They are mobilising *Pacific Glory*,' said Lucas. 'The boat is in poor condition. It will need much work to make her sea-worthy.'

'Is she still alongside? I didn't notice her this morning.'

A sudden thought occurred to Lucas that they must have sailed early—a tip off from someone in the museum. Jim suggested they bring their departure forward. Lucas asked him what time was the next high tide.

'High water is six o'clock this evening. But we need to top up the fuel, so we can't leave before seven.'

'Okay, we aim for seven. *Merde*! What a nightmare.'

Only the ship's crew stayed on board during the vessel's transit to the Philippines—a time of anticlimax for Michael as he waited for the boat to reach Zamboanga. The vessel had left Singapore late on Saturday. Depending on weather, the transit should take about two weeks. Monday was always a quiet day. No sign of Lucas, but that was no surprise. He only turned up at the office if there was a need. Danica would check the mail every morning and if, like today, there were no tenders to prepare, she would let him know. At least Michael could complete the outstanding survey reports, and he enjoyed the quiet moments when he and Danica were alone. To avoid distracting thoughts from the sight of Danica's tight denim jeans, Michael made her a sweet, strong coffee. She left the draughting bench, and they sat together in Lucas's empty office.

Danica said she planned to visit her sister in Perth, who was in her last year at the University of Western Australia.

'Wow. Australia's a long way. Have you been there before?'

He lit a cigarette, smoking surreptitiously. He knew it annoyed her so he pushed the overflowing ashtray, already full of Gitanes stubs, to the end of the desk and blew the smoke away from her. It amused her, his fussy concern.

'This will be my last chance. Maybe I will find an attractive Australian. Australian men are damn *shiok*.'

'But you have a boyfriend in the Singapore navy?'

Danica's face crinkled with distaste. 'Long story. We split a month ago. A possessive guy—not keen on my working late with you.'

'I understand. Sorry if I am to blame.'

'No, I'm exaggerating. Let's say there were issues, and I decided too young and immature for me. These Chinese boys have these awful mothers. Auntie Lee—a real drama mama! So controlling, lah! I need an older man.'

Michael listened, amazed at her outburst. Although she made light of the situation, it upset her. Fighting to control her emotions, she sunk her face into his shoulder and he inhaled a sensual fragrance of patchouli, jasmine and other mysterious notes. It was Chanel's latest perfume "Chance"— an improvement on the chocolate orange scent from a few days ago. He could always rely on Danica to match her attractions to an appropriate aroma. Neither hurried to break the spell, but they pulled away as Lucas might return at any moment.

Danica usually skipped lunch, but she took up Michael's offer to drive into Changi Village for a late bite. Both desired escape from the office. Her confession needed a pause in the schedule to unwind and think. Michael loved to frequent the hawker stalls or Charlie's bar. But he decided the Changi Sailing Club was a more private setting. The Coachman Inn restaurant was famous for its stunning views across the sea to Pulau Ubin and Pulau Tekong. He liked its old-fashioned ambience and relaxed atmosphere. In Singapore, people were always in a hurry, rushing, bolting down food and dashing to collect children from school. Never at a slow pace.

'Amazing, I never knew this place existed. So *atas.*'

Like an excited kid, she stared, open-mouthed, at the cross-section of patrons at the restaurant: a mix of expatriates and locals, informally dressed yachters, business people from the Marine Base and a noisy crowd from one of the seismic boats.

Michael smiled at her childish joy. *Atas* in Singlish meant high class or sophisticated. Compared to the average hawker stall he supposed Changi Sailing Club was *atas* but, to him, it was nothing of the sort. He buried himself in the menu and ordered Hainanese chicken rice for himself and a nasi lemak for Danica.

'The Royal Air Force started the club, I guess, before the war. Lucas is a member. We sometimes come for a drink in the evening.'

'So you are not a member?'

'No. They never challenge me. If you arrive by yacht, they give you a temporary pass for a few dollars a day.'

'Do you go sailing often?'

'No, I hate all things to do with the sea, especially swimming, getting wet and cold.'

Danica laughed. 'You are such a fraud. What other clubs do you hang out in without a membership?'

Michael admitted he crashed the Singapore Cricket Club, although he used to be a member. Fortunately, some of his friends would invite him for a drink. They set the fees at a reasonable level, with a concessionary reduced rate until you reached forty, after which they soared sky high.

'They expect no one over forty can still play sports.'

'Eh. Forty years old, is it? My God, that is so impressive.'

'You are mocking me. I am only just forty.'

She laughed and touched his hand in reassurance. 'But I am sure you are fit enough for energetic sport.'

Their food and drinks arrived. The *ang mohs* went for beer, so Danica ordered a Tiger to keep him company. She quite liked it and giggled too much.

'*Wah*, Michael, you getting me *mabuk*.'

'One drink can't make you tipsy,' he laughed.

She adored his shy smile, although blue eyes in a man were *bapok*, like a doll. But cute in a baby. Danica toyed with her nasi lemak—no match to one at half the price from Changi Point hawker stall. And how could you eat with a spoon and fork! Michael's chicken rice looked disgusting. The Hainanese cooking method boiled the chicken in stock, leaving the breast meat under-cooked. Correct for purists but liable to infect with salmonella. Michael made a pile of pink flesh at the side of his plate.

She loved the sea view across to the nearby islands, so untouched and natural, with no ugly high-rise buildings. The old-fashioned bungalows, their hard edges softened by age and the luxuriant trees, must have a store of memories! Michael said these were former married quarters for the families of the British military dating from before the war. They had converted many to secluded chalets with barbecue pits for holiday rentals. Very popular with government employees. Modest and cheap, aimed at Singaporeans rather than tourists, so possible to rent just for a weekend if she ever wanted to escape her Housing and Development Board high-rise.

'Like on holiday, but still Singapore, lah. Away from stuffy office, relaxing here is a good feeling.'

But she wondered if he was hitting on her? A married man talking of renting a chalet. Dangerous stuff. His next comment seemed to confirm it.

'I must bring you here one night after work. Friday nights are best. If it's a nice evening, I love to sit outside with an ice-cold beer and watch the sunset.'

The waiter cleared their main course and handed over the menus in case they opted for a dessert. In no hurry, Michael ordered another beer, so she asked for a lime juice and an ice cream. Perhaps she was wrong, and he was just being friendly.

Lucas and Jim met up with Davinder for a leisurely lunch at a seafood restaurant in Changi Village. That their vessels were competing on adjacent surveys for the same wreck was weird.

'At least I am getting paid. I guarantee you guys lose money.'

'You are correct, but a risk worth taking. Our research found the cargo manifest has 250,000 pieces of porcelain. We are looking at a return of several million dollars at auction.'

'So Lucas, okay to lose money on the boat and team, is it?' said Davinder. 'Most likely, none of us find the wreck. At least Tong has paid 50,000 dollars upfront.'

'That's an excellent result. It will be all you pick up as the longer the job runs, without success, he won't pay you anymore. If I were you, I would cash the cheque quickly.'

'No need. His associate, Yap, handed me the money in cash yesterday.'

There was an amazed silence.

'You realise Tong heads a Triad organisation involved in many rackets,' said Jim, with a mischievous grin. 'Don't mess with those guys.'

'One hears rumours—best not believe.' Davinder recognised the scar-faced gangster, Yap, when he handed over the money at his bar in Bugis. The same man who had offered him protection. He knew he was playing a dangerous game dealing with these people, but he kept this secret.

'I think the biggest problem in the Sulu Sea is piracy. Jim, are you taking armed guards?'

'That's another fallacy. Why attack an old survey boat with a crew of youngsters? There is nothing of value. Even if we recover antique china, it still has no value to those people.'

'You forget our team is a prized resource,' said Lucas. 'Any foreigner is at risk of kidnap and ransom, so we plan to use security. What about *Pacific Glory*?'

'Tong has an armed henchman called Yap. Foolishly, I recommended *Eastern Pearl* to you. But, by the time you fly your team to Zamboanga and get stuck in port, we will start before you.'

'I'm surprised you got arms on board in Singapore,' said Jim.

'I didn't say that.'

'Sorry, I thought you did.'

'They plan to source AK47s. As long as they don't involve me. I can reassure you the vessel carried no guns when they left.'

'Okay, Davinder—it's not our business,' said Lucas. 'I expect they will arrange for a boat-to-boat transfer in International waters.'

'I see the police are not getting anywhere with that case of the drowned diver,' said Jim. Lucas frowned at him. Although they suspected a link between Tong and the death of the diver, Mitch Austin, Lucas did not want these fears passed on to Davinder.

'*Certainement*, just an accident,' Lucas interrupted. 'My contact in the police confirmed the diver's blood tests were well over the limit. The cops believe he fell into the canal. One theory is he hit his head on a lamp post and toppled in the drink.'

'Sounds like a typical drunk diver,' said Davinder.

Lucas relaxed. No hurry—his office was in the capable hands of Michael and Danica—so fortunate to have such a dedicated pair!

'Let's get another beer and toast our mutual success. The best solution is the boat broke in two with half the treasure in your block and half in ours. Everyone goes home happy,' Davinder grinned. He called the waitress over and ordered three more bottles of Tiger.

Chapter 16

By Friday, August 16, the survey crew had checked into the Lantaka Hotel in Zamboanga City to await *Eastern Pearl's* arrival. Despite its recommendation as the best hotel in Zamboanga, it was empty of guests apart from a few American divers headed for Santa Cruz. Jim reckoned the transit to take at least thirteen days and more if they ran into poor weather or strong currents. She was running a day later than forecast. The team sat at the terrace bar, lingering over beers, overlooking the seafront, enjoying the calm after a chaotic stopover in Manila.

After a drink, the men wandered around town and the barter market at the wharf-side, glancing over the native crafts from Sabah and Borneo, including batik, tribal carvings and Moro brass. Motorboats called kumpits, traded between Zamboanga and the neighbouring countries. By the hotel's seawall, there was a flotilla of small craft with families of Badjau or sea gipsies with cowrie shells and coral necklaces for sale. Their children jumped, giggling, into the harbour to retrieve coins thrown by the tourists. The Badjau originated from Borneo back in the eleventh century, and their way of life has hardly changed since. They settle in crude stilt houses near shore, to dry the fish they catch. Most of them are born, live, and die on their boats.

Vargas had found a local guard for security protection. Lucas and Jim set off to meet the man at Rio Hondo, a Muslim village built on stilts near to Fort Pilar. At sunset, they arrived at the settlement, walking across a network of catwalks, which connected the chaotic dwellings. Birds and rats teemed over the mudflats at low tide amid a stench of raw sewage. The wafted smell of dried fish merged with the muddy ooze of human excrement, the noxious stink making them gag.

Lucas and Jim entered a labyrinth of shacks, most with tin roofs apart from the mosque, which had a traditional ornate dome.

After a quick walk, the men arrived at a seafood restaurant next to a provisions store. Young children, playing outside, smiled a shy greeting, gazing at the tall, white foreigners with fascination. Vargas sat at a table where he could view their approach. With him was a muscular, dark-skinned man with a shaved head. Vargas rose and introduced him as Hamza, a member of the militant group calling themselves the Moro Islamic Liberation Front.

Hamza stared at the two Caucasians, and then relaxed. Vargas ordered beers. Four bottles of lukewarm San Miguel arrived in an instant, accompanied by prawn crackers. The owner fetched out a bucket of ice cubes to add to the warm beer. They passed cigarettes, and the tension eased.

Hamza had worked on similar protection jobs offshore Kalimantan for the oil companies. He knew what the job entailed: alert, armed protection around the clock, working back-to-back with another guard. Mostly the risk was low and he could afford to relax, but it depended on where this group was working. Lucas showed him a map of the survey zone, and he became animated when he saw how close it was to

Basilan Island, under the control of the militant group, Abu Sayyaf.

'Abu Sayyaf means father of the swordsman,' said Vargas. 'It refers to a mujahedin fighter in Afghanistan in the 1980s called Abubakar Janjalani, the founder of Abu Sayyaf. After the security forces killed him in 1998, his brother, Khadaffy Janjalani, took control. This evil man targets missionaries, aid workers, mariners and foreign tourists. The Americans claim Osama Bin Laden sends funds to the group.'

'Will Abu Sayyaf be here?' asked Lucas, pointing on the map to their exploration site.

'Yes—they have a camp on Basilan Island. If they catch you, cut the throat.'

'Hamza is right,' said Vargas. 'The fishermen will inform Abu Sayyaf to get a reward. You cannot trust anyone or relax anywhere in the Sulu Sea.'

'If Hamza comes with us, can he offer security?'

'They are less likely to attack you. Best hire two guards for protection night and day. If you have the Moro on your side, it may deter them. There are only four hundred Abu Sayyaf, but thousands of Moro.'

'Could we manage with one guard?' asked Lucas.

'Two is better, each working a shift to give you total cover,' said Jim.

'Okay,' Lucas turned to Vargas. 'Can you see if he is available?'

Hamza and Vargas discussed the terms in Tausog, the local Muslim dialect, with much hand-waving. Hamza folded his muscular arms and leant back in his chair, making it creak under his large frame. Jim held a peculiar fascination for him.

'Monsieur Miffré, he says, their food must be halal. Also, he is not happy you have a woman on board. Is this true?'

'We have an Indonesian cook—a Muslim, so no food will be haram. Yes, Christina Velasco, a scientist from the

National Museum in Manila, is coming with us. If it gives him a problem, we can stagger meal times.'

'He asks if she is Muslim or Christian?'

'Christian, I believe. She dresses in western style.'

'He says she must dress with modesty. He has a friend called Abdul. They will supply arms and ammunition. They have AK47s.'

The men agreed on the financial terms. Hamza spat on his open palm before clasping Lucas's hand in an iron grip. Vargas rubbed the sweat from his brow and replaced his glasses. He never enjoyed dealing with the Moro. Beneath a blank stare, they were unpredictable. Vargas asked when they expected their boat to arrive. After consulting Jim, Lucas said the arrival time in Zamboanga should be about 8 p.m.

'Vargas, I don't understand why she needs to come alongside,' said Jim. 'If she stays offshore, we can join her from a small craft. No need to pay harbour dues and go through the hassle of customs clearance.'

'True. If your boat calls at Zamboanga, she cannot leave until immigration gives authorisation. They will delay you to sort out the paperwork.'

The longer they held a boat in port, the more commission for him, but he reassured them that, as he knew the officials, he could get them away within 24 hours. Jim suggested they call the captain—he might be in range—and tell him to standby offshore. Lucas saw his phone receiving a poor signal and called the boat at once. Jaffar confirmed he was three hours away and running late. He doubted if he could make it alongside that evening so best for the survey team to join tomorrow. It was not urgent, but they needed to take on more supplies and fuel. Jaffar told Jim that they had overtaken *Pacific Glory* two days ago.

Lucas and Jim smiled; relieved the pieces of the jigsaw were in place. The group split up and Hamza left to find Abdul. They expected Christina Velasco's flight from Manila at nine o'clock, and Vargas agreed to bring her to the hotel. In the pitch-blackness, the walkways were even more hazardous, but Lucas asked a boy to show them the way. For twenty pesos, he scampered ahead, flashing his torch, and pointing out loose or missing planks. His younger brother, just a toddler, ran along with them. Jim pressed a coin into his hand, and his face erupted in a grin.

Michael and Alex had wandered off with George to look around the town and find some food. George remembered a seafood restaurant he liked but, predictably, it had changed management, installed air-conditioning and had no customers. Nearby, a humbler establishment met his approval. The condemned seafood was swimming in glass tanks lining the side of the restaurant. The choice was not large. It pleased George to see several large *lapu-lapu*, monkfish, pomfrets, prawns, squid and crabs. Alex looked slightly sick. George ordered a mix of dishes: rice, noodles and a delicious chicken dish called *Inasal na Manokay* comprising chicken pieces marinated in soya sauce, brown sugar, shallots and the juice of *calamansi,* a type of lime, for several hours before cooking over hot charcoal. The chickens were tough kampong chickens, small and wiry, but full of flavour. George had selected a *lapu-lapu,* or grouper, for the house speciality, *lapu-lapu Badjao,* cooked in the style of the sea gipsies. They served the large fish, with head and tail still intact, stuffed with a rich mixture of clams, prawns and mussels, onions, chillies, peppers, herbs and the ubiquitous *calamansi* juice. Alex joked it looked like the fish's last meal had been paella. On George's urging, he gingerly sampled a small portion. The restaurant proprietor divulged *Lapu-lapu* was also the name of a Filipino chieftain who killed Portuguese navigator Ferdinand Magellan in 1521.

'This job will go well,' George predicted. 'Lucas understands survey.'

'I am worried about this other group. Jim thinks Tong is head of a Triad gang in Singapore! How unbelievable can you get?' said Michael.

'No,' said George. 'It is quite possible. The Singapore government may be free of corruption but a lot goes on hidden from view. The Triads have infiltrated every Chinatown in the world. Why should Singapore be free of this virus?'

'So, you think we might have problems?'

'I can't see how. Tong has a separate survey area. They will be too busy with their block to worry about us.'

'Hey, this is a good meal,' Alex said. He had overcome his initial revulsion at the live seafood. Laughing, Michael and George told him it would probably be his last decent meal. Neither of them expected much of the ship's food.

'I can't get a signal,' said Michael, checking his cell phone. Both George and Alex tried their phones, but no one was picking up a signal.

Washing down the food with generous gulps of San Miguel, they demurred on coffee or tea and found a provisions shop for last-minute supplies such as cigarettes, sweets and chewing gum.

Michael felt an impulse to move to a better cell phone reception area, worried in case Lucas was trying to reach them.

It had been a frustrating journey for Tong. He suffered from seasickness. There had been a steady swell for the first six days as they passed from Singapore across to East Malaysia and Brunei. After a rushed job to get the vessel ready in time, the ship's owners had excelled themselves. Not perfect, but Tong was not interested in the cosmetic look or in conforming to burdensome health and safety rules. As long as the engines functioned, he could relax.

Onboard the team comprised a six-man survey crew and four divers. Although Tong had expressed a preference for Asians, the team was Caucasian, apart from two Singaporean engineers and the Malaysian divers. He found the Scottish Party Chief—an uncouth, red-haired, abrasive, crew cut youth, to be irritating. Their dislike was mutual, judging by the surly looks between them over breakfast. He went by the name of Sandy.

The two Australian navigators appeared jokey and friendly on the surface. Both fresh from college and still wide-eyed and incredulous at everything they saw, they regarded the boat with horror and mocked the marine crew behind their back. They kept to themselves and avoided the geophysicist, Tony, who ignored them.

It had incensed Tong when he found out his rivals chased the same shipwreck. Mitch had blabbered too freely to the wrong people. Fortunately, the director at the museum had been helpful after the merits of supporting the cultural integrity of the Wah Chan Clan had been explained. The exploration permits were fast-tracked, but this did not stop PanAsia winning the adjacent block. Unjust that a bunch of *gwailos*, or red-haired devils, should make a fortune from the Chinese heritage. The ancient trade routes from China had stretched throughout the South China Sea and beyond the Sulu Sea. It was a travesty of justice that the colonial exploiters should once again profit. He intended to do everything in his power to prevent it.

When the *Eastern Pearl* sailed arrogantly past them, it had cancelled the advantage of their quick exit from Singapore. Obviously, the survey team would join the vessel in Zamboanga. Although the cheapest way, it might be the slowest if the authorities delayed them in port.

Chapter 17

Vargas had a fruitless trip to the airport, waiting in vain at the arrival hall for Christina. He called Lucas to break the unwelcome news. The next flight was not until the following day. Lucas groaned and handed his phone to Michael to call Christina. Christina answered.

'Michael, thank God! So sorry, I missed my flight so still in Manila! I left in plenty of time, but this crazy taxi driver ignored me and took the worst route possible and we got stuck in a traffic jam for ages.'

'Christina, don't worry. We checked. There are no more flights tonight. Vargas will meet you at the airport tomorrow. Try to get the first flight in the morning.'

'Are you waiting for me?'

'Well, we planned to leave tonight but the boat won't be alongside until tomorrow morning so there is no problem.'

'Listen—someone paid the driver to obstruct me. I ordered the taxi straight from work at the museum. They knew when I was leaving.'

'It sounds far-fetched, Christina. You were unlucky. Let's talk later. Stay cool.'

Christina's suspicion of a plot to cause her delay was far-fetched. Jim laughed, claiming the girl had a fantastic imagination. But Lucas looked pensive. He said the Triads had a web of influence worldwide. It was clear that Tong had influenced the museum to favour him and would try to hinder them. Easy to arrange for a contact at the museum to make sure Christina missed her flight with a small payment to a taxi driver. Jim gave a nervous cough at the ridiculous conspiracy theory.

'Lucas, this delay means the vessel best come alongside tomorrow to pick up the team. No point trying to rush.'

'That makes sense. I'll call Captain Jaffar. If he is nearby, he should stay moving and not drop anchor. A ship at anchor in these waters is a tasty relish in a sandwich.'

The Lantaka was full and unable to extend their booking, so the party transferred to the City Inn—a low budget dive in the downtown district. The hotel found a more expensive suite for Lucas, and he remained to keep an eye out for boat arrivals from his perch in the terrace bar.

It was a relief to Captain Jaffar to receive explicit instructions at last. Best to make full steam ahead and standby near the port for greatest safety. He hoped that was the end of changes; it upset the crew. Now the girl from the museum had missed her flight! This proved his premonition of disaster was well founded. To allow a woman on board was asking for trouble. From the bridge he saw the watchman walk the decks, eyes focused on the horizon for passing vessels. In these dangerous waters, they must keep a keen eye open for threats. Their boat was as conspicuous as a worm on a hook. Jaffar was aware they had no defence apart from aiming the fire hoses at attackers—no match for determined pirates.

The ship picked up speed, cutting through the calm sea as a surgeon's knife parts flesh. Jaffar admired the majestic still evening with a clear sky lit by a full moon. High above, a passenger jet idled past, the travellers gazing at the flotilla of fishing boats, each illuminated by powerful lights as they worked—insignificant specks on the vast canvas of the world. Apart from the fishermen, a few unlit motorboats powered through the darkness as quietly as stealthy sharks—smugglers, running goods to and from Sabah and Kalimantan, their diverse cargoes hidden from view.

One lean old man, thin as a skeleton, lit up a cheroot as his skiff passed close. A blaze of sparks and the aroma carried across the waters. The fellow's searching stare locked onto the captain's eyes. The glowing cheroot glinted off stained, crooked-set teeth in a grinning mouth. With a humped back and gnarled hands resting on the rudder, the ghostly rider stalked the waves, a harbinger of the Apocalypse, bringer of doom. For a few moments, they ran alongside each other until he spun the tiller to starboard, and left as suddenly as he came.

Jaffar shivered. The memory of the staring eyes and mocking grin lingered and troubled him. Was the apparition real? He had a grim feeling. Much better to work with his usual crew running supplies to the oil platforms or ferrying cargoes across to Malaysia and Indonesia. Instead, fate had dealt him a bad hand: a bunch of young surveyors fresh out of college with no idea of life at sea. Moreover, a female onboard! Young men carelessly wandering along the corridors for a shower best cover up. Imagine the fuss when this lady came to use the latrine after the mariners. Jaffar turned on the kettle for a calming cup of tea, needing a brew to quieten his nerves. Never a smoker, he forbade smoking on the bridge or in the galley during meal times. Why the weird compulsion to fill the lungs with poisonous smoke? He had never understood it. Most mariners smoked like dirty chimneys, so the ban was unpopular.

The brew drew flavour from the bland Lipton's tea bag while he updated the ship's position on the nautical chart. Distracted by the framed family photos in Ipoh, the tension eased. Thinking of them made him smile. Homework completed, his youngest daughter tucked up in bed, the older boy watching television or playing a computer game. His wife ironing clothes for school tomorrow and running the washing machine, never a break for leisure. Sometimes he yearned to be home and away from jobs like this.

Jaffar estimated arrival at Zamboanga by midnight. Too late to land at the jetty. Early morning the best time to contact the Port Authorities and request a berth. And a chance to order fresh victuals, fuel and water, and to stretch his limbs with a quick walk into town.

As Jaffar steered towards Zamboanga, Captain Singh, at the wheel of *Pacific Glory*, looked pained as Tong hovered at his shoulder, a whiff of brandy on his stale breath. The man still had not found his sea-legs and, unsteady on his feet, lumbered around as the ship rocked from side-to-side. Tong insisted on wearing a formal black suit as if attending a funeral. The sole concession to the sticky heat was to remove his tie in a gesture of informality.

'Can't this crate go any faster?'

They had had this conversation several times. In theory, ten knots should have been within their ability, but given the age and state of the engines, the captain had instructed the chief engineer not to exceed seven knots. Even that was pushing it.

'We are at top speed and cannot go any quicker into the strong current. It will switch when the tide changes, and we should make better progress.'

'Let's hope so. When will we reach the survey site?'

'ETA by first light tomorrow. Pointless to start work at night. First check for reefs in daylight,' said Singh.

Yap appeared on the bridge during their conversation. He kept a stoic silence apart from respectful talks with Tong, in a Chinese dialect. Yap cast an expressionless eye out to sea at the calm conditions, but both men were unsteady and clumsy. Singh saw them use strange hand signals to each other—the code of the secret societies. The Chinese as a race seldom shake hands like westerners, but Triad gang members communicate with the universal sign of greeting which involves joining the thumb and first finger of the right hand into a circle to overlap the top joint of the first finger and extend the other three fingers. To get rid of them, Singh changed the heading and made the vessel roll. Tong and Yap staggered to the back of the bridge. At least he had forced them to move. He hated it when passengers got in the way. The two Chinese gave up the pretence of looking at the marine chart and descended the stairs to their cabins.

Relishing peace, it annoyed Singh when Sandy sidled up next to him at the wheel just after the Chinese left. The men eyed each other, like foreign species thrown together in a zoo. Good—if he could persuade Sandy to leave, life would be perfect. The best thing was to ignore him. While Sandy stood alongside him, Singh stayed alert, focused on the dangers. Vessels sometimes ran on autopilot with the crew asleep, so he kept a keen eye on the radar.

'It's a right bonny night.'

Since Sandy had lived in the Tropics, he liked to emphasise his Scottish accent. He tolerated most races, except the English, proud of his tough, working-class origins from Glasgow. Recalling the Massacre of Amritsar in 1919, when British and Gurkha troops massacred 379 defenceless Sikhs, Singh had inherited an ingrained hatred of the British. The same brush of colonial aggressors tarred the Scots. Lost in his thoughts, Singh was half-listening to Sandy, who was complaining about the job, rattling off a series of gripes: Wreck hunting was a dicey business. If you found nothing, no one was paid, but if you discovered a shipwreck, then count on the sharks to steal it from under your nose—the human ones, not the timid blacktip reef sharks, which cruised these waters. This was a dull job. No TV, no games—just an ancient recorder playing old films of Bruce Willis. Ignored by the captain, Sandy left the bridge. Captain Singh sighed with relief. Free of interruptions, the time he liked best when he poured himself a generous shot of Johnnie Walker whisky diluted with a splash of icy water. The ship's owners allowed no alcohol, but what they did not know would not hurt them. He extracted a Benson and Hedges from a fresh crisp pack. Such sensual anticipation tearing off the plastic wrapping to push up one of the filter-tipped smokes with its smell of tobacco, which he craved. Pure happiness. Answerable to nobody, Singh had no family concerns. He took each day as it came; each job brought its problems, which he overcame with calm. His turban was too tight, and the ball of hair uncomfortable beneath it. He rubbed a nicotine-stained finger to release the tension at the nape of his neck. His finger came away drenched in sweat despite the coolness of the night.

Chapter 18

Mornings in Zamboanga began with the call of the imam, summoning the faithful to prayer. Alex buried his head under the pillow with a groan. The loudspeaker sang out the hypnotic refrain, which rolled out on the still morning air to merge with other chants simultaneously from other mosques scattered through the city. As early birdsong annoys, the port stirred to life at its own tired pace. This display of faith reasserted the force of Islam, a power the Catholic Church had never countered in the southern Philippines.

Father and son were sharing a cheap room at the City Inn. Michael woke up with a start, his eyes darting around as he tried to find an angry wasp, ringing and vibrating. He sunk back as his dulled senses focused on his phone, jumping on the bedside table next to Alex, who grunted but ignored it. Michael hurried to pick it up, thinking it might be from Julie, but it was Lucas updating them on the plans for the day. The vessel was expected alongside soon, and the customs officials and agent at ten o'clock. He suggested they take a leisurely breakfast.

'How long before we can turn the boat around and leave?' asked Michael.

'It won't happen before mid-afternoon at the earliest. The captain has to stock up on supplies, fuel and water. And immigration may delay us. Join the vessel about ten. I'll have a better idea after I have seen Vargas.'

Michael and Alex arrived downstairs to find the survey team had finished most of the noodles and strong coffee laid out on the buffet. The staff served the late arrivals more food and drink with bad grace. As daylight dawned, the wake-up call from the mosque faded and the rumble of traffic and blaring of horns reached a crescendo. Checking out, the survey team squashed into taxis and hurried to join the queue converging on the road to the quayside. Zamboanga had transport connections far and wide to Sandakan, Santa Cruz Island, Jolo and even Manila. The taxi driver was amazed they had stayed at the City Inn—a rough dive, more suitable for students and backpackers. Business people, such as them, should stay at the prestigious Lantaka and relax in style.

On arrival beside the jetty, there was no sign of *Eastern Pearl,* so they moved to the Lantaka's palatial lounge bar and terrace to await developments. Lucas was enjoying a hearty breakfast in the restaurant with Vargas and Christina, who had just arrived from the airport.

At ten o'clock, the customs and immigration officer appeared on the quayside as the boat moored up alongside. The survey team grabbed their bags and hurried to board the boat, eager to secure the best accommodation. Captain Jaffar assigned the cabins and forced the team to share cramped quarters, each equipped with bunk beds and a small desk with communal showers and toilets outside in the corridor. Jim, Michael and Christina were lucky to claim single berth rooms.

The quick arrival did not herald a quick departure. The official was in no hurry. Exhaustive checks of the pro-forma invoice convinced him that duty was not payable on the survey equipment as long as the gear checked in left the country at the end of the job. They showed him the document from the National Museum, but he waved it aside, unread. Paperwork from Manila angered him more than a red flag to a bull. He kept demanding where their destination was. Jim explained they had permission to work near Brutus Reef, but he cautioned this was too close to Basilan Island, where the security forces patrolled and a no-go area.

At this point, Hamza and his partner arrived on the quayside, loaded with gun-belts and an arsenal of weapons. Hamza acknowledged the official with a curt wave, in no way subservient. The customs agent knew him and showed no surprise. He relaxed, as if any venture involving the Moro guard was okay with him. Vargas and Jim convened to meet the immigration officer in the mess room. After a long meeting and a gift of two hundred cigarettes, he promised to sign the paperwork off by sunset. He warned we were on our own and could not expect help from the navy.

Hamza introduced his colleague, Raspal, as the second security man.

'What happened to Abdul?' asked Jim.

Raspal was a menacing boy, only sixteen years old, scowling with an insolent grin. Dressed in paramilitary uniform, an old AK47 slung over his shoulder like an extra arm. The threatening image was let down by the boy's lack of boots—his bare feet protruded from over-large rubber flip-flops.

'Away on another job up north. Raspal is his son,' said Hamza.

Lucas and Christina Velasco arrived last of all. Christina was staggering under the weight of two heavy packs and a large rucksack packed with storage sacks, chemicals, reference books, not to mention hammers, chisels, rubber tubing, pipettes and cling film. The last surprise—a diving wetsuit and gas bottles. No one had expected her to dive, but she intended to do so.

Michael helped Christina find her cabin and the nearby shower and toilet reserved for her sole use. Irked, she said she expected no special favours. Captain Jaffar, in an agitated state, was holding her luggage.

'My dear lady, I notice you have an umbrella. I request you do not erect it. An unfurled umbrella on a boat is unlucky, but if activated onboard will precipitate certain disaster.'

Christina's mouth fell open in amazement. To distract her, Michael introduced Captain Jaffar. He did not dare tell her the superstition that a lady on a boat was an ill omen. But naked women on board were welcome, as superstitious mariners claimed this could calm the oceans. Hence figurines of topless ladies, affixed to the bow of a ship, placating troublesome seas to reach safe harbours.

'Whatever you do, don't whistle or hum any tunes,' Michael warned her. 'Mariners hate that—it's the worst thing possible and guaranteed to bring rotten luck.'

Christina cast a critical eye at the compact cabin space. They packed her cases in a steep pile beside the bunk and blocked her escape.

'Well, Michael, whistling a cheerful tune, is not my highest priority. And rather than unfurl my umbrella, I am more likely to use it to smack that rude captain if he gives me any more superstitious nonsense.'

'Oh. I agree. Stand none of Jaffar's rubbish! There are loads of stupid traditions. After you settle in, I will tell you of others. Many are funny, but you should not take them literally.'

Despite the guarantees, *Eastern Pearl* remained in Zamboanga, as the officials had turned obdurate. The promise to release them by sunset looked unlikely; Vargas needed a vital rubber stamp, but the man responsible for signing the papers had not come back from lunch.

At last, when hope appeared dashed, the official returned with the paperwork and permission to sail. A relief for Lucas; able to leave operations in the capable hands of Jim and return to Singapore. He stood on the quayside and watched them cast off, trying to quell an uneasy sense of concern for the uncertain future.

With the frustrating delays behind them, the tension eased as the vessel left the quayside. Crowds of small boys assembled to watch the drama unfold and cheered as the survey boat headed to starboard, cutting a swathe through the dugout canoes and fishing boats. Captain Jaffar found himself on the same course as the old battered Sandakan ferry. The two vessels converged on the congested sea-lane and the ferry passengers, jostling to see the action, waved, shouted and clapped their hands in a friendly frenzy. Jaffar swung the wheel sharply to port and cut his speed to give way to the bigger boat. *Eastern Pearl* pitched in the wake, like a cork in a whirlpool. The ferry gave a triumphant blast on its foghorn as it sped away.

'What's that ship called?' asked Jim.

'*Magnolia Grandiflora*,' said the captain. 'When you are a big bully, the minnows must scatter.'

'Strewth, what a ridiculous name. More suitable for an exhibit in a flower show. Let's hope we get a smoother run to site.'

The shipping movements remained busy with a large variety of small coastal fishing craft trawling for shrimp. Further offshore the traffic became scarcer replaced by occasional cargo boats, tugs, barges, tankers and container vessels. On the rear deck, Hamza and Raspal changed into military camouflage uniforms and brandished their weapons to the amusement of the crew. It distressed Christina to see armed guards onboard. She disappeared to her cabin without a word. Despite the calm seas, the wind and sea state increased as they passed into deeper waters.

After a four-hour transit, they arrived at the south of Sakulakit Island.

'We can start at first light, providing it stays fine. But the weather looks threatening,' said Jim.

He gazed with concern at the ominous black clouds sweeping in from the north. The flat calm of the morning had waned. The wind direction had switched as fresher squally conditions rolled in with gathering gloom on the horizon.

Suddenly it was if someone had emptied a bathtub of water as heavy drops of rain fell on the deck and rebounded. A thunderclap followed, so loud they looked up in alarm. Just in time, they reached cover as lightning hit the mast. For several seconds, a glowing ring of light formed on the boat before dissipating into a dark void. The forces of nature played with them as a cat toys with a mouse. Leaks spurted through the weak spots in the instrument room as the crew rushed to plug the holes.

'Crikey,' said Jim. 'I was ready to start the computer. The lightning surge might have burnt out the motherboard.'

Multiple thunderclaps and flashes discharged in the clouds above or struck the sea. When the storm waned, it gathered strength for a fresh onslaught, running a circuit with their vessel one moment at the epicentre and then at the edge. There was no boundary between the waves and sky as sheets of rain merged the two battering the boat like a volley of bullets against a tin roof. Heartened that conditions would be much worse on *Pacific Glory*, they braced themselves to ride out the storm. Christina was seasick as soon as they left port. Now, in the rough weather, she felt like death. Also, both Hamza and Raspal were queasy and retired to their cabin. Captain Jaffar muttered of ill omens as he held the boat steady into the seas.

As the wind subsided, the sea state remained choppy, so they anchored at the southern fringe of the site, ready to start work the following day.

Michael, Alex and George played a round of whist in the flood-free comfort of the ship's recreation room. The fit enjoyed the dinner choices of roast lamb or curried chicken, preceded by soup or salad, and finished with tinned fruit. Alex had a hearty appetite, happy to embrace this harsh regime. The remaining survey crew gathered in the mess room to watch a movie.

Christina came in for a chat. The noise from the film was too much to bear in her frail state. Michael stood up and asked if she was feeling better.

'Yes, I'm sorry; I am not used to the motion. Why didn't you tell me we had armed guards?'

'Nothing to do with me. Lucas and Vargas arranged it in Zamboanga. I understand it's normal practice. Customs and immigration took no notice of the museum permit and tried to prevent us from leaving, but the guards helped persuade them.'

'Weapons on board are a provocation. The groups will suspect we have a valuable cargo.'

'I am more concerned about the other survey boat. Lucas thinks the Chinese are Triad gang leaders. Maybe we need protection against them.'

'I agree they are suspicious. To make me miss my flight was a deliberate ploy for Tong to get started first.'

'They have only gained a few hours on us. We will soon overtake them.'

Of *Pacific Glory*, there was no sight because of poor visibility. Captain Jaffar listened in on the VHF to discover if they had any problems, but there was no radio traffic from the boat.

Chapter 19

Pacific Glory had arrived on site while the immigration officials in Zamboanga delayed *Eastern Pearl*. Despite overtaking their rivals, there was little progress. It was a sultry afternoon with the sun sparkling on the wave ripples as the stirring kiss of a breeze flutters the ripening barley. The fishing fleet rushed home with their catch, pursued by excited gulls. A few flying fish darted out of the water, alarmed by the boat.

On the back deck, Tong and Yap waited impatiently for the job to begin as the survey team checked and calibrated their equipment, a long-winded exercise. Sandy explained they needed to verify accuracy before they could start. But there was no air of urgency.

Sandy and the captain consulted the marine chart to plan for the day. Singh frowned as he studied the many shoals surrounding the islands. The hazard of hidden reefs was a risk to the towed equipment. They agreed to inspect the seabed using an inflatable dinghy, without risking the mother vessel. While the team lashed the equipment in position, Singh scanned the horizon with his binoculars.

'What's up, skipper, worried about pirates?' asked Sandy.

'These waters have seen so many incidents that the tears and blood of victims stain the sea. It pays to be cautious.'

Sandy laughed in disbelief, suspecting the problem to be imaginary.

'Singh, people always tell these stories, but you meet no one that scary pirates have robbed—not in this day and age.'

'No, you are wrong. It is a common occurrence. They show no mercy. Women, children, old and young—it doesn't matter who you are. If you have no value to them, they force you to walk the plank and feed you to the sharks! That is your fate, if you are lucky. However, if the militants take you hostage, they drag you through the jungle to their camp. Many disappear for months or even years, and their family does not know if they are dead or alive. For rich and important people, they demand a ransom. If your relatives can't pay, the savages will chop off your head!'

Sandy laughed again, but with less conviction.

'In that case, we better get cracking and leave before we become another statistic.'

Picking up the glasses, he scanned the horizon ranging them over every boat and motor launch, convinced ruthless pirates waited for them like hungry hyenas.

By evening, they completed the reconnaissance survey. They ceased operations and anchored up in deeper seas. During the day, the wind direction had switched and gradually increased in force. Close to midnight, they noticed lights of an approaching vessel headed their way at full speed. Crowded around the radar, they watched the worrying shape come closer. Once she was within VHF range, they heard *Eastern Pearl* call out a friendly greeting. Tong told Singh to ignore him and keep radio silence.

The seas increased to a Sumatra storm, battering *Pacific Glory* with such force that multiple leaks opened draining water through the roof. The instrument room flooded, causing electrical shorts to cables and damage to recorders. Floodwater entered the cabins. The overpowering smell from the ruined carpets mixed with the odour of stale sweat, foetid socks and the contents of the overflowing toilets. Thunder and lightning crashed around them. With zero visibility, sea and sky merged into one curtain of foam and noise backlit by flashes exposing their scared faces. When the storm was imminent, Singh had lifted the anchor to ride out the high seas. The boat surged over the white caps and dived into the troughs. Singh struggled to keep her head into the wind. The tempest towered above them and broke against the bridge, leaving the deck awash. The crew sighed with relief when the boat rose above the waves and held their breath when vast waves smashed into the bridge.

By morning, the storm ran out of enthusiasm. The wind direction had changed. The vessel was several miles away from the site. Singh turned about and headed slowly back. Although the storm was over, a high swell persisted. Brown-coloured water raced past full of suspended vegetation, including entire tree trunks and many coconuts, bobbing like lottery balls. The weather delay pushed them on the back-foot, with nothing to show. Drained by lack of sleep, the survey team lay unconscious in their bunks.

Ever the optimist, Sandy believed they could fix everything. Spares backed up most items, but they could not afford further incidents. The ship's crew rigged up tarpaulins over leaky roofs and sealed up various gaps.

'Davinder won't pay you guys the full charter rate with these unpleasant conditions,' said Sandy.

'Foul weather is an act of God. In severe storms, any vessel comes under pressure and springs a few leaks. As you can see, we rode out the storm with flying colours with no injury to the crew or damage to the boat.'

'Captain, this boat has useless air-conditioning and disgusting toilets which won't flush—basic requirements.'

'I heartily agree with you. I have recommended to Mr Tong we head into Sandakan, which you must know, and sort the problems out, but he said no. Why don't you have a word and make him change his mind?'

'And what makes you think he will listen?'

'Perhaps they lighten up when you are finding the treasure?'

'Yes—and pigs might fly.'

By nightfall, *Pacific Glory* had surveyed most of the western half of their block. The side-scan captured sonar images. The seabed was sandy, sometimes forming thick dune deposits with ripples. Of the wreck, there was no sign. The magnetometer read out showed three anomalies, possibly buried metallic targets. Tong stopped work to switch to diving. Although it was night, Mahmood and Suleiman agreed to dive to escape from the squalid conditions on board.

The divers spent thirty minutes on the first descent, over a featureless, flat seafloor. Initially, they used metal probes to detect buried objects. The next shift deployed an airlift to blow off the sand and search deeper for artefacts. Gradually they removed the upper layers of sediment and opened a trench. Just before their time was up, a diver met a hard level, but the visibility was deteriorating with the ebb tide, so they stopped operations.

The following day Tony implored Sandy to restart the survey. Conditions were ideal. He wanted to delay diving until they had completed the geophysics. But Tong and Yap were eager to complete work on the trench. Once again, Mahmood and Suleiman used the airlift. Visibility had improved, but the excavation had filled up with fresh sediment, undoing their earlier effort. They added another diver to the shift. With dwindling gas supplies, Mahmood exposed the hard level. It contained coarse coral fragments, and as he forced a sample into a plastic bag, his fingers closed around a piece of blue and white porcelain. It was a base plate with mid-eighteenth century hallmarks. The date of this shard confirmed it matched the age of the *Siren*—a discovery that overjoyed the entire team. The broken fragment was consistent with the wreck breaking up and spilling its cargo over a wide zone. They found no metallic debris to explain the magnetometer anomaly. The geophysicist was backtracking on his original interpretation, claiming it was just noise.

This find raised morale, but not enough to counter the unrest over the dreadful living conditions. Although the crew had unblocked the toilets, the failure of the air-conditioning was unbearable as the unrelenting sun burnt them alive.

At midday, they damaged the magnetometer sensor, snagged on an object on the seabed. While the engineers repaired the cable Sandy met up with Tony, Tong and Yap on the bridge for a progress update. They had only completed twenty-four kilometres of geophysics because switching to and from diving operations was wasting time. Much better to run the survey through to completion and increase the production rate.

'How long to survey the remaining lines?' asked Tong.

'To complete the entire block may take three weeks.'

'Far too slow. What if you reduce coverage to fifty metres spacing?'

Sandy looked at Tony for a comment.

'Yes, it's possible. You might miss the magnetometer contacts. Try a wider interval and add infill if we get a contact.'

'Will the sonar density be okay at a larger line separation?' said Sandy.

'Keeping the range at 100 metres should still give enough coverage.'

Tong and Yap talked together in their Chinese dialect while the others doodled on their pads. Tong followed Sandy's advice to complete the survey work as a priority. This would free them to concentrate on diving over the most promising areas. Tony was impatient to show them the data.

'I examined the geophysics in the trench where we discovered the pottery shard. The coral level shows up on records as a strong seismic reflector with this diffraction.'

'What do you mean by diffractions?' asked Tong.

'Any larger material such as pieces of coral, cobbles or objects of debris such as crates of porcelain can give these chaotic patterns,' said Tony. 'I believe we have found the old seabed of 1764. If we follow this reflector, it deepens to the north and shallows heading south. It's possible the 1764 level outcrops at the southern limit of our block. Between the mid-eighteenth century and today, the sand has shifted. Most likely sand buried the wreck in the dunes. Our best bet of finding it will be where the cover is thinnest. That is in the trough areas of the sand waves. Or we could find some vestige of the wreck still intact at seabed.'

Tong studied a section of the record, which looked chaotic. 'I can see what you mean, so this part might contain part of the wreck?'

'It's possible.'

Encouraged, Tong called the meeting to a close and a faint smile of optimism lit up his face.

Chapter 20

Julie replaced the telephone after a brief conversation with Lucas to update her on the last few days' events. She loved his descriptions of Rio Hondo, the Muslim town built on stilts, of Christina, missing her flight and the vessel's dramatic departure from Zamboanga. It sounded like an exciting place. Julie wished she could have been there. Michael said he did not want her worrying, so Lucas omitted the details of the armed guards and the rival group searching for the same wreck. They agreed to filter out any information that might alarm her. Alex had settled in well and was sharing a cabin with George Choy.

She always enjoyed shopping in Cold Storage. Such a brilliant store, and it stocked a vast range of items. If a trip to Jelita was the highlight of her day, her life needed a change. With her men away, she had better chase up her female friends to relieve the boredom—a safer course than pursuing the elusive Luigi. After helping her start the Volvo and a chat beside the pool one evening, he had vanished. No longer did he appear for his flashy evening swim or jog about the grounds.

Annoying to think she qualified as one of those long-term expatriates she despised when she first came to Singapore. After living here for ages, the UK was a fading memory—a place to visit parents on dutiful vacations. Friendships, which there took forever to build up, flourished here in days. It surprised her how much she missed Michael and Alex and the chance to share the discoveries of each day. She willed them to come home again, concerned they might run into problems. No doubt about it, living alone in paradise could be dull. Without the family, her life was as unbalanced as a toppling table with broken legs. Pathetic—she must pick herself up and forge independence. If the rumour mill was correct, pirates and terrorists roamed the Sulu Sea searching for gullible foreigners to kidnap. She suspected both Michael and Lucas had been less than candid with her. No point dwelling on it, but of the two scenarios—either successful and finding a valuable cargo worth millions or not—the only outcome of interest was their safe return.

The family next door asked Julie along on a day trip to Singapore's resort island of Sentosa—a budget Disneyland of dreams. Despite living next door to the Teos for two years, this was the first social invitation to join them and their two teenage boys. Previously, contact was the odd, casual greeting across the balcony or a friendly nod in passing. Most of the Fletcher's social life centred on fellow expatriates. When Alex was a baby, everyone was much more friendly, with weekly invitations to birthday parties and barbecues with their neighbours and school friends. As Alex grew older, the dynamic changed as he asserted his independence and new friendships. Of course, this was inevitable, but maybe, she wondered, both she and Michael had failed to adapt to the changes.

Sentosa was not somewhere she liked, but with nothing else to do, she accepted. She preferred the less commercialised parts such as the jungle walks and nature trails, ignored by the public, marshalled from one contrived attraction to another. It was such an exhausting resort, and the Teos insisted on trudging to every point of interest including the museums, Butterfly Park, Sea World and many more. They stopped at the Rasa Sentosa food centre for expensive hawker fare inflated for the captive tourist market. Afterwards Julie tried to escape alone on the ferry, but the friendly neighbours ignored her pleas for early release and urged her to take in one last show—the famous Musical Fountains—a dramatic display of dancing jets of water coordinated to music. They jollied Julie out of her zombified state and made her follow them. Just a quick walk away. Everyone who visited Singapore must see the fountains.

Much later, Julie fell out of her taxi at Pagoda Villas in a disjointed, half-blind state. The driver waited, watching the ghostly sleepwalker stagger up the steps to her apartment, where she crashed with a tired groan. Once inside, the stale heat hit her like a wall of treacle. She dropped, fully clothed, on top of the bed, kicking off her shoes for blessed relief to her sore feet. With a superhuman effort, she removed her clothes but lacked the energy to get under the covers. Besides, even the weight of a single sheet felt too oppressive.

The red light of the answerphone flashed with insistence. She tottered over, half asleep, to listen to the messages: A call from Michael to say everything was going well. God, the heat. With the air-conditioning off, it was a stifling oven. Even breathing required a conscious effort to extract oxygen out of the stale air, so thick and clammy. She fetched a can of Tiger from the fridge, ice-cold to the touch, and dabbed it over her forehead to ease the knot of a growing headache. It seemed a shame to waste it so she tossed it down her throat, enjoying the sharp edge of hoppy bitterness and the cold relief as the gas bubbles exploded in her mouth.

Despite being tired, she felt restless and could not sleep for ages. On the bedside table, she noticed Michael had emptied his pockets of a pile of receipts. She idly looked through them and noticed one for a meal for two at the

Changi Sailing Club. The chicken rice was obviously Michael's choice and someone else selected the nasi lemak followed by an ice cream. In fact, three beers—typical of Michael, and the mystery guest drank lime juice. Was this for lunch or dinner? The date from 3rd August tallied with just before the team sailed to the Philippines. Michael had been late back one night after working late at the office with Danica on his 'reports.' It did not occur to Julie that the guest consumed a beer and the lime juice, but she was certain Danica was the mystery partner!

Night slid away as a guilty lover, and the rising sun encircled the apartment in its torrid embrace. A laser shaft of sunlight seared across Julie's pale face as she buried herself under the sheet. Late morning, and already the bedroom was a warm, damp glove enveloping her in a fog with no escape from its oppressive weight. Unable to rise, she drifted back to semi-sleep.

Much later, she woke to a cracking migraine—a piercing pain. Bright lights aggravated her condition, so only darkness helped. The amah noisily shifted furniture and bashed the floor with a brush. To add more torment, she switched the television to the MTV music channel running a music video of the Spice Girls big hit 'Spice up your Life'. Bedraggled, Julie hauled herself up to turn the set off.

The maid came three mornings a week to help tidy. Michael and Alex, the chief mess-makers, were away, so she had little to do. Julie groaned, pointing at her head and rolling her eyes with a grimace to show she had a severe headache. The girl smiled nervously and carried on watering the plants.

Julie returned to bed; maybe she needed a few more minutes. Peace at last. But she was too anxious and wound up to relax, annoyed at discovering that receipt for a cosy meal at the yacht club. She dragged herself into the bathroom for a cold shower.

Her surge of activity, or the effect of the pills, eased her headache. She slipped into her favourite white Japanese dressing gown, still dripping wet. The blinking answerphone light alerted her to an incoming call from Michael, leaving a message:

'Hello, only me—a quick call to see how you are. We can only get reception in the far north. We are heading south, so I expect to lose the signal soon.' Julie picked up the telephone. It was not the right time to raise the mystery receipt. That could wait until Michael returned.

'Sorry—just taking a shower. I heard your message late after I got back. The Teos next door asked me to join them on a trip to Sentosa with their two teenagers. I'm not sure which is the more tiring—walking in the heat for miles or dealing with moody teens. I have a migraine this morning.'

'Sentosa is an exhausting place. If you have a headache, it's likely to be a reaction to MSG in Chinese food.'

'We ate my favourite kailan in oyster sauce. Perhaps that is the culprit. Have you found the wreck?'

'No, not yet. Tomorrow we look at one of the earlier anomaly areas near the centre of the block. I hope it will be more promising. Early days. The weather is wonderful today, but a storm hit us yesterday. Alex is doing well.'

'Lucas called me with a full update. Zamboanga sounds a colourful place. I expect you took Alex out for a nice meal somewhere?' He could not hear until the line came back. 'Michael, the line is fading—speak to you later. Bye.'

Julie replaced the telephone. Enough on his plate without worrying about her. These snatched conversations were unsatisfactory. Shortly after Michael's call, her headache eased. She dressed in shorts and a casual T-shirt—no point in worrying who might see her. She planned a dull day alone at home. The amah was packing up, ready to leave. With so little work, she considered giving her a break. And less pressure on her to clear up before she came. The light on the phone was still glowing red, and she saw another missed call. Someone must have phoned yesterday.

When she played it back, the caller left no message. How strange. Perhaps it was Luigi? She hadn't given him her number, or had she? If Michael and the draughtswoman were

taking romantic dinners, perhaps she should pursue Luigi
more vigorously.

Chapter 21

Julie headed to Changi Village for early morning breakfast at the hawker stalls. The village was still half-asleep, with several open-air restaurants too tired to tout for the passing trade. Most of the shops opened at 11 o'clock.

Stray cats and dogs scuttled through the legs of a group of small boys as they kicked a football along the pavement. The outside seating of the restaurants was crowded with groups of locals and tourists lingering over coffee, but Julie ignored this area and headed towards the hawker centre which offered better value. The pensioner sweeping up the paper plates and half-eaten chips smiled a welcome. Nearby the all-night 7-Eleven store was the hub for the young, partying crowd who tolerated its high prices to purchase cigarettes, snacks and Mr Softee ice cream. With daylight, the old Chinese provision shop, Khiann Whatt, lifted its blinds on another hot and humid morning. The owner arranged some of his goods outside the shop in the 'five-foot way' to catch the eye of passers-by. At this time of the morning, many families came by for drinks and snacks for boat trips across to

Pulau Ubin or Pengerang in Malaysia.

A short walk through the village brought Julie to a covered market. Inside was a vast array of tropical fruit of every conceivable variety. She walked along the aisles, inhaling the aromas from green coconuts, deep yellow bananas, rambutans, star fruit, mangosteens and the putrid, rotten smell of durian, which had the odour of a dead dog in a storm drain. Durians had a tough carapace with studded spikes like medieval battle clubs. It amused Julie to see a group intensely sniffing the fruit like connoisseurs comparing the subtleties of each one.

Malay matrons, formally dressed in colourful *baju kurung*, laughed as they bartered over bananas and limes. Young Chinese and Malays, in western style jeans, wandered past the stalls, some come to buy, some to look. The names of many vegetables and herbs were still foreign to her, despite living in Singapore for many years, although she recognised the familiar ginger, garlic and the Chinese cabbage they called kailan. From the Malaysian hills came carrots, tomatoes, French beans and small waxy potatoes.

Julie wandered past stalls with live crabs, prawns and exotic fish such as grouper, pomfret and stingray. Large fish heads of red snappers stared out of a bucket used to make the famous fish head curry. The eyes of the fish were about the same size as a human eye, and the highlight of the meal was to crunch into the eyeball enjoying the strange juxtaposition of the fluid-filled aqueous humour contrasting with the chewy membrane covering the cornea and iris. Julie gagged at the powerful smell and looked in distaste, vowing never to eat fish again. Even the prospect of a hot coffee and breakfast lost its appeal.

Hurrying through the market, she rushed out into the fresh air and headed off in search of the ferry port. To take her mind off things a ferry trip to the nearby island of Pulau Ubin would be fun. She would have preferred Alex and Michael with her to share the experience, but she had made the trip before and liked to wander around alone. There was a brand new ferry terminal, still using the old bumboats. Each boat carried up to twelve people on the short sea route to the nearby island. Passing down a footpath lined with huge, willowy angsana trees Julie boarded a small yellow painted bumboat, and, once it was half-full, they left the jetty, raising an impressive wake as they sped out to sea, bumping in the swell and raising a fine mist of spray.

On arrival on Pulau Ubin, a few minutes later, she walked up the single scruffy street lined by provisions shops and seafood restaurants, taking a few photographs. The only form of transport on the island was to hire a bike or an old and dilapidated, but expensive taxi. Julie preferred to walk and take in the sights. Compared to modern Singapore, the island was a throwback to a quieter pace of life. She spent an enjoyable few hours walking through the jungle marvelling at the huge butterflies and discovering small attap palm roofed houses nestling in smalholdings with fruit trees of papaya, wild chickens and smiling children.

Later that day, feeling energised by her trip to the island, Julie organised a barbecue for the weekend. The wreck search was a good excuse for a party. Lucas Miffré said he would bring along an acquaintance from Ang Mo Kio, a waitress called Kim Choo. Julie invited two of Michael's oldest friends and cricket club contacts, Andy and Beryl. The remaining guests were friendships nurtured beside the pool over leisurely evening swims or other parents from Alex's school.

Apart from the locals, there was a mix of expatriates from Japan, Germany, France and the United States—a surprising range of different nationalities to choose from, and they were brilliantly friendly. After an absence, the young Italian from Block 42 had resumed his evening swims in the pool most evenings. He always seemed to be alone, so she delivered an invitation for her barbecue party with a hand-written note slipped under his door. After all, he had been so helpful fixing the problem with the Volvo. It was a bold step, but annoyingly he had not bothered to reply.

Saturday evening and Julie assembled all she needed for the party. The communal barbecue pits were on a grassed pitch near to the pool complex. Her apartment was nearby, and the provisions shop supplied essential items. Julie sourced succulent fresh tiger prawns, mixed satay, sirloin steaks and chicken marinated in chilli, galangal, coriander and cumin. Her friends contributed salads, coleslaw, plovers' eggs and wine. She borrowed iceboxes from the neighbours and filled them with cans of beer, coke, and whatever else people brought in contributions. In no time, someone fired the barbecue up, its smoke rising in high anti-social clouds. As the charcoal glowed, the smoke faded. The glowing embers yielded a fragrant aroma, wafted on the breeze to entice hungry children out onto their balconies until their mothers cuffed them back to their homework. Julie drew her guests together in a warm huddle as she tossed a few chicken breasts and steaks on the barbecue.

Lucas arrived with a strikingly attractive Chinese girl, young enough to be his daughter.

'Julie, let me introduce Kim Choo.'

'I am so glad to meet you,' said Julie.

Flustered, she asked her what she wanted to drink, but they hung back awkwardly, undecided.

'Kim Choo works at Jack's Steak restaurant in Ang Mo Kio.'

Lucas passed over a bag containing some delicious New Zealand fillet steaks. He grabbed a beer for himself and an orange juice for Kim Choo.

'Thank you—it's lovely of you, but you shouldn't have bothered. We have tons of food,' said Julie.

'It's one of the perks of working at a steakhouse. I hear your husband is out in the Philippines on a treasure hunt for Lucas?'

'Yes, and my son, Alex.'

She had not got used to the idea, and the way Kim Choo described it made it sound like a tough assignment her beloved Lucas should avoid.

'You must miss them.'

'It's a worry. Piracy is active in the Sulu Sea.'

'And you have other children?'

'No, just Alex.'

She did not see why she should justify having one child in eighteen years. It was none of anyone's business. Well, it was one more than Kim Choo. Judging by her boyish figure, she had borne no children. An awkward silence developed—where nobody talks until they all talk at once.

'And do you ever return to England?'

'Occasionally, for vacations and for Alex to see his grandparents.'

The barrage of questions was faintly annoying, but Kim Choo was not listening. Absorbed with Lucas, she poured him red wine, making the glass gush over and splash his hand. They both giggled at her endearing clumsiness. Amazing how a mature man was so besotted by youth and beauty!

Andy and Beryl were wandering about, looking for the party. Julie gave a friendly shout to redirect them up the steps. Andy worked for an international property company, specialising in expensive rentals to expatriates. It sounded a glamorous job meeting wealthy bankers and business executives, showing them around opulent apartments and earning a hefty commission when he tempted them to commit to their dream home. Andy's best attribute was never to discuss work, but his favourite topic of cricket could bore anyone to tears.

Lucas poured Julie a glass of wine as he wandered over to chat, leaving Kim Choo talking to Andy and Beryl.

'I got an update from Jim this morning. They have made excellent progress and completed the first phase geophysical survey. The divers have started work. At this rate they should finish within a week or two.'

'I haven't heard a word for days. To be exact, not since the first day they started work when Michael called. I suppose they are out of the range of phone signals?'

The phone coverage was intermittent according to Lucas, but he received a satellite call every morning from Jim to update their progress.

'And have they found anything?'

'They have located parts of the wreck, but the trouble is the sand has buried everything. Jim says the other boat, the *Pacific Glory*, located a trail of broken debris which may be from the *Siren*. The interesting news is they reckon both the hull and stern sections are in our block. Let's hope they are intact and contain the porcelain.'

'I didn't know you hired two boats to look for the wreck.'

'No—we are only running the one boat. The other one is another group from Singapore searching a different patch.'

Julie could not recall Michael mentioning this, so why the secrecy? Two boats searching different areas for the same wreck must mean at least one of them was looking in the wrong place, and maybe both of them would return empty-handed.

'It's such a shame if all this hard effort is in vain.'

'If we have found nothing within two weeks, I will call them back,' said Lucas. 'We hope to make a profit from the film Alex is making for us: "The Search for the *Siren*". We can sell it to the Discovery channel; even failure sells.'

'What a suitable name. We are all searchers after something, aren't we? Money, fame, love...,' her voice trailed off.

Andy and Beryl broke away from Kim Choo to greet Julie as she was turning the steaks over on the barbecue.

'My that smells gorgeous,' said Beryl. 'What a shame Michael is missing this. It's very enterprising of you to throw a party on your own. Are you celebrating anything special?'

'Not really. Just freedom. I will pursue my dreams. If Michael wants to take part in a risky enterprise with Alex, then I am free to be reckless.'

She meant the words to be throwaway and light, but judging by the shocked faces of Andy and Beryl, she had caused a stir. Beryl coughed and changed the subject.

'Well said, Julie. It's a marvellous opportunity for shopping or visiting places of interest.'

'Can't stand shopping,' said Andy. 'An over-rated pastime and Singapore is no longer cheap. We are cross with Michael as he has missed most of the cricket season. You used to love coming to the Padang to watch Michael play.'

'Andy, you know I was just a cricket widow. When we were first married, Michael was so keen, but I was fed up with wasting every weekend watching slow, boring games. The only highlights were the cricket teas and a few jugs of beer at the end, but even then the only topic of conversation was cricket.'

'I hope we can talk him into a game when he gets back. Young Alex as well, if he is interested. He's a tall lad, so he should be a good fast bowler.'

Julie wasn't listening. She had other things on her mind and smiled with pleasure, as she noticed Luigi mounting the steps holding a bottle of Chianti and a package of something long, which turned out to be a saucisson and a block of Pecorino Romano, the delicious hard, salty cheese. Luigi was floating along, a shy smile on his face. Such an attractive man, dressed casually but with style.

Chapter 22

Late morning the day after the barbecue and Julie stretched out her long legs, enjoying the freedom of the double bed without Michael beside her. The heat of the day suggested it must be close to midday. It was delicious with no pressing agenda, no work and no one to cater for. Better, though, it was a weekend devoid of plans. The maid came on Mondays, Wednesdays and Fridays so there would be no noisy interruptions. Her party had been brilliant. The problem was getting rid of Andy, Beryl and Luigi—happy to stay and finish the beer.

Unfortunately, Andy and Luigi had dominated the conversation into the small hours with Andy attempting to explain the laws of cricket to the Italian while he countered with long details about his work. He was a consulting engineer for a French company for the construction of the world's first fully automatic Mass Rapid Transit link called the North-East line running underground from near the old World Trade centre in the southwest to Punggol in the northeast. Singapore was always extending their network with more stations saturating their small island, reaching ever further afield like the tentacles of an octopus. Many of the stops were at obscure satellite towns where the population lived in conformable high-rise Housing and Development Board flats, the ubiquitous HDB.

Julie said it was such a shame to eradicate so much of the former secondary jungle and relaxed kampong houses with their small plots of fruit trees and chickens just to install yet more rail networks and stations, but progress and modernity was to benefit the many and not the few rooted in the past.

Luigi told her the North-East MRT line would have minimal impact being underground apart from the 16 stations along the route. It was unavoidable to have some surface infrastructure, including car parking and roads, but there would still be plenty of trees and greenery to soften the concrete impact. He was proud to specialise in tunnelling and making sure all the tunnels joined up so the MRT trains could run along happily. It was an important and well-paid job. Few consulting engineers could match his experience. Sadly, his contract only had six more months to go, and then it would be somewhere else that needed him, like Dubai or Qatar. If not tunnels, he could do bridges.

Even yawning and tidying up did not budge them until the small hours when they took the hint to leave. Taxi prices increased after midnight, but Andy and Beryl were too mean to take one, preferring to totter home inebriated. One day they might trip into a storm drain—deep hazards risky for the young and alert and potentially fatal for the old and complacent.

Luigi proved more difficult to persuade to leave. He lived alone in a third-floor flat in Block 42 of Pagoda Villas, just a short walk away. Apart from his sole topic of conversation relating to the MRT system which he returned to with boyish enthusiasm he, somewhat weirdly, kept taking loads of pictures on his new digital camera—a recent purchase from Sim Lim Towers, where he said prices were much lower than the so-called duty-free deals at Changi. Proudly, he drew her attention to its superior resolution and how it packed more megapixels than cheaper cameras. Julie yawned at the tedious monologue, but he found that entrancing and an excuse to shoot close-ups of her frowning face. He was great fun, although slightly tiring.

Eleven o'clock already. Reluctantly, she pulled herself together, put filter coffee on, threw on a top and cleared up the mess from last night. She laughed when she saw Luigi's beloved camera tucked into the side of the settee. No doubt a deliberate ploy. Time for a little joke. How amusing to hide it and deny he had left it behind! As Luigi only lived a few blocks away, he would probably call by on the off chance. Energised by the thought, she stripped off for a quick shower and a change into something appropriate.

After her shower, she dug out an old pair of Jordache jeans, surprised they still fit after so many years. Jeans were not too comfortable in the constant humidity of Singapore, but just right for relaxing inside her apartment with the air-conditioning turned high. She had not decided on a top when the doorbell rang, so it rushed her into throwing on yesterday's T-shirt and a spot of Armani to freshen up. As expected, Luigi was on the threshold. So predictable. On seeing Julie, he broke into a warm smile. He slipped out of his trainers, conforming to local practice in Singapore of never wearing outside shoes inside dwellings.

'I am so sorry, but last night I think I left my camera behind. Silly me!'

'Really! I can't say I have seen it. You had better have a search. I have just made coffee. Would you like a cup? It's Lavazza.'

Luigi had the typical Italian prejudice that only Italians could make decent coffee and habitually refused such offers as they only led to disappointment. But he risked it on this occasion.

'Lavazza espresso from Turin is marvellous.'

'This is only a filter version from my machine so it won't be that great.'

'No problem. Made by you will be *eccellente*. I am on my way for a run. I try to complete some circuits of the grounds to keep fit. It is so nice here with the bougainvillea and palm trees. Like on a permanent holiday! At my office there is no chance of exercise so I have a swim when I get home, but at the weekend I jog a lot more.'

'Yes, your swimming prowess is impressive. Hmm, and jogging is so useful for all round fitness. Although I am much too shy to do any running myself.'

'So kind. And your son—he is how old now?'

'Alex—just 18.'

'No, unbelievable—but you are so young.'

Luigi searched the sofa for his camera, without success. Panicking, he looked around everywhere and bent over on his hands and knees, peering under the furniture when Julie calmly handed it over. She rather liked that view of him. Relieved, he sat back and sipped his coffee with hearty glugs.

'Would you like sugar?'

'*Si grazie.* Sorry I should not talk Italian. It's force of habit.'

'No, I *love* it,' she handed him a bowl of sugar.

Julie became conscious of her inappropriate clothes—a bit too informal for a lone male Italian she had only just met. But Michael and Alex were away on their little adventure. Best to act as normal.

'You caught me by surprise. I threw on the nearest things when the doorbell rang.'

'So sorry. I should have phoned first, but I do not have your number.'

'Yes,' she said. 'That would be a problem.'

He played back the photos on his camera. There were many of the party guests, which he passed over quickly until he found several close-ups of Julie. She sat next to him and admired them politely. It felt awkward sitting so close, so she got up for another cup of coffee.

'This one of you frowning is my favourite.'

She agreed it was typical of her severe look when annoyed by childish behaviour.

The situation was developing too fast for her. She broke away, looking at her watch in alarm.

'I'm so sorry, Luigi, but the maid is due any minute. I really need to tidy up before she comes or she will resign!'

He looked crestfallen and unbelieving of this lie. Maids seldom worked on Sundays, as he well knew. She went to collect his trainers from the hallway and he reluctantly stood up.

'Well, Julie. Thank you for a wonderful party and looking after my camera. And not forgetting the excellent coffee! I had better take my regular exercise. See you next time!' He fumbled with the laces of his trainers in a hurry to leave.

Julie was feeling stunned by all this attention from an attractive man at least ten years younger than herself when the phone interrupted her thoughts. It was Beryl thanking her for the brilliant barbecue party and asking her if she wanted to join them for a curry lunch at Samy's in Dempsey Road.

Samy's Curry Restaurant was an institution in Singapore. Since its founding in 1963 at the Civil Service Sport's Club, the colonial building formerly used by the British Military, had served an unchanging Southern Indian style curry served on banana leaves and eaten, traditionally, with the hand.

At 1 o'clock, Julie met up with Andy and Beryl at an outside table on the small hillside terrace on Dempsey Road.

'I haven't been here for years,' said Julie. 'We used to come here for Sunday lunch and combine it with a trip to the Botanic Gardens. Alex was just a baby, but he loved eating his rice off a banana leaf! '

Andy and Beryl reminisced on many previous happy visits. Over the years, the staff and menu remained unchanged. They replaced only the worn chairs and tables.

'This is on us,' said Andy. 'You are our guest.'

Julie tried to resist his offer, but Beryl said Andy had just found a tenant for a long idle apartment off Farrer Road for a banker and his much younger wife, and he could look forward to a handsome commission. So they would love to share their good fortune with Julie, especially as Michael and Alex were away at sea.

'In the good times the monthly rental was 10,000 dollars a month, so I was pleased to get 8,000 in today's depressed market.'

'Yes, it was lucky,' said Beryl. 'Those older apartments are much nicer than the horrible ones at Bayshore Park. Also, Farrer Road is so convenient for shopping.'

Andy did not rate this as an essential consideration. In his opinion, they should represent shopping among the Ten Courts of Hell at Haw Par Villa theme park.

'Many of the younger crowd prefer the East Coast for the Tanah Merah Country Club and the proximity to the sea and seafood restaurants, although I don't reckon the facilities are anything special.'

'Yes,' agreed Beryl. 'Not our sort of area.'

A waiter placed a banana leaf in front of each of the diners and another waiter offered a choice of white rice or biryani rice. The third waiter served cabbage dhal, cucumber salad, potato marsala and papadums. A jug of Tiger beer materialised as if by magic. Main course options added to the banana leaf included sambal prawn, chicken marsala and mutton curry. Andy told them to avoid the fish head curry, which he considered too hot and over-priced. It was a sultry afternoon, but the overhead ceiling fans stirred the air. When Andy disappeared to the washroom at the end of the meal, Beryl started discussing the barbecue party.

'We *so* enjoyed your barbecue yesterday. I am sorry it took so long to get rid of us but Andy and your young friend, Luigi, couldn't stop talking!'

Julie laughed. 'I got him to leave just after you left. He was so boring talking about his work the whole time. He lives in one of the high-rise apartments at Pagoda and is always at the poolside every night. That's how we know him. He is so friendly to Michael and helps fix his car.'

'That's reassuring,' said Beryl. 'We thought you two were having a wild affair.'

Chapter 23

This morning, a scorching sun rose over a flat, calm sea—ideal conditions for the survey—and *Pacific Glory* was making fair progress. They completed work on the eastern flank with no useful results, so they moved to the western side, bordering Lucas Miffré's block, which looked more promising. Tony planned to trace the archaeological level where they had found the single shard of porcelain. When he plotted up the magnetometer contacts, he noticed they formed an arc-shaped trail from the northwestern edge, and then circled towards the centre before turning back to exit in the west. The distribution showed the wreck must have broken up, spilling its cargo, which the currents spread out. Tony hoped there was still a sizable chunk of the wreckage buried somewhere in their area. It would be brilliant to uncover the stern or hull section, but there was a strong possibility it was in *Eastern Pearl*'s block.

At the midday meeting on the bridge, Tony said he expected to finish the geophysics soon and restart the diving programme. He had found weak magnetic anomalies, which he suspected to be modern metallic debris rather than objects from a shipwreck, but they should check.

Tong had spotted a light glowing from Sakulakit Island, the largest of a group of small islands clustered nearby. This was disturbing news. Steep volcanic outcrops stuck up like a dragon's teeth, sheer from the ocean. Such land was unsuitable for settlement as the rocky knolls were devoid of vegetation, apart from a few twisted shrubs fighting for a roothold in the hostile terrain. The summit was an excellent vantage point to see both the survey vessels and the sparse trees on the slopes provided cover. Who could be there? And were they spying on them?

Captain Singh had noticed a fishing skiff in the area. As the fishermen cast their nets or laid their traps, they always seemed to stare at them in fascination. The crew of six followed their every move. Singh suspected they could be agents for Abu Sayyaf tasked with spying on them. Once they found the treasure, the fishermen would alert the militants and Yap with his old gun would be no match for the ruthless brigands.

The team laughed off the captain's concerns as fear-mongering, but their nervous glances belied their words. Sandy suggested they increase security, placing lookouts round the clock. Singh kept his binoculars trained on the fishing boat, searching for weapons, but, apart from their knives for gutting fish, he saw nothing suspicious. After the meeting, Yap returned to his cabin. He had spent a restless night and wanted to catch an hour's break before lunch. But Tong had other ideas. He hammered on Yap's door and walked in without waiting for an answer.

'I want you to visit Sakulakit Island. I need you to investigate this strange light at the summit. The captain says no one inhabits these islands. Best you go with Mahmood and Suleiman to check.'

'What now?' Yap rose from his bunk, startled at the intrusion.

'It's likely the fishermen use the island for storage and supplies. Also possible the security forces or terrorists may be there, so be careful. The captain is a nervous wreck who sees militants on every boat, so I think it most likely the fishermen are just inquisitive and not spying on us.'

'Should I take the AK47?' Yap opened the cupboard where he stored the rugged Kalashnikov machine gun, wrapped in oilcloth.

'Yes, but keep the gun hidden from our team. Brandish the weapon when you approach the fishing boat to see how they react.'

Tong suggested Yap inspect the chart on the bridge as there was only one logical place to land—an inlet on the south side with a sheltered bay. The rest of the island was an exposed rock outcrop rising vertically from the sea.

'Check for signs of recent visits such as empty drink cans and rubbish. Ask the crew to lower the zodiac at the end of this survey line.'

'Okay, boss.'

Yap put on his walking shoes and dark glasses. Conscious of Tong's impatient stare, he bungled the lace-ups, which tripped him up in the doorway as he grabbed the AK47. The rifle barrel smashed into the doorframe.

'Take care with the gun,' snapped Tong, losing patience. 'I said keep it hidden from the crew. First, sort out the boat. Don't put it in the zodiac until departure.'

In the instrument room, Sandy was checking the progress of the current survey line on the computer monitor. It was great when everything ran smoothly. He could turn off his brain and relax, happy to suffer discomfort and the demands of annoying clients. He had a large mug of coffee and was smoking a hand-rolled cigarette—essential props to allay boredom. A tight, self-satisfied smile creased his blotchy, unshaven face. Once he had this awful job completed, he could look forward to a break in Songkhla, his favourite destination for cheap living, wonderful food and girls.

Mahmood came into the instrument room, admiring the relaxed way Sandy planned the survey lines.

'Hi, Sandy. Tong asked us to ferry Yap across to Sakulakit. Can you ask Singh to standby for the crew to lower the zodiac once they finish the current line?'

'Yea, no problem. Why go there? It's only a lump of rock.'

'Tong saw a glimmer of light last night and thinks the fishing boat is suspicious. According to him, it is waiting for us to find the treasure and call in the militants to attack us.'

'Yea, he mentioned that at the morning meeting. What a waste of time. Check out the fishermen if that's what he wants. At least you get a break from this boring grind and escape to shore. Why do you get the best jobs, Mahmood?'

One of the ship's crew joined the men in the zodiac, and they cast off from the mother boat. Yap kept the AK47 hidden inside a sports bag along with canned drinks and sandwiches in case they missed lunch. The crewman opened the throttle, and the nose lifted as they flew over the waves, falling back with a breath-taking thud into the troughs before surging forward. They headed straight at the fishing craft but pulled away at the last moment to divert to Sakulakit. Although Yap wanted to flaunt his weapon, he was too slow to assemble it, being thrown around in the dinghy. The close approach caused a nervous wave from the fisherman setting their traps on the seabed to catch crabs and lobsters. Tong's suspicions appeared groundless.

They rounded the island, approaching a rocky inlet from where the crags rose steeply to a tree-covered hill and tied the boat up on a convenient rock after beaching on a gravelly foreshore. No one expected to find anything, but they welcomed the break to stretch their legs.

Yap unwrapped the Kalashnikov, and they climbed up the volcanic rocks, scrambling across deep fissures. Several caves, eroded by the sea, indented the coastline. Snakes lay trapped in shady nooks and crannies. The same species of a banded snake were everywhere, even in the rock pools or curled up asleep in the sun.

'There are hundreds. I have never seen so many.' Suleiman backed off, as a black and white serpent raised its head to study him.

'Don't worry—only sea snakes,' said Mahmood. 'They have a small mouth and won't bite unless you put your hand close or stand on them.'

'I've never heard of sea snakes on land. Are you sure?'

'Yes, they are poisonous sea kraits. They come ashore to rest, mate, and lay their eggs. I have seen them on the east coast Malaysian islands close to Rawa. Still, take care as their venom can kill you in thirty minutes.'

After a short, tiring climb to the top of the hill, they came upon a few trees clustered near the summit. If they walked on the ridges, they could avoid the coiled-up snakes in the hollows. Scraggy grasses and plants had established a precarious threshold, growing out of cracks in the rock. With the aid of binoculars, they saw *Eastern Pearl* surveying at Brutus Reef and their vessel to the north. An excellent vantage point and others had been standing here judging by an empty pack of Marlboro duty-free cigarettes and a few cigarette ends. Captain Singh had warned them that American advisers were helping the Filipino security forces on Basilan, so a group of commandos might have been on Sakulakit on a training mission. Who knows? There were many possibilities.

'Why come here?' persisted Yap. 'There is nothing on the island.'

'Smugglers could hide out in the caves below,' said Mahmood.

'No way. Only snakes live here,' said Suleiman, shivering. He hated snakes. 'Let's leave.'

'Where did that fishing boat go?' Yap scanned the sea with his binoculars. A worried frown crossed his face.

'They must be behind the rocks. Do you think they are following us?'

In answer, Yap cocked the Soviet machine gun, and the men hurried after him in Indian file, as they retraced their steps back to their landing place. With a fresh sense of urgency, they reached an inlet next to the one where they had come ashore. The cliff was too sheer and lacked footholds, so it was impossible to reach their boat. They climbed up the hill again to search for a suitable route. Twenty minutes later, they showed up, hot and flustered, at their landfall. But their zodiac had vanished. All that remained was a section of cut rope and a snake curled up on a rock.

Chapter 24

In the adjacent survey block, the proximity to shallow reefs had meant a cautious start. After a reconnaissance, George and Alex lowered the side-scan sonar into the sea. Michael switched on the thermal recorder, and a detailed image of the seafloor appeared. The data showed trains of large sand waves and coral. With excellent results, there was a heightened sense of optimism.

At the end of the first line, next to the reef, it shocked Jaffar at how abruptly the seabed shallowed. The Admiralty chart depicted a shoal with only one metre of water, and his vessel's draught was three metres. He turned the ship to port to keep away from the hazard. Close to this point in 1764, the *Siren* had hit the rocks and sunk. The weather had been as kind as a silk glove on a lady's hand, but, to an unfamiliar crew, the strength of the currents near-shore was a surprise.

The PanAsia team ran a survey line to locate the site of Mitch's plate, but it gave no magnetic or sonar contact. Perhaps more sand had accumulated over the last twenty years covering the wreck. Michael discussed this problem with Jim and Christina.

'How long to finish the lines?' Christina was impatient to dive.

'At this rate, it should take another five days,' said Jim.

'What should we do?' The prospect of such a long period of inaction was boring for Christina.

'The logical thing is to check out the seabed contacts,' said Michael. 'If no luck, follow up with the magnetometer. The water depths from the 1986 survey don't match, so either the sand cover is thicker, or we are in the wrong place.'

Jim's patience, never one of his virtues, was running on empty. 'After your trip to London, you were sure we had the right spot, mate.'

Christina came to Michael's defence. 'We can't be certain—that's the purpose of the survey. Tong's team is looking elsewhere, so that shows how difficult the job is. Conditions are ideal at the moment—couldn't we do a quick dive?'

'No worries. We should examine "Mitch's plate" target as a priority,' agreed Jim. 'We know Mitch found a dinkum dish, so the wreck is here somewhere. What if the airlift breaks or the sea gets too rough? There's no point wasting time on other stuff. If we get a breakdown, we might never have the chance to explore our best lead.'

'I hear what you say,' said Michael. 'But we have no leads. Let's check the surface contacts first. It should be quick. Most will be modern metallic debris. Then we can use the airlift to investigate deeper anomalies at Mitch's location.'

The men dispersed to the bridge to instruct Jaffar. Christina disappeared to her cabin.

As they resumed the survey, a small fishing boat approached alongside. The fishermen called out greetings and held up wriggling fish for sale. After brisk bartering, the cook took groupers, stingrays and a barracuda. They agreed to call again with chickens or goat meat from the nearby islands. The visit raised morale at the prospect of fresh food.

Captain Jaffar noticed the flashing blips of distant boats to the west on the ship's radar. The prime fishing ground was near to the Pilas Island chain, and coastal traffic kept to the Basilan Strait. The radar traces streaked out, leaving blue, tadpole-like trails as the vessels crossed the screen. No ships approached these shallow waters. In the early hours of the morning, while others slept, he was alone on the bridge, exposed. He dimmed the lights, trying to melt away and become invisible.

At night, Jaffar closed off the desk at the back with thick curtains to hide the glow of the computer monitors. When the ship was at anchor, it was vital to keep a watch, always alert; it was their most vulnerable time. In theory, Hamza and Raspal gave security protection round the clock, although Jaffar considered their services useless. During daylight hours, they strolled the decks, stopping to scan the horizon with suspicion. After lunch, they took a long siesta on the old sofas thrown out on the back deck, waiting for their next meal. At supper, they were first to the galley where they lingered over their food. After mealtime, another stroll, smoking to control the mosquitoes. In the evening, they ran a vigilant patrol—they thought dusk was the most dangerous time for an attack. Once night fell, their vigilance relaxed to an on-call basis. The captain called them if he saw any suspicious activities. Although still a vulnerable stage, the guards loved videos; never tiring of Bruce Willis or Sylvester Stallone movies. Their casual style implied that the risk of piracy, or the threats of an Abu Sayyaf attack, was over-stated. That was until Captain Singh made a courtesy call on the VHF to warn Jaffar to be extra cautious. The fishermen had stolen their inflatable. The theft had marooned Yap on snake-infested Sakulakit Island for six hours. It worried Jim, and he advised the captain to increase the night watch.

Christina's early enthusiasm and optimism turned to boredom at the monotony of each day. Tonight, she sat on the steps leading from the bridge deck, and admired the sunset. She was at peace, satisfied they were, at last, making progress. The geophysical survey was complete. Tomorrow the divers could start work and, hopefully, she would have something to look at. The sudden noise of the anchor drop startled her. The iron links of the chains rattled and clanked, grinding until the barnacled shaft bit into the seabed, gripping the vessel taut as she settled to a well-earned rest.

Christina admired the red-shot sun sink against the stark black outline of volcanic rocks sticking out of the water like the charred roots of tall buildings left after the ravages of a nuclear attack.

'Stunning, isn't it?' Michael crept up, unseen behind her. At sunset, the flickering sea reflected the sky, which took on ever-changing hues of orange and purple. Overhead, thin grey clouds drifted and filled.

'Impressive—yes,' agreed Christina. 'But menacing and cruel, like a stark landscape scorched by fire. I was thinking of Hiroshima after they dropped the atomic bomb and killed thousands of civilians.'

'I know what you mean. It's staggering to think such things happened not so long ago—not in our lifetime, but in our parent's time. What capacity for evil. Might it happen again?'

'Michael. It is in our nature—wars, murder. It only requires one person to trigger the madness and others to stand by and do nothing.'

'A depressing thought. Why must malign forces always overpower our good intentions? Are we focusing on the battle lost, the negative stuff, and ignoring a slow trend towards an improvement—a time when such things will become archaic and feudal? The nuclear threat has diminished. Nations have stepped back from the abyss. Now our concerns are minor issues such as global warming and recycling old tins.'

'Minor to you maybe, but my friends take that stuff seriously. I see a black cloud on the horizon—an ill omen for tomorrow.'

'I am sorry it has taken so long for the survey. It has been tedious for you.'

'I have had nothing to do, except read books. Now I expect to be busy.'

'Alex can help during the recovery and logging phase. Lucas has asked him to make a documentary film of the job.'

'Wow, we will be film stars.' Christina took a childish delight in this news.

'And anything you need, just ask.'

'Thank you.'

'Don't mention it.' Michael was curt. He switched back to his professional role as if he had shown too much of himself. To relieve the awkward moment, Christina asked after Julie and the family.

'We have a brilliant place to live, and she loves Singapore.'

'Is she alone a lot?'

'No, not these days. I used to work in the oil and gas sector when we first arrived in Singapore. I was often away on jobs overseas for one or two months, so that was hard for her, especially with a young baby. With PanAsia, we mainly concentrate on near-shore jobs and I am mostly office-based. This job is a change; it's nice to travel to unfamiliar areas.'

'Things seldom work out the way we plan,' said Christina. 'Forgive me for saying so, but you are older than most of your colleagues and more mature and calmer than them.'

'Older, yes, but your analysis is too flattering! Since I started at PanAsia two years ago, I have only seen Singapore and Malaysia, so great to have a fresh challenge.'

'I admire anyone who follows their heart to do what they want. Look, it's getting chilly, I'm going back inside.' Christina shivered. The wind had freshened and the wave height was increasing with white foam breaking and driving across the bow of their boat.

After Christina left, Michael remained on the steps alone with his thoughts. The lack of success was troubling. He felt the force of the unspoken questions. His research in London pointed to the south of Brutus Reef as the most promising, but reefs fringed the coastline. Was it possible they had the wrong one? On a whim, he walked up to the bridge and asked Captain Jaffar to put a call through to *Pacific Glory* to have a chat with his opposite number, Tony, the geophysicist. After a brief delay, they brought him to the VHF radio.

Tony reported success, but it worried him they were working in the incorrect place. He believed the trail of anomalies extended across both their blocks, and he thought the stern and hull sections could be in their concession. Tony urged Michael to concentrate his efforts on his eastern boundary to pick up the same archaeological horizon.

'I shouldn't tell you this as we are rivals. But it makes sense to share information. For God's sake, keep quiet.'

'Fair enough, I hear Mr Tong is scary.'

'Not only him. Yap, his sidekick, is even worse.'

'I hope they aren't listening!'

'No, they are on the back deck looking at cannon we have just recovered,' said Tony. 'Tong's on his mobile to Singapore, as usual.'

'Cannon—that's an impressive find.'

'Tong and Yap search for something specific. For them, the cannon will be a poor reward. I must go. They are returning to the bridge.'

Chapter 25

Mahmood climbed back on board with greater urgency than usual and snapped off his facemask, sending spray towards Tong who backed off in distaste. Mahmood gave the thumbs up as he told him they had found two cannons, already hooked up to the HIAB crane and ascending from the seabed. Although heavily encrusted, after cleaning, the markings would confirm the maker and the vessel—a significant find. But Tong shrugged, indifferent to the discovery. Only the porcelain was valuable. He waited with nervous anticipation as they hauled another basket up. Since resuming diving operations, they discovered a rich seam of wreck artefacts from the archaeological layer of broken porcelain. The only undamaged items were several bars of iron ballast, a bronze seal, a few hundred silver coins, and the best prize so far: three ingots of Chinese gold. At each find, morale improved. In the mid-eighteenth century, gold from China was the cheapest source. Perhaps the East Indiaman was heading to Batavia, the present-day Jakarta, to realise a quick profit? At auction, the ingots would fetch a high price, but they needed to recover more than this. Sandy approached Tong on the back deck. Lately, he had become almost civil.

'Any more gold bullion in this lift?'

'No, only broken porcelain,' said Tong, scowling at the crew as they washed and sorted the latest haul. Yap scrutinised the work keenly as a hawk.

> 'Surely we must arrange for the man from the National Museum to board the boat?' 'Yes, yes. When I'm ready.' Tong was unwilling to act. He needed longer to hunt for

the Imperial porcelain.

'If I call Manila today, they could send someone out tomorrow. By then, we should have more finds.'

'Go on, if you must. But, I need another two full days at least without them sticking their noses in.'

Downcast, Tong moved off towards his cabin, worried at this costly disaster. His business interests in Singapore needed his attention. Although the boat had a satellite phone, the calls were expensive and the connection poor. Sandy followed a few paces behind, mounting the steps to the bridge. He wanted to involve the National Museum sooner rather than later because he distrusted Tong. He suggested to Singh they could make a port call to Zamboanga to pick up the museum representative, but the captain reminded Sandy that was not viable with immigration hassles and port delays. Instead, the museum should hire a pilot boat in Zamboanga to ferry the person out to join their vessel at sea.

Tony studied the latest dive recoveries without enthusiasm. All the porcelain pieces were mass-produced, inferior quality stuff in standard blue and white enamel from Jingdezhen, in Jiangxi province, sent to Nanking for trans-shipment via a canal, to the port of Canton for the *Siren* to load up along with a cargo of tea. In parts, the old archaeological level coincided with the present-day seabed to create a still-stand—an area stable for hundreds of years with no significant deposition or erosion. These locations were promising for artefacts but not for best quality. The sea action would break the ceramics and corrode the metallic objects, such as cannon. Preservation of buried objects, trapped in a time capsule, was usually better. On the western side, advancing dunes must have buried any wreck. This was the most promising area to search. Although they had a few rich pickings, he suspected the most valuable cargo was in the PanAsia block.

Captain Singh heard a report, on Radio Mindanao, of an attack on a police station in Davao City. The incident killed two young children playing outside the front gate, but it only damaged the target with no fatalities. Details were sparse, but Abu Sayyaf claimed responsibility for the indiscriminate slaughter, achieving nothing save publicity for their twisted cause. The terrorists escaped seawards via fast boat towards Basilan close to their survey zone. Singh assumed the security forces would send gunboats to search for them—reassuring in some respects but troubling if this was an active area because it heightened the risks to innocent bystanders. The light they had seen on Sakulakit and the discarded cigarette took on new significance. Perhaps there was an Abu Sayyaf cell on the island? In his fertile imagination, terrorists hid in the network of caves and tunnels incised into the island. In fact, every boat picked up on the radar was a potential enemy. Were these people crazy to survey in such a tricky area with no armed guards? Yap with his AK47 was not a comforting vision of reassurance. As Singh squeezed a Lipton tea bag into his cup, ever hopeful the brew might rise above its usual mediocrity, Sandy requested they lift anchors from the four-point mooring pattern. The divers had found nothing after twelve hours of excavation, another failure. Singh saw them crawling out of their wetsuits, depressed, as a steady rain fell around them from the gloomy clouds. Their optimism melted away, discarded with their crumbled diving suits tossed onto the back deck. Morale was sinking fast. His fervent wish was for them to recognise failure and abandon the pointless survey.

The continued lack of success was also troubling Tong when every dive came up empty. Their early luck faded, with little of value found for days. Sandy kept pressing him to collect the junior researcher from the museum, a colleague of Christina's, but the desultory discoveries of porcelain shards and a clutch of silver coins, welded together, were the only meagre rewards and it seemed pointless to call out the museum to record such finds. Monitoring the weather forecasts, Sandy saw that the wind was due to pick up. It made sense to use the break in operations to fetch the representative and avoid loss of operational time. Reluctantly Tong agreed. The three gold bars were the most valuable finds, and Tong took the best-looking ingot for himself. They logged all finds and sent to Manila with a share apportioned to the Museum and a share to him, so best hide one while he had the opportunity. Yap might need a quiet word to Tony and Sandy to make sure they understood.

Tong ordered Yap to keep an eagle eye on the divers, who he suspected of hiding objects stuck to the hull for retrieval later. He demanded Yap go on the next dive, a prospect which filled him with horror. Yap's blind panic amused Sandy. He savoured his discomfort until Tony volunteered instead. After diving lessons, he was proficient enough. Tong reluctantly agreed he should take Yap's place and confided his distrust of Mahmood and Suleiman.

Tony dived alongside the Malaysian brothers, following a knotted rope guide to the seabed. On the descent, the strength of the buffeting current amazed him. At the seafloor, the forces were even stronger—to stand upright required a tremendous effort. The earlier shift had opened a large trench that they needed to deepen by another metre. The airlift acted like a giant vacuum cleaner to lift the sand, but the grains spilt out, reducing visibility to zero. Once free of the trench, the strong current dispersed the sand. While the men worked, Tony swam around the periphery marvelling at the abundant marine life until he remembered Tong's order to inspect the ship's hull. He carried out a quick visual check of the barnacled hull and found no hidden treasures strapped under the boat. Tong's suspicions were groundless.

Later that evening Sandy and Tony met Tong and Yap to work out the future programme. The survey team had achieved all the original objectives. Despite many finds, they had run out of ideas.

It was obvious that the wreck had broken up, and there was nothing of significance left to discover. The best discovery was the gold bars, and if they trawled with a fine-tooth comb, they might find more. However, even that would not pay for the cost of continuing the survey. It was best to admit defeat and call it off.

Tong and Yap exchanged uncomfortable glances. Tony suggested they return to successful locations and widen the search, starting at the cannon site to enlarge the trench.

'The trench will have collapsed by now,' said Sandy. 'It'll take two further days to settle.'

'Forget the cannon site,' said Tong. He knew that gold ingots were rare, and one of similar age had fetched a huge price at auction somewhere in Europe. 'Send the divers back to where we found the gold bars. You can get started straight away.'

Tony looked thoughtful.

'If the wreck extends into the PanAsia block, we could strike a deal with them. We have the resources of a diving team and support. If we pool our capabilities with theirs, the chances of success are greater.'

Yap's eyes popped out of his head like a startled prawn. However, Tong considered the matter. His brow creased in a frown.

'If we joint venture, the artefacts we have found stay ours. The museum still has their share, as agreed.'

'Reasonable enough,' said Sandy. 'But what if they refuse your overtures?'

'Best to hold back and watch their progress,' said Yap. Tong looked at Yap, surprised he was speaking English, instead of his usual dialect, and come up with a sensible suggestion. Tony told them he could call the Party Chief onboard *Eastern Pearl* and discuss the possibility of cooperation informally. This offer met with silence, and Tony suspected Tong and Yap had their own agenda and talk of a joint venture was likely to fail.

Chapter 26

Jim stood alongside the captain on the bridge, both deep in concentration, focused on keeping the anchor pattern taut in the variable currents. As the boat stood at anchor, the divers explored a promising anomaly, a buried target which needed a few more hours' work before moving to the next location. The sultry morning ended with a brief rainsquall before the wind dropped, and a wispy mist engulfed everything in a thin white film, wrapping itself with ghostly tendrils around the islands, so only the dark peaks protruded. Over the horizon, the orange-shot sunset lit the sea and sky, but with fading brilliance. Jim noticed a new radar blip off the Lakit chain and drew it to Captain Jaffar's attention.

'Crikey! It's approaching fast,' said Jim. Jaffar raised his binoculars, but the mist hid the distant view. The men stared at the trace advancing across the screen like an angry bee. Straining their eyes and ears in the boat's direction, they heard the roar of the powerful engines long before a patrol boat broke through the haze. Jaffar's heart was racing as he reached for the alarm to summon the guards. Jim stayed his hand with gentle pressure.

'Philippine navy.'

The gunboat eased her throttle, standing off as their commander noted the registered Singaporean flag. He only relaxed when he saw them at anchor and posing no threat. Fortunately, Hamza and Raspal were off duty and relaxing on the back deck with guns out of sight. The navy marines, all armed and kitted out in oversized camouflage uniforms, came alongside to board. The young men, clumsy and as self-conscious as part-time film extras, tripped up the stairs to the bridge, swivelling about and alert for an ambush at any moment.

'Good evening, captain,' the officer, a short, well-dressed man with a loud voice, introduced himself politely. 'What are you doing here?'

Captain Jaffar explained their mission and showed them the permit issued by the museum in Manila. The officer scarcely glanced at the paper before pushing it back, unread.

'Do you not realise you are in a high-risk area? Terrorists who committed the bomb attack in Davao City escaped to these islands. Who sent you here? Where are you from?' The questions came thick and fast.

'In Zamboanga, they advised us to hire these two men for protection,' Jim said as he showed them the names of the Moro guards on the crew list and pointed them out on the back deck.

'Foreigners should apply to the navy for security. Navy marines are available for protection duties and are cheaper and better than these mercenaries.'

The navy man stared with distaste at the guards, who had noticed the gunboat and were at least standing by the guardrail and looking alert.

'Sorry we didn't realise that was possible. We will contact your HQ if this project runs for a long time.'

'I recommend you contact our home base in Zamboanga. How long will your survey last?'

'That depends. Not too long because it's an expensive business for the boat and team. Another week or two at the most.'

'It is best to complete your work as soon as possible. Time is of the essence and the longer you stay here the more likely they will attack you.'

Out of politeness, the captain invited them for food in the mess-room. The smell of fresh cooked noodles and satay chicken wafting up from the galley drew the navy men below. Jim handed out cans of iced cold drink and cigarettes. Christina drifted in to grab a coffee, giving the officers a cursory glance. Jim introduced her to the men and explained she was the official museum representative from Manila. Christina was in a hurry for her next dive; she had to rush off. It was an important location where Mitch Austin may have discovered the priceless Ch'ing dynasty plate. The sight of a Filipina, in this company, unsettled their preconceptions and dampened their swagger. It was amazing that these people were unaware of their vulnerability. On departure, they repeated their warnings about the Abu Sayyaf group, who had a camp on Dassalan Island to the north and other camps on Basilan. After the recent attack in Davao, they needed to be alert. The navy men glanced disdainfully at the marine crew curled up asleep by an old tyre on the deck. Compared to a navy vessel, this was a tired old boat manned by amateurs.

'Captain—a quick word of advice,' the naval officer stood next to Jaffar. Although a short man, he had a forceful personality made more impressive by a slow and measured speech delivery. 'Be aware these islands are home to several militant camps. They are here because they feel safe. The jungle is their friend, so if I send in our security forces they will laugh at us and kill all my men. You are rich foreigners. Keep a diligent lookout night and day. If Abu Sayyaf takes an interest in you, no effective protection is possible. I trust you have heard of this ruthless band?'

Captain Jaffar made light of the warnings. 'The client has taken on two competent local men for security, so we can relax and do our jobs with confidence. My marine crew run watches around the clock. All the pirates, villains and bad hats in the region can take us on, and we will be ready for them; I assure you.'

The naval officer smiled thinly. 'Well, good luck, captain. If you need help, use VHF Channel 16 straight to our patrol boat, the *Minerva*. We patrol these waters regularly.'

'And we are the *Eastern Pearl*. Another vessel called the *Pacific Glory* works nearby, but they have nothing to do with us. We are competitors.'

The officer looked surprised. 'Are you both treasure hunters from Singapore?'

The captain glanced at Jim, standing next to him, showing by an uplift of his eyebrows that he should field this question. Jim explained they were on an official archaeological search sanctioned by the Philippine Government—the authority was in the papers he had shown them. The *Pacific Glory* survey was a separate group to them. Perhaps the navy could monitor them?

The navy men frowned. They had no orders to get involved with foreigners, and with a curt goodbye, returned to their boat. Something was not right.

Christina dived on "Mitch's location" along with Nick. The microwave positioning, in use twenty-five years ago, was less accurate than the differential GPS they were using today. So far the dives had examined the side-scan sonar contacts—objects such as anchors, metal drums and chains. The only exciting find was a massive magnetometer anomaly from the remains of a World War II Japanese warship encrusted in coral by Brutus Reef and just inside their survey block. This discovery fascinated the divers with its excellent state of preservation, but Jim told them not to waste time on it. Christina said they must keep focused on finding the *Siren*.

After a quick dive, Christina re-boarded the boat. After removing her facemask and the hood of the wetsuit, her black hair cascaded over her face. Her eyes were glowing as she smiled and beckoned Michael.

'See what I found?' In her hand, she clutched two silver Spanish dollars known as pieces of eight. 'Maybe we have a galleon?'

Michael looked at the coins and shook his head. 'Doubtful. In the eighteenth century, they traded gold and silver coins of different nations. The *Siren* called at various ports to buy fresh supplies and received the change in a range of currencies such as Dutch ducats, French Louis D'Or and Spanish dollars. The money is not a reliable indicator of origin.'

'I found them in the trench. At least it proves we have the right level. We excavated it to a depth of three metres and the magnetometer gave a positive signal from the coins. But that's all.'

Jim appeared at the handrail of the bridge. 'G'day, Michael. The captain wants to anchor up at the next location. How deep do you reckon?'

'Excavate to two-and-a-half metres to find the archaeological level.'

Jim pushed back in exasperation. 'That will take hours, mate. As it's calm, the divers could continue through the night.'

'The problem is getting enough rest time.'

'My last dive was only thirty minutes,' said Christina. 'I can put in a shift for you later.'

'Great. Are you happy to work with Nick at midnight? I know it's a helluva lot to ask. No one enjoys being so late,' said Jim.

'Sure, can do. Will you be topside on my shift?'

'I guess so; I am the only one to help. We can't trust the local boys yet.'

'I'm not an experienced night diver. I need a trustworthy dive supervisor.'

'Check the time and follow procedures. Safety is our first concern. I should train Michael up so I can catch sleep.'

'He told me he hates swimming. The thought of diving fills him with terror. Somehow I don't think he is the right person to teach.'

'Before we complete this job, people will need new skills just to survive,' Jim cast a thoughtful eye over the too calm sea. It worried him. He stared in all directions, but there was not a single boat in sight. They were alone and vulnerable.

Chapter 27

Christina regretted volunteering for the midnight shift. Night diving felt alien; the enveloping darkness was claustrophobic. As she slipped below the surface, the water crushed her in an ever-tighter grip. She pumped her legs, dropping deeper, the faint light from her torch probing for the seabed, and kept one hand wrapped around her knife, fearful of sharks.

A passing shadow, then a pack of angelfish in a rush, had her turning in panic, and she looked for Nick in reassurance, but he had streaked ahead. Someone told her sharks never attack when fish are abundant, but humans got bored with the same diet, so maybe a shark might fancy a change?

Christina's fear eased as she reached the seabed. They set up the airline, in reality, a giant vacuum cleaner, to shift the sand and dispel the grains, the speckles dancing in the light of their torches. Conditions were ideal with a moderate southerly current carrying the excavated sediment away from the trench edge.

Onboard Jim was monitoring the diver's progress. It was the first time Christina had dived at night, so he might abort the dive early. Michael stayed to help Jim on the back deck.

The sound of a ship's engine disturbed them, and they noticed a small vessel approach. Most likely another fishing boat trying to sell their catch. They were on the opposite beam to the divers, so Jim gave them a friendly wave and beckoned them to come alongside on the port side. Why had the fishermen called at night?

Michael was heading for the bridge when a gunshot shattered the peace. He wheeled around, stunned, as a large group of men swarmed over the stern, brandishing guns and knives. Their frenzied screaming, a chilling primitive battle cry, rooted him to the spot for precious seconds until his brain kicked in with an adrenalin rush to propel him up the steps. The captain was shouting his name, and someone tugged him through space to land in a heap on the floor. The crew secured the wheelhouse from attack, locking and bolting the doors just as the furious attackers shoved against it like angry wasps. He noticed Alex cowering at the side, having rushed up from his cabin, dressed only in a white top and pants.

When the panel door stood firm, they abandoned the onslaught and headed off to find another entry point. With the speed of the invasion, it had been impossible to batten the hatches. The invaders streamed inside the lower deck, yelling and shouting as they hammered on the cabin doors with their weapons and dragged everyone from their bunks at gunpoint.

The guards struggled to rouse themselves. Raspal, the younger and fitter, grabbed his AK47 as he swung off the top bunk. He flung open the door, pointing his gun out towards the noise of intruders. But this was a fatal error. A lone raider, armed with a sabre, loomed out of the dark on the right. As he turned around, the pirate plunged the blade deep into Raspal's back and through his heart in one fluid, two-handed lunge. Hamza was still on the edge of his bed as Raspal collapsed in the corridor as his life drained away. It was pointless to resist; he surrendered, stepping over the body of his friend, whose warm blood was pumping over the floor as his eyes faded.

Another man, armed with a short-barrelled shotgun of ancient vintage, gathered up the fallen trophies of the two AK47s discarded by the Moro guards. The pirates herded the team, like pigs to slaughter, towards the back deck.

Gunfire burst out again, unnaturally loud, as they shot open a locked cabin and the dark-skinned youth who had killed Raspal motioned the two Australian surveyors, cowering by the porthole, forward with his bloodstained sword.

Jim knew it was vital to find the leader of the twenty-strong group fast to calm the over-excited attackers. The onslaught had swept past him in a rush to take the bridge. He fell in with the rest of the ship's crew on the back deck, feeling there was safety in numbers.

Battle still raged over control of the wheelhouse, the nerve centre of the boat. The captain rushed out a message, via the Inmarsat, to Singapore. Just as he completed his call, a fresh onslaught on the port side door splintered the frame. He remembered the look of hate and wild staring eyes of a guy with a red bandana. The butt of a gun smashed into his skull, and he fell into a sea of darkness.

An older man, with an air of authority, entered the bridge. He spoke good English.

'My name is Aziz. Let me reassure you I will harm none of you if you cooperate. Is he the captain?' He asked, pointing at the prone figure on the floor.

Jaffar lay in a pool of blood seeping over the floor from a gash across his skull. His attacker with the red headband examined the damage with cursory disinterest. Another man knelt beside the body and checked for breathing and pulse rate. During the examination, Jaffar regained consciousness with a groan.

'You should not have defied us.'

'Nothing of value on board,' said Michael. 'This boat is conducting a survey on behalf of the museum in Manila. We have to recover our divers from the sea at the end of their shift.'

'Are you in charge?' asked Aziz.

'No, I am a scientist. Jim is our party chief. He is on the back deck.'

'We need to leave. Your leader must get the divers onboard.'

Jaffar had hauled himself up and was fumbling in the first aid box, looking for a bandage to staunch the blood flow. One of the younger pirates tried to help him, but he shrugged away the offer with contempt. Another man wagged a dagger under Michael's nose and pushed him to join the others. Michael grabbed hold of Alex's hand and they headed for the back deck to join Jim and the others.

The captain slumped back to the floor; the effort to treat his wounds had left him faint. He dropped his head between his knees to stem nausea. Aziz ignored his distress as he calmly thumbed through the ship's logbook.

Unaware of the attack, the divers cleared the base of the trench. They exposed a set of curved wooden spines—one flank of an old ship. With mounting excitement, they widened the excavation and found a solid timber floor. The loose sand fell away from the wood timbers with surprising ease. After more work to widen the trench, they spotted a trap door with rusted hinges, which they forced open. Shining their torches into the void revealed a hollowed out chamber with a mass of a brown glutinous material surging up and clogging their masks.

Nick directed the airlift into the opening to draw up what looked like old tea leaves, but this was a helpless task that dislodged yet more of the leaves. The divers backed off to let the cloud settle and anxiously looked at their watches to see how much time they had left. Nick shone a torch into the hold and saw packed stacks of porcelain peering out from the brown sludge.

There was just enough room for Christina to dive through the hatch, but it was not wide enough for Nick to follow her. It was a dangerous manoeuvre akin to swimming into a dark cupboard with no room to turn and made more hazardous by the poor visibility and the swirling tea leaves. Christina counted several sealed crates of cargo in a pristine state. They had found it! Crate after perfect crate packed in a time capsule. Thousands of mint condition Ch'ing dynasty plates, saucers, tea sets, servers, bowls and carvings. The blue Chinese characters were staring back at her startled gaze—the first sighting in over two hundred years. The hold space extended, undisturbed for many metres with crates too many to count. She looked at her watch. Their time was nearly was up. Normally Jim would tug twice on the rope Nick was holding to warn them to start the ascent. He was making urgent hand signals and flashing the torch to alert her. The only exit was to retreat backwards on the same line as her entrance. But first, she stretched out and grasped a small saucer. On the way out, she was stuck and panicked, kicking up more brown sludge until she lost sight of her entry point. Sensing her panic, Nick widened the hatch by smashing the rotten wood and grabbed a flailing leg to pull her free. Exhilarated, they started a slow climb back to the boat.

The divers waited below the sea surface, ignorant of the pirate attack, and let their bodies adjust to atmospheric pressure, although the depths were so shallow this was not strictly necessary.

On the back deck, the team huddled together in protective groups, whispering to each other as they checked who was missing. It was best to avoid eye contact with the assailants. Alex noted the cruel, intense gaze from the man with the red headband. Other members of the gang relaxed as they laughed and joked amongst themselves.

The pirates looted every cabin, ransacking. Nothing escaped their attention as they picked each one clean. Alex had his wallet and passport in his pocket, but no one took them. Jim said this was a well-known trait—even pirates had standards—they never searched their victims. If they spotted a watch, they liked they might ask the owner to make them a present. They did not perceive it as theft. Michael updated Jim on the events on the bridge.

'Jaffar has a savage head wound. Although he is conscious, he may get a concussion. They cracked his head with a rifle butt—I thought they had killed him. Fortunately, he got a message off to Singapore. They will know what has happened.'

'Why didn't the guards repel the attack?' Alex looked across at Hamza, squatting, dazed, on the floor by the handrail.

Jim told him Raspal had died in the attack. He pointed out the killer standing close by with his bloodstained knife.

'Their men call him Gerardo,' said George. 'Someone to avoid, and the one with the red headband is the brother of Aziz.'

The pirates filled cases bursting with the crew's personal effects. Clothes, watches, phones, cameras, shoes, even wash bags with shaving kit and toothbrushes. Nothing was too insignificant. From the galley, they concentrated on tinned goods, biscuits and chocolate and canned drinks. A group carried away the fridge, still full of perishable food and drinks, and manhandled it up to the main deck.

'Once they finish looting, do you think they will leave?' Alex asked his father.

'Maybe. Let's hope so.'

'Remember, the ship may be valuable to them,' said George.

'Why take the boat? We have no cargo,' replied Jim. 'Only survey equipment of no use to them.'

'Whatever their plans, we will soon find out.' Michael noticed Aziz was issuing commands to his men.

Jim looked at his watch with a start. After the mêlée, he had forgotten the dive team. By the deck lights, they saw the reassuring train of bubbles rising from the divers. Jim was ready to don his diving suit to fetch them up when both bobbed to the surface.

Christina was clutching an antique saucer in her hand, keen to burst out the good news when she froze. An armed stranger was aiming a gun at her head.

Jim reassured her. 'Don't worry. We have had a visit. Come up nice and slow.'

Christina could only mouth the silent question, pirates? But no sound came from her. She had enough sense to keep the saucer concealed in her hand as she climbed up the rope ladder. As she reached the top, the pirate with the gun tugged her arm and dragged her onboard with such force she collapsed on the wooden deck to the amusement of the pirates. Michael picked her up. After a dive, she took off her wetsuit, had a shower and put on casual jeans and T-shirt. Michael restrained her with a warning to stay put with them. He did not want her going to her cabin alone with the pirates still looting.

Of the original group of twenty attackers, only five remained. After an orgy of looting, fifteen re-boarded their boat and disappeared into the night. The youth, with the red headband who attacked Jaffar, left with them, so Michael felt more relaxed at the removal of one threat. Aziz trusted this man. Later they learnt George was correct—he was Aziz's younger brother. However, the killer of Raspal—the man they called Gerardo—remained.

The pirate's parting gesture had been to load the galley fridge into their boat, still packed with frozen provisions. A pointless action—when the scorching sun thawed out the food.

Aziz left the bridge and arrived on the back deck. He told everyone to get ready to leave the boat.

'They might as well scuttle the boat,' said Alex. 'They have taken our food and belongings.'

'And my clothes,' added George. 'They took my safety boots, shoes and T-shirts. I only have these left,' he pointed to his flip-flops and worn shorts.

Jim confronted Aziz. 'Are you pirates or Abu Sayyaf terrorists?'

Aziz looked at him with contempt. 'We are poor fishermen. You are colonial thieves come to exploit us.'

Jim shrugged as if this was predictable. 'No, we are not exploiting you. The National Museum of the Philippines hired us to hunt for an old shipwreck. It is an approved search. If we find the wreck, they will display the cargo in the museum in Manila.'

'We know what you do. We have watched you and the other boat. What you say is lies. None of the money comes to Mindanao! The government in Manila will pay back their loans to the World Bank before they give a peso to us.'

'It's no justification to rob and kill innocent people. We are here to do a job.'

'Yes, you are mercenaries. I tell you my plan. Get your men together to take to the lifeboat—the sea is calm tonight, so you reach Zamboanga in a few hours. Except you, you stay with me,' he pointed to Michael. 'And the girl diver—she must come with us. The captain can stay. I need a skeleton crew. The rest of you can go.'

'Leave the young woman. She is a museum assistant. Take me instead,' said Jim.

'Sure, we get bigger ransom, but the lady can cook and serve my brothers. Our fighters need such a desirable bride, and, *inshallah*, raise many children.'

Christina could scarcely believe her ears.

'If anyone harms Miss Velasco, the security forces will be on you like a ton of bricks,' said Michael.

'Do as we say, Englishman, and she comes to no harm. This ton of bricks you talk of—I hardly think so.'

'How far do you want to sail?' asked Jim. 'We have only limited supplies. You have stolen most of our food.'

'How many days' fuel and water have you cruising at top speed?'

'At full pace, say eight knots, we have just enough to reach Labuan,' lied Jim. In fact, fuel was not an issue as they had plenty. And despite losing provisions, there were stores the pirates had not discovered.

'Labuan is the right direction. Order the captain to disembark your people, including you. We keep our word and have not harmed you. Everyone will leave except the hostages.'

Captain Jaffar was on his feet when they returned to the bridge, scowling at the bodyguard. He took over command and issued orders.

'They tell me you and the museum girl are prisoners. God save us. I prefer they let that woman go; she is bad luck. Look, I must have the Chief Engineer and one seaman stay. The rest of you escape with the survey party in the lifeboat. You have enough fuel to reach Zamboanga. Summon your squad to muster and disembark on the port side and you will reach port by midday.'

'What of Hamza? Does he leave or stay?' asked Michael.

'Let him leave. He's no use to man or beast!'

'And the cook—we need him to stay?'

'No, let him go. We can manage without him. Your boy too—make sure he leaves on the lifeboat.'

'When we reach Zamboanga, we will check into the Lantaka and call Lucas and the agent,' Jim shouted up to Michael.

During the commotion on deck, Christina hid the blue and white porcelain saucer in her cabin. It was the only proof they had discovered the wreck of the *Siren*.

Chapter 28

Julie heard the persistent call of the phone competing with the dull throb of the air-conditioner and the thrash of the monsoon against the rattan blinds. In that haze, neither half-awake nor half-asleep, she waited, irritated, for it to stop to resume her flight from reality back to her dreams.

Who rings in the small hours? She wrestled with the dilemma on an anxious knife-edge of indecision whether to answer the phone or go back to sleep. The call cut off as the machine recorded a message. This was no dream.

In a panicky sweat, she sat bolt upright and listened to the recording, her voice so forced and artificial, 'I'm sorry no one is here to take your call, please leave a message after the pip, and we will get back to you.' But the caller said nothing— a wrong number at this late hour. Then the phone rang again. With a jolt, she stared at the space in the bed beside her. It must be Michael calling. Frantically, she dashed across the lounge to answer it, hands shaking, fumbling with the cradle, her eyes unable to see in the darkness. In a rush, she caught the side of a coffee table. A painful scratch on her leg drew blood. The handset crashed onto the tiled floor, the cord twisting away from her fingers like a snake. 'Hallo, Mrs Fletcher?' from a smooth, well-spoken voice, calm but firm.

'Julie Fletcher? Sorry to wake you so early in the morning. My name is Peter Dempsey; I am an attaché at the British High Commission in Singapore.'

'What's the problem?'

'First, we have no cause for concern. We just received a report of an incident in the Sulu Sea, off the Philippines, of an illegal boarding of your husband's boat, the *Eastern Pearl*. Both your husband and son, Alex, are fine, but in these circumstances the embassy likes to call the nearest relatives as soon as possible.'

'Do you mean refugees clambering on board?'

'No, not refugees. A group of armed men boarded their vessel. The captain sent an alert to Singapore.'

'So, a case of piracy?'

'Well, we aren't too keen to use that label until we are sure. It's too emotive and gives people the wrong impression. Philippine naval patrols are heading for the location.' He mumbled on, trying to calm her, aware his platitudes fell on deaf ears. 'Often, these are opportunist attacks. The attackers ransack the boat for money and personal effects and then jump ship fast. Do you know if the vessel was carrying any cargo?'

'No,' said Julie. 'They're searching for an old shipwreck—an East Indiaman called the *Siren*. They hadn't found the wreck yet, as far as I know.'

'An East Indiaman? One of the tea clippers trading with China?'

'Yes, tea was the main cargo, but also porcelain and gold. The survey had permission to search from the Philippine Government.'

'They will not harm the team unless the crew put up resistance. Modern-day pirates are often local fishermen supplementing their income.'

'But they may hold them hostage!' Ransom demands were a possibility, conceded Peter Dempsey, but he stressed pirates were more likely to make a quick raid and escape.

'Mrs Fletcher, please can we count on your discretion? Don't speak to the Singapore press. In fact, it's best not to discuss it with anyone until we get a better idea of whom we are dealing with. Any news is better coming from us. Negotiations will stand a stronger chance of success if we keep a tight lid on it. You do not want media intrusion at such a tough time. Let me make it clear right at the outset, Her Majesty's Government position is never to pay to secure the release of hostages.'

There was a pause as Julie reeled back in shock at the diplomat's clinical dissection. She was familiar with the official line of no negotiation with terrorists—a mantra Governments churned out to the media while conducting secret calls. She didn't believe a word of it and ignored it.

'It may be a "story" to you, but this concerns my husband and my son. Is this secrecy thing your standard procedure?'

'Yes, most cases sort out fast, so don't worry. Carry on as normal. If they take any hostages, we will support you to secure a quick release. My role as security attaché is to help British citizens when they get into difficulties.'

Easy for him to say, thought Julie. His smooth patter roused her to anger. Unknown to her, Peter Dempsey dealt with many similar attacks—piracy in his patch was common. Long haul yachtsmen sailing in the Malacca Straits, off Sabah and Brunei or the Sulu Sea, were high-risk areas. Other British nationals affected included merchant seamen, or divers and travellers visiting remote locations. Peter was an expert at finding solutions, without the news reaching the press.

'I notice you have lived here for a long time, Mrs Fletcher. We registered the birth of your son, Alex, in 1984. You are welcome to meet me at the embassy on Tanglin Road.'

'Yes, thank you. Singapore is very much our home. And please stop calling me Mrs Fletcher; Julie is fine.'

'Julie. Don't worry, we will sort this out,' said Peter, ringing off.

Julie paced around her apartment, frightened and angry; an icy knot of fear centred in her stomach. She ached to talk to someone. How to keep this secret? The telephone rang again, causing her to start. Lucas Miffré's distinctive French accent was a relief after that long-winded man from the embassy.

'Julie, has Peter Dempsey from your Foreign Office called? Have you heard what has happened?' Lucas' melodic words crammed more feeling than a native English speaker—a reassuring Gallic charm.

'Yes, Lucas, he just phoned with news of the attack. What a shock!'

'We're not sure of the details. But it's a dangerous place to work, so we put two armed guards on board. The incident was early morning today, and they overpowered the guards, but the captain got a voice message to our office to warn of an assault by over twenty pirates. Just by luck, the caretaker was doing his rounds, saw the answerphone blinking and had the sense to call me straight away.'

'Oh, my God. What will happen, Lucas?'

'Ransack the boat for items of value such as watches, money, cameras—whatever they find; a nasty fright, no more. Soon they will leave and the survey can continue.'

'What if they take hostages?'

'Sure, it happens—but that is more the style of Abu Sayyaf.'

'How do you know it wasn't them?'

'We only have the captain's account. *Certainement*—his impression. Let's hope he's right. Piracy we can cope with, but Abu Sayyaf is more difficult. That's why we took on Moro security guards on board. The Moro is the Islamic Independence group, but Abu Sayyaf is a more extreme bunch with affiliation to Al-Qaeda,' Lucas was unsure how much she knew of the local politics.

'So you mean because the Moro were protecting you, the terrorists kept away?'

'Yes, exactly,' said Lucas.

'Why is Abu Sayyaf worse?'

Lucas coughed to hide his embarrassment. The group had a track record for taking hostages for ransom and beheading their victims if large payments were not forthcoming, but he did not want to alarm Julie. He mumbled reassurances, and hopeful of a quick resolution, advised her to keep in touch.

Julie gazed outside her apartment at the deserted swimming pool lit by security lights. The monsoon wind was racing through the shrubs and bending the palm trees, sending broken branches falling. She pulled on her white dressing gown with a shiver and tied the cord tight before sliding through the veranda doors and walking out onto the balcony. Her bare feet felt the damp coolness of the tiles.

Besides the high wind, it was raining hard, and a powerful gust unravelled her robe. The gown blew away, but she didn't care. She let the rain course over her body; a numbing cold was all she desired. She drank in the chilly air with deep gasps and gazed upon the darkness and the wild night.

Sometime later, she sat inside the apartment, exhausted, as rational thought returned. Michael told her they planned to use armed guards for protection, but that had been ineffective. Had an exciting project made them blind to risk? He had soothed away her doubts. Even when Alex joined the search, they accepted it as an adventure. Only eighteen-years-old! Why allow him to go on this mad caper? The lure of the fantastic wealth from the Ch'ing dynasty cargo drove them on, against her better judgement, but the Sulu Sea was one of the most dangerous seas in Asia. How she wished to rewind the clock! The dull and predictable past with its boring daily routine was so claustrophobic. Now her world was spinning into chaos and disorder, with this manic scheme endangering their lives and unsettling her mundane existence. How could she face this nightmare alone?

Chapter 29

Aziz swung around on the swivel chair on the bridge. His feet just reached the floor, making him look like a restless schoolboy as he leaned back, languidly, staring with disdain at Michael and Christina, trussed in a sitting position, arms tied behind to a metal pole and legs roped together. He cultivated a slow and menacing approach, drawing deeply on a cigarette and exhaling the smoke towards the sulky captain.

Beside Aziz was a young, turbaned youth, no older than seventeen, who held the sawn-off shotgun levelled at Michael and Christina. The sweaty finger on the trigger flexed impatiently as he struggled to resist the urge to kill them. The youth's staring eyes looked unnaturally bright, as if the thrill of command conferred status and manhood. Aziz ordered the captain to head southwest at full speed. He refused to divulge their destination, so it was not clear whether they were heading for Sabah, Indonesia or one of the Sulu Sea islands. Aziz told the youth to relax and stop pointing his gun at the hostages.

'Trussed up like a chicken is uncomfortable,' said Michael, with a sigh of relief that Aziz had called off the youth with the gun. 'Surely we can't be any threat? Please let us move to our cabins.'

Christina was desperate for the toilet, but Aziz ignored her pleas.

'Aziz, why attack our survey boat? Our team is a group of scientists working from a Singapore registered boat with full approval of your government and the Manila Museum. Nearby is another boat, *Pacific Glory*, north of Sakulakit. Why did you not attack them?'

'The Chinese gangsters who came to Sakulakit Island? Their men were on guard. But you were an easy target.'

'A bad mistake! They salvaged cannon, gold bars and silver coins from a wreck but we have discovered nothing.'

'Ah. So you are mercenary treasure hunters.'

'Search the boat. We have no hoard of gold.'

'The navy knows our position,' said Christina. 'The security forces will hunt you down.'

Aziz walked over to Christina and knelt on one knee to stare at her. She stared back defiantly, daring him to slap her. The moment passed, and Aziz returned to stand beside the youth with the gun.

'For your freedom, we demand a ransom. Let's see if your employer values your life.'

'That's a problem. My boss cannot afford to pay. This job has cost a fortune—and with no gain.'

'He will raise the cash from the insurance company.'

'Wrong, no one can get insurance cover for piracy anymore,' said Christina.

'We are not greedy—forty million pesos to surrender you both.'

'And the vessel?'

'I will release the vessel when it has served its purpose.'

'If they pay anything, it will be less than that. We are private citizens with families, not rich businessmen. However, an honourable solution is that we offer you a fee to complete our project in peace,' said Michael.

Aziz looked amused at the aggressor becoming the policeman. But the flicker of interest Michael had ignited faded fast.

'This is my plan. You come to my island. It is one of many with low hills and forests. Lots of islands—over three hundred, but small and uninhabited. My people are the Samals—we live on houses built on stilts or boats moored alongside each other. You foreigners call us the sea gipsies. We only move to land when it is time to die.'

'We saw some in Zamboanga,' said Michael.

'Oh, they are Badjaos—something for the tourists. They trade in the marketplace and beg on the streets.'

'Why visit your island?'

'It sounds like we are heading to Tawi-Tawi Island—a very remote island near Sabah,' said Jaffar.

Aziz looked furious. It was essential to keep radio silence so as not to alert the security forces, which was why their destination was secret. He conceded the captain was right, but ordered Jaffar to keep off the radio channels and ignore any incoming calls.

Jaffar was keeping the speed as low as possible. Although the boat could manage 10 knots, he kept below 6 knots, hoping the navy would locate them. At the present speed, Jaffar reckoned they would reach Tawi-Tawi within 15 hours in the late afternoon or early evening.

'No problem. I have turned off our Automatic Identification System,' lied Jaffar. 'No one knows our position and I will ignore incoming calls on the VSAT.' This seemed to satisfy Aziz, but Jaffar had not turned off the AIS and hoped help would arrive.

'My island is part of a free Muslim Mindanao. Manila does not exist for us. I can hold you hostage for as long as it takes and we will look after you and let you convert to our religion. We make the woman a bride for our warriors. The security forces will get bored and abandon the hunt. Years will roll by and your families and loved ones will forget all about you. They will assume you are dead. No one will find you. That is your future unless they pay a ransom.'

Christina looked appalled. Michael caught her eye and flashed a message to ignore this provocation.

'Okay. It's a haven for you, but the future you outline is impossible for us. Why so much money? Is it to spend on arms to fight your government or build schools or a hospital for your people?'

'I don't have to account to you. Our proceeds go to finance the armed struggle.'

'So you are Abu Sayyaf?' replied Michael, pleased with himself at provoking Aziz.

'You say that, but I told you before we are poor fishermen. The only pirates around here are you who come to steal our treasures and sell them for mega-dollars in New York.'

Aziz instructed Gerardo to take them to their cabins. On the way, he let them visit the toilet. Gerardo locked Michael in his cabin on the lower deck. In a mean gesture, he severed the electric flex from the air conditioner. He coiled the cord in his hand and led Christina to a small empty cabin vacated by the cook.

He had other plans for the girl. There was a calm silence; just him and the vulnerable young woman who stared at him with fear and revulsion. He shoved her through the door, so roughly she crashed on the floor, stunning her head. The sight of her groaning at his feet excited him. He tied her hands together in front of her, using the electric lead. He left a length of the cable free and used it to swing her onto the lower bunk. To stifle her cries, he thrust a dirty rag in her mouth. She kicked out and hit him in the mouth, drawing blood. Enraged, he slapped her across the face.

Gerardo ripped up a bed sheet for a makeshift rope and wrapped the cotton sheet around each of her ankles, fixing them to the steel supports at the end of the bed and tightened up the slack to force her legs apart. He took his time to carefully knot the sheets so they held firm and resisted her futile attempts at kicking. Her struggles merely stretched the straps, which bound her legs. He tugged her arms to the head of the bed and lashed each wrist firmly to the metal support with the loose electrical cord, first using a knife to divide the flex into two equal lengths. It was a professional job, and he stood back to admire his handiwork.

Spread-eagled flat on her back, she wriggled about, angry and powerless to move arms or legs. Such a fighting spirit! The rag in her mouth suppressed her cries for help. No one could hear her. Before he could take his plan further there was a shouted command from Aziz on the bridge. Unhurried, Gerardo stared at Christina with a smug leer.

'You heard Aziz call for me. Soon you will be my bride. Wait for me here. Do not leave,' he laughed.

He left her trussed up and locked the cabin door behind him. He listened at the door and could just hear her gasps, but the rag in her mouth was doing its job. The adjacent cabins belonging to the departed marine crew were all empty, and the position of the cabin at the end of the corridor was perfect. No one would pass by. Next, he went to Christina's former cabin. Fortunately, the key was in the lock, so he locked that door as well. Anyone looking for her would think she was asleep and not know Gerardo locked her prisoner in another cabin. When Aziz was asleep, he would return for his reward.

Vargas waited for the survey crew to arrive in Zamboanga. It was his job to know everything, to cooperate and smooth the way. It was a profitable business. Besides his fees to broker the release of the hostages, he expected a cut for providing the Moro guards. The first demand was unrealistically high—they always were—but bit-by-bit, they would reach an acceptable figure, a sum to match the worth of the prisoner and respect for the system. There was no hurry. Hostage negotiations were like a game of chess. How much would the

Frenchman pay? It depended on the insurance cover. The insurers might be awkward and reluctant to settle.

Vargas sat in the restaurant of the Lantaka, glancing at his watch every few minutes as he scanned the horizon for any sign of the small boat. He expected a tired bunch, but elated at their survival. Still a need for caution, as there was no shortage of villains attracted to a boatload of foreigners. Next time, he must persuade Aziz to drop the crew off on a deserted island for pick up from a trusted boatman.

Whilst Vargas waited in Zamboanga, the hijacked *Eastern Pearl* continued in transit to Tawi-Tawi. It had rained that evening on Tawi-Tawi, as if the waters could wash away the sad events. A few hours earlier, as the heat of the day faded, a blood-red sunset filled the sky—the vast orb hung over the horizon like a waiting predator.

Captain Ramos was on patrol off Tawi-Tawi when he received a call about an attack on a survey vessel close to Basilan. Pirates had taken a foreigner and a Filipina as hostages and were last seen heading south-west. Unfortunately, the report failed to mention the name of the vessel. Pointless to pursue with so little information, so Ramos instructed the patrol boat to head towards Languyan, the village by the inlet to Puerto dos Amigos, as part of their normal patrol. The helmsman yawned, annoyed at such a futile exercise. Best return to base at Batu-Batu than waste time on a token gesture.

Ramos was no longer youthful; his black hair was grey-streaked, and he was overweight from too much rich food and lazy, office-based life. A gradual decline from the young and assertive officer to the dull and predictable captain. His colleague on patrol was a new posting from Manila—a Lieutenant Fernandez, eager and dynamic, and thirty years his junior. An uneasy partnership between the older man of experience and the youngster trying to upstage him.

Their patrol boat idled over the mirror-flat sea, close to shore, and relaxed. There was no need to hurry. They noticed a small fishing boat sweep in from the northeast following the coast on a parallel course. The boat skimmed the waters, bobbing up and down. Captain Ramos ordered the helmsman to pick up speed to follow them. If innocent fishermen returning to port, why such a rush? As they closed in, the fading sun glinted off a metallic object in the stern.

'I can see a refrigerator,' Lieutenant Fernandez stared, panning over the boat's occupants to count the number of heads. 'And thirteen people on the back deck plus two more up front.'

Captain Ramos looked inside the boat—sometimes the waves turned the vessel to the port and, besides the chest or refrigerator, he suspected weapons.

'I can't see any nets. I don't think they have been fishing,' said Ramos as he directed the helmsman to increase speed. The patrol boat swung in an arc and started in pursuit.

'Perhaps they are smuggling drugs?'

Ramos looked doubtful. But, against his better judgement, he instructed the lieutenant to go on the offensive.

'Okay, ready the deck gun and we can inspect.' Afterwards, he regretted encouraging the young man. If he had been on duty with his usual team, they would have approached more cautiously. Maybe things would have turned out differently. Fernandez responded with enthusiasm, even removing his designer dark glasses for an unobstructed view of the target. The late afternoon sun slanted low on the horizon behind them, giving them an advantage as they sped towards the fishing boat.

'Let's go in fast!' Fernandez ordered the helmsman, who looked across to the captain for confirmation. Even now, Ramos hesitated. What if they were harmless fishermen? However, the pilot took the lack of response as approval and opened the throttle, lining up to achieve a clear line of fire. Speeding up, the boat's prow lifted in the sky like a sleek thoroughbred and raced towards the group before they could detect the throaty roar of the engines.

One man, hearing the noise of the vessel, produced an AK47. He wheeled round, in panic, to confront the navy, but was too slow. The lieutenant discharged a volley. The pirates, in the stern, took the full force and fell to the deck where their bodies continued to dance as the lieutenant pumped more bullets into their corpses. Captain Ramos shouted for him to stop. In his frenzy, Fernandez could not, or would not, hear him. Ramos rushed over and pushed the deck gun aside, forcing him to stop the massacre.

The groans of the injured men merged with the startled cries of green, gold and white coloured parrots, disturbed by the gunfight. Monkeys jumped from the trees, eager to see the latest antics of their civilised cousins.

A search of the boat revealed bags of looted booty. The door of the fridge swung open, spilling out once frozen food to mix with the blood of the boys lying in the boat's pit.

They trussed the eleven survivors, circling rope around their legs and torsos to immobilise them. They entwined dead and living, as in a grim dance—all teenagers, no older than the captains' sons. It sickened Ramos. He placed the loot on the chart table of the bridge. A few cans of drink fell out of the rucksack of one dead youth, sporting a red headband. In death, his lips curled up in a hideous and defiant snarl. What a pathetic waste! They must be part of the band involved in the pirate attack. At base, they would work on them. Yes, they would reveal everything they knew and more after encouragement.

After taking the boat in-tow, they sped off, the surging engine lifting the nose of the boat out of the water, causing the pirates to slide further astern into the pile of corpses.

Chapter 30

After the call about the attack, Julie could not get back to sleep until she cried herself to oblivion. When she awoke, she sat bolt upright in bed—her eyes red-rimmed, cheeks hollow and hair a straggly mess. She vowed to keep the incident secret, as if denial made it better. Play along with it, as the embassy man had suggested. With a bleak late morning, her resolve failed her. The view across to the pool looked wild, with a howling wind and debris-tossed vegetation. She saw her white dressing gown impaled against a dragon pot on the next door balcony and ran to retrieve it before they noticed. The phone rang again with hateful insistence, and Julie hurtled to pick it up in time.

'Julie. It's Lucas. Splendid news from our agent—the pirates have released Alex and the survey team. They are unharmed and have arrived back in Zamboanga.'

'Alex is free! But what of Michael?'

'Don't worry. The pirates are holding some ship's crew along with Michael and Christina. We know they roughed up the captain, but he will be okay. As we suspected, they took everything of any value. Alex got off lightly. He kept hold of his passport and money, and passed the video camera over to Jaffar, who has it hidden.'

'But they still have Michael! Will they release him soon?'

'Julie, if I learn more, I'll let you know. Peter Dempsey at the embassy is waiting for an update, so I will give him the news. Maybe you could call him later. He is very experienced in dealing with these situations. I had not realised how many piracy incidents there are every year. According to Peter, he resolves the vast majority peacefully with no loss of life. Oh, I forgot to mention that the girl from the museum, Christina, was on a dive when the pirates boarded the boat and discovered a hoard of porcelain in great condition. Success, then this happens!'

'Well, I am pleased for you,' said Julie, sarcastically. 'Help me get him back.'

'Don't worry. I am flying out to Manila on the next flight and onto Zamboanga to see Jim and Vargas. The guys will stay overnight at the hotel so I can get an update.'

'Okay. Lucas. And when does Alex return to Singapore?'

'We will try to arrange flights for tomorrow. The only problem is if the Philippine authorities cause a delay. Don't worry, they will be safe.'

'Bye—and thanks for calling. Wait, you say they released Jim. Isn't that unexpected? Surely he is worth more to them than the museum girl?'

'Yes, I agree. Perhaps money is not the major concern. Julie—keep calm, we will get them back,' Lucas felt guilty for not being honest and mentioning the death of one of the security guards. What was the point? It was best not to raise her fears even more. Julie let the phone fall to the floor without replacing the receiver. She crumpled in the nearby papasan, its deep cushion comforting her like a baby in the womb.

They selected the most important people for ransom, such as Michael, but why not Jim? She expected an Australian to be higher in the pecking order than a humble Filipina. Why pick Christina? Obviously, she was young and attractive, or a valuable member of staff who would command a high price. Julie ran to the bathroom and was violently sick. It was out of her hands now. She had to have faith that this man at the embassy and Lucas could secure their release. It was a waiting game.

Julie put the phone back on in case Lucas or Peter Dempsey called, but the constant ringing was driving her mad. At first, she welcomed the press intrusion. Better than tense inactivity and brooding silence——a welcome change of pace. Later, she escaped to brave the poolside and familiar faces. The news was too fresh to have filtered through to Pagoda Villas so she carried on as normal, enjoying the pool, taking a chicken rice lunch and trying to concentrate on a slushy novel. However, the reality kept intruding to force out the fiction. Her thoughts tried to imagine what it was like to be held hostage by ruthless pirates. Something different—a mixture of pure fear and elation if you survived. She imagined Michael trussed up next to the young Filipina and offering her comfort and reassurance. Certain to reinforce his ego unbearably. On his return, she would never hear the end of his heroic efforts to survive against all the odds.

Michael might return a new man, with revived interest in saving their marriage and abandoning furtive affairs with youngsters, just as she might rediscover her love for him so that each could forgive each other and move on joyfully together into a comfortable middle age. The trashy novel she was reading was heading for a happy conclusion, but Life was seldom so straightforward. It was strange that the poolside was normal and various neighbours greeted her or made small talk. All the time she felt the tension rising like champagne held back by the wire cage trapping the cork. When she could stand no more, she headed back to the apartment. A check of the phone messages showed several calls from the UK press.

How did they know her number? She wondered if Peter Dempsey had released it. The last message was from Peter asking her to call him on his personal number.

'Julie here, just returning your call. Have you any updates?'

'No, nothing new since Lucas called me earlier. You know they released Alex? That is a very positive result.'

She agreed but needed some advice.

'They tell me to expect a ransom demand and then a period of bartering. I don't have a clue who will pay any ransom. For a start, we have no savings and I can hardly bother my parents or Michael's parents over this.'

'No need. The insurance companies will pay out. Lucas can arrange any payment and then claim from them.'

'But imagine if he can't pay in time, or the insurance turns the claim down? It isn't fair for him to foot the bill.'

'I am sure these points will become clearer tomorrow. Don't concern yourself with the money side. The important thing is getting Michael and the girl back alive.'

For her sanity, she did not want to think about it anymore. Peter suggested they go out somewhere discrete for dinner and a few drinks as tomorrow she would be headline news and it was best for him to brief her on how to handle the press.

'I am so churned up. I don't know what to do,' said Julie. 'But thank you for the offer of dinner. It may take my mind off things.'

Peter booked a table for dinner at Hua Yu Wee, an old-fashioned Bugis-style seafood restaurant on Upper East Coast Road. The colonial bungalow had not changed in years, except the seaside location was long gone because of land reclamation. Now inland, it was a forgotten oasis of calm, deserted by the throngs who demand a sea view. Julie caught a taxi and met the attaché. The meeting in such a pleasant location, away from the embassy, was a welcome surprise. In other circumstances, she would have enjoyed sitting outside enjoying the cool night air amongst the other diners as they feasted on chilli crab, lobster and pomfret. But she was too tense. It did not seem right to be enjoying a meal with another man while they held Michael captive. Peter explained how he hoped to interview Alex when he returned to Singapore to gain a valuable insight into the events up to the attack on the vessel. Any descriptions of Aziz and his gang would be helpful. Also, Peter was interested in any insights into Vargas, as this was the man they were all trusting to conduct the negotiations. He recommended Lucas hire a professional broker and had even suggested an ex Army man who had an excellent record of success. Of course, such men were expensive.

Peter warned Julie there would also be a small press conference, but they would not spring this on her unprepared. It was very important not to talk directly to the press on the phone, or in person. She should assume they would discover her address and come and make a nuisance, so if she had any friends to stay with, this might be a good time. It was all predictable stuff, so they hurried the meal and Peter dropped her back at her apartment.

'I know it's pointless to say don't worry, but we are doing all we can to get Michael released,' said Peter opening the passenger door. He looked at the layout of the ground floor apartments with their balconies overlooking the pool and frowned.

'The trouble with these condominiums is they are not very secure. I'm worried that the press can easily harass you. If you are going to stay here, would you like me to arrange a guard?'

'Thanks for the offer, but Alex will be back so I think we can manage. If there's a problem, we can think again. Thank you for a lovely meal and for cheering me up. I'm very grateful.'

Peter walked back to the car.

This was something she had to face alone.

Chapter 31

Vargas waited on the restaurant balcony, staring out at sea with unfocused eyes. The balloon glass contained a fine brandy and the colours of the liquor enriched the drab surroundings. Cupping the drink with the touch of a gentle lover and swirling the contents, he studied the liquid, as if answers lay hidden within, but, with concentration, a solution would emerge. He abstained from the cigar, a selfish pleasure he liked to indulge on special occasions, but rolled the Havana between his fingers, caressing it with a passion his wife could not rouse, before returning it to his jacket pocket with a sigh. It must wait for future celebrations. Best not to appear too relaxed when he met Lucas Miffré.

He had trouble dealing with immigration—Zamboanga was not a recognised entry port because of the security problems. The slip-up was with the marine crew when they landed illegally in the lifeboat at midday. It surprised Vargas that the authorities made more fuss over the breach of immigration procedures than the piracy incident. Piracy was so common the authorities just regarded it as a minor crime.

Provided the parties knew the rules of engagement, they could leave the negotiations to the professionals and concentrate on the fight against the militant groups such as Abu Sayyaf.

Once more Vargas booked the team into the Lantaka hotel. He was in no hurry to send them back to Singapore. Best to keep the news out of the press and delay them from broadcasting their story. Also, unwise to call in the armed forces. With their reputation for ineffective attacks they might jeopardise, rather than help, the rescue of the hostages.

In the past, Vargas brokered many deals with pirate groups. Aziz was one of several privateers who followed the age-old traditions going back hundreds of years. Abu Sayyaf was the first to take prisoners for political purposes. For them, the monetary gain was less significant than the spread of terror and to win publicity for their cause—the goal to achieve a separatist Muslim state. This ruthless rabble had the blood of countless innocent victims on their hands.

It had been a big mistake to abduct the Filipina—they should have taken the Australian for a decent ransom. A female government researcher did not come high in the pecking order unless she was from a rich family. The girl was in a dangerous situation; her only hope was for her family to pay up.

Vargas called Aziz on the vessel's Satcom to inform him the marine crew and survey team had reached Zamboanga. He expected to meet Lucas that evening to broker a deal for the release of the hostages. While he was talking, he glanced out of the window and saw Lucas hurrying towards the entrance earlier than expected, so he rushed to the hotel lobby to meet him.

'Where is the team?' asked Lucas.

'Most of them are catching sleep. They landed just before midday, but there was a hassle with customs and immigration for the marine crew. No problem for the survey team. The trip back exhausted them. But I can call Jim if you wish.'

'No, leave him be. Let's take a table in the terrace bar and you can fill me in on the details.'

The men sat at a table overlooking the port and ordered beers.

'Why didn't the Moro guards protect them?' Lucas was short-tempered and aggressive. 'They were ineffective. Where are Hamza and Raspal?'

'Raspal put up a defence and died of his wounds. Hamza resisted but could not stop twenty armed pirates. He has returned to Rio Hondo to break the news to Raspal's family and will be back here tomorrow.'

'You should have told me about Raspal straight away. The security forces need this intelligence.'

'Mr Miffré, best not involve the navy until we discover these people's demands. We are sorry, but the Sulu Sea is a dangerous waterway.'

Peter Dempsey could not get involved in hostage dealings, but he had passed Lucas the name of a professional negotiator. By this stage, Vargas was acting as self-appointed intermediary. Dempsey had warned him this might happen. As the agent was best placed to deal with the abductors, he was probably in cahoots with them to enjoy payments from both sides. They must drive the ransom demand to a reasonable figure.

Vargas revealed the opening bid from Aziz was for fifty million pesos to release the hostages and vessel and, true to prediction, stipulated no security force involvement.

'It's too neat. You act as our agent and have the ear of Aziz. Perhaps he is a friend of yours?'

Vargas smiled. 'I agree it looks suspicious. But it's easily explained. As soon as I heard what happened, I put a call through to the satellite phone on the bridge. Captain Jaffar answered with reluctance as they are keeping a radio silence, but I convinced him to pass me to the pirate leader, Aziz. Now he has my number so we can make a deal. Simple.'

Lucas doubted this version of the story but played along with it for the time being. He explained the world press was aware of the attack and there was pressure for the security services to react with a robust plan.

'The British, Australian and American consular services know of the incident. The Singaporean, Malaysian, Indonesian and Philippine governments are in the picture. Even if we wanted to, we can't stop this. How the various countries in the region respond is up to them.'

'No one has any idea where they are,' said Vargas. 'They could be in the Sunda Islands, off Sabah, in Kalimantan, or a deserted island in the Sulu Sea. There are a million places to hide. Abu Sayyaf has terrorist camps on Basilan Island and Jolo, yet five thousand troops cannot find them.'

'Possibly a lack of will or resources. This demand is ridiculous. We cannot pay fifty million pesos.' Lucas got his calculator out. '*Incroyable,* that is nine hundred thousand US dollars. For a start, the marine insurance will not settle because this region is uninsurable. Who is this man, Aziz? Is he ruthless?'

'I hear of him by reputation. Yes, a well-known bandit, but honourable, not ruthless. Are you sure about the insurance? I don't believe the ship would sail without it.'

Lucas confirmed he had chartered the vessel from a company in Singapore on a day rate basis. The responsibility for insurance was with the hiring company. However, it was a worry, as he had not checked the contract fine print.

'This whole business stinks of a set-up. This group knew we were coming, just waiting for us. If I find you are involved in this racket, I will inform the authorities.'

Vargas pushed his chair back and got up to leave.

'Mr Miffré, do you want your people back alive or not? We are the best agency in Mindanao, and we only represent our clients—that means you, and not those of criminal gangs. One life lost—I don't think you need any more unnecessary casualties, do you?'

'Casualties! Is that how you see them? What is your cut? Ten per cent or twenty per cent?'

'Aziz first demanded forty million for each of the hostages. Already I have driven him down to fifty for both—not a bad deal!'

Vargas turned on his heel and stormed off to his room. Let them stew overnight. It was often like this—the intense emotion, the accusations. Tomorrow Lucas would see it his way.

Meanwhile, Lucas regretted his outburst. To call in a professional negotiator was an expensive choice. Best to work through the agent—the only course open to them. He put a call through to Singapore and asked Danica to read the vessel charter agreement carefully for any clauses relating to the insurance cover. On second thoughts, he asked her for the number of Wong Kai Chee Marine. He would contact Philip Wong and demand to know if they had insurance risk coverage for ransom payments.

Captain Singh and Sandy stood on the bridge, confused, as *Eastern Pearl* had vanished. Sandy grinned; happy to see them abandon the hunt with no chance of an unworkable cooperation pact. He patiently explained the latest developments to Tong. Recent progress showed better results with successful dives to recover two more gold bars, several hundred gold and silver coins, and more pottery artefacts. The strong currents had broken the porcelain to fragments. After the museum took its percentage, there was precious little to defray the costs. The operation would incur a significant loss.

Tong felt deflated and cheated. If the valuable hull or stern sections were still intact and buried in the adjacent block, why had *Eastern Pearl* abandoned the search? Sandy suggested they could switch blocks and Tony supported the move. Tong was not keen. To waste more time was pointless. Tong instructed the captain to set sail for Zamboanga to off load the survey crew and the man from the museum. He and Yap would depart in port.

'I'm sorry they do not let Mr Tong disembark from the sea,' said Singh. 'You must know this. The immigration authorities do not allow sea entry to the Philippines from Zamboanga.'

'He's right. You can fly into Zamboanga City without a problem, but you cannot arrive by boat. We might be gun-running to the Muslim insurgents or smuggling whisky,' said Sandy.

'The only person permitted leaving is the Filipino museum wallah,' said Singh. 'We can transfer him to a kumpit. I can't land in Zamboanga.'

'We will go with him,' repeated Tong. 'Yap and I will travel by kumpit. I must get back to Singapore as soon as possible. I have contacts. The immigration authorities will be no problem. You can return to Singapore once you have dropped us.'

Captain Singh instructed the crew full ahead to Zamboanga to dispatch the Chinese gangsters and museum man. Good riddance, he hurried to get rid of them. With luck, they would arrest Tong and Yap for illegal entry.

Chapter 32

Captain Jaffar recognised the northeastern edge of Tawi-Tawi Island, the main island of a group of 307 islands, two hours' sailing time from Sabah. It was an idyllic island fringed by sandbars of white coral sand and mangrove rising to a forested hinterland in the hills. If they made good progress, he could make the port of Bongao by 5 p.m, but it was a surprise when Aziz told him to head for the closer port of Languyan.

Jaffar had slipped away from the bridge at midday when one of the crew relieved him. Neither Michael nor Christina had appeared at breakfast. He heard Michael banging on his door. Fortunately, the key was in the lock. Jaffar found him desperate and faint from lack of water in the stifling hot cabin. The temperature inside was over one hundred degrees. Jaffar took Michael to the galley and gave him water. He sat next to a fan, stained with sweat and incapable of movement.

Jaffar, increasingly worried, found Christina's cabin locked, and there was no sound from within. He fetched a master key from the bridge, but the cabin was empty. No sign of her in the galley, so he widened the search, trying all the empty cabins. Still he could not find her. Had she been lost at sea? Finally, he tried the cook's cabin at the end of the corridor below the bridge deck. The key was missing from the locked door, but he could hear faint cries from within. Jaffar threw his weight against the door and forced it open.

Christina was in an awful state—tethered to her bunk, with lashings around her wrists and ankles. The cabin was without air-conditioning and like an oven. She told him Gerardo had stuffed a rag into her mouth and tied her up. She had not slept a wink for fear of his return. Jaffar freed her and took her through to the mess room for water and food.

The vessel followed the north coastline of the island, past occasional fishing villages with houses built on stilts. Most of the population lived on the coast, busy with fishing and seaweed farming. The scene was dramatic with the waxy green leaves of the mangrove spread like a carpet above the sea. Vertical taproots supported the lush vegetation above, like the spindly legs of a flamingo, anchored to the muddy seabed. The sun burnt down from a cloudless sky as they nudged inshore towards an inlet. The port of Languyan came into view.

Aziz apologised for Gerardo ill-treating Christina. In recompense, they would give Gerardo an appropriate punishment at their base camp. He was sleeping late after the night watch, but Aziz promised to question him when he came on duty.

'In your culture, what is the usual punishment for violating a young woman?' Michael asked.

Aziz was aware this was a pointed question, but he did not want to be too harsh on Gerardo.

'Gerardo is just a boy. If the lady cannot forgive him, we will give him a severe beating to teach him a lesson.'

'Why discipline him with barbarity? All we ask is that you treat us with respect, and Gerardo leaves Christina alone.'

'No, they should punish him, as you say. It is justice,' said Christina.

'*Inshallah*, we shall decide later. Meanwhile, I regret we have to restrain you again.'

They tied up Christina and Michael, back to back, around a metal pillar on the bridge. At least it was possible to see outside and offer each other reassurance. The vessel passed Languyan and headed inland into a shallow inlet towards Puerto dos Amigos. Rhizophora and nipa palms, fringing the coastline, formed impenetrable thickets. The mangrove was teeming with bird life such as kingfisher, yellow bulbul and many-coloured sunbirds of which the most striking was the small crimson sunbird, whose Malay name is *burong sepah raja*.

Captain Jaffar put on the reverse thrusters, throwing up black ooze from the seabed.

'We cannot go much further. We will run aground,' Jaffar warned as he forced the engines into reverse with a grinding whine. He looked at the ship's echo sounder. There was less than one metre of water below the boat. Possibly this was already too far, and the falling tide might ground them. As the vessel reversed, she threw up mud to discolour the water. Fragments of sea snakes appeared as the vessel props chopped and threw out the still twisting segments. Large forms, possibly submerged logs or crocodiles, glided by at the surface of the seething sea.

Captain Jaffar noticed a deeper channel shown on the marine chart extending towards Puerto dos Amigos, but he did not trust the accuracy of the map and was unwilling to risk the survey boat.

'There's no way we go further without grounding.'

Aziz reached a decision. 'We can use the inflatable dinghy to run ashore. Captain, we will take the hostages and you can have your boat back.'

After his night watch, Gerardo had slept late, but now he returned to the bridge, irritable as his plans to follow up with the girl had failed. What an idiot to prepare the dish but miss the meal! Aziz had forced him to stay up all night, keeping watch for navy vessels. He planned to return to her cabin at dawn at the end of his shift but, befuddled by lack of sleep, he had crashed out in the mess room. It was a missed opportunity, but at the base camp, there would be better prospects.

Aziz said the plan was to disembark with the hostages at Puerto dos Amigos and free the ship's crew. Gerardo objected and said the crew would alert the security forces who might attack them before they had time to reach their camp in the hills. He suggested they drain the boat's fuel and leave them stranded out to sea. Aziz agreed this was a good plan. It would gain them time. Also, best to destroy the radios. At his command, the gang went off to pump out the fuel and muster on the back deck to await instructions. It did not concern the captain. He had spare fuel stashed away—enough to make it to the capital town of Bongao and alert the Philippine navy.

Aziz had used the vessel's Satcom to open the ransom negotiations through the agent in Zamboanga. Before cutting the satellite cables, he called to see what the response had been. Predictably, they had refused the opening offer. The boss had demanded proof Michael and Christina were alive, but it would be best to keep him guessing. There was a hard trek ahead to reach their camp in the hills via a circuitous route to avoid Abu Sayyaf strongholds. The militants had many sympathisers and, given an opportunity, would try to take their hostages.

The pirates moved Michael and Christina to the zodiac. Once onboard the rubber craft, they bound their hands and feet, gagged their mouths and draped them in shawls. It was unnecessary for such a quiet area. Small slits in the hoods afforded a glimpse of the sea streaming by as the zodiac hurtled, like a spinning top, crammed to bursting point with the five pirates squashed against them.

The rubber boat sped past several canoes and small fishing craft, but no one gave them a second glance. Arriving at the barangay of Puerto dos Amigos, the zodiac beached in a clearing in the mangrove. The men bustled them into a single file with guards at the front and rear. They attached a line of rope to the hostages secured to their shorts and followed a rough track to avoid the village.

They passed through thick, low-lying shrub, which soon gave way to the tall forest, full of brown and white monkeys swinging through the trees. The oppressive heat and humidity caused sweat to pour off Michael's brow into his eyes, making him cry in pain. Christina was wheezing, unable to catch her breath through the facemask. It took a one-hour slog to reach the ridge where Aziz called a quick break for water.

Aziz removed their masks and untied the ropes. They followed the ridge north for another hour. It was hard going because of clumps of thorny cycads with razor-sharp stems. Apart from the hazardous plant life, the leaf litter at their feet was crawling with giant stinging ants.

'Michael, will Lucas pay the ransom?' Christina asked.

'I wouldn't bet on it. Lucas won't give in to their demands unless they reduce to a token face-saving amount.'

'Can he afford to pay?'

'He is a millionaire. He can afford it. But he won't pay.'

'All we can do is pray. Michael, they are ruthless thugs, not English gentlemen. You cannot reason with them. Remember, they killed Raspal and nearly killed the captain. Now they have a taste for it. Why stop there? It's only a matter of time before that goon who tied me up rapes me. The only thing stopping him before was Aziz calling him up to the bridge.'

'I will have another word with Aziz and make sure Gerardo keeps away from you.'

They walked on in silence, Michael intent on protecting Christina. It was dusk, and they passed into a thickly forested region before breaking into a clearing at the top of the ridge.

As the men approached closer to their camp, they bound the captives' hands and wrapped scarves over their eyes to blindfold them again. Cycad palms lacerated Michael's arms, as he stumbled through the undergrowth, pulled along on a tethered rope in single file. Christina followed close behind and doubled up low whenever Michael warned her of more thorns. Torrential rains soaked their clothes to the skin. Michael's salty sweat mingled with the rain, making the scars on his legs and arms throb with pain. They forced him to walk in a pair of trainers after stealing his stout walking boots. Blisters on his feet caused a constant agony. Gasping, they struggled up a steep muddy hill, the tree-draped slopes crisscrossed by a network of twisted roots.

Michael, exhausted, tripped over the roots, made slippery by rain. He lay still on the ground trying to regain his strength when one guard kicked him before beating him across the back with a stick grabbed from the forest. As he staggered forward, the guard continued slashing him across the back of his bare legs. Christina rushed back to help, and the guard started thrashing her as well.

At a steep point, where a false step might have plunged them into a ravine, the men undid their blindfolds. In horror, they saw fat leeches gorging on their flesh. One man removed them using a lighted match until the matches ran out and then resorted to squeezing to detach them from sucking blood. Aziz said they were wasting time, as the leeches would drop off after taking a blood meal. At last, in total darkness, they reached the pirate camp.

Chapter 33

Two days after the attack, the team including Alex left on the domestic flight to Manila for onward transfer to Singapore, and Lucas hurried to another meeting with the agent. Vargas sat on the hotel terrace with Hamza, both uneasy.

As Lucas approached, the Moro guard rose to his feet. Lucas joined the men on the terrace overlooking the busy port. The intense late morning heat hung heavy. He needed a cool drink. Because of Raspal's death, it was not right to criticise Hamza.

. 'Sorry—the men got onboard so fast; we could not repel them,' said Hamza.

'Now we must save Christina and Michael,' said Lucas.

'When you make a deal with Aziz, I will take the money in for you.'

He felt bad for the guard, but was he trustworthy? He might be in league with Vargas and Aziz. Therefore, he shrugged, uncertain how to respond. He questioned both men further.

'Yes, Aziz is the leader,' confirmed Vargas. 'He is a well-known pirate. His men are brazen.'

'And is hostage-taking normal for this group?'

'No. It is a new trend to copy Abu Sayyaf.'

Preoccupied with his thoughts, Lucas discarded the menu placed in front of him by the waitress. He opted for a large bottle of San Miguel. By now, the staff knew he liked his beer freezing, but an unfamiliar girl served a lukewarm bottle and opened it. Another disaster! The solution was a bowl of ice cubes, which Lucas accepted without enthusiasm.

'I hope they'll want a quick settlement,' he said.

'The pressure is on us—there's no hurry—quite the reverse; like a cat with a mouse, they can wait for as long as it takes. Weeks, months, even years. It is no concern to them.'

It shocked Lucas. Unbelievable. The stress was too intense to stomach. He wanted to get this nonsense settled fast. He requested an update from Vargas.

'Yes, we have progress. I told Aziz fifty million pesos was out of the question. He has already reduced by half. For only twenty-five million pesos they will hand back Michael and the girl. That's a big concession.'

Lucas drummed his fingers on the table, before reaching into his case for his calculator. The sum sounded larger when quoted in millions of pesos but, even with such a large reduction, it was too much.

'Hmm. It's good they are listening. Ten million pesos is our top price. So much for Michael and Christina? How much more to return the vessel and crew?'

'In fact, nothing extra. As a gesture of good faith, Aziz released the boat and crew unharmed. The pirates abandoned it yesterday and have taken the hostages to their camp in the hills.'

'How do you know this?'

'Captain Jaffar sailed into Bongao early this morning. It is the biggest town and port on the southwest side of the island.'

'Bongao? What island is this?'

'Tawi-Tawi Island.'

'Never heard of it. Where is it?'

'A small island around fifteen miles long. Near Sabah although it belongs to the Philippines.'

'Tawi-Tawi Island,' Lucas ran the unfamiliar name over thoughtfully.

'The remote island is Muslim and sympathetic to Abu Sayyaf. Captain Jaffar called me, so my news is bang up-to-date. I'm sorry I should have mentioned it to you at once, but I was dealing with your questions first.'

'And the ship's crew, are they safe?'

'Yes, all accounted.'

'Where are the hostages?'

'According to Captain Jaffar, the pirates took them off, in the ship's zodiac, at a place near Languyan,' Vargas was enjoying his role—like a conductor of an orchestra, with a wave of his baton engaging the musicians alert to his every command. Without him, no solution was possible; only he had the complete picture.

'Thank God. If Michael and Christina are on this island, why don't the security forces find them?'

'The forest is thick with a shoreline fringed by mangrove swamps—like finding a cicada in a banyan tree. Many of these cases settle for around twenty million. I think your offer of ten million is too low, but we can see if he bites. If we keep the negotiations rolling, we may get a quick settlement.'

Lucas entered the conversion rate on his calculator and gave a gasp when the sum came to two hundred and seventy thousand US dollars. Still too much.

'But an insignificant price for two people's lives,' said Vargas. 'A few years ago pirates kidnapped a group of Malaysians from a resort in Sabah and held them hostage on Tawi-Tawi. The families called in a Malaysian emissary, an experienced man, for the ransom negotiations, but he kept haggling even when close to agreement. It was ridiculous. They were not demanding much. He drove the figure lower and lower as if bargaining with his own money—such a *kiasu* attitude. The kidnappers lost patience, and ordered the hostages to make a dash for freedom, giving them a start of a count of ten. As they ran away, they shot them dead. Only one person escaped to tell the tale.'

'Was Aziz involved?'

'No. But you need to appreciate how things go wrong if not handled with the benefit of local knowledge. Agree a price and trade fast. There is a risk the thrill of killing becomes more attractive than money. You are not dealing with normal, rational people.'

'My problem is we are not sure the insurance will cover the ransom. I have to pay out and claim it back. Every time someone pays, it makes it harder to do business. The British embassy's advice is never to pay a ransom—that is the official view.'

Vargas laughed. 'But acceptable for diplomats to take a hard stance. They are not in the firing line. Since when do you listen to the British?'

'Okay, we play it your way. Offer Aziz ten million pesos as our last offer. If he agrees, I will go to Singapore tomorrow to raise the money. Keep in touch in case of any developments.'

Vargas frowned. It seemed a pointless offer, bound to fail, but he would pass it on. He explained how Aziz used a satellite phone from a logging base near to his camp in the hills. Tawi-Tawi had no cell phone service, and the satellite link was useful to avoid misunderstandings. After Vargas had left, Lucas talked further with Hamza, eager to keep him involved, but wary of any dramatic rescue. Once they agreed on a price, he could withdraw funds from his bank, return to Zamboanga and, together with Hamza, rejoin the vessel in Bongao. It was a sketchy idea, but meant he was on hand to pay the ransom and free the hostages. The best choice was to play it straight.

Back in his hotel room, Vargas smiled at his deception. He had elaborated on the graphic story of the Malaysian emissary and the explicit details of the imaginary slaughter of the captives to convince the Frenchman to pay. The case was genuine, but they had solved it with no fatalities.

Lucas tried to reach Julie to give her an update, but her telephone was engaged, or maybe she had taken it off the hook. Exasperated, he slumped back in the chair when his mobile sprang to life. It was Captain Jaffar calling from the vessel in Bongao, where the port authorities had given them a good grilling.

'Did they tell you that dastard killed young Raspal? As Raspal was a Muslim, we must bury him within twenty-four hours. So we wrap in a white sheet and commit him to the sea for the sharks to eat. Have I done the right thing?'

'What you did was for the best. Raspal's family will appreciate you followed the Muslim traditions. I hear they hurt you during the attack?'

'One of them cracked me over the head—nearly fractured my skull. Aziz is a cool customer. He is only just in control. The younger thugs are trigger-happy.'

'Will they harm Christina and Michael?'

There was a lengthy pause, as if Jaffar was choosing his words with care.

'They are animals. The evil guy who whacked me over the skull has a red headband. He sailed off in their longboat. But the boy who killed Raspal is even worse. They call him Gerardo—a vicious, sadistic psychopath. He trussed up the girl from the museum in her bunk, planning to rape her. Lucky for her Aziz called him up to the bridge and put a stop to his mischief.'

'*Mon Dieu*, how terrible.'

'Aziz kept Michael and Christina bound to the bridge stanchion for hours on end. I dread what they must endure in the jungle camp.'

'Thank you, captain. I'm sorry you had to suffer such an ordeal.'

Lucas stood up to release the pent-up tension and paced around the room, lighting up another Gitanes and dragging the smoke into his lungs before expelling it in a cloud. The situation was worse than he had imagined.

'I took a video film of the gang when they left at Languyan. We can bring the rogues to justice with my evidence.'

Lucas sat back on the bed, much relieved by this news. Jaffar loved to use old language such as rascals or bad hats. He asked Jaffar to make a list of the equipment and personal effects stolen or destroyed for the insurance claim. Lucas hoped to see the captain next week in port.

'Boss, the ship needs fuel and victuals, and none of us has any money.'

Lucas was calmer as the full extent of their losses emerged. On the positive side, the ship was undamaged, and the marine crew were unharmed. They could refuel the boat, secure the release of the hostages, and return to the shipwreck. As a carrot to make sure of future trouble-free survey, they could hire Aziz to act as their security. There was no need for violence or dramatic rescue attempts.

The ransom demands were immaterial—just a hiccup along the way to successful business cooperation. With millions generated from the sale of the porcelain, they could expect revenue from the book and film rights of the search. Aziz was only seeking a fairer deal for his people, and once he understood the positive benefits that must flow to Tawi-Tawi, then he would cooperate with them.

Chapter 34

The High Commissioner had finished reading the Straits Times. There was a low-key mention of the piracy incident, but they could not rely on the UK press to exercise the same restraint as the Singapore press. In a minute, he would call Peter Dempsey for an update. Doubtless, the news had hit the headlines, with the switchboard under storm from reporters. The eight-hour time difference from London gave them breathing space to work out the best approach.

'Margery, please ask Peter to come to my office at ten thirty. I will expect a full update on the Sulu Sea incident.'

'Yes, sir—I saw him in the tearoom. I'll let him know right away.'

'Fine. Also, Margery, I will take lunch at the cricket club so inform the driver to pick me up at midday. The embassy team is playing against Singapore Cricket Club, but we have had to call up two players from the Australian High Commission. I prefer to lose the game than share the honours with them.'

Margery allowed herself a thin smile. The familiar repetition—the stoic flying the flag, the public school banter she despised. Peter Dempsey she liked. He was very smooth, too young for her, but efficient and unflustered. Best of all, he was keen to help with every task they handed him. Peter had sorted out a few piracies. One incident, an attack in the Malacca Straits, involved a group of merchant seamen, including British nationals. He had picked up the pieces and got the crew released. Unfortunately, the next day, the police found the corpses of two Indonesians locked up in a frozen food cabinet. Peter said the pirates fled the scene after stabbing the men and throwing them in the freezer, still alive. Despite this, Peter gained a reputation for successful repatriations. If anyone could free Michael Fletcher, he was the fellow to do it.

'Peter, the old man wants to see you at ten thirty for an update on the Philippine piracy case. He thinks the UK press will splash the story tomorrow morning.'

'Oh God, Margery—that loose French cannon, Lucas Miffré, has gone rushing down to Zamboanga. I told him to hire a proper negotiator, but he prefers to do it on the cheap and work through their agent. The agent's half the problem. I hate it when amateurs take over.'

'He won't like that,' Margery dipped her head towards the High Commissioner's ever-shut door.

Peter looked at his watch with irritation. Less than fifteen minutes before a stressful meeting. He returned to his office to check his emails.

Margery enjoyed the power of her position, the organiser, the only person party to all sides, the silent confidante, and trusted servant of the Crown. By quarter past ten, the High Commissioner would have finished the morning phone call to his wife and be ready for another cup of tea. She liked to keep him waiting. His desk was always clear; they let nothing important interfere with his day. As for computers, the High Commissioner had no use for them. He scribbled his letters in longhand for her to interpret and type. He held emails in particular contempt and left her to deal with the replies.

With a sigh, Margery studied the empty calendar for the day with half an ear, listening for the intercom, ordering up another tea.

She peeked at her watch. Nearly ten thirty and, as usual, Peter would be bang on time. She relaxed, relishing his imminent arrival at the old man's study like a naughty boy called in to see the headmaster. She was smiling when he tiptoed up, straightened his tie, and with a complicit grin in her direction, knocked on the door. In deference to the tropical heat, he wore a short-sleeved blue striped shirt tucked into black trousers, which emphasised his trim waist and tight bottom.

The High Commissioner sat at his overlarge desk poring over a manila file in a show of being busy. He ignored the timid knock from his attaché until Peter repeated it.

'Enter,' he boomed grandly. Looking up as the attaché entered the room; he removed his reading glasses, pointing them at Peter like a weapon. 'Look, we need to discuss this man's abduction in the Philippines. They are holding a British subject for ransom.'

'Yes, sir, that is correct. Mr Michael Fletcher, a treasure hunter from Singapore. I have already spoken with his wife and reassured her we are doing all we can.'

Although not invited, Peter sat down in the Regency chair over the desk from the High Commissioner. From this point, he struggled to appear on top of the situation. Two photo frames of the High Commissioner's wife and dog blocked his view, so Peter moved the chair to the side, a movement that annoyed the commissioner. He preferred some obstacles in the way of communication with junior officers. Drumming his fingers on the desk, he closed the file and rescued his paper pad and pen from beneath the Straits Times.

'She won't blab to the press, I hope.'

'Oh no, I'm sure she will be discrete.'

'Good. A treasure hunter? Damn fools, sounds like he deserved it. Do we know where they are holding the captives?'

Peter squirmed in his chair, struggling to steer the conversation back on track. Why did the High Commissioner behave like an upper-class amateur from a bygone age?

'Yes, sir. We have evidence they are in a jungle camp on the island of Tawi-Tawi.'

'Tawi-Tawi? I have never heard of it. Where is it?'

'It's a small island at the southwestern limits of the Philippines, close to Sabah,' said Peter. 'A beautiful place, but off the tourist track and the Foreign Office advises foreigners to avoid it because of terrorism fears. It was a legitimate and sanctioned survey to locate an old shipwreck in the Sulu Sea. They even have a Filipina museum researcher assigned to the job. But, unfortunately, the pirates have kidnapped her as well.'

'A girl! No one told me this. What are we doing about it?' The High Commissioner left his chair to pace around the room. This information was too startling to take sitting down.

'As you might expect, sir, the pirates are demanding a large ransom. I have been in contact with the Frenchman, Lucas Miffré, who organised the expedition. They are negotiating with the group, via an intermediary, and have not asked for our help. I explained we do not get involved in ransom demands.'

'Damn right we don't. We are not a soft touch.'

'Yes, sir. I told the Frenchman we only repatriate British subjects.'

The High Commissioner looked startled, 'Did I miss something? Where does this Frenchman fit in?'

Peter held back a wish to throttle him.

'The French gentleman is a Monsieur Lucas Miffré. He is the backer, the moneyman, behind this expedition to locate a valuable shipwreck off the Philippines. The ship was one of the China tea traders of the East India Company. She sank in a typhoon in the 1700s. Monsieur Miffré's survey boat was working at the site when pirates attacked and boarded it. Naturally, he wants his people free. Also, I should mention another point…'

The High Commissioner glanced at his watch. 'Well, get a shift on. I have a cricket game at the Padang later, so let's not take all day. It looks like rain—always does on the rare occasions when I play.'

He had just remembered he had left his cricket whites in Eden Hall, which meant a detour home before rushing to the club for lunch. If his wife were in, she would want to go shopping or ask him to walk the dog. He had already set out alibis for the afternoon in the morning call home. Why did Peter drone on with these lengthy explanations?

'It seems our American friends have expressed interest. They believe this abduction involves the Islamist terrorist group, Abu Sayyaf. An elite band of commandos from the US forces is on duty with the Philippine security services, in an advisory role. This is off the record. The Americans want us to put them in the picture, and they will help with any rescue attempt.'

'Really? Not a direction we wish to take, surely? Can't we send in a bunch of our own SAS chaps? Keep the show in our hands.'

'We have no arrangements in place. We can't just march in and interfere.'

'Hmm. More's the pity. Well, if you cooperate with the Americans on this, Peter, be careful. I don't need our hostage slaughtered in a "friendly fire" incident. Another thing that concerns me is this Frenchman has arranged this foolhardy search for a valuable English wreck.'

'British, actually,' said Peter. Aware of the bemusement on the High Commissioner's face, he enlightened him. 'The 1707 Ratification of the Union—creation of the British state if you recall your history. It is not correct to refer to the shipwreck as English. And according to Lucas, the *Siren* was originally a French vessel.'

'Stop being so bloody pedantic. The point is, why doesn't this Frenchie get help from *his* embassy? Why come to us? Is he playing both parties along? It wouldn't surprise me.'

'I know it's irregular, sir, but I think our prime consideration is for the British subjects—Michael Fletcher and his son, Alex.'

'I thought you said one British hostage. Now you tell me there are two.'

'No sir, you misunderstand—there is only the *one* British hostage. I hadn't mentioned the boy because they released him and he is en route to Singapore. I plan a thorough debriefing tomorrow. The experience may traumatise him. If you wish to attend the debrief, I will hold it at the embassy on Sunday afternoon.'

'Normally, I'd love to, but Sunday is awkward. I'm sure you can manage without me. See Margery and get an expenses chit. Put the lad in a decent hotel, it's the least we can do. Try the Goodwood Park.'

'It's unnecessary—the family live in Singapore. He stays in an apartment in Changi with his parents.'

'Oh, I see. I naturally assumed being British subjects they were out here on some caper. If they live here, that's different. We still need to debrief the lad. Are you able to meet the boy's flight and bring him straight to the embassy?'

'Yes, sir, an excellent idea. But I expect his mother will want to welcome him home. I'll get in touch with her this evening to arrange something.'

'Good, I'll leave you to handle this with your safe pair of hands. Come up with the standard press briefing and keep me informed. I should be home by eight tonight, so call me with an update. On your way out, please ask Margery to bring me a cup of tea.'

'Yes, sir, thank you for your help.'

It had thrilled Margery when Peter asked her to show up at the office on Sunday morning, even though it was the weekend. She agreed to cancel her tennis game with the Ford-Smyffes.

'I have to conduct a debriefing of that young lad from the piracy case. Sorry to interrupt your weekend, but I was wondering if you could be here for eleven o'clock? His flight is due in at nine-thirty, so I will bring Alex and his mother straight here. I would appreciate it if you keep Julie company while I question the boy alone. Will it suit you, Margery? I'm sorry to mess up your Sunday. When we have finished, we can go to my club for a bite of lunch.'

Margery felt honoured to attend the debriefing session, and lunch afterwards. For the first time, she wondered if those conspiratorial glances and ready jokes at the old man's expense were Peter signalling an attraction towards her. A youth ten years younger than her would be a splendid catch.

Nervously, she reviewed what would be the most appropriate dress for the Sunday session before deciding on a severe-looking little black number she reserved for special occasions. Maybe a trifle obvious, but it exuded firm confidence, and, from experience, she knew it would appeal to a young man, such as Peter Dempsey. The poor chap seemed permanently on the back foot with his dealings with the High Commissioner, but perhaps that was a submissive position he enjoyed.

Peter cut short her day dreaming by demanding she phone Julie Fletcher and invite her to meet him at Changi Airport late morning to greet Alex's flight from Manila. He suspected Julie was not keen on a joint meeting, but it might help to deflect the press interest. Margery relayed the message that both of them should attend a debrief at the embassy, followed by a short press interview with selected correspondents of the world media. Afterwards Peter Fletcher invited them to lunch at the British Club.

Chapter 35

A small team of old men and women maintained the pirate's camp at the summit of a hill. There was no sign of the fifteen-strong band from the fishing boat or their hoard of booty, stolen from the survey vessel. Aziz suspected moving the large refrigerator had delayed them. It had been a stupid move to bring the heavy item and useless without electrical power. The news that the navy had attacked and killed five of their comrades at the same time as they trekked up the hill had not yet reached them. Such devastating news might imperil the sensitive hostage negotiations.

They imprisoned Michael and Christina inside a crude hut built of nipa palm and bamboo. A faint light from a narrow opening, guarded by a metal grill and chick wire, gave a limited view outside to the forest. The interior was dark, hot and oppressive. No fresh air circulated and the stale conditions attracted blood-sucking flies and mosquitoes. The dirt floor was alive with ants drawn to remains of rotting fruit.

'The hut looks as if they have used it recently,' said Christina. 'Perhaps another poor captive.' Exhausted, Michael sat on the earth floor. The camp, on a flat clearing at the top of a hill, connected via a high ridge to the thick jungle on one side and provided an excellent vantage point to see anyone approaching from far off. Michael observed the hill gave a good defence against attack apart from an airborne onslaught by helicopters.

'This will not happen. Have you forgotten no one knows we are here?'

Michael looked thoughtful.

'The view outside is fine if you like the rain forest, but the facilities inside the accommodation are a bit lacking.'

There was a raised wooden platform, presumably a crude bed at one side—at least it was clear of the insect life populating the floor. Narrow and short, the bed was big enough for one person, but not for two. Michael volunteered to sleep on the floor in the small corner space next to a large bucket. On closer inspection, this was the toilet served by a jug of cloudy water full of twitching mosquito larvae. An unpleasant smell spread out, becoming more noxious closer to the bucket.

'That's disgusting,' said Christina. 'I refuse to use that thing.'

Michael was rummaging in his pockets to retrieve a damp packet of cigarettes.

'I thought you had given up smoking?'

The cigarettes disintegrated as he vainly tried to salvage one, making them laugh. Best to put a brave face on their predicament. Michael moved the pack to the window space and jammed it behind the wire to dry. Their laughter cut off when Aziz stormed up to their hut. He stared in at the prisoners as if they were mad dogs in a kennel.

'Mr Lucas refused our first ransom demand. As a token of good faith and to conclude this business, we then made a large reduction. We have just received his counter offer, which values your lives at only ten million pesos. This is a surprising and insulting price. Our cards are on the table; we are acting straight with him.'

Michael was unfamiliar with the value of the peso, but a figure in millions sounded impressive. Catching Christina's eye, he saw his assumption was a mistake.

'Sounds reasonable. Initial bargaining before eventual agreement on a new bid.'

Aziz's glacial green eyes never blinked and stared through narrow slits like a lizard. He addressed this threat to Michael.

'Ten million is only enough to free one, so the other must die unless we get a better price. Tonight we punish Gerardo for his disrespect to the girl on the boat. Note the punishment because you will receive the same tomorrow night, if your people cannot increase their payment.'

Aziz turned to stare at Christina, bringing his face and bulging eyes close enough to the grill for the foetid sweat of his body to make her gag.

'Each of us gets what he or she deserves in our society. We mean business—get that into your head, you stupid girl. Tomorrow you write to your museum and tell them we are serious. Our messenger will take your letter, in person, to Manila.'

'But, the director has no authority to negotiate for my release. As you know, our government does not bargain with criminals.'

'That's right. We are just the victims, but when you talk to Lucas, strike an agreement that covers both of us,' said Michael.

'Your agent, Vargas, has taken on this task. We trust him to make your boss come to his senses. Maybe we cut off one of the girl's fingers to convince them we are ruthless pirates.' With these chilling words, Aziz left them.

'He's vicious.' Christina sunk onto the floor in the corner, drawing her knees up to her face. 'He means it—I am everything they hate—an educated woman, a Christian, a westernised university graduate. You are a valuable commodity to them. Your people can pay the ransom and let you go, but my family cannot afford to raise enough money for my release. A gipsy once read my palm and declared my lifeline is so short I should get married and have children while I was young. I should have listened to her, shouldn't I?'

Michael was not sure where the money was coming from. Perhaps there was a contingency fund for British subjects in distress they could turn to. Also, likely that Lucas had arranged an insurance policy, but this might not cover Christina. Everything she said might be correct, but they needed to stay positive and focused on how to escape. She sunk her head against his shoulder and sobbed, her whole frame shaking. He hugged her to ease her suffering and stayed with her until exhaustion overcame them both, and they fell asleep leaning against the wall, oblivious to the ants and cockroaches crawling over them.

The women had prepared a meal for the group—a stew of wild boar and spit-roasted jungle fowl served with copious supplies of tuba, an alcoholic drink made from the fermented sap of the coconut palm. The men gathered around the fire for their food. Everyone except Aziz drank of the liquor, which roused them to a loud frenzy of shouting, singing and drunken celebration. Later, a woman squeezed rice through the wires of the grill. She noticed the prisoners were sleeping, so rattled on the grill.

Michael awoke with a start and ran over to scoop up the rice, which had fallen to the floor. The woman smiled, revealing a mouth of gappy teeth in a wizened old face. She forced a chicken leg through at a spot where the wire was wider—a routine she was familiar with from former prisoners. If the gang had imprisoned others, what had happened to them? Had the pirates released them or killed them without mercy? Michael shared the meal with Christina. As they tore the chicken apart, Michael was studying the hut carefully. He gouged out a depression in the earth near the wall to discover if there was a foundation. He moved to the back of the shack and clawed at the soil with his bare hands, but the thin soil passed to red laterite, and it was impossible to make any headway.

'The hard red clay is the weathered top of bedrock,' said Michael. 'We cannot dig out of here without tools.'

'We could try the sides of the hut—they're bamboo.'

Michael shook the walls. Although the canes moved, they held firm. The construction was simple but secure, with wire strands binding them together.

'Hmm, a good shove might weaken it enough to break. But the camp is outside, and it would alert the guards.'

The drinking and laughter from the men clustered by the fire decreased and they fell silent. Michael and Christina stared through the grill, and what they saw in the dying embers of the blaze filled them with horror.

Gerardo, stripped to the waist, was face up against a tree beside the fireside with his arms tied to the lower branches and suspended, so his feet dangled. He hung there in the flickering firelight as if crucified. A man passed Aziz the long flex of a broken fan belt, which he cracked against Gerardo's arched back. He put more force into each successive stroke, raising angry red ridges as Gerardo twisted and writhed. With surgical precision, he varied each strike, moving from the shoulders downwards like a metronome. Everyone watched, shocked by the savagery at each lingering snap and wondering how much Gerardo could stand without crying out. Despite the unbearable pain, he uttered no sound. After thirty-six lashes, they cut him down, and a woman rushed up to bandage his wounds. The men dispersed, uneasy, staring at the ground. Gerardo had endured the punishment. The hatred he felt for the girl burnt strong as he vowed revenge.

'If they punish their own, they are capable of much worse with us,' said Michael.

Christina had crumbled to the earth floor, unable to watch. Hardest to bear was the realisation it was she who had insisted on this cruel travesty of justice.

'Oh My God! Aziz threatened you with the same punishment tomorrow.'

'Just an idle threat, I hope.'

'After this Gerardo will get even—he will kill me.'

Chapter 36

Julie met up with Peter Dempsey waiting for Alex's flight arrival at Changi late morning. Alex had received an upgrade to business class. He was one of the first off the Singapore Airlines flight. After the introductions, a police officer took them on a fast track out of the airport. Peter offered a lift in the limousine, but Julie had come in her car and followed on to the British Consulate.

She wanted to go straight home with Alex, but it made sense to attend his debriefing if it helped release Michael. At the embassy, Peter escorted them to his office, a sparsely furnished room dominated by a picture of a youthful Queen and a large map of Singapore. A pleasant woman, called Margery, came through with tea and biscuits.

'Julie—the good news is that negotiations are ongoing. Both sides are talking, so we should secure the release of Michael soon.'

Peter ushered them to a modern two-seater settee, rather upright and uncomfortable, and drew up a chair to sit opposite. Julie politely admired the room, but it was over-furnished. A single window faced out towards the road, although shutters subdued the traffic noise. Through the doorway, she glimpsed much grander rooms for other staff.

'Things are at a delicate stage,' said Peter. 'As you know from the press reports, there was a fatality during the assault—the attackers killed a security guard. Unfortunate, but a peripheral casualty and your husband is not at risk. They should look after him well, as he is a valuable commodity.'

Julie looked strained and bewildered. So insulting to call anyone a commodity, but she let the glib statement go.

'We plan a brief meeting with the press in a few minutes. They are certain to ask if we will settle a ransom, but all I want you to say is that dialogue is ongoing with the kidnappers and they have released the vessel and marine crew unharmed. We paid nothing. It was a goodwill gesture by the gang, so we are dealing with reasonable people rather than fanatics.'

'Where is Michael? Are you certain he is alive?'

'We cannot be specific, but he is being held somewhere in the Philippines. Yesterday we had an update from Lucas that his agent has established contact with their leader, Aziz. It is excellent news.'

Alex felt left out of the conversation. Peter Dempsey was focusing all his attention on his mother. He interrupted them to ask if anyone was negotiating for the release of Christina. It was shocking they had kidnapped her. Was the agent helping?

'Well, yes, we hope so,' stuttered Peter. 'Her case is outside our jurisdiction. In theory, their policy is the same as ours. The Philippine Government refuses to sanction payments. What usually happens is the victim's family puts up a moderate sum to free the hostage.'

'It seems so callous to ignore Christina,' said Julie.

'I understand steps are in hand, via the agent to offer a token payment for goodwill to cover both the hostages, but the British Government's policy is not to yield to terrorism, and we never agree to such demands. It is a matter outside our jurisdiction. Singapore's approach is the same as ours, so you must not divulge these plans. If you do, it might put the hostages at risk. My view is they are safe because the group holding them don't have a track record for K and R.'

'You've lost me there,' said Julie. 'What are K and R?'

'I'm sorry for slipping into jargon—it stands for kidnap and ransom. This group's *modus operandi* is minor theft from their piracy exploits. We believe there was an opportunist sequence of events developed out of the attack on the boat. It isn't their normal pattern.'

'A copycat of the Abu Sayyaf?'

'I want to ask a favour,' Peter looked uncomfortable. 'As the press are branding this an Abu Sayyaf terrorist attack, rather than straight piracy, we should go along with this analysis. So do not mention Aziz. He is insisting Lucas and the agent do not contact the security forces, and if press reports name him, it could put the hostages at risk.'

'Why do you blame Abu Sayyaf when you haven't any evidence?' demanded Alex.

'We can't be certain this was piracy. Abu Sayyaf might be behind it. In our view it is better to implicate that organisation. You know this war on terror thing. It makes the public keep their guard up and not become complacent.'

'Why do you embroider the truth?' replied Julie. 'Is it to control the media?'

'I agree with you. This is the official line. Abu Sayyaf is the greater enemy to democracy than a group of pirates.'

'Oh, I see,' said Alex. 'So the security forces have an excuse to go in heavy.' Peter Dempsey looked uncomfortable. Alex's analysis was more accurate than he cared to admit. As a mere attaché, he must follow the line that was most expedient. With increasing acts of terrorism worldwide from Islamist extremists, it was possible it involved the Abu Sayyaf group. He hoped that was not the case, but you could never be certain.

'Michael and Christina are just pawns in a game for you.' Julie rose to her feet, drawing Alex to her side.

Peter squeezed her arm. 'Remember, we have the experience. We have been here many times. Kidnap cases happen every year, and most never reach the ears of the public. Play it our way, and we will get Michael and the girl out alive.'

'Okay, I believe you. Can you let go of my arm?' Julie was pale and rattled.

As she entered the press room, a hundred flashlights exploded in her brain. Peter led Alex and Julie to a long table facing a crowd of over thirty reporters and photographers. Peter raised his hands for calm to read a prepared statement, after which they were free to ask a few questions.

'Two days ago, a survey vessel called the *Eastern Pearl* from Singapore was working in the Sulu Sea in the southern Philippines. A group of twenty armed assailants attacked the boat. The boat was carrying out a geophysical survey project under a permit issued by the Philippine Government. The attackers killed one of the security guards, but this was the only fatality. Mrs Fletcher's husband, Michael Fletcher, a geophysicist based in Singapore and a Filipina research worker, were taken hostage along with the crew. The assailants released the rest of the surveyors and most of the marine crew to return to the port of Zamboanga by the ship's lifeboat.'

The press all started shouting questions at once. Peter paused until the room was quiet again before continuing.

'Amongst those freed was Michael's son Alex, who is here with Mrs Fletcher. Please keep questions brief and respect their feelings. Following this release, only two hostages, Michael Fletcher and Christina Velasco stay captive. It is important to stress we have made no payments to facilitate the safe return of the team onboard the *Eastern Pearl*. The attackers have stolen personal effects and we hope we can free the remaining two hostages. I repeat, the united position of all the governments involved in this case is not to give in to ransom demands. Dialogue lines of communications are in place, and we expect a quick resolution and release of the hostages.'

The room erupted with everyone shouting. Peter selected the BBC news reporter as most likely to ask sympathetic questions.

'This must have been a horrifying experience for you, Alex. Did you witness the attack?'

Alex saw Peter glance anxiously. His mother looked across and smiled, so Alex replied.

'It was two in the morning, so I was asleep. The shouting and running feet woke me up as the attackers boarded. Someone yelled at my cabin door to go to the bridge. The captain had secured the outside doors. They fired shots, the door splintered and broke open, and they swarmed onto the bridge. They hit Captain Jaffar with the butt of a gun and knocked him out cold. Finally, they ordered us to collect on the back deck while they ransacked the cabins, stealing anything of value, including my toothbrush. It was a terrifying time.'

After this account, Julie reached out and squeezed Alex's hand in reassurance. His graphic report had shocked the room.

The BBC news reporter continued. 'What more can you tell us of the security guard who died in the attack? Was he a hired professional, and how did the events unfold?'

Peter fielded this question. 'The man was an experienced, locally hired Filipino professional. He died doing his job protecting the team. A second guard was unharmed and released.'

A reporter from CNN shot off another question. 'Julie, have the pirates been in touch to ask for ransom money?'

Peter jumped in before Julie could reply.

'I can answer that for Mrs Fletcher. Michael Fletcher is a British subject, and our Government's policy is never to pay ransom for the release of prisoners. We cannot categorise this as a pirate attack at this stage without more evidence.' Julie put her hand on Peter's arm, interrupting him.

'As you put the question to me, I am happy to answer it. First, it is our firm impression that there is sufficient evidence to categorise this as a pirate attack. Second, I agree that payment of any ransom merely empowers the attackers to continue their crimes and I believe it best to secure the release of my husband and the Filipina research worker by other means such as prisoner exchanges or political concessions rather than large payments of money.'

'That is a very brave statement. But has there been an approach?' persisted the reporter.

'The Abu Sayyaf terrorist group are active in the Sulu Sea area, and we cannot discount their involvement in this attack,' Peter Dempsey repeated.

'But that's awful,' a middle-aged American woman from Time Magazine interrupted.

'Abu Sayyaf kidnapped some God-fearing, peaceful American missionaries last year, as I recall.'

She paused and resumed when she remembered the names. Many were aware of the case and nodded in recognition as she continued.

'Yes, the missionaries were Martin and Grace Burnham, and there was a guy from California who they beheaded.'

Peter rose from his chair to quell the uproar as the room exploded with indignant shouts. 'Gentlemen, ladies, we better stop there. I caution you against writing any ill-considered inflammatory accounts without evidence. Best let things develop to a solution. I must request balanced reporting and not to exceed the guidelines of responsible journalism. The Singapore Government can be prickly and will block any articles they take exception to and may ban the guilty parties from the country.'

The press conference left Julie shaken, but Peter was even more appalled at her interruption. He summoned an embassy limousine and whisked them off for lunch to the British Club in Bukit Timah. Margery came along too, at Peter's invitation. A drink and delicious food in a calm setting would do wonders to defuse the tensions. It had been a mistake to throw them into the press pack without more preparation. He should have kept to the original plan of debriefing Alex on his own, but they had been running late, forcing him to change plans. He hoped the quiet setting of the British Club would relax Julie. They sat outside in the decorative garden surrounded by hibiscus on a terraced hillside. Often you could see a bright yellow golden oriole flying past, heading for the nearby Bukit Timah Nature Reserve. However, Julie was still seething and blind to the peaceful scene. Peter persuaded her and Margery to have a gin and tonic, and the men had beers. She glanced at the menu and tossed it aside with no appetite. The men looked disappointed, but Peter rallied and ordered bread and olives.

'You deliberately made the press think this was an attack by Abu Sayyaf when you know it's a pirate gang led by Aziz. Lucas Miffré is negotiating with this Aziz via the local agent Vargas. Why do you have to lie? Is it because you *hope* it involves Abu Sayyaf? Is this a personal ego trip, Peter?'

She was so cross she had raised her voice, and one or two heads turned to look at the group. Peter winced in embarrassment and lowered his voice to reply.

'No. We discussed this at the embassy. It's too early to name the gang holding your husband. We cannot release names or discuss the bartering going on behind the scenes. These press conferences are unavoidable. I can assure you there was no deliberate intention to bring Abu Sayyaf into this. If you remember it was the correspondent from Time Magazine, who blurted out the case of the missionaries, the Burnhams.'

'So that's true, is it? I recall terrorists kidnapped tourists from a resort island and beheaded one of the Americans.'

'Yes. Abu Sayyaf went on a rampage and held over one hundred hostages at one time. You are right; they executed an American tourist, Guillermo Sobero, in October last year. Finally, the security forces attacked and rescued Gracia

Burnham, but they shot her husband Martin dead during the assault. The security forces deployed over one thousand American troops to Basilan to wipe out Abu Sayyaf, but they still survive and are active, although not on the same level as back in 2001. Even during those horrific times, the terrorists released most of their hostages unharmed.'

Julie and Alex fell silent. It was clear the press focus would be on Abu Sayyaf as a target for righteous indignation. Margery concentrated on getting a fuller description of the pirates from Alex. They got on well and discovered a common interest in tennis. She even asked him to make up a mixed double with Peter, Margery and a secretary. Julie felt sidelined. Even Alex was warming to the group and drinking far too much beer. The limousine took the party back to the High Commission after lunch, and the Fletchers returned home to Pagoda Villas.

Peter and Margery sighed with relief after the Fletchers had left. It was a novel experience to wander through the empty rooms and corridors. Apart from the man at the front gate, the embassy was as quiet as a grand hotel out-of-season. They walked side by side, their feet echoing in unison.

'That didn't go too well,' conceded Peter, as he accepted a cup of tea from Margery. Cheekily they had taken over the old man's office, enjoying possession, knowing that none of the staff was likely to turn up on a Sunday. The air conditioning was off, but Margery helped Peter to remove his jacket.

'Thanks, Margery. It's hot in here.'

'I thought you handled things very well. A tough position with lots of stress. And I am sure the press conference was a nightmare!'

'It was. I wanted to keep you away from that circus.'

'The families don't understand that we have to be uncompromising in these situations. It is in their best interests!'

'How right you are, Margery. The official line is no deal. Discrete dealings can proceed. That is the first time I can remember a wife saying don't pay the ransom.'

'What! She said that?'

'Yes.'

'But that's what you wanted!'

'Margery, the *official* line is one of no negotiation but the *reality* is we pay a ransom. If you adopt a rigorous no pay policy like the Russians, then you are condemning the hostage to death.'

'I am sure you are taking her too literally. I think she was just backing up the official line. Well, enough talk of work!'

Margery daringly perched on the High Commissioner's desk. From his lower vantage point in a Regency upholstered chair, Peter admired her elegant long legs. She relaxed against the edge of the desk facing him, her legs crossed to raise her patented leather black stiletto shoes into view. As the tight shoes were hurting, she rubbed a finger across the arch and bridge of her foot.

'Sorry, it's agony. Do you mind?'

She slipped off her shoes. They fell with a thud.

Getting more comfortable, she lent backwards, and her hand dislodged a pen, which crashed to the floor. Margery laughed as she bent over to retrieve it, flashing those nice legs and a shapely backside peeping out of black lace lingerie. She spun back onto the desk. It was uncluttered apart from pictures of the High Commissioner's wife and his dog, Mountbatten. As if reading her thoughts, Peter stood up and removed the framed photos to a side table, turning them away to face the wall.

'The old man keeps a good malt whisky.' He twisted the cork with an audible squeak from a bottle of 21-year-old Glenfarclas Glenlivet. 'I am sure he wouldn't mind us having a taster.'

'Really, Peter, I never knew you could be so reckless!'

Peter filled two generous tumblers of neat malt. He sunk into the plush leather chair with his whisky and watched Margery as she relaxed full length across the desk and then turned, with her chin supported by her hand.

'Bottoms up.' She raised her glass and took a large gulp, clumsily spilling a few drops over the immaculate, polished table. Surprised, she ran a finger over the spillage and sucked her finger dry. For greater comfort on the hard surface, she bent one leg, leaving it swaying in the air, and stretched out the other so her toes could reach his arm.

'You look reckless yourself spread out on the High Commissioner's desk.'

Peter drained his whisky.

'Peter,' she purred, 'I have given up my Sunday to debrief this lad rescued from pirates. I'm sorry you have had all the hard work and I feel I have done nothing.'

'No, you were useful in getting the young man to relax. It was my fault for not following up to extract more information from him. You put him at ease.'

'That's what I'm good at—putting people at ease. Your resolve dealing with those poor people was *so* impressive. But, as you say, sometimes a firm hand is the best approach.'

Peter was sweating in the stuffy atmosphere. 'It's boiling in here,' he wiped his forehead with a handkerchief.

'Yes. You need some fresh air and you have had a tense time.' She slipped off the desk and hoisted him out of his chair to stand face-to-face. He smelt and then tasted a wave of malt whisky as their mouths merged and her fingers released the buckle of his brown leather belt. Carefully she extracted the strap, twisting it in fascination before discarding it on the desktop behind her. Her graceful actions mesmerised Peter. He stared ahead at the disapproving picture of the Queen staring down from the wall as Margery followed his gaze.

'Don't worry about her,' she reassured him with a laugh. 'Anyhow, there are *no* security cameras in here.'

Chapter 37

The SEAAIR eighteen seater twin prop flew in low over Tawi-Tawi. Lucas was gripping the locked pilot bag containing 230,000 dollars equivalent to ten million pesos. It had been impossible to source enough one thousand peso notes from Singapore, so he had opted for fifty, and one hundred US dollar used bills, which packed neatly into his case. The weight was about thirteen kilogrammes—light for so much cash. Vargas expected another day before Aziz decided. If he held out for more money, Lucas was a quick ferry trip away from Labuan to draw out extra to complete the deal.

Tawi-Tawi was a hilly island covered in a thick shroud of trees. At the water's edge, a stretch of white coral sand glistened as the sea rolled into shore. In the distance, more low-lying elongate islands of the Sulu Archipelago stretched out to infinity. On first sight, it looked green, which surprised Lucas as Hamza had told him the government had cleared over ninety-five per cent of the forests in a felling programme in the 1960s and 1970s. Many of the congressional representatives, who were also landowners or part of the supply chain, destroyed valuable forest for the fine furniture trade.

'It looks green,' said Hamza. 'But it's all palm oil trees they plant to replace the forest.'

'I suppose the changes killed most of the bird life and animals.'

'Yes, they kill many rare birds. The brown turtle dove only lives on Tawi-Tawi. Now less than ten survive. They ruin our land. That is why we want our freedom.'

The plane descended to the short airstrip at Bongao, the capital of Tawi-Tawi. The grass was close-cropped by grazing cattle. Sanga-Sanga airport was small and basic and even lacked an X-ray machine to check passenger's baggage. The lack of scrutiny attracted the terrorist groups such as Abu Sayyaf, secure knowing the island was a useful haven with fast ferry and flight connections for travel to Sabah, Malaysia and Kalimantan. The locals greeted Lucas with polite smiles, always inquisitive of new arrivals. A few adventurous tourists sought this location off the beaten track, ignoring the stark warnings by foreign governments to avoid such a high-risk region. Those that did come were young back-packers, divers and bird spotters.

Hamza fielded a few questions, and the men hired a tricycle taxi to town—a colourful motorbike with an attached sidecar. The driver sped off in a sweep of dust, avoiding a cow, and merged into a chaotic cluster of identical tricycles. The fifteen-minute journey to the commercial jetty was noisy and dangerous. As they approached the port, the welcome sight of *Eastern Pearl* unrolled before them. It was the largest boat amongst a sea of small wooden craft and shoppers crowding the quayside for the vast range of merchandise from the market stalls. They arrived in time to see two naval officers climbing up the gangway. Hamza looked nervous and refused to board until the navy men left. Lucas handed him a 100-peso note to buy chicken and noodles for lunch from the market stalls. More than enough for a feast for both of them.

Lucas hurried onboard and found the captain and the navy men on the bridge.

'Mr Miffré, sir,' said Jaffar. 'We have a visit from the navy, a lucky coincidence.' Lucas noticed a thick, bloodstained bandage covering the crown of his head. It needed a fresh dressing. However, before he could commiserate, the visitors, standing by the chart table, walked forward.

'I am Captain Ramos, and my colleague is Lieutenant Fernandez,' he motioned towards a junior man in dark glasses who stayed back, refusing to acknowledge the introduction. 'I understand you are the owner of this boat?'

'No. We have chartered it from the owners in Singapore. My name is Lucas Miffré. We are doing a project on behalf of your National Museum in Manila. At least we were until this pirate attack.'

'Mr Miffré. We know your situation. I came to inform you of the latest news.'

To ease the tension, Lucas offered the men cigarettes. Captain Ramos accepted, but the lieutenant waved the offer aside. Jaffar ran up with a lighter, ever the attentive acolyte.

'Thank you, I am fond of French cigarettes,' he exhaled deeply. 'I think we are nearer to getting the release of your friends. On Sunday, a patrol launch intercepted the bandit's boat near Languyan. There was a brief exchange of fire, killing four and eleven more surrendered. One of these later died of his injuries. We took the prisoners to our base at Batu-Batu and interrogated them. They admit belonging to Aziz's gang. As they have proved cooperative, we know where Aziz is holding your people.'

'What wonderful news!' said Jaffar.

'A needless loss of life.'

Captain Ramos cast an accusing glance at his lieutenant, who snapped his head back in surprise, the rebuke like a slap. 'It will not be easy. The pirate's camp is high in the hills, in thick forest and well protected, so we cannot risk an assault—a foolhardy venture. In any confrontation, we lose many men.'

Lucas looked worried. He agreed a head-on attack was too risky and might endanger the lives of the prisoners.

'It can happen. You know the case of the American missionaries—the Burnhams? We rescued the man's wife, but sadly, Martin Burnham and another hostage died during our rescue attempt in June. But our security forces lost twenty-two men on attacks against Abu Sayyaf to free them. Too high a price to pay! Now we prefer to give time for these things to work out.'

'So what is the solution?' Lucas shrugged. 'From your experience, what's the best course of action?'

'Do nothing. Mr Miffré, has Aziz contacted you for a ransom payment?'

'Yes, he has been in touch with our agent in Zamboanga. The first demand was for fifty million pesos. They reduced by half, and then we counter-offered with ten million. I am still waiting to hear if that is acceptable.'

Distracted, Lucas looked from the bridge at the hectic activities in the port. Hard to imagine beneath this veneer of normality men would spy on them. The mere fact of naval officers boarding a commercial vessel was enough for rumours to fly. By now press reports of the pirate attack near Basilan had circulated around the world. The navy attack on the gang close to Tawi-Tawi would be big news. Despite efforts to stop speculation in the press, some in Tawi-Tawi would know where they were and who was holding them.

'Good. Are you negotiating for both hostages?'

'The offer is a package to include both prisoners. If your people want to add something, I'm sure it can help.'

'Keep them talking, but our government won't get involved. When Aziz hears what has happened, he may settle. But only ten million pesos for two hostages is too low. Better, give them "face." I doubt if they accept this.'

'Perhaps he will kill the hostages in revenge?'

'No, Mr Miffré. It is not their way. But one of the slain criminals was the brother of Aziz. This makes it more difficult to settle. And they have a youth called Gerardo. He used to be with Abu Sayyaf until his cruelty was too much for them. This man is dangerous—a murderous psychopath. He murdered captives on this island two years ago, even though a ransom deal was in progress. A sadistic killer, he loves to torture and then behead his victims. The lives of your friends are at risk unless the group can control him.'

Lucas looked horrified at these fresh revelations.

'Was he the one who forced his prisoners to run away? A chance for freedom, but he shot them as they ran?'

Ramos laughed. 'No, I don't think so. It must be another case. No, Gerardo always severs the heads of his victims. He never wastes bullets.'

Ramos wanted to save Michael and the girl, but the capture of Aziz and Gerardo was most important. The lieutenant glanced at his watch; they were wasting valuable time. Jaffar hovered nearby, and in the brief interlude, he seized an opportunity to interrupt.

'Mr Miffré, we need fuel and water most urgently. However, the lack of funds has prevented me from proceeding with a top-up of supplies.'

'I meant to ask Vargas to sort this out. Will they accept payment on a credit card?'

'No, sir—I asked them. They say it has to be cash—pesos, ringitts or Singapore dollars are fine. I have to manage with the chief engineer, and one AB to run the whole boat. We haven't even got a cook.'

'Don't worry,' said Lucas, 'I'll contact the agent. With luck, the original team will return.'

Jaffar gave a resigned sigh. He wanted crew familiar with the vessel. No way would he sail for Singapore without them.

Lucas peeled off a wad of dollar bills from his wallet for Jaffar to arrange bunkering. As the officers were leaving, Ramos held back to let Fernandez walk ahead, stopping in the doorway to the bridge. He gestured Lucas over, handing him a pen and a writing pad. He requested Lucas write the contact details of the agent. Lucas always carried a notebook with essential phone numbers and email addresses, although in Tawi-Tawi with no mobile phone coverage and only a few internet cafes in Bongao communication was a low priority. Ramos recognised the name and told Lucas they considered Vargas trustworthy. In the trade of barter and brokering for life and survival, it was best to have an excellent negotiator and listen to his advice.

Chapter 38

Since the ill-fated press conference at the British High Commission, the headlines had been all about Julie. The right-wing papers praised her stand to resist payment of a ransom as a heroic, unselfish gesture, but others questioned the motive behind her principled stance. One suggested an unsatisfactory marriage and an attempt to get revenge on a selfish husband. Another suggested she was pursuing an affair—a rumour based on a trusted source. This lie enraged Julie. Someone must have seen her by the poolside talking to Luigi.

Journalists clamoured to get past the guard post at Pagoda Villas—not a difficult condominium to enter, and some found an unguarded exit gate where they gained entry when a resident left to go shopping. The telephone kept ringing. At first, Julie let the answerphone take the calls, and then listened to the frantic offers of exclusive deals. After the dust settled, an arrangement to publish her side of the story to the likes of the Daily Mail was a choice as appealing as standing on cut glass, or jumping in a scalding hot bath. She would resist such offers regardless of the promised payment. According to the tearful phone calls from her mother back home, the UK press picked up on the story in a big way. Well-wishers plus a few negative trolls besieged her poor parents. Worse, though, the intrusive press were turning up at their home in Sussex for comments. But this attention should not have surprised Julie. At least the local media, as represented by the Straits Times, was careful not to upset the Singapore government, ruled ever since independence by the People's Action Party. It constrained their journalists to keep to party politics, such as covering the latest visit to a housing development estate by a PAP Minister. No chance of groundbreaking journalism here. This government control extended to the television, which broadcast the dullest news showing a controlled upbeat view of life in Singapore contrasted to the chaos of the rest of the world. Michael joked that the manipulated propaganda was close to becoming reality. In his view, Singapore really was the perfect country.

Julie put the phone back in case Lucas or Peter Dempsey called. The constant ringing was driving her crazy. At first, she tolerated the press intrusion. Better than tense inactivity and brooding silence—a welcome change of pace. She longed to visit the poolside, or just wander in the grounds, but did not dare.

Alex joined her to watch dramatic footage on the six o'clock news of the Philippine navy gloating over four corpses involved in the attack on the *Eastern Pearl*. An officer regretted another man had since died of his injuries. The group were part of the attack party on the vessel but then had left loaded up with booty. By luck, the Philippine navy had caught them before they could reach safety in Tawi-Tawi. The security forces welcomed any intelligence on the hostages.

Julie rubbed her forehead to relieve the searing pain rolling over her. Mentally and physically, she had reached a breaking point. Events had overtaken her appeal to Peter Dempsey that security forces exercise restraint and give negotiations a chance. It was out of control, like a driverless car plunging off a hillside. It appalled Julie at the way the Abu Sayyaf issue dominated the coverage.

'This is just a game to them. Those poor boys were teenagers,' said Julie.

'But they were killers,' said Alex. 'The one with the red headband cracked Jaffar over the head—he was Aziz's younger brother.'

Julie winced, unable to watch more. 'Did he kill the guard?'

'No, that was Gerardo—he stayed on board the boat with Aziz. I guess he is guarding Pa and Christina.'

'Turn it off before they interview another bloody expert. I can't hang around here; surely we can do something?'

'Why not call Peter Dempsey for an update? He was helpful.'

'I'm not so sure. I found him insincere at the embassy meeting. It was a surprise because he came over and took me out for dinner the previous day and seemed genuinely concerned, but I think he has his own agenda.'

'He is keen on Margery,' said Alex. 'Like a Miss Moneypenny to James Bond relationship, if you ask me. I'm looking forward to our tennis game, mind you.'

'Peter Dempsey's inclinations are of no concern. Margery and Peter probably deserve each other! I am more worried about his role in this business. No—we are on our own and have to rely on Lucas to raise the ransom money. Also, don't you dare hobnob with the embassy staff over tennis and Pimms until they release Michael!'

'Oh, Ma, you are such a spoil-sport.'

'When we refused to tow the Abu Sayyaf line, they dropped us.'

'Yes. Like a hot brick. And your remark about not wishing to pay the ransom really surprised Peter.'

Julie conceded that caused quite a stir. The world press was treating her as a hero or a villain, depending on their stance. She suggested they drive to Orchard Road after lunch to buy the international editions to find out the latest stories they were inventing. It had been a mad moment, and Peter Dempsey's attitude provoked her to repudiate his lies and to follow up with the stunning statement that she did not approve of giving in to ransom demands. Was that the explanation, or did she mean those harsh words?

'Just to reassure you, I was trying to be helpful and follow the official line on no ransom stuff. Their reaction proves how hypocritical they are.'

'So you *do* want Pa back?'

'Naturally! I had a chat with Lucas and he reassured me they are in negotiations with Aziz and the insurance company has agreed to pay, but I don't know what their limit is. Lucas said my comments were helpful and may push Aziz into a quick agreement.'

Alex suggested that could provoke the pirates into violence against the hostages. Julie looked thoughtful and admitted that was a regrettable possibility—she never thought through the implications. That the non-payment might lead to the death of Michael and Christina was appalling.

'I haven't heard from Lucas today. Yesterday he was visiting the boat in Bongao in Tawi-Tawi, sorting it out. They are in the harbour with no money or food, and low on fuel. Once they reach a deal, they aim to use the *Eastern Pearl* to rendezvous with Aziz somewhere safe, pay the ransom and we get Michael and Christina released. That is the plan.'

'Good in theory, but it depends on trust and no double crosses,' said Alex.

Julie had an idea. She leapt up, pacing around the room. 'Let's do what they least expect. Alex, how do you get to Tawi-Tawi?'

'You can't just fly there. It's a wild place, and the airfares cost a bomb.'

'That is no problem,' Julie dismissed his concerns with a wave of her hand. 'Maybe Aziz will see us if we appeal in person to his better nature. Am I being too naïve?'

'Yes, but it's worth a shot, isn't it?'

'When the navy slaughtered those pirates, they raised the stakes. Your father and the girl are at greater risk. What if my comments on not paying a ransom reach Aziz? He might react badly. We need to be close at hand to influence a successful outcome.'

'A hands-on approach by the concerned wife might defuse those newspapers, giving you a hard time.'

'You're right, but I don't want Peter Dempsey or Lucas interfering.'

Alex went to research flights on the internet to this obscure island where they held his father prisoner. He found out plenty of flights were available at a reasonable price, but as he suspected, nothing direct. The best plan was a flight from Singapore to Manila and connection from Manila to Zamboanga, followed by another flight from Zamboanga to Sanga Sanga airport on Tawi-Tawi. The entire trip would take at least 15 hours with delays at each of the stops. Alternatively, there was the option to take the fast ferry from Zamboanga to Tawi-Tawi. Alex suggested they contact Lucas to arrange the flights as they might get a discount using his travel agent. Julie knew Lucas was away in Bongao and hard to reach when she had the brilliant idea to ask Danica to arrange flights. She dialled PanAsia's office. Danica was alone in charge and happy to oblige. She could not have been more helpful and agreed to research the best flight options and cheapest price. Julie felt tempted to ask her if she had enjoyed her dinner date with Michael at the Changi Sailing Club, but that was unnecessary. Danica told Julie how helpful Michael had been after the recent breakup with her Singaporean boyfriend.

'So sympathetic, lah. You are *so* lucky to have such a devoted husband. I was *so* upset when my relationship with Daniel broke up, but Michael took me out for lunch at the Changi Sailing Club and helped me get over it. Next week I was planning to fly to Perth to see my sister but I may rebook as I can't stand leaving while Michael is still a prisoner!'

Chapter 39

After the failure of the Philippines venture, Tong delayed his return to Singapore and diverted to Taiwan. He tried to visit the country every year. Taipei, a bustling modern town of two million, was not yet on the radar of the foreign dealers, so prices were low for rare antiques. The quality was similar to China, but much easier to arrange export licences and shipments to Singapore. Frequently, he had bought enough at rock-bottom prices to fill a twenty-foot container. Kaohsiung in the island's south was a promising destination, especially for old marine collectibles. The attractions of Kaohsiung included the good but reasonably priced hotels and the services of a discrete mistress; a woman whose skilled attentions would let him forget the unsuccessful search for the *Siren*. But, despite parading all her seductive charms, Song Lee did not excite Tong. When Song Lee glanced at her watch with a barely concealed yawn, Tong surrendered to a restless sleep. Even a visit to local antique shops yielded little of interest. In a foul mood, he checked out of the hotel to take the train back to Taipei and connect to the Sunday morning flight to Singapore.

 Back home, he felt more relaxed as he unlocked the door to the Wah Chan Clan headquarters in Chinatown. Empty, at this early hour, apart from the girl who came to clean the meeting room and make tea, if required. He loved the old lodge with the grand table and rosewood chairs. Faded pictures of his ancestors stared from the walls. The rumble of traffic and visitors increased in intensity. But it had always been so. The barred windows faced a more restless and modern Singapore, one in which opportunities grew more productive every year.

Tong opened the black pilot case, which never left his side. He unfurled the cloth, which concealed a 10 tael gold ingot, and drew the anglepoise lamp close to the tarnished metal to illuminate the Chinese hallmarks. Despite lying on the seabed for over two hundred years, the gold looked fresh and only slightly mottled. Such a surprise when he saw the gold bar because, at that time, silver was the standard high value currency in China. He checked one of his reference books to see if there were any plates of Chinese ingots from the period and found a single example of a precious ingot, but the markings were different. Tong copied the Chinese characters onto a card with the careful and practised brush stroke of a calligrapher. He planned to show the marks to an expert in Chinatown to identify the foundry and date of manufacture. It was too risky to display the ingot openly. If, as he suspected, the ingot dated from about 1750, it could fetch 20,000 US dollars at the Beijing auction house, possibly even more in New York.

He had recovered only this piece from the expedition, but was optimistic it would fetch a high price. The National Museum in Manila held the other finds until approval of an export licence—supposedly a straightforward process. Proceeds from the sale of the gold and cannon would help defray his costs. It would haunt him that a hoard of Imperial porcelain still lay buried beneath the seabed.

The girl entered the room, interrupting his thoughts. Unbidden, she poured out a cup with a unique and expensive amber tea from the island of Hainan, leaving silently. He returned to the delicate task of copying the marks and stood up to compare the results. An excellent copy. Satisfied, he rang a handbell on the desk, his signal for the young lady to return. She arrived at once as if expecting his call. Wordlessly he tapped the top of his cup, and she refilled it.

On a tray, she carried a large pile of mail and placed them by his hand. He studied the envelopes, judging which letters to open and which to ignore. The invoice from Davinder's company fell into the latter category. The survey vessel had not returned to Singapore, and they were issuing more bills despite demanding payment up-front. With the lack of success, why pay them another dollar?

One letter from the museum in Kuala Lumpur caught his attention. He presumed it must be from Dr Chiew, sending an invoice for attending the permit application meeting in Manila. Tong picked up an antique paper knife with its ivory dragon's head handle and slit it open. Like Pandora's Box, the dry words marked the death of a dream.

Dr Chiew had received a reply from the porcelain expert studying the Imperial porcelain marks. The expert's opinion, the leading man in his field, was the plate was an excellent copy but not authentic. In plain words, a fake. He believed a rival factory of the contemporary age made them. It was worth a little. The expert noticed a subtle difference in the fourth hallmark—a disparity seen before in other forgeries. Tong looked up bleakly at the window. He wondered if the Australian diver knew this? Probably not. Not that it mattered anymore.

The room turned drab from a massive cloud passing overhead—precursor to an immediate downfall. Too early for the monsoon, but these days Singapore's weather was unpredictable. Hot and dry for the last week, and the ancient wooden shutters swayed in the swift breeze, soaking up the waters. Old houses were like people: they got thirsty and needed to slake their thirst. Although one dream was dead, his lifelong quest to gain Chinese antiquities remained undimmed, and there would be other enterprises and successful acquisitions.

He walked to the sideboard. On the wall above, a black and white clan portrait of his father stared at Tong. He removed the picture, placing it on the table, to disclose a safe. A glance confirmed the room was empty. Sometimes the girl came in to clear the tea things, gliding as quietly as a nurse, eager not to wake her patients. Reassured he was alone; Tong dialled the combination numbers and opened the door. After replacing the gold bar inside, he lifted out the so-called Kangxi plate—the impostor—the crude forgery.

A final sad glance and he dropped it to the marble floor where it smashed into a thousand pieces. A crack of thunder split the air. But in Tong's mind, he saw the grinning, drunken face of the fat Australian diver as he raised an accusing finger to lay a curse upon him. At that instant, the picture of his father shot off the table and shattered, mixing with the broken shards of the worthless plate.

Tong shivered, but the death of Mitch was not his fault. Yes, he sent Yap to check up on Mohamed and Suleiman on the same night as they questioned Mitch, but Yap had acted on his initiative—it worried him that others might question the diver and discover the wreck's name and location. The divers had given an honest account and left the club. Throughout, Yap had lingered in the shadows, wearing dark glasses to avoid recognition. When the Australian left the bar, he caught up with him and got into conversation. Mitch was quite drunk and wanted to go to Newton Circus for food. But he didn't have enough money for the taxi, so Yap had offered him a lift, pretending he was heading in the same direction.

At such a late hour, the food court was quiet. Although Newton is open all night, many of the hawkers close up, especially if business is slow. Some, such as the Malaysian satay stall, always stay open. It was at the satay stall Mitch had his last meal on earth washed down with a bottle of Tiger beer. Yap paid for their food and drinks. The grateful Australian boasted about the fabulous treasure on a shipwreck called the *Siren* in the Sulu Sea. Did Mr Yap know the legend of the Sirens? Beautiful, seductive maidens, part human and part bird who called mariners onto the rocks with their bewitching songs? That happened to the East Indiaman in 1764. She sailed around the world from London to Canton without a problem. But as she neared Brutus Reef, the sailors heard the song of the Sirens, and the boat sunk in a tempest! Not only the *Siren* claimed Mitch—the area was like the Bermuda Triangle with many other ships shattered against the rocks. Talking to the Malaysian divers had brought all those memories flooding back. Along with his new friends, he planned to retrieve the priceless cargo. Even though he had revealed all he knew, including the name of the wreck and its location, he was not sure whether he could trust them. Although he had dived on the wreck site 15 years ago, he could still remember every detail and undulation of the seabed. It was so fresh in his memory. He could find it again. But they would have to hurry—some Chinese investor had caught wind of things and was planning another expedition! Yap could not believe his luck. The diver was a mine of information, but such loose talk was a risk.

After their meal, Yap agreed to drive him back to the Mitre. Once in the car, he took a deliberate wrong turning towards the canal and, laughing, both men went to relieve themselves. A quick shove from Yap in the back propelled Mitch over the railings and into the water—a neat end to the problem. If the Malaysian divers planned to double-cross Tong, they would meet a similar fate.

Chapter 40

Bongao was not yet on the tourist map. There were only three hotels on offer. The Beachside Inn was the top recommendation, and if Lucas had seen the others, he would know this was the right choice. But the hot water was lukewarm, and he could not get the cable TV to work. He was so tired he slept well, retiring to bed early because there was nothing else to do. Its best feature was the peaceful setting with a view of the volcanic peak at Bud Bongao, the highest point. Lucas hired a tricycle and took a brief look around town. For security, he had left the case with the ransom money on board the boat, locked in the safe. The sparse eating-places did not appeal, and with no bars or fellow tourists, he felt exposed and returned to his hotel.

The next morning Lucas raised the Venetian blind, and a wave of heat and light invaded his bedroom. Sunbirds, with their fast wing beats, danced around the hibiscus, sipping on the nectar. A young smiling girl served him murtabak with strong local coffee and orange juice, and he was alone in the enclosed garden with the staccato rhythm of cicadas.

Vargas was due on the Zamboanga to Bongao ferry at lunchtime, so he had a few hours to kill with simple choices: either take a gentle stroll or return to the boat. Instead, he picked up an East Malaysia Daily Express abandoned on an adjoining table. The police were searching Tawi-Tawi for two Malaysian fishermen abducted by bandits believed to be Abu Sayyaf. It shocked him to read they had been missing for ten months. New intelligence suggested they had recently transferred to Tawi-Tawi from Basilan Island. So long, and no deal. How naïve he was to get involved with this foolhardy venture.

Vargas had caught the ferry at five in the morning from Zamboanga and seven hours later disembarked at Bongao. He preferred the ship to the plane, even though the flight was only forty-five minutes. The boat had stopped at Jolo to drop off and pick up fresh passengers. First-class in air-conditioned comfort and a high price meant there were few customers. The alternative slow ferry was much cheaper, but took seventeen hours on a roundabout tour of several islands in the Archipelago. Okay, for a leisurely tourist on a budget.

Lucas met the ferry, and the men found a proper taxi rather than the basic tricycles favoured by the locals. They went back to the Beachside Inn for a bite of lunch. Tension built like the taut bow of an arrow. When Vargas had tried to discuss the case, Lucas had stopped him, raising a finger to his lips, signifying silence.

'We can talk now. I didn't want the driver to listen to our conversation.'

Lucas escorted him to the gardened terrace, as an aggressive mynah bird, legs astride finished leftover noodles. 'Have you heard from Aziz?'

'Yes, he rejects your offer and insists on twenty million for a ransom deal—that is, five million less. At least you guys are moving closer together.'

'Vargas, to get this business settled fast, I have two hundred and seventy thousand dollars in used notes with me.'

Vargas looked impressed and took his calculator out.

'At the current exchange rate that's ten million pesos—the same as your original offer which he has refused.'

'But used US dollars are a big bonus. It is a stronger currency than the peso.'

'What denomination notes do you have?'

'They are fifty or one hundred.'

'Can you show me?'

'They are on board the boat; check later.'

It concerned Vargas as there were several counterfeits in circulation. Years ago, perfect forgeries of one-hundred-dollar bills turned up in the Middle East. The forgers put in a deliberate mistake.

'They left a minor detail wrong on the face of the note because in most Arab countries, counterfeiting currency carries the death penalty. Forgers can claim they weren't making a real forgery.'

'Can you spot forgeries?'

'No, that's a job for an expert, but the point is people don't trust a hundred dollar note, and Aziz might not accept them, even if they are genuine.'

Lucas groaned at the prospect of changing his high-value notes into smaller denominations. What a nightmare! It would increase the weight and need several cases to transport.

'Can you raise to fifteen million? Maybe Aziz will settle for a deal.'

'I want to stick with my original bid of ten million cash, which he can have tomorrow when he hands back Michael and Christina.'

Vargas' mouth was gaping open in disbelief. Lucas touched his arm to calm him. 'And add an extra five million as the fee for providing security for us when we return to complete our mission.'

'Oh no, he will not accept that.'

'Why not? He gets what he wants, and we finish the job. We are on the cusp of finding a significant cache of porcelain, one that will at least equal, if not surpass, the Mike Hatcher salvage from the *Geldermalsen*.'

Vargas looked interested and requested more details about the value of the cargo rescued from the shipwreck.

'Going by memory, I believe the Christie's sale raised twenty-five million dollars, but since then Hatcher found the wreck of the Chinese junk the *Tek Sing* in the South China Sea. She had a cargo of 350,000 pieces of Chinese porcelain. When she sunk on a reef over two thousand people drowned—a loss of life greater than the *Titanic*.'

'Incredible.'

'Aziz needs to understand the bigger picture, and I need you to convince him.'

Captain Ramos stood next to the helmsman as they came alongside Batu-Batu naval base, ready to disembark after a routine patrol of the borders with Sabah and Indonesia. Their ex-US navy Swift patrol boat bristled with twin Browning heavy machine guns, two grenade launchers, and a crew of six. Since Lieutenant Fernandez had joined the unit, these trips were a strain. Fernandez was a sullen youth who had ingratiated himself with the other men, but resented and disliked Ramos. The dislike was mutual. Ramos considered the man was not officer material, and he was not sure he could trust him.

As Ramos strode up the jetty towards his office, the recent action near Languyan against the pirate gang preoccupied his mind. The men captured from the longboat confirmed they planned to join Aziz. They claimed to be from Jolo Island. Being unfamiliar with Tawi-Tawi, a guide was meant to take them to the jungle camp. They admitted the attack on the Frenchmen's boat but said it had been a random raid as they chanced upon the vessel. If they had seen the Moro guards onboard, they would have left them alone. Lieutenant Fernandez had been questioning them with little success, and they had no more to give. This case, plus a long-running abduction of two Malaysians believed held somewhere in Tawi-Tawi, was giving him a headache.

'Captain, the commander, wants to have a word.'

It was the duty-officer staffing the front desk who spoke, a middle-aged woman who had worked at the Batu-Batu base ever since Ramos could remember. It was unusual for a formal request like that because the command base was fairly informal. Normally if you had a question, you wandered into the commander's office as his door was always open.

'Captain, I have seen your report on this latest hostage-taking incident. Sit down and update me with any fresh developments.' The commander was pacing the room impatiently.

'Right, sir. I believe our prisoners haven't been forthcoming.'

'And that's another problem. You have given this junior lieutenant a free hand to interrogate them.'

'But I expected him to act with restraint.'

'Well, one prisoner has sustained a fractured skull from a nasty fall against the wall. He is not likely to survive.'

Ramos stood up, alarmed. 'When did this happen?'

'This morning, while you were on patrol. If we had useful intelligence, that is one thing, but this looks like pointless violence. There are no witnesses, so it ties my hands.'

'I think the lieutenant over-reacted during the recent action. I had to restrain him from killing all the pirates.'

'Did you put this in your report? I don't recall it.'

'No, not in so many words.'

'We must shift him to other duties. He is off active patrols. There may be disciplinary procedures, and if the prisoner dies, there will be lots of reports to write.'

'Yes, sir. I will see to it.'

He was secretly pleased. It looked like Fernandez would not be bothering him much longer. The commander came and sat down opposite Ramos and offered him a cigarette.

'In January, the Americans sent one hundred US Special Forces to the Philippines as advisers to help train our team. George Bush, the US President, agreed this after the kidnap of the Burnhams. They base the Americans in Basilan to help us fight Abu Sayyaf.'

Captain Ramos pretended surprise even though he knew this. 'Surely they cannot get involved in the fighting?'

'Correct, our Philippine constitution will not permit. However, they can assist technically and logistically. If attacked, they can defend themselves. Since the Twin Towers attack last year, President Arroyo is looking to cement relations with America and is seeking more US aid to deal with our Muslim insurgency.'

'How does this affect us?'

'The Americans know of the assault on the *Eastern Pearl*. They blame Abu Sayyaf, despite evidence to the contrary. As a result, they are sending a squad of marines over from the Basilan contingent. Expect them here tomorrow.'

The commander walked over to the window, gazing out thoughtfully. 'Pointless trying to make them see sense. They won't listen, so why waste our breath? How can we use this to our best advantage? A force that cannot fight is less than useless, but we may achieve a beneficial strategy. Our objectives are to secure the safe release of the hostages and capture of Aziz and his little group. Do you not agree?'

'Do we have a name for the leader of this American contingent?' asked Ramos. The commander rifled through the papers on his desk.

'Yes, the squad is under the command of a Captain Leroy—a decorated Gulf War veteran. That does not impress me. Tawi-Tawi is no desert.'

'Right, sir,' said Ramos. 'The terrain is not unlike Vietnam and may prove just as lethal for our American friends.'

Chapter 41

Another day dawned over the forest after heavy rainfall lifted. The delicate filigree of a thousand enmeshed spiders clung to the jungle canopy. Michael stared through the barred window of his hut as shafts of sunlight, magnified through the prism of web-trapped raindrops, pierced through the trees to dissipate, so only a few beams penetrated. On the nearest bush, he saw a small-bodied spider with elongated, hairy legs, spread-eagled in its trap, motionless, waiting for its victim.

A swallowtail butterfly was flitting towards the blood-red hibiscus, next to the web, and Michael tried to distract it in case it was caught. Bitterly, he knew it was his greed and stupidity that had led him into this foolish venture. Like the butterfly careless of danger, they had succumbed to Lucas's manic plan. His most significant concerns were for Julie and Alex, dragged along as victims and now Christina, an innocent party, just trying to do her job.

Overhead, the chorus of birds surpassed each other in their preening beauty and song. He recognised the bluster of the racket-tailed drongo as the bird flashed through the trees, unfurling its fan-shaped tail. Michael drank in the scene with a heightened awareness, conscious that the birth of this fresh day could be his last on earth. He consoled himself as they had survived the most critical period. Since his punishment, Gerardo was less of a threat, banished to other tasks. After the unsuccessful attempt to burrow out of their prison, they locked Christina up in a separate hut. Fortunately, they were close enough to communicate. The guards only opened to bring them food or release them for a toilet call.

However, Gerardo often squatted outside Christina's hut staring in through the bars directing his hatred like a piercing light, so strong she was forced to sit with her back against the door.

With each day of their survival, Michael was more optimistic. Either Lucas would pay the ransom, or the security forces might attempt a rescue. Christina had told him the most dangerous situation was if the army mounted an assault. The last thing they needed was raw recruits firing off volleys from their M16s and wiping out anyone that moved.

Left unattended for lengthy periods, the unrelenting boredom of their imprisonment depressed them. With inactivity came no chance of escape. Sometimes the men foraged for wild game and left them alone, apart from the old retainers. Using every opportunity, they shouted themselves hoarse, hoping a passing patrol might find them.

This morning there was a distinct mood in the camp with everyone up early, moving with urgency and packing up rucksacks.

'Michael, something's up. I think they are about to leave.'

Deep in the forest, a sudden surge in activity from the macaque monkeys alarmed the guard, who rushed to the edge of the hill to see what could have disturbed them.

'Let's hope it's an attack,' said Michael, beyond caring anymore. Anything to end the nightmare was welcome. 'This place will swarm with crack troops.'

The guard ran off to join his comrades, grouping beside the cluster of attap huts to draw out more arms and ammunition. Another false alarm, like many others. Whatever had jinxed the monkeys had gone, and the jungle canopy closed once more to hide its secrets.

The woman brought them breakfast. Gruel made of manioc, a bowl of rice flavoured with pieces of pork, and a mug of rainwater tasting earthy.

'Aziz isn't around this morning,' said Michael, looking across at the cluster of unshaven figures, eating *Pancit Bihon*, a noodle dish with chunks of wild boar.

'He left at first light to make a call from a satellite station they use nearby. He went yesterday to discuss a deal.'

Christina raised her voice. It was a mystery to Michael how she always found out information before him.

'How do you know this?'

'When he came back, he was angry, marching about, and stared across at our huts. I think they must be near to an agreement.' Christina broke off as she noticed Aziz walking towards Michael's hut.

'Your boss does not value your life or the life of the museum girl. So what to do?' Aziz glared at Michael through the wire grill.

'These negotiations take time. They want a deal.'

'Yes, you are right, but they think we make empty threats. So we step up the pressure. This afternoon is their last chance. If no agreement, then we keep our promise to give you a beating. It will be just like for Gerardo. Except maybe more. So tonight we see how brave you are.' He had raised his voice so Christina could hear. Best to let them feel the fear.

An hour later, after Aziz had left, Gerardo approached Christina's hut.

'You need to get cleaned up. I take you to the river for a wash and make you smell better. You first. Then I return for your friend.'

He aimed the gun at Christina and pushed her down the hill. Christina was nervous as they walked the short distance from the camp, his gun trained on her back. When they reached the river, he told her to wash. He even handed her a bar of soap and a towel.

The river opened into a shallow lagoon shaded by overhanging trees dappled by sunshine. The main thrust of the stream followed a deeper channel with a strong current. She squatted at the rocky edge, soaking her feet, but with Gerardo so close, it concerned her. Christina moved further away and paddled in the shallows, letting the water wash out the ingrained dirt and filth of the camp. Meanwhile Gerardo sat preoccupied whittling a stick with a knife, indifferent to her. His preoccupation reassured her and she relaxed and enjoyed the cool water.

She wandered further from the bank towards a cluster of rocks to give her more privacy. The water was deeper, the rough riverbed more uneven, with sudden drops enticing her to swim away. Now that Gerardo was far off, she washed the grime out of her matted hair using the block of hard soap, which lathered well in the soft water. After rinsing, she submerged her face, loving the refreshing sensation as her clean tresses flowed out with the current.

Preoccupied, she did not see him wade into the river. He came up alongside her, swimming quickly, with a few powerful strokes. Blinking the water out of her eyes, she saw him looming over her. With one hand, he gripped her hair, and the other toppled her off balance and forced her underwater until her terrified struggle ceased. Dragged back from unconsciousness, Gerardo pulled Christina up and hauled her into the shallows by the bank. As she staggered backwards, he drew out a short-bladed knife from his pocket and held it against her neck.

Now he turned his attention to her T-shirt, pulling it up, so it caught her arms in a vice. She managed a single stark cry before his hand locked over her mouth, stifling all noise. Christina freed one arm and scratched his face, causing him to yell with pain and gain her precious seconds. She broke away, but in her confusion ran towards the steep riverbank. With no escape, he drove her back against the rocks and pushed her into a fissure, so she was cornered. Powerless to retreat, the rock hemmed her in a trap.

In midstream, the water surged past with high pressure from the recent rains and Christina knew a dash into the deep waters was her only chance. He watched her fear as he pressed down on her. No hurry, he could take his time. Gerardo placed one hand, gripping the knife, next to her throat while his other loosened his shorts. She bit into his arm, drawing blood. With a cry, he dropped the knife and slapped her hard across the face. He renewed his attack. She countered and forced her knee up, jabbing between his legs. Although winded, he fell on top of her, allowing his strength to overpower her. Crushed and trapped, she felt a wave of nausea roll over her, overwhelmed by his animal stench. Panicky, her breath came in frightened bursts as fight drained away. Her well-aimed kick had won her more time, and he took a minute to recover.

'We are alone. No one can help you. Now I make you pay for your lies to Aziz.'

Gerardo adjusted his position, pinning her tighter into the rock cleft as he searched for the knife he had dropped. With a grunt of satisfaction, he retrieved it from a crack in the rocks.

'When I have finished, I will slit your throat and watch you die!'

His rank, stale breath surged over her like chloroform deadening a butterfly. She turned her head against the rock—anything to avoid him.

'The river will carry your body away and out to sea for the sharks. They will never find you. I warned you not to go too deep in the strong current.'

He was laughing in a sarcastic, taunting tone as the end of his knife cut her neck. Only a scratch, but enough to stain the water red. She toyed with an idea to drive her neck into the knife to end her life quickly, but he withdrew the knife as he fumbled with her clothes. She swung her head round to face him, to curse him; defiant in death. Her last memories were of his cruel smile.

Chapter 42

Vargas had arranged an afternoon call to a secure VSAT station at a logging camp near Aziz's hideout in the hills. He organised their calls early to avoid the workers, but today was a holiday, and the camp was empty. Aziz came with armed men. The guard, a trusted contact, met them at the gate and unlocked the office, urging them to be quick. Right on time, Vargas rang. It was a weak signal, but it was the only choice with no cell phone connections to these outlying islands.

'I'm spelling out the facts for you,' said Vargas. 'Once you seized hostages you entered a different league. Have you considered this suggestion from the Frenchman?'

'What his offer of ten million pesos plus another five million if we guard him as he continues his search? We cannot work with these people. Our only deal is to return one hostage for ten million and the other we keep until he pays the full ransom. If you double cross us, we kill both the hostages.'

'I thought you agreed to settle for fifteen million for both captives?'

'That was yesterday. Now you must pay the same price for the second person, or we make a trade with Khadaffy Janjalani.'

'I doubt if the leader of Abu Sayyaf is keen when his followers can take a foreigner for ransom any day of the week. Will you release the woman but keep the Englishman back?'

'I did not say that. The man is worth more because of the press interest, so his value increases.'

'Aziz, it's only a matter of time before the marines find your camp. I told you yesterday they captured your men. We assume they have talked.'

'None of them know the location. If anyone finds us, we can fight.'

'You think you are secure, but you are not. They are planning an attack—possibly by helicopter. So best settle. Lucas has raised the money. The security forces will allow the hostage exchange to go ahead without interference.'

'And you believe them?' Aziz shouted in contempt.

Vargas ignored this outburst.

'Yes, I trust Captain Ramos. The arrangement is simple. The Frenchman pays you ten million pesos to release the Englishman and the girl unharmed. He has it in US dollars in Tawi-Tawi.'

'He is here?'

'Listen, it's a good plan. But Lucas wants your help. Offer them protection when they go back to search for the shipwreck. He settles the ransom for the release of both the hostages. Then you earn another five million standing by while they finish their work. If he recovers it, everyone benefits.'

'Good for him, yes. No way the navy will let us stay and protect them while they continue with their treasure hunt.'

'He wants you to use the second payment for a worthy cause, such as building a school or a clinic to help the poor people of Tawi-Tawi. It is an excellent scheme.'

'Now he tells me how to spend my money. There is no way this will work.'

'He has drawn out ten million in cash. It is all he can raise. Not possible for him to go higher. Let's settle this now, I urge you to accept it.'

'If they continue to look for the wreck, Abu Sayyaf will attack them next time,' said Aziz. 'Okay, tell him to contact us in Puerto dos Amigos with the money—but not ten million. It has to be fifteen million, and we walk away afterwards with no protection for them. Best they leave our lands and never return. If they decide to continue their survey, they do so at their own risk. But we guarantee not to interfere with them again.'

'That is not much of a concession. I doubt if he can raise the extra cash just like that. Stay where you are as he is waiting to hear from me. I hope to get a decision.'

The fast developments surprised Aziz. 'Okay. Let Mr Miffré meet two days from now at the earliest. Or we make them sweat for another week. He should come, unarmed, to Puerto dos Amigos to a safe point for the exchange. If we see anyone else with him, we will execute the hostages. I am only settling for such a low figure because I, too, want a quick solution. Also, we demand the release of my brothers.'

'Aziz the navy won't agree to these terms, as you know. Cooperate, and we may get them off without a capital sentence. It was foolish of your man to kill Raspal. How do I explain this to his family?'

'Tell Hamza to meet us in peace, and we give him money for Raspal's family. We do not argue with our Muslim brothers, but they must come unarmed.'

'They mean business this time, Aziz. Because they believe you are Abu Sayyaf, they will hunt you down without mercy. If the Americans get involved, I fear for the lives of the hostages. The Philippine forces will sweep through the villages as they did before, with indiscriminate slaughter. I hear reports you have mistreated the prisoners. Do not harm them—we cannot tolerate that. Cooperate, or we walk away from this.'

'One of my brothers, just a youngster, upset the girl, and we punished him. It has caused unrest amongst my men, and they wish to punish the foreigners. We wish justice for those that have died. I am resisting their demands to kill a hostage, but I may have to give the man a beating to satisfy them.'

It appalled Vargas. He ordered Aziz to exercise restraint when they were so close to a solution.

'Aziz, I am calling Mr Miffré now with your last offer of 15 million pesos plus your promise of non-interference if they choose to continue the survey. We will arrange another call at the same time tomorrow to let you know his reply.'

Aziz and his gang hurried through the jungle back to their camp. He was losing appetite for this business. Navy marines were hunting them. Tawi-Tawi was too small to evade the security forces. He should move. Easy to hire a launch in Languyan and hide on one of the nearby islets. They were many low-lying and forested coral atolls, although none were suitable for a lengthy stay. Once they agreed on the ransom the next challenge was the tricky business of completing the handover and escaping.

Back at the camp, Aziz walked over to the hut where they kept Michael imprisoned. In his mind, he had decided they must punish him. It was necessary to prove his authority because Gerardo was a challenge, winning the men with his passionate cruelty and religious bigotry. Despite being close to a deal, he had to do this. The men were itching to harm the captives, so giving in to their demands by flogging the man was the best solution.

It surprised Aziz to see the door of the girl's cell wide open. He asked where she was. To him, she was the unlawful representative of the Christian Philippines of Manila, the colonial power and occupying force.

'Gerardo took her to the river for a wash half an hour ago. Someone should find out if she's all right,' said Michael, looking worried. It alarmed Aziz, as he had not ordered Gerardo to do this. After the earlier episode, they did not allow him near the girl. He was too unpredictable.

'I will check on her myself. Come with me,' Aziz unbolted the door to let Michael out and they ran through the bush to the river.

Christina must have blacked out. When she came round, she felt the firm pressure of Gerardo's body relax as he slid away into the current. In his hand, he still gripped the knife. A pool of blood stained the surrounding water. She thought it was hers and her hand ran along her neck where he had cut her, but the wound was slight. Gerardo lay floating face down and motionless, the back of his skull hammered open by a rock held by someone crouched nearby in the shallows. As her eyes focused, she noticed a short, wiry man, heavily tanned— a hunter or forest dweller. Silently he handed over her wet clothes and by sign language showed she should get dressed.

'Is he dead?' she asked, fearful even now, he would regain consciousness.

The hunter understood her and nodded. He turned his back while she pulled on her top, sensitive to her feelings, and when she next looked up, he had vanished, melting away into the trees like a ghost.

Gerardo drifted into deeper water in the channel. Free of the rocks, his body gained speed and disappeared out of sight—all evidence lost. The only sign of the attack was the knife wound to her neck. Turning slowly, she wandered to the bank and was standing, still dazed, gazing at the river when Aziz and Michael found her.

'Where is Gerardo?' said Aziz.

She was too shocked to speak but pointed at the river. Aziz ran to higher ground, looking downstream as far as the waterfall, but there was no sign of Gerardo in the water.

'What happened to you?' Michael looked at the wound to her neck. 'Did he attack you?'

'Yes—he tried to rape me. And then he was going to slit my throat. I passed out. When I came to, he was lying dead in the water. A bushman stood over him holding a rock so he must have killed Gerardo.'

When Aziz returned from searching for Gerardo, Michael repeated Christina's explanation.

'*Inshallah*,' Aziz shrugged. As they walked back to the camp, Aziz told Michael that Vargas was completing a deal with an exchange to take place in Puerto dos Amigos in two day's time. Lucas Miffré was already in Tawi-Tawi and planned to bring along the cash in person. They could leave with him onboard their boat.

'*Eastern Pearl* is still here?'

'Yes, she is at berth in Bongao according to your agent. Although we have agreed, it is most likely your people will double cross us. With Gerardo's death, my men will clamour for revenge. I may have to subject you to a beating to satisfy them. This is a dangerous time for you, so I will assign one of my trusted men to guard you.'

Chapter 43

At last, Vargas had negotiated a deal with Aziz for both the hostages for fifteen million pesos—a fraction of the original asking price, so he was well pleased. Lucas had no guarantee for protection for future work, just a tacit agreement that Aziz would tolerate them without interference. Lucas was too tired to keep the negotiations running *ad infinitum*. He had no enthusiasm to continue the survey so best to settle. With his team back in Singapore, it was no longer a feasible option.

Lucas transferred funds from his Singapore bank to the Standard Chartered in Sandakan. He took a long ferry trip from Bongao to Sabah to collect the money in US dollars late in the afternoon. With no return sailing until the following day, he stayed at a budget hotel, the Hotel London, and filled in time visiting the orangutan sanctuary at Sepilok. He caught a report on BBC World Service of Julie and Alex's arrival in Manila, en route to Tawi-Tawi. Julie had broadcast a personal appeal to the kidnappers to release Michael and Christina. They hoped to meet with officials in Bongao. This latest move surprised and worried him. Julie was proving to be a loose cannon. In her press conference at the British High Commission, she condemned ransom negotiations—a stance which had gained her both approval and condemnation in the press. However, in a private call, she had clarified how she was under pressure from the British Embassy and hoped covert negotiations and a ransom payment could lead to success. What did she hope to achieve in Tawi-Tawi when they already had the bones of an agreement in place?

The return ferry trip was a disaster; an engine failed, and it took seven hours at reduced speed, herded into the first-class upper decks like cattle. Tired, he held onto the case of money with grim determination. After the early evening arrival, he went straight to the boat to liaise with the team over plans for hostage exchange.

While watching the sunrise over the Chinese jetty from the bridge of *Eastern Pearl*, Lucas waited for an update. They refuelled the boat and were ready to leave. He did not have to wait long. Vargas phoned, happy that Lucas had raised more money but worried that Julie and Alex were heading for Tawi-Tawi. The story had been on the world news and might complicate their delicate negotiations. There was even a rumour that she planned to prevent any ransom payment and wanted to discuss satisfactory solutions with Aziz. How naïve! Lucas reassured Vargas that the press had misquoted her—she was in favour of a ransom to release Michael. No one knew how the pair were travelling from Zamboanga. There was the fast ferry direct to Bongao arriving midday or else they might catch a flight to Sanga Sanga. Either way, they should reach Bongao by early afternoon.

'Julie has got courage,' Lucas said to Captain Jaffar. 'Wait for their arrival so they can join the boat. It may help the exchange, and we don't want them rushing around with a different plan, sowing confusion. If Aziz hears they are here, it could delay the handover and encourage him to push for more money.'

Jaffar turned from the chart table and raised a quizzical eyebrow. 'Look what happened when I took on the museum girl as crew. I told you it was unlucky to have a woman on board and now you tempt fate again with this lady from England.'

'Captain, that's an old seaman's superstition.'

'Maybe, but I am not sailing blindly up to Puerto dos Amigos until I know what the plan is.'

Lucas and Hamza crowded near Jaffar as he pulled out a large-scale chart of Tawi-Tawi.

'Captain Ramos paid us another visit yesterday. He wanted information on the exchange and promised the navy would not interfere until after they release the hostages. They plan to patrol to the north of the island because they think Aziz will break out that way.'

'There's no guarantee—he could head west towards Sabah or south to Kalimantan,' said Lucas. 'Or stay on Tawi-Tawi.'

'Ramos gave me a tracker device to put in the case lining with the money. They will follow it and catch the villains,' said Jaffar. 'It's easy to activate. I can show you later.'

'I'm impressed—I didn't think they had that technology out here.'

'They don't, it comes from the Americans.'

'The Americans?'

'The American technical advisers are working with the Philippine security forces in Basilan, trying to find Khadaffy Janjalani and his mob.'

'Did you tell Ramos they plan the handover somewhere near Puerto dos Amigos?' asked Lucas, looking worried.

'Yes, was that wrong?'

'No. But with the Americans running around like headless chickens, who knows what their agenda will be?' Jaffar raised an eyebrow. He unrolled a marine chart, and they gathered around the table.

'There's only one direct route in, and that's here at Languyan and the channel towards Puerto dos Amigos.'

Lucas studied the map for suitable landfall. He felt nervous of a double-cross by the security forces. Aziz would avoid the busy port of Languyan. He was more likely to arrange the handover somewhere closer to Puerto dos Amigos. Lucas noticed an inlet to the west, which might be accessible via a small boat. It should be possible to land and move to the rendezvous point. Captain Jaffar was unwilling to sail *Eastern Pearl* too far in the shallow mangrove.

'It's a good plan,' said Lucas. 'From the chart, it looks as if we can reach the shore. The navy will stay away waiting for Aziz to escape after he has the money and handed back the hostages. Their Swift Patrol boats can reach 32 knots. We assume Aziz will escape by a fast dinghy and most likely have at least two craft hidden. If they have twin engines those things can go fast but the navy has an advantage with 50 calibre machine guns.'

'They have no chance unless they keep to the shallows. Mangrove is bad news,' said Hamza. 'If you go too far the mud can swallow you up like a hungry python.'

Lucas and Jaffar only had to look beyond the Commercial Port to see the thick mangrove swamps of the shoreline.

'Hamza, on arrival we should run a reccy with the inflatable to discover if the Americans are in the vicinity.'

The ship's satellite radio startled the men with its persistent call. It was Vargas calling, seeking an update on their departure time. Lucas said they should wait for Julie and Alex.

'I suggest they join our team on the vessel, but not to get involved in any of the action onshore, do you understand?'

'They must stay away. If Michael's wife and son go ashore, the pirates might grab them and use them as human shields.'

'What do you mean? Does Aziz know they are here?'

'We have to assume he will. They have the VSAT phone and many contacts. Nevertheless, we expect everything to run smoothly. When you reach Languyan, wait for me to confirm the time and place of the handover.'

'Should we call him as soon as we arrive?' asked Jaffar.

'Yes, captain, I heard your question. That's an excellent idea. What is your ETA?'

Jaffar and Lucas looked at each other, and after a quick consultation, they decided on five o'clock in the afternoon. If Julie and Alex were running late, they should leave without them. The midday flight was usually reliable, so that should ensure arrival in good time.

Lucas replaced the handset, a deep frown creasing his forehead. Something was not right. Sighing, he sat on the stool vacated by the captain. Jaffar was pacing, working off the tension, and wondering why he was wasting time with these mad people. Pirates, treasure hunters, Islamic fundamentalists, security forces, and now he must take on board this English woman. No one could convince him this was not inviting bad luck.

Captain Ramos tried to keep a lid on the situation. He resented outsiders homing in on his patch. He wanted the credit for capturing Aziz and Gerardo; it might lead to promotion. An unfortunate development was that Lieutenant Fernandez had ingratiated himself with Captain Leroy and the Americans. After Fernandez's behaviour in assaulting a prisoner, Ramos hoped his criticism to the provincial commander would bar him from active duties. But his role in gunning down the pirates had sparked the admiration of this Captain Leroy, a tall gum-chewing Texan, straight from central casting. They had assigned Fernandez to assist the American squad on one of their patrol boats.

Ramos stood at the doorway of his office, suppressing his anger as he saw the American soldiers, kitted out in full jungle fatigues with blackened faces, leaving with Fernandez. The Americans had blundered about and ignored him, although he was the senior officer present. Captain Leroy may have excelled in the desert campaign in the Gulf War, but the jungles of Tawi-Tawi were a different proposition. The mangrove swamps and an invisible enemy were a frustrating web to overcome. Should his men need to defend themselves, Ramos suspected Leroy's squad would shoot first and ask questions later.

Chapter 44

Finally, the boat was underway, leaving Bongao at full speed. Despite a fresh wind, with white caps cresting the waves, the vessel ploughed a steady path. The sky's colour was a deep blue with wispy clouds strung out along the receding shoreline.

They rounded the island, heading northeast past fishing villages built on stilts. Radiating out from the shore, fish traps marked by stakes sunk into the seabed formed long fences far out to sea. The lines, regimented and uniform, delineated separate territories, patrolled by small canoes, manned by women or children, while the larger boats ventured further seaward. The haunting songs of the fishermen, releasing their nets, carried on the breeze as they toiled and beat the waters with paddles, driving the fish into the nets. Their singing only ceased when they heaved the catch aboard.

Julie and Alex stared at the surging sea as the salt-licked wind sprayed over them. For Julie, this was a novel experience enjoying the exhilaration of a fast passage to meet an enemy, an outcome unknown, riding to confront evil and to overcome impossible odds. Alex had been on edge and drained by the nervous tension of the last week. Overhead a frigate bird soared high; immobile, its long slender wings hardly moved as it rode the thermals, keeping pace with the boat. Notorious for attacking boobies and terns to pinch their food, the frigate bird is also known as the pirate bird.

While Julie and Alex stood at the stern, Lucas handed them drinks.

'Thank you,' said Julie, 'so lucky to bump into you at the ferry terminal. I couldn't believe it.'

'Sorry, I meant to call and update you with the negotiations. But I have been busy trying to raise the ransom money.'

'It's so unjust having to settle these demands. On the one hand, the government is saying don't pay, and, on the other, they give the nod to our negotiations to save lives which perpetuates the cycle to repeat for future innocent victims. It is madness.'

'True, but the safe return of Michael and Christina is the priority.'

'I appreciate that. But the British High Commission in Singapore has a different agenda.'

'How do you mean?'

'An agenda to blame Abu Sayyaf,' said Alex, 'The hostage incident is a trigger to wage a fresh campaign against the terrorists.'

'Alex, they need no excuse to go after Abu Sayyaf. Peter Dempsey has been helpful, and we all agree we don't want Filipino forces barging in the middle of delicate negotiations. They don't hold a great record for rescuing hostages alive.'

'So we head to Puerto dos Amigos, give Aziz a trunkful of money, and he hands back Michael and Christina. Forgive me, but it sounds too easy.'

'If you follow the script, there should be no problem,' said Lucas. He was tired of trying to justify his actions when Julie and Alex questioned every move.

He counted out the cash in high denomination US dollar notes one last time and packed a large suitcase full. To control the weight as low as possible, he avoided smaller denominations. Now, alone, he pondered the enormous risk—a buffeting trip up the inlet to the barangay of Puerto dos Amigos followed by a secret exchange point with security forces monitoring every movement. In reality, a nervous and anxious journey with no plan.

Two hours later, Captain Jaffar slowed the engine speed to a crawl. Close inshore, near to the carpet of mangrove and in the lee of foliage cover, he paused, not daring to approach closer. Five hundred metres from a landfall east of Puerto dos Amigos, he cut the engines and dropped anchor, a noisy procedure, which caused the birds to fly out of the trees in alarm. The racket annoyed Lucas, nervous of hidden watchers in the trees. They held station for thirty minutes and searched the shore through field glasses for any sign of life. The thick, tangled mangrove was an impenetrable fortress, defying them to breach the green barbed defences.

'Let's send two of the crew ashore with Hamza,' said Lucas.

They lowered the inflatable to the water with the crewmen aboard using the small deck crane. After starting the outboard motor, the little craft sped off from the mother vessel.

Lieutenant Fernandez was with the American contingent a few hundred yards from Languyan. The Americans had set up camp within a tree-draped hollow above the town. It was a useful vantage point to monitor the marine traffic passing en route to Puerto dos Amigos.

Captain Ramos resented the role that his lieutenant held with the special American unit. He put a call through from base to Fernandez and demanded to speak to Captain Leroy. The American was standing alongside Fernandez, a pair of binoculars to his eyes as he searched the vista.

'Captain Leroy, sir, Captain Ramos—I was at the Batu-Batu base when your team arrived this morning. As the senior officer, it surprised me you didn't come and see me before leaving.'

Evidently, Leroy had rubbed this guy up the wrong way, but he did not have time for all these courtesies.

'Apologies, Captain. Lieutenant Fernandez gave us a briefing. We understood he was following your instructions. The lieutenant said not to bother you.'

'My lieutenant is not aware of the full picture. Captain, *Eastern Pearl* left Bongao at thirteen hundred. Have you spotted the boat yet?'

'No, captain, only small fishing boats in the last few hours.'

'How long have you been there?'

'We set up camp at fifteen hundred hours.'

'Languyan is only one hour sailing from Bongao. By now she might be in Puerto dos Amigos.'

Leroy scowled at Lieutenant Fernandez. 'Thanks for the warning; I guess we need to move to Puerto dos Amigos, wherever that is.'

'Right, but keep your options open.'

He cut the line before Leroy had time to reply.

'Shouldn't we take our boat up there?' asked one soldier, eager to avoid the jungle trek to Puerto dos Amigos, as they studied the map. They had a patrol boat moored up at Languyan so that might be the quickest option.

'No, the chart shows very shallow water depths. It's a quick hike by foot. If we meet this Aziz gang, I want to be on firm land and not in a tin-pot boat as if we are going duck shooting on the bayou.'

'Yeah, we'd be the sitting ducks.' The soldier joked, but his smile faded when he saw the tight set to Leroy's face.

A short time after Ramos called from Batu-Batu, Hamza ran a quick reconnaissance around Puerto dos Amigos. There were a few villagers and they noticed a busy road used by lorries transporting felled timber from the forest. A steep hill skirted the highway, with impenetrable jungle. A small mosque served the local population of fishermen and seaweed farmers.

An hour later, they rejoined their vessel and reported the area free of soldiers.

'We arrived earlier than they expected, ahead of the Americans. We should hang around here until we hear from Vargas,' said Lucas. 'Relax—take lunch and keep alert.'

'Yes,' said Alex. 'There's no sign of those American commandos.'

'I reckon they'll stake out Puerto dos Amigos. If they land at Languyan, they will have to trek across the jungle.'

'That's a crazy plan,' said Jaffar. 'Have you seen how thick the mangrove is? It's slow going and hazardous with many coral snakes.' He huffed at this complexity. 'You shouted at me for dropping the anchor. Now you want me to stay anchored under their noses?'

'Before we needed secrecy. Now it doesn't matter.'

Vargas had rung Ramos with the news that Aziz wanted the hostage exchange to take place at the mosque in Puerto dos Amigos. After Ramos conveyed the intelligence to Captain Leroy, he was pleased to gain the upper hand and push Fernandez out of the picture. He had reminded Leroy that the American squad should see the handover covertly.

When Aziz escaped out to sea, Ramos planned to have a navy patrol boat standing by to intercept them. It was handy talking to the parties as it avoided any chance of a slip-up, but the Americans were impulsive, young and undisciplined. Away from their homes, everything was strange to them, the heat, the jungle, the invisible enemy.

Vargas sat in his usual seat on the terrace of the Lantaka in Zamboanga, sipping a beer as he puzzled over the various possibilities. The highest level of the Filipino forces had guaranteed not to jeopardise the hostages. Now it was Aziz's problem. He was just the broker, marshalling the players to the dance. It startled him when his cell phone rang with a call from the commander of the navy base at Batu-Batu.

'Captain Ramos has given me an update. Your plan is unravelling,' said the commander, barely suppressing his rage. 'Mr Miffré has smelt a rat. The boat headed into the swap zone much earlier than planned.'

Vargas feigned surprise. 'Why are you so sure?'

'Not complicated, my friend. The whole of Bongao saw them leave port, full steam ahead at one o'clock. We reckon they arrived on the scene before the Special Forces. If this goes wrong, it will not look good because the Englishman's wife and son are on the boat.'

'There should be no problem if the forces exercise the restraint promised us,' said Vargas.

'We know the Americans regard the hostages as a peripheral issue. The major prize is to target Aziz. If the man's family gets hurt or even worse, killed, this will be a political disaster.'

'Commander, I urge you to do everything you can to make sure the Americans do not overreact.'

'For the future, the last thing we need is to involve foreign forces—especially the Americans.'

'I agree totally, commander. I want the business sorted out.'

Aziz had arranged for the prisoner exchange to be at six o'clock outside the mosque. The pirates were still in the hills above Puerto dos Amigos. It elated Michael and Christina when they spotted the *Eastern Pearl*'s arrival offshore Languyan, a long-lost friend. Once the boat had entered the inlet towards Puerto dos Amigos, she disappeared behind the forest of trees.

Aziz summoned his group together to sit in the shade of a large eucalyptus tree. Michael and Christina appreciated a break from the tiring trek. Aziz told his men of the proposed transaction. If forces had staked out the mosque, the imam planned to call the evening prayers ten minutes too early. This was to warn of danger. If the prayer summons was at six, it meant there were no marines.

'We may walk into a trap. We expect a minor force of American marines at the mosque. Vargas says they are hunting for Abu Sayyaf so they will assume we are terrorists. We have a promise of non-interference from our navy, and the Americans are under their command. They do not allow the Americans to interfere, so do not fire at them. If you do, they will attack.'

'It is a double-cross!' cried one man. 'Kill the captives and escape from here.'

'Brave words,' Aziz replied, 'That is the Abu Sayyaf way to execute their hostages and win publicity for their cause. But we gain nothing by slaying them.'

'We need revenge for Gerardo,' the man persisted, casting a hostile glance at Christina. 'And you promised to lash the Englishman just like you did to Gerardo, but you feed and protect him.'

'Enough,' Aziz raised his hand. 'Forget Gerardo. It is pointless to kill them when we are due to collect the ransom money. We follow through our plan as agreed.'

Michael and Christina exchanged glances of relief. The conversation reverted to Taurog as the men continued to discuss their plans.

'Do you think it will happen, Michael? We have been through so much together. Dare we hope?'

'Stay close. If there's a chance to break away and run into the jungle, we should take it.'

'Thank you for looking after me.'

'You had a terrible time with the attacks from Gerardo. I'm sorry I could do nothing to protect you.'

'No, you kept my spirits up and made me strong. Memories fade, and I will only have this scar to remind me of the horror.' Christina let her fingers run over the red line left by the knife cut across her neck. A few centimetres more and the blade might have severed her carotid artery, releasing spouts of blood and killing her instantly. Michael reached out and gave her hand a gentle squeeze in reassurance.

Chapter 45

An hour before the rendezvous, Aziz contacted the boat via the satellite radio. Jaffar thrust the handset over to Lucas as if it was a hot plate burning his hands.

'You are on time. Can you confirm you have the package?'

'We do,' replied Lucas. 'But first I want to speak to Michael and Christina.'

'I assure you they are well. But you double-crossed us. The forest is swarming with mercenaries. You have the Englishman's wife and boy with you?'

Lucas drew in his breath, shocked Aziz was aware Julie and Alex were onboard. Vargas must have warned him.

'The commander has ordered the marines to let our exchange go ahead without interference. They are only observers. Mrs Fletcher and her son are with us, and the world's TV and press watch you keep your word and do not harm the hostages.'

'So be it. No doubt this call is not secure, so your soldiers hear our plan. Go to the mosque for the evening prayers at six o'clock, but do not enter. Wait outside for further instructions. How will you get there?'

'We will take the inflatable boat to shore. I believe the mosque is a short walk away?'

'Yes, moor up by the small jetty beside the road to Darussalam. You will see the minaret of the mosque sticking above the trees—tie up and go to the front door. Mr Lucas, carry the suitcase with the money. Place it on the ground next to you. There must be no one else with you except for Hamza and the man's wife. Do you understand?'

'Why bring Mrs Fletcher?'

'The foreigners are trigger-happy. If they see a white woman, it may restrain them. She is our guarantee against treachery. We kill the hostages if you double-cross us.'

'Julie agrees, but first, she wants to speak to her husband.' There was a lengthy pause. Julie looked concerned, wondering why such a simple task should pose a problem. Aziz returned to the radio. After a muffled exchange, Michael came on the line.

'Michael, we are calling from the boat. Julie and Alex are with me—you can speak to them in a minute. We are going to pay the ransom, which involves me, Julie and Hamza handing over the money to Aziz. Once the pirates check it, they will release both of you. It's as simple as that. Is Christina with you?'

'Yes, Lucas. She's just coming. We are both coping, but it hasn't been a picnic.'

'Do what they say. No heroics. Neither of you is in danger provided you follow the plan.'

Lucas passed the handset over to Julie. She managed a few snatches of conversation with Michael before Aziz broke the connection.

The team compared watches and lowered the ship's inflatable over the side. Hamza tugged the outboard, and the motor purred into life with a satisfying explosion. The blades made the water boil as acrid smoke poured out of the exhaust. Mud from the seabed churned up and stained the sea a murky black. Hamza opened the throttle, and the prow of the boat bucked, throwing Julie in the air before rebounding off Lucas like a colliding pinball. The rapid acceleration pinioned them to the floor as sea spray spume seared their eyes.

Approaching the shore, Hamza slowed to a more sedate pace. Lucas scoured the shoreline for evidence of the marines. Aziz's insistence on bringing Julie along made sense from a tactical point of view. It might restrain the military; she was so fearless and happy to come ashore if it could help secure Michael's release. She was filming with the video camera as if this was a tourist outing. As they neared land, Hamza cut the boat's motor, pointing out three of the soldier's hideouts.

They were ten minutes early as they moored up, just as the imam broke into his haunting call to prayer. His beautiful chant, a song of peace, called the faithful. Robed figures disgorged from every house in the village. They strolled, chatting, as they drifted towards the place of worship. Several of the brothers realised they were too early. They looked at their watches and shook their heads, disturbed by the change of routine. Lucas held Julie back to let them pass. She received many curious glances in her western-style clothes.

'It was stupid of me to have overlooked this. We should have covered you in a shawl.'

'Okay, I'm not decently dressed, but no need for them to stare at me. Has Aziz planned this to make us conspicuous?'

Once the entire village had passed into the mosque, Lucas and Julie remained on the steps by the heavy teak door. To keep busy, Julie studied the ornate carvings, marvelling at the craftsmanship.

'Look more concerned,' said Lucas. 'They watch our every move.'

A short distance away, Hamza joined in the prayers, prostrating himself on the ground. He was observant enough to note a glowing cigarette through the distant trees. There were four contacts in his field of vision, and others hidden behind the mosque to cover the route up to the hill. Time passed. The sound of the prayer chants, a sibilant wave, swept across the land, suffusing calm upon man and nature alike. The chatter of the monkeys and songs of the birds ceased. Fishermen out at sea cut their motors, letting their boats drift. The sun's great orange orb cast its final fleeting glow, fading, as it sunk below the horizon, a weary harbinger condemned for eternity to recycling repetition, an endless rotation of death and rebirth.

On the seaward-facing slope, Captain Leroy occupied high ground overlooking the mosque. It puzzled him when the entire village descended on the building, just as the hostage exchange was about to take place. The terrorists had slipped in along with the worshippers. That suitcase full of money was the focus. He guessed the gang had hog-tied the hostages somewhere nearby in the bush—dead or alive; it didn't matter too much. Better if they were still living. One solution was to rush the mosque now, close off the doors and windows and seize everyone for questioning, but he had insufficient men to cope with so many rebels masquerading as local villagers. Captain Leroy radioed his men to cover him as he advanced towards the building, gun at the ready. Lucas and Julie looked on in disbelief as he approached.

'Hi you guys,' he adopted a friendly tone to help them relax. Sometimes he intimidated folks when his six-foot-six-inch frame, in full military fatigues and blackened face, confronted them. 'My name is Captain Leroy. We are here in our capacity as advisors to the Filipino security forces. It's a high priority strategy to locate the Aboos.'

'Lucas Miffré—and Michael Fletcher's wife, Julie,' Lucas introduced themselves but met a blank stare. Could it be Leroy was unaware of the full picture? Possibly no one had briefed him. 'The pirates took Michael Fletcher, a marine geophysicist. As you must know, we are here on an agreed mission to bring him and an employee of the museum in

Manila out alive. When you talk of the "Aboos" do you mean the Abu Sayyaf?'

'Affirmative, our intelligence is the Islamist terrorists are responsible.'

'No! Aziz is not a terrorist. This business is a plot by the Western governments to pin the blame onto Abu Sayyaf,' said Julie.

'I don't know who you've been talking to, ma'am, but I have my orders. When they come out of their prayers, we can see who picks up the ransom money.'

'The pickup is only half the story. First, they check if it is correct, and only then release the captives. If you guys interfere, they will kill the hostages. Just seeing you here may scupper our chances.'

They waited in an uneasy silence. Captain Leroy disliked this arrogant man. Inside the mosque, the sound of prayers merged with the clicking sounds of cicadas echoing through the raintrees by the shoreline.

Impatiently Lucas looked at his watch and reached a decision.

'Aziz must have called it off—it's ten past six. They have taken fright. The worst case is they kill the hostages. Captain Leroy—you have undone our hard work. Julie, we are wasting our time, let's return to the boat.' Lucas made to pick up the case, but Julie resisted, ignoring Lucas's fingers digging into her arm.

'Call yourselves professionals,' said Lucas. 'Our boatman spotted the positions of three of your men as we arrived.'

'They will kill Michael now,' Julie sank to the ground, tears welling up in her eyes, 'Why are you all so stupid?'

Captain Leroy looked embarrassed as Julie gave vent to great sobs, which racked her chest. In between her cries, she gasped for air like an asthmatic. Leroy hated girls crying.

The mosque was disgorging the villagers at the end of prayers. It surprised the people to see the tall soldier and the man with a case next to a distressed woman. The villager's route back to their houses took them past the group, and several tried to comfort her as they cast suspicious and distrustful glances at the captain.

'Look, if you don't believe me, stay out of sight and see if anyone approaches me for the suitcase.'

Lucas placed the suitcase at his feet and folded his arms. The crowd continued to mill past the strange group. Captain Leroy shook his head, puzzled, and concealed himself in the shade of a large angsana tree from where he had a good vantage point. The captain, gun at the ready, focused his attention on the case full of money and called up his team on the walkie-talkie.

'Number two. If anyone, other than that guy in the jacket, picks up the suitcase, shoot—go for a leg shot as I will want to interrogate him. Do you copy?'

Leroy noticed that Lucas's position gave a perfect line of fire for only this man. A stray shot might hit the Frenchman, but the collateral damage was always a risk.

The entire village filed past with a curious glance, but no one hesitated. Captain Leroy had doubts. He had expected things to be more clear-cut with a warm welcome from the locals, appreciative of their mission to eradicate a dangerous terrorist force. Instead, the enemy was hiding in the jungle and tolerated by a compliant population. They claimed Aziz was just a small-time hoodlum, a pirate leader. What bullshit!

Suddenly, some action! A tall robed figure approached Lucas. It was the imam of the mosque; the holy one himself. He was a lanky, lean man with a short grey beard.

'Number two. Aim to take out the Ayrab with the beard the moment he touches that case.'

The imam smiled as he greeted Lucas. 'Forgive me, I did not notice you within the mosque. Is there someone you seek? Can I be of help?'

This development was a worry. Maybe the imam had a message? Had there been a change of plan? Lucas hoped he would not pick up the case.

'Thank you. I planned to meet my contact here, but I think I missed him. Possibly I am too late.'

'I understand,' said the imam, looking at the case on the ground. Lucas willed him to go away, trying to warn him of the soldiers nearby.

Lucas could tell he understood. Both took their time, holding the soldier's attention for as long as possible. He bowed to Lucas.

'*Inshallah*, I hope you find your friend.' He strolled back to the mosque. Lucas stood alone by the suitcase; tense and sweating. When no one picked up the case, Leroy relaxed. At least the woman was calmer. He was sorry for her; she was out of her depth.

With a glare towards the tree where Leroy stayed hidden, Lucas plucked up the case and headed back to their inflatable. Hamza fell in step behind them. They must abandon the mission.

Meanwhile, Leroy organised a search for the hostages as he suspected the terrorists were still here.

On the trip back, none of them spoke. The disappointment was too much to bear. Julie cried to herself, hunched in front, staring unfocused towards the receding shoreline.

The shadowy shape of *Eastern Pearl* loomed up, and Hamza cut the engine to bring the zodiac alongside. To her astonishment, she heard laughter. Turning in surprise, she saw the deck rail lined with the crew. It was too dark to make out their faces, but then she heard Michael call her name. Lucas switched on the torch to light up the grinning faces of Michael and Christina.

'My God, it's you.' Julie had no memory of climbing out of the inflatable. One moment she was in the small boat, depressed and confused, and the next she was in Michael's arms in a firm embrace, so tight it took her breath away.

'How did you escape? We thought the exchange had failed because of the soldiers.'

'No,' said Michael. 'The suitcase was a ploy. There was no money in it, only old telephone directories. Aziz made an alternative plan with Captain Jaffar. While you distracted the Americans at the mosque, Aziz took us directly to our boat. The villagers had hidden two fast escape dinghies in the mangrove to the north. Aziz didn't have to set foot in the village. Captain Jaffar handed over the actual money in another case, and we boarded the vessel.'

'That's right,' said Captain Jaffar. 'It went like clockwork. No need to check the money. They were in too much of a hurry to bother. Aziz threw the case to a man in the second boat.'

Julie confronted Lucas, 'I suppose you were in on this subterfuge as well?'

'Yes, I had to prepare two cases—one full of the ransom money and the other packed with the phone directories. The case with the money has a GPS tracker hidden so the navy patrol can follow them. Even now, they should be in pursuit.'

Captain Jaffar was nervous; their sounds of celebration might stir up the Americans. Best to cast off immediately and head back to Bongao. The soldiers might get angry when they realised Aziz had fled, leaving them to chase shadows. Leroy still believed the place was crawling with Abu Sayyaf terrorists.

The boat started up her engines and stirred up the brackish waters of the mangrove. Over the shoreline, darkness had fallen. Faint lights from the village of Languyan blinked their farewells. In Puerto dos Amigos the Americans were sweeping through the jungle, stabbing their guns through the dense foliage, alert as cats after rats for any motion in the undergrowth. A frustrated Captain Leroy, exposed and foolish, turned his attention to the mosque. The imam spoke English and knew the island, so he might have useful intelligence worth pursuing.

Chapter 46

The pirates grabbed the ransom money and sped off towards the girdle of uninhabited islands. Aziz headed for the nearest island, fringed by coral, which was inaccessible from the navy gunboats. The channel into the bay was shallow and only navigable at high tide—a secure hideout until the fuss had abated.

As they hurtled along, the helmsman was counting the money—jubilantly cheering and punching the air in victory. He opened the throttle to come alongside Aziz, but did not notice the shoal ahead. Aziz saw the danger in time and peeled off into deeper water, but the other boat hit the bank. It launched into the sky for a few seconds until the weight of the outboard motor forced the stern onto the sandbank. Sliding backwards, the propellers sheared off, and the boat's crew tumbled out. The man at the helm took a higher and faster trajectory, and smashed his head against a mound of coral. He might have survived the skull fracture, but not the broken neck. As his body jerked like a discarded puppet, blood seeped, a crimson stain cloud mixing with the sea and drifting over the red anemones anchored to the seabed.

A furious Aziz threw a line across to take the crippled boat in tow. The ransom money flew in the wind, billowing out of its cracked case and lodged against the lifeless body of the helmsman, whose splayed arms trapped it, bobbing in rhythm to the waves.

Captain Ramos was patrolling the approaches to the inlet at Languyan, expecting Aziz to break out and head to one of the many uninhabited islands for a potential hideout. Ramos spotted two crowded longboats in the distance. At once, a beeper sounded from the detector, picking up on the GPS signal hidden in the suitcase lining.

As the patrol boat sped towards the target, it surprised Ramos to see a longboat tossed into the sky, its crew flying out. As the navy boat raced towards him, Aziz broke free from the stricken craft, abandoning the money, and escaped to the shallows where the patrol boat could not follow. But relief was short-lived when the navy manned the 50 calibre foredeck gun.

A few rounds peppered around, landing short. The plumes of water crisscrossed, edging ever nearer. But as Aziz closed on the island, the navy eased off, wary of running aground. Captain Ramos dealt with the damaged vessel first— a wise choice—one survivor bundled up a handful of wet dollar bills and ran towards the shore, but the rest of the crew clinging to the wreckage surrendered. Ramos recovered the case of money and they dragged the body of the dead pirate onboard. Aziz had escaped today, but not tomorrow—there was no escape from the small island. Ramos called up another patrol boat from Batu-Batu base to take over and guard the channel. When Aziz tried to break out, they would be ready for him.

A short time later, Ramos overtook *Eastern Pearl* on her way at full speed to Bongao. Lucas and the captain were still on the bridge when the patrol boat came alongside.

'Here is the case of money,' Ramos threw it onto the back deck. 'It broke open, but most of the money is there. You won't find a berth tonight—too late. Anchor up and call the harbour master in the morning, but stay onboard as I will need to come and take statements.'

'Thank you,' said Lucas. 'What will happen to Aziz and his gang?'

'Aziz escaped, but not for long. We capture most of his men and one is dead.' Ramos pointed to the prisoners tied up in the patrol boat and the lifeless corpse at their feet. 'We hope their sentence will match the severity of the crime, but that depends on the judge. The judiciary on this island may be sympathetic because they are so young. Best to transfer them to the mainland for a tougher penalty. Goodnight, I must return to Batu-Batu. Don't leave before I see you tomorrow.'

Captain Ramos arranged for one of the navy guards to jump across to *Eastern Pearl* to give them more protection. With so much money, it was best to take care.

Early the next morning, when Michael surfaced, the vessel lay at anchorage outside Bongao. On the bridge was Lucas, Christina and the captain, sipping champagne. With plenty of spare bunk space, Julie had taken a cabin next to Alex rather than sharing Michael's cramped cabin. Besides, she wasn't keen on any close encounters until she could resolve outstanding issues, not least of which was the dirt and smell hanging over him, no doubt from the unsanitary conditions imprisoned at their jungle camp.

Lucas held up the suitcase and updated them with the latest news—the capture of the pirates, the return of the ransom money, and the escape of Aziz.

'Good that he's free,' said Michael. 'He never meant to harm us, but things were getting out of hand because his men were too militant—as bad as Abu Sayyaf. Eventually Gerardo might have ousted Aziz, and we wouldn't be here.'

'You are very forgiving,' said Christina. 'Don't forget he wanted to flog you just like he did to Gerardo.'

'Really?' said Julie, who had just joined them on the bridge, along with Alex. 'You probably deserved it!'

'Just an idle threat. He also promised to chop off one of Christina's fingers and send it to the museum.'

'Gross,' asserted Christina. 'But I never believed him—just a bluff. Fanatics only see the world from their narrow and twisted viewpoint.'

'Like Gerardo?' asked Julie.

'No, he was a sadistic psychopath and killer,' said Michael.

'Will you come back if Lucas wants to resume the survey?'

Michael gave a wry smile. However, by his silence, she knew he would return.

Christina was standing alone. Michael wrapped his arm around her, recognising their shared sufferings.

'Julie, Michael was a rock of strength. He saved my life.'

'Hell, I can't do this emotional stuff. Come, drink up and finish the bottle,' Lucas topped up their cups.

The vessel was ready to follow the pilot launch into the port. As their ship nudged closer to the pier and the end of their ordeal, Julie joined Alex alone on the back deck. The two gathered to look at the risen sun dispersing the mist, which hung over the sleepy harbour. Overhead a frigate bird loomed, circling the boat for a few turns before soaring away.

Lucas emerged with more champagne for breakfast. With no cook, Lucas had thrown together instant noodles, scrambled egg, sausages and pancakes—an eclectic mix.

Kim Choo had donated a few bottles to celebrate in style when they located the wreck of the *Siren*. In the circumstances, Lucas said they should rejoice in their rescue.

'And I have another piece of news. Captain, can you call everyone up to the deck?'

'The best plan is to sound the alarm. We are long overdue for an emergency drill,' said Jaffar, sounding a few blasts on the klaxon. The piercing and insistent ringing brought the whole of the ship's crew scrambling to the muster station. Relief replaced panic when they realised it was only a drill.

Lucas thanked everyone and explained the latest development of the capture of the pirates and recovery of the money. He was also pleased to announce his engagement to Kim Choo. No details yet, but most likely, everyone would receive invitations to a quiet ceremony in Singapore. All agreed this was amazing and a good excuse to finish the champagne.

'I don't want to dampen your spirits. Maybe too early to discuss this, but our search for the *Siren* was successful. We found the cargo. So let's return to finish the job.'

Everyone groaned.

'Not right this minute. We no longer have a survey team. Next time I organise things better. With *bonne chance*, our mission will succeed.'

'Before you rush back, you may need to do more research,' said Christina. 'Nick and I dived on the wreck and found a large hoard of porcelain in mint condition. But all we have is this small saucer.' Christina held up the dish which she passed around for everyone to examine.

'Like you, I assumed this was a Ch'ing dynasty piece matching the age of the *Siren*. But the base marks contradict this. The saucer is earlier Ming—a much more exciting and valuable find.'

'You mean this came from an older wreck and not the *Siren*?' asked Lucas.

'Most likely, yes. Or the captain purchased it in Canton in preference to the off-the-shelf stock.'

Lucas reckoned they should stick with their original interpretation. Possibly, there were two wrecks: The *Siren* and another older vessel of even greater value. When they resumed the survey, he planned a more professional approach with more robust security. Things could have been worse if Abu Sayyaf had captured them, but next time would be easier.

Captain Ramos agreed they were free to leave, and Lucas arranged the travel arrangements for the team, booking flights back to Singapore for the following day. Christina wanted to show Alex around Manila, and he jumped at the chance, so they arranged an earlier flight from Bongao to Zamboanga and then onto Manila. In a quiet moment, Julie found Alex staring into the sea at the bow of the vessel. Strange to see the rapid transition from moody teenager to a mature adult compressed into such a short time frame.

'Looking thoughtful?' Julie stood by her son. So easy to imagine life here was normal with boats plying their trade. The threat of piracy and the Abu Sayyaf militants were far away.

'Have you caught the bug for this wreck hunting business?'

'No way! I'm not cut out for this adventurous lifestyle. After university, who knows? I have no set plans—best to live for the moment.'

'Live for the moment sounds a practical philosophy. I cannot go through this again if your father returns. Two people living together and a close-knit, loving family is fine, but we need to be open to change and fresh challenges—fly free like the birds.'

Alex looked up sharply, worrying his mother was leading up to a revelation. She smiled, squeezed his arm and wandered off to join Michael, who was standing alone looking at the busy crowds on the quayside.

'Sorry to have caused you such trouble. But survival is a rebirth. When pirates threaten your life, you appreciate a reprieve. I don't have the right words.'

'Did you know the British High Commission in Singapore told me they are not in favour of paying out ransom payments for the release of hostages?'

Michael was well aware of the official position, but in reality someone usually paid. Otherwise, hostages could stay captive for years or might lose their lives.

'That's right, Michael. I understand, but I better tell you this. It has been all over the papers. There was a press conference at the embassy where a reporter asked me the question. In reply, I said I supported the principle of non-payment because whenever they pay a ransom it only encourages more attacks and doesn't get to the root of the problem. We need to understand why is piracy happening. Is it just for monetary gain–a criminal act–or is it for political purposes?'

'I can't believe I am hearing this. You were prepared to sacrifice my life on a principle?' Michael was about to storm off, but Julie touched his arm to make him stay.

'I want to apologise for getting a few things wrong. The mixed messages from the British Embassy put me under a lot of stress. The press briefing was a disaster. But you are alive and well and we are together. That is all that matters.'

Michael relaxed, prepared to listen and look at the situation from Julie's perspective. Lucas had overheard and backed up Julie, explaining how she had to follow the line imposed by the British High Commission on the one hand, while covertly pursuing active negotiations through Vargas.

'I have got a few other things wrong as well,' admitted Julie. 'Like failing to appreciate what we have, being jealous and cranky.'

Michael interrupted her flow. He drew Julie to his side and kissed her so that her words died on her lips.

Two men attended Friday prayers at the Sheik Karimol Makhdum mosque on Siminul Island—a quick boat trip from Bongao. It was the first mosque erected in the Philippines in 1380 by an Arabic missionary who introduced Islam and Sharia law to Tawi-Tawi. Neither man prayed from the heart. Their actions were hollow to disguise the real motive for their meeting.

'The only remains of the original building are the pillars,' explained the man garbed in flowing robes. The man had a price on his head, so it was a surprise he was talking on friendly terms to an officer of the Philippine navy. Khadaffy Janjalani, the leader of Abu Sayyaf and mastermind involving countless terrorist atrocities, left the mosque with the naval officer at his side. The men had hired a boat to return to Bongao, ignoring the public ferry that carried most of the pilgrims over for prayers. To keep inconspicuous, they dressed the navy officer in Arabic garb. His name was Lieutenant Fernandez.

'So they moor their boat up at the Chinese pier?' Janjalani asked.

'Yes. There is one navy man and one Moro guard onboard—both armed. Survival relaxes the westerners, and they are happy. Easy to board and retake prisoners.'

'So you say. That is how many?'

'There is the Englishman, his wife and son, and the French boss, Lucas Miffré. Also, the ransom money of 350,000 dollars. The total package is ready for plucking,' said Fernandez.

'And what of the marine crew?'

'A Malaysian captain, a Singaporean engineer, and the rest of the crew are local islanders they hired when the original team returned to Singapore.'

Fernandez did not mention Christina Velasco, as he was sure she must have returned to Manila.

'Hmm. It is tempting,' agreed Janjalani. 'But the window of opportunity is small. It needs careful planning, and I doubt if we have enough time.'

'A quick strike to collect the money?'

'Why leave infidels unharmed? The best course is to kill them. Are you certain the money is on the boat?'

'Yes, Ramos handed it back to them. It is onboard.'

'A tempting present with minimal risk. But you are a valuable asset, and I do not want your cover blown. If I go ahead, the navy might discover your involvement. You should stay in your job and watch what is happening with the Americans. I must know their plans.'

'Whatever is your will.'

'Thank you for this information.' Janjalani passed the Lieutenant a roll of notes. By its thickness, Fernandez knew it was a sizeable sum.

Chapter 47

The High Commissioner requested an immediate meeting with Dempsey at nine o'clock. Such an unusual summons shook Margery first thing in the morning, and before his usual cup of tea and a leisurely read of the papers. Peter suspected it must concern the Tawi-Tawi hostage issue. However, he was aware the pirates had freed Michael, and the security forces had captured many of the gang and recovered the money—so a successful outcome. The meeting, most likely, was to commend him for a job well done.

Margery looked tense when Peter knocked on the old man's door. Apart from a nervous glance, she concentrated on the typewriter, clattering away as if her life depended on it. Since that afternoon of abandon in the old man's office, both of them had reverted to their normal professional relationship as if nothing had happened. But keeping up appearances was very frustrating. Once they sorted out this hostage business, she hoped Peter would relax. The immediate problem was something had gone wrong with the operation to free the Fletchers. The High Commissioner had been reticent but admitted the American ambassador had phoned him at Eden Hall late at night with some development on the Tawi-Tawi operation. This morning he had stormed straight into his office without a morning greeting and was on the intercom at once demanding to see Dempsey.

The High Commissioner looked bleak as he motioned the nervous security attaché to sit in the Regency chair beside his massive mahogany desk. From his low seat, Peter squinted, blinded by the sun, as he looked up at the angry man behind the desk.

'This Tawi-Tawi caper has gone ape-shit, do you realise the problem?'

'No, sir. All went to plan and I believe they freed the hostages unharmed. Also, we retrieved the ransom money, and the navy apprehended most of the gang.'

'Yes, this French fellow, Lucas Miffré, aided by the agent and Mrs Fletcher, who bravely travelled to the scene at her own expense, secured the return of the hostages. But, it is your involvement that has given us the problem! Remind me; what was the role of this elite group of American commandos who staked out the village with the Spanish sounding name?'

'Puerto dos Amigos—the port of two friends, you mean, sir?'

'Yes, yes, I know what it means. And who are these friends?'

'No idea, sir—perhaps two friendly fisherfolk decided it was a splendid place for a port.'

'Don't be an idiot and answer my question.'

'Oh. Yes, the role of the Americans—as far as I can recall it was nothing specific. We briefed them to allow the hostage exchange, but to follow up and capture the gang. Strike into the hills and eradicate any terrorist camps. Really, I think, quite a simple strategy.'

The High Commissioner's frown meant there must be something else, a detail Peter had missed.

'So when Captain Leroy destroyed the mosque in Puerto dos Amigos, burning the imam to death, was that a measured response?'

'My God, how did that happen? The Americans could only act in self-defence. Did they come under fire?'

The High Commissioner paced the room, only the angry sound of his footsteps on the wooden flooring breaking the silence.

'It was an unprovoked attack by the Americans. Peter, you appear to have conjured up this whole Abu Sayyaf nonsense to justify a dubious and risky military enterprise.'

'I consider, sir, it was a logical deduction. Someone convinced the press it was a terrorist kidnapping. If you recall, we discussed it, and we made a policy decision to run with the popular consensus.'

'No. I suggest you conjured up this fantasy and directed the media to follow your lead.'

The High Commissioner looked triumphant. He had the attaché on the rack and enjoyed watching him squirm in discomfort.

'Obviously, there's a way to play this: One solution is to disown our part in this fiasco and explain it as the deranged act of an out-of-control individual, Captain Leroy. But Leroy is a much-respected Gulf War veteran, so that will not run. Alternatively, we can argue justification, such as an arms' dump found in the mosque, followed by an accidental fire and death of the holy man. This is the approach the Americans favour. Finally, pretend it never happened and keep it under wraps—HM government is keen on that approach. Leroy's rampage was after the Philippine navy left. It should be possible to suppress the news from the press as it's a remote place.'

Peter sensed the fault for the fiasco was shifting away from him. He felt emboldened enough to point out another solution.

'We could say the decision to blame Abu Sayyaf, which led to the over-zealous actions of the American forces, was excusable because of mistaken intelligence.'

'Ha, ha. Where have I heard that one?'

The High Commissioner allowed himself a wry smile, stopped pacing, and walked to the sideboard to pour a drink. He noticed the level in the bottle was lower than expected and the photo of Mountbatten was beside the whisky instead of its usual place on his desk.

'How strange! I am getting absent-minded.' He returned the photo of his dog to its proper place, beside a smaller photo of his wife.

'I'm sorry I forgot to ask, do you fancy one?'

'It's early for me, sir, but in the circumstances, yes, thank you.'

The High Commissioner poured two generous tumblers of malt whisky.

'An incident on an obscure island hardly embarrasses.'

'It shows the continued fruits of the tarnished British-American alliance as in our unpopular and disastrous sortie into Iraq?'

'Steady on—you are following the populist line again. I warned you we create perceptions, but we do not have to believe them. The best course is to do nothing. One should plan any exposures to achieve the greatest embarrassment.'

Peter's mouth gaped open in surprise, shocked at these words.

'When retirement looms, one gains courage—a need to redress the balance for all those years of discretion. Besides, it will spice up my memoirs. I am looking forward to lifting the lid on an awful lot of issues. Just watch this space!'

'It's not disloyal. Revealing the facts is what politicians love to do when it suits them.'

'Yes, how right you are. That is the case when helpful—lies and truth masquerade for total confusion. Before you go, I had a further update this morning from the French chappie, Lucas.'

Peter sensed something else had gone wrong.

'There was an attack yesterday evening on the boat in Bongao. The objective was to kill the hostages and take back the ransom money.'

'My God, how terrible.'

'Fortunately, Captain Ramos and the navy men were still onboard, taking food in the galley and repulsed the attackers.'

'Are the Fletchers safe?'

'Yes—all the team, except for the marine crew, had left the boat and checked into local hotels ready to fly out the following day. And Lucas Miffré had the ransom money safe in a suitcase under his bed in the hotel.'

'Well, splendid news.'

The High Commissioner took Peter's empty whisky glass from him and put it back on the sideboard.

'Not really. They killed two people on our side—a navy man, and a fellow called Hamza. A six-man suicide squad carried out the raid. The sole survivor admitted they acted on the orders of Janjalani.'

'So I was correct! It *did* involve Abu Sayyaf.'

'More of a spur-of-the-moment decision due to leaked intelligence. Maybe we have given you too much leeway. I should add that for a man of your talents, another arena of operations might beckon. Perhaps a spell in Egypt at our Cairo office would suit?'

Peter looked put out; conscious the High Commissioner was not as dumb as he appeared.

'Egypt would be a challenge, sir.'

He could imagine nothing worse.

'Oh. Good. I am glad a change of scene appeals to you. Just so happens that we have a vacancy coming up. The last chap caught bilharzia and made a tremendous fuss. Stupid, I believe it's only a parasitic worm and seldom fatal. I will confirm your availability with Cairo tomorrow so you can pack up your things next week; take a spot of leave and start next month. Lovely place. I'm afraid you will be on the same pay grade at attaché level, but the cost of living is so cheap.'

Margery sailed in with a cup of tea as Peter departed in a daze. The Commissioner dialled a number on his mobile phone.

'Hallo Bill—yes, we can rely on him to keep mum about the Filipino business. Bill, I was wondering how to tweak this. Let's go with your idea of linking the imam's death to the discovery of weapons at the mosque as the pretext to weed out the Abu Sayyaf camps in Tawi-Tawi.'

'Situations change. There is no mosque. Look at the map on Google Earth on your computer.'

'I don't understand,' said the High Commissioner. What was this Google Earth? If this was a computer thingummy, Margery was the one to ask.

'I will explain. For Tawi-Tawi Island, Google Earth is full of errors. That mosque you thought I mentioned. Look on the Google map and a mosque in Puerto dos Amigos does not exist. Therefore, any alleged incident to a so-called imam, or holy man, is a figment of someone's heated imagination. End of story.'

'That's a splendid solution.' The High Commissioner agreed, wiping away the nervous sweat from his forehead. 'Your unit has done well with only a limited aim. If we persuade your people to mobilise more firepower, we could clean up the Muslim insurgents from Tawi-Tawi and Basilan. No hurry, let's meet up at my club sometime next week and discuss it further,' said the High Commissioner.

'And what action are you taking with your attaché, Peter Dempsey?'

'Don't worry—we are transferring him to a new posting. He seems keen.'

'Well, you still need him to keep a lid on things. They are flying back to Singapore today. We thought it best to get them out of the country as fast as possible so we pushed this Lucas guy to cooperate. Your man must meet them at Changi and make sure no word of the American involvement leaks to the press.'

This development worried the High Commissioner. Not content with messing up the hostage exchange, the Americans now wanted him to cover up for them!

Peter had stopped off to see Margery, and they wandered outside to the Reception area for greater privacy.

'Given my marching orders,' he said. 'They have made me the scapegoat for the diplomatic incident caused by the Americans. I wonder if there was a hidden agenda. To kill a harmless cleric is too stupid for words.'

'It's so unfair. I heard you might leave us. Is that confirmed?'

'They are moving me to Cairo. He is fast tracking it, so I start next month.'

It appalled Margery. 'So unjust after your excellent work—ask him to reconsider. At least he knows you—an unfamiliar person might be a disaster.'

'You know I expected a commendation for a job well done—even a promotion. I mean, the hostages are alive. We lost a few guards, and the pirates got what they deserved. Apart from that problem with the imam which was nothing to do with me. And the treasure hunter's search was successful.'

'Yes, that's the most important thing, isn't it? You keep looking, but sometimes you don't recognise it when you have found what you are seeking.'

'I'm not sure what you mean.'

She looked downcast, feeling sad at the realisation that Peter was leaving. It was only now she realised how stupid and slow she had been to ignore the attraction between them.

'How soon before you go?'

'He just said to pack up next week.'

'Don't worry—I will get him to change his mind.'

'That's good of you, but they have made their decision. The embassy needs a scapegoat.'

'I'll threaten to resign if they move you. That will alarm him—he totally depends on me. He can't do anything without my help.'

Margery's intercom bleeped from the High Commissioner.

'Margery, is Peter still around?'

'Yes, sir. He is standing right next to me.'

'Ask him to come and see me pronto. He needs to be at the airport tonight to meet up with this Michael Fletcher and the crowd we just rescued. Got to get our story straight before the press descend, you know.'

Chapter 48

The team had flown into Manila International Airport ready to catch the first flight to Singapore when Vargas called Lucas. The American Embassy had booked them overnight into expensive suites at the Makati Shangri-La and would pick up the bill. Transport with armed protection and onward flights were arranged for the next day. Because of the likely press interest, he suggested they keep a low profile and avoid leaving the hotel. Michael was too tired to argue and keen to take advantage of the free hospitality. Lucas and Julie suspected the motives. What was the latest agenda?

'It's nothing sinister,' said Michael. 'The Americans are cooperating with the government. Just a courtesy.'

'I am not so sure. The British Embassy handles you two, so I expected Peter Dempsey to give us some support.'

Lucas stared out of the window of the high-rise hotel, looking peeved at the sound of workers hammering on an upper floor. They were rewiring the broadband and renovating the rooms and restaurants. But compared to the hotels in Zamboanga, this was impressive.

'No mention in the local papers,' said Lucas. 'I'll check the international editions later. I think the bookshop gets airmail copies about 5 p.m. But often the Western newspapers are a day late.'

'Nothing on the TV channels,' said Julie. 'The fact that all went well and we survived dampens their enthusiasm. It takes time for news to filter through from Tawi-Tawi. Surely we merit a paragraph or two?'

Lucas shrugged and looked at his watch. They agreed to visit the bar, followed by dinner.

Fifty-six years after the war, Manila was a typical southeast Asian city with huge high-rise office blocks and hotels with congested roads teeming with chaotic traffic. Not an attractive destination for the tourists seeking the history of the early Spanish founders. Christina was keen to show Alex parts that had survived the bombing in World War II. They walked through the Walled City of Intramuros to San Agustin church—an impressive structure built in 1607.

'This is the oldest surviving stone building in the whole of the Philippines. Your country captured Manila in 1762 during a conflict against the Spanish. I believe they looted the church for souvenirs.'

'I have never heard of this,' said Alex.

'Few are aware of our history,' said Christina. 'The British occupied us for two years and then gave it back. I guess we were just a gambling chip, in their colonial master plan. This is a sacred place. It has survived several earthquakes, and during the Japanese occupation, they turned it into a concentration camp. Many perished within these walls during the last days of the war.'

After the recent tensions, Alex savoured the simple joys of walking in tropical gardens and visiting the tourist sites. They had flown to Manila on the first flight from Bongao. Alex helped Christina with her equipment and diving gear and, in return, she promised to take time off work to show him the sights of the city. Christina's parents had a massive villa in the outskirts and they gave him a palatial room overlooking beautiful gardens. Alex hoped to stay for several days but, with the team heading to Singapore, this might not be possible. Somehow, in the rush to leave Bongao he had lost his mobile phone, so no one could reach him. Keen to preserve his newfound freedom, he was in no hurry to replace it even though cheap phones with local SIM cards were available. In an emergency, his father had Christina's number, so he relaxed. As if by telepathy, Christina's phone rang. It was Michael tracking him down.

'Have you seen the news this morning?' Michael asked, without preamble. 'After we left the boat in Bongao, we stayed overnight in a local hotel. Just as well we did! There was an attack on the *Eastern Pearl* by a squad of six terrorists. The Abu Sayyaf group claim responsibility. The plan was to recapture or kill us and reclaim the ransom money. Fortunately, Captain Ramos and his force were onboard at the time and repulsed the attack.'

'My God, how amazing! Were there any fatalities?'

'Oh, yes—the security forces killed all the attackers, except one. Our losses were one navy guard and Hamza.'

'No. Not Hamza! What happens now?'

'Where are you and why are you not answering your phone?'

'Sorry, Dad. In the rush, I left it on the boat. I am staying at Christina's parents' house and she has been brilliant showing me around places off the usual tourist trail.'

Michael suggested it was not the best time for sight-seeing. He explained how the American Embassy was keen to get them to leave the country fast. They had arranged flights for the afternoon, but they needed to head to the airport at 2 p.m latest.

'The press will wait for us in Singapore, so best to delay your return and stay out-of-the-way until all this blows over. Unless you want to travel with us.'

'Two o'clock is pushing it. We are in the old city. I would have to fetch my bags. I don't even have a ticket.'

Tickets were no problem. They could buy one at the airport. Alex should come to the Makati Shangri-La by two o'clock latest or else stay in Manila for a few more days to let things cool off. The decision was his.

'And one more news item for you from Vargas,' said Michael. 'Aziz escaped from the island where the Filipino forces had him surrounded. They believe he is back on Tawi-Tawi.'

The American Embassy left nothing to chance. They escorted their limousine to the airport between two light armoured vehicles manned with marines. In addition, an armed guard travelled with them in the car. With much blaring of horns and fast driving, the convoy jumped traffic lights, attracting inquisitive stares. The guard assigned to them explained this was a normal defensive strategy. The tinted windows hid their identities from the curious.

'Madness,' said Lucas. 'Such a show attracts an attack. We would be better just taking a regular taxi.' His words cut short as they came to a shuddering halt. The advance patrol had crashed into a jeepney. They blocked their limousine in, sandwiched between the two armoured vehicles. Marines rushed out, waving their guns. Crowds gathered to watch the unfolding drama. After a few minutes of standoff and angry shouting, they continued the journey, leaving a smashed jeepney and enraged passengers behind in a swirl of dust.

At the International airport, they were fast-tracked to the business class lounge of the Singapore Airlines flight. A chance to relax at last.

'Very dramatic trip,' laughed Julie, helping herself to snacks and a glass of red wine.

'It is all an act they play,' said Lucas. 'The pirates, the security forces, the embassy people—they all contrive to follow the script. We are just the pawns in their game!'

On arrival at Changi, they passed effortlessly through the immigration counter to collect their cases. Peter Dempsey flashed his pass at a police officer on the Arrivals gate and waited at the baggage belt. Crowding the glass window, the press posse struggled to see the rescued hostages. As Lucas, Michael and Julie searched for their bags, Peter approached them.

'It's good to have you back,' he shook their hands awkwardly. 'To avoid the press pack, we will leave by a side door. If you can come with me, I will give you an update on the latest developments. It is quite a delicate situation.'

'We heard about the attack,' said Lucas. 'It's all over the TV and newspapers in Manila.'

'That's right. It was a shock, and so lucky you had left the boat. The embassy invites you to the Goodwood Hotel for drinks and food. It will be a chance to bring you up to speed. And, if you feel up to it, we can have a brief press briefing; but I understand if you are too tired.'

Peter remembered the previous press event had not been a success. He smiled grimly at the memory.

'If you all approve, we can meet the press such as the Straits Times, STV, BBC and one or two of the UK newspapers. I would say a maximum of six.'

'What about that lady from Time Magazine who nearly caused a riot?' laughed Julie.

'Probably not a good idea,' conceded Peter.

'It has got to be done,' said Lucas. 'Say little and get them off our back. My office tells me we have had loads of work enquiries over the last fortnight so all publicity helps.'

Peter briefed them during the drive to Scott's Road. He explained that the High Commissioner favoured the Goodwood Park Hotel for accommodating embassy staff and important guests. The facilities were excellent, although a bit faded from the ravages of time since it was first built in 1900. Prima ballerina Anna Pavlova performed there in December 1922 but its chief claim to fame was to build the first outdoor swimming pool in a hotel in Singapore in 1963. During the war, the Japanese high command requisitioned the hotel for their senior officers.

'The old man likes the tartan wallpapered bar downstairs and its fine range of malt whiskies.'

'A good reason for recommendation,' agreed Lucas. 'But who is this "old man" you refer to?'

'The High Commissioner. My boss, you could say. But not for much longer. Since this piracy escapade, I will leave for a new post in Cairo. But no matter. Back to the present. The key point to stress is we had to pay a token amount to break the deadlock. However, security forces were on hand to recover the money as soon as they released you. They have rounded up the gang and we are confident they will not pose any future risk to mariners.'

'A happy conclusion,' said Michael, sarcastically.

'Indeed. Keep it light without too many details.'

'And is the loss of life worth it, in your pursuit of Abu Sayyaf? Losing Raspal, Hamza, most of the pirate gang of fifteen, a navy guard and not forgetting, Mitch,' said Julie, opening the door of the limousine as they arrived outside the Goodwood Park. She looked around, tempted to catch a taxi home and leave them, but Michael restrained her. It was something they had to do.

The meeting room was the scene of a cheerful party. As a parting gesture, Peter Dempsey had invited all the team from the PanAsia office plus a few of their associated friends. In fact, anyone he could think of, including a few of the embassy staff. A pleasant surprise for the High Commissioner when the bill landed on his desk after Peter's departure to Cairo. After the generosity of the Americans, it was only fair to reciprocate. The survey team were tucking into the beer and shovelling up the buffet spread. Danica and Kim Choo were sipping wine, keeping some distance from the boisterous youngsters. Phillip Wong of Wong Kai Chee Marine drew Lucas aside from the welcoming throng.

'*Eastern Pearl* should leave Bongao tomorrow, if all goes to plan. I arranged for the usual crew to travel yesterday and join the boat, so Captain Jaffar has everything he needs.'

'That's great news,' said Lucas. 'I was afraid the incident would delay them. I hope the vessel did not sustain too much damage.'

'A few bullet holes, but the greater problem is the needless loss of life. Jaffar was quite shocked. This has been a traumatic job for him, poor chap. We can inspect the boat together when she returns to Loyang in two weeks' time. The best news is you are all back safely.'

Lucas noticed Jim hovering nearby. It surprised Lucas that the freelancers were still in Singapore. With the failure of the job, he expected Jim to send them home. Jim explained they had lots of work to keep them all busy. The press interest had led to many enquiries and new survey projects. None involved treasure hunting!

Margery sidled up to Peter as they both admired the happy homecoming.

'Well done, Peter—a brilliant party to welcome the hostages back to freedom!'

'Margery, I plan to invite the press to mingle with us. They can question Lucas, Michael and Julie without the formality of an official briefing. Do you consider that could work?'

'I think so. The danger is that Julie will shoot off her mouth. In an informal setting without an audience that may be less likely and the others should restrain her.'

'None of them knows about the atrocity carried out by Captain Leroy at the mosque. Our prime objective is to suppress that news breaking out. Anything else they say we can handle.'

They agreed that was the best way forward. Peter topped up Margery's glass with more champagne.

'If I have too much of this, I won't be able to drive home,' she laughed.

'No problem, I have booked a suite with the embassy discount. It would be a pity to waste it.' Peter discreetly passed her the electronic card to one of the best ground floor suites overlooking the swimming pool.

'Peter, how considerate!' Margery handed the card back. 'Best you keep hold of it and show me to the room later. We should both take full advantage of the generosity of the High Commissioner!'

Jim tugged Lucas by the sleeve and drew him aside to a quiet spot in a corner. His ever-full glass of beer wobbled until Jim sank a few gulps to restore equilibrium.

'Great do, mate. All worked out nicely in the end.'

'Yes,' agreed Lucas, sensing Jim had more to say.

'Felt you should know. I was in Holland Village yesterday at Mr Meng's antique shop where Mitch sold his plate to Tong. Guess what? I saw another plate, just like it, in the window. It has six marks on the base and Meng told me it was Ming Dynasty and priced at $300. He claims it was a special issue for the Emperor of China. Thinking I am a gullible tourist, he tells me he got it from a young archaeologist diving on a secret wreck site. All *bona fide*, of course, but for a quick sale he could reduce the price to $250!'

'Clearly a forgery,' said Lucas. 'Meng must have a cupboard full!'

'Tong would go mental if he knew he had been cheated!'

Lucas had forgotten about Tong's hunt for the *Siren*. Vargas had seen Tong and Yap land at Zamboanga in a hurry to return. Jim said he had called Davinder and understood they had terminated the survey and the boat was in transit to Singapore. Tong's failure was satisfying in light of the partial success of the PanAsia survey.

'So, did Mitch *really* find a Ming dynasty plate?' Lucas took a thoughtful sip of champagne and selected a stick of chicken satay from the buffet.

'Perhaps he did, and the genuine serving dish was used to make the copies?' suggested Jim.

'We will never know for sure, but we have found a huge hoard of valuable porcelain—maybe from the *Siren,* or from another East Indiaman, who knows? When the security situation improves, we will return.'

THE END

EPILOGUE

Nearly twenty years after these events not a lot has changed. The security situation in the Sulu Sea in 2021 remains high-risk for mariners, with dangers from piracy and the Abu Sayyaf. The targets most at risk are seafarers of commercial and leisure vessels, foreign aid workers, Christians and tourists. At present, any enterprise to salvage the valuable cargo of the *Siren* is doomed to failure.

Since the time in which I set this fictional work in 2002, the catalogue of crimes over the years includes the following horrific examples:

- In January 2002, Abu Sayyaf kidnapped two male and four female Jehovah witnesses selling Avon cosmetics on Jolo Island. They beheaded the men two days later and left their heads in a marketplace with a tag saying "infidels".
- A bomb placed outside the old terminal building at Davao International airport in March 2003, killed twenty-one people and injured 148.

- In February 2004, Abu Sayyaf leader Khadaffy Janjalani, hatched the worst marine terrorist attack in history when a bomb on board the SuperFerry 14 from Manila to Cagayan de Oro City caused a fire that led to the loss of 116 killed. The ferry owners had refused to pay him protection money.

- Abu Sayyaf gunmen raided a farm in Mindanao in February 2006 and killed six Christians, including a nine-month-old baby girl.

- In January 2008, Abu Sayyaf attacked a convent in Tawi-Tawi and killed the Catholic priest, Father Rey Roda.

- A month later there was a foiled assassination attempt on the life of the Philippine's President, Gloria Arroyo.

- A landmine killed two US soldiers in Jolo in September 2009 — the first US fatalities since 2002—when a series of bombings in Zamboanga killed an American Green Beret commando.

- The terrorists captured a school head teacher in Jolo in October 2009 and beheaded him three weeks later.

- In February 2012, the group abducted two birdwatchers on Tawi-Tawi—Swiss citizen Lorenzo Vinciguerra and Dutch Ewold Horn. Joint Task Force troops rescued Lorenzo. They held Ewold Horn captive for seven years until he was shot dead by his captors in May 2019 during an attack by the army.

- A group of militants infiltrated a holiday resort on Samal Island in September 2015 and kidnapped Canadians Robert Hall and John Ridsdel, Norwegian Kjartan Sekkingstad and a Filipina woman, Manites Flor. They beheaded the Canadians in 2016 after the authorities refused to make a deal. They freed the other two hostages after payment from their respective governments.

- In November 2015, an armed gang grabbed a 39-year-old Malaysian electrical engineer, Bernard Then, from a seafood restaurant in Sandakan while enjoying a meal with a friend. They released his friend but increased their ransom demand for Then to US$6.5 million—a sum his relatives could not pay. A street cleaner found his severed head inside a sack outside a council building on Jolo Island.
- In an attack at sea offshore Sabah in November 2016, German yachtswoman, Sabina Wetch, died of her wounds. The assailants abducted her friend, Jurgen Kuntner—a 70-year-old sailor, and held him for a high ransom of US$600,000. Three months later, Abu Sayyaf beheaded him.

In February 2017 Abu Sayyaf were holding 27 foreign hostages of Dutch, German, Korean, Indonesian, Malaysian and Filipino nationalities, including a nine-year-old girl. About 400 terrorists continue to be active. The cases mentioned are just the tip of the iceberg. The Filipinos have lost hundreds of soldiers over the years besides many civilian deaths. In the west, we hear little of these atrocities unless it involves one of our nationals. Although security forces killed Khadaffy Janjalani in 2006, there is always a ruthless leader to carry on the fight.

In 2018, the southern Philippines backed Muslim self-rule in a landslide vote in favour of a new autonomous region covering five provinces, including Tawi-Tawi. Hopefully, this will lead to the demobilisation of 30,000-40,000 forces of the Moro Islamic Front. However, this welcome end to a conflict that has cost over 150,000 lives after decades of fighting was short-lived. On 27 January 2019, Abu Sayyaf militants slaughtered twenty people in bomb blasts at the Catholic cathedral in Jolo during Sunday Mass. On August 24 2020, two female suicide bombers detonated bombs in Jolo killing 15 citizens and wounding 72 in another Abu Sayyaf attack. The saga of violence continues and militants are still holding many hostages in their jungle bases.

ABOUT THE AUTHOR

Over the years, I have been lucky enough to visit many countries of the world as a marine geologist. From 1983 to 1994, I lived in Singapore and experienced some high-risk jobs, such as the subject of this book.

Since our family's return to the UK, I have continued to work on additional challenging projects worldwide, including offshore Iran, Iraq and western Africa—areas where armed guards are considered a wise precaution. In particular, I experienced a pirate attack on MV *Askelad* near Forçacdos, Nigeria in 1998. The attackers took two of our team prisoner to a local camp where they were well-treated and played football with the villagers. After payment of a ransom, they were released.

Special thanks are due to all those who have made useful suggestions for revisions, including my beta reader, Abigail Teeder, and Nicola and Seb for editing.

Thanks also to Ari Suonpää for his artwork, *'The Siren's Cove'* used on the front cover and to Hammad at HMD publishing, Kuching, Malaysia for final cover design.

This novel is dedicated to my wife, Barbara, especially for her patience when I spent so much time on revisions and fine-tuning. It has taken many years to complete. To you, the reader, thanks for reading my debut novel, which I hope you enjoyed. There is another novel in progress, '*The Sussex Pond Murders*' when Michael and Julie first meet up in the UK. I hope to release this next year.

Richard Sorapure, June 2021

Printed in Great Britain
by Amazon